Praise for *Whe* 

"*When She Was Me* is eerie, captivating, and full of twists. I gasped out loud multiple times."

—Darcy Coates, *USA Today* bestselling author of *Dead of Winter*

"A mesmerizing, addictive thriller that will keep readers guessing from start to jaw-dropping finish. Told in vibrant, hypnotic prose, with complex relationships and haunting secrets at its core, *When She Was Me* is a standout debut from a wildly talented new author. Marlee Bush is one to watch."

—Laurie Elizabeth Flynn, author of *The Girls Are All So Nice Here*

"A nail-biting story of sisterhood, suspicion, and suspense. *When She Was Me* weaves together past and present seamlessly to create a twist you won't see coming. I couldn't put it down!"

—Tracy Sierra, author of *Nightwatching*

"A searing, blistering thriller that grabs you and doesn't let you go until its final, dizzying twist. Beautifully written and as tender as it is terrifying, Marlee Bush is a breakout new voice to watch."

—Jenny Hollander, author of *Everyone Who Can Forgive Me Is Dead*

"*When She Was Me* is a powerfully gripping debut. Atmospheric and lushly described, it reads like a tense, vivid dream. The serpentine twists and nuanced character relationships will haunt you long after you turn the last page."

—R. J. Jacobs, author of
This Is How We End Things

"I tore through *When She Was Me* with my heart in my throat—the prose was cunning and beautiful, the atmosphere was claustrophobic and unsettling, the imagery was dark and vibrant, and the strange dynamic between the sisters was hard to look away from. In short, Marlee Bush has crafted one of the most mesmerizing psychological thrillers I have ever read."

—Ashley Tate, author of
Twenty-Seven Minutes

"*When She Was Me* is a thrilling debut. Creepy and utterly compelling, these twin sisters will have you second-guessing everything."

—Paula Gleeson, author of
Original Twin

WHEN SHE WAS ME

MARLEE BUSH

Cover design by Caroline Teagle Johnson
Cover photographs © Sue Anne Hodges/Arcangel
(cabin), Creatopic/Shutterstock (women)
Internal design by Laura Boren/Sourcebooks
Internal illustrations by Laura Boren/Sourcebooks

Published by Poisoned Pen Press, an imprint of Sourcebooks
P.O. Box 4410, Naperville, Illinois 60567–4410
(630) 961-3900
sourcebooks.com

Cataloging-in-Publication Data is on file with the Library of Congress.

Printed and bound in the United States of America.
VP 10 9 8 7 6 5 4 3 2 1

For Craton,

because my most important story began with you.

PROLOGUE

I watch you because I don't have a choice. That's my job, isn't it? Even while you're sleeping, I'm left awake and wondering. Your head rests on your pillow, your hair fanned around you like a halo. And it's all so deceiving. The beauty of you. The peace of you. I want to pluck your brain out and put it under a microscope. Roll it around my fingers and feel your thoughts.

But I can only watch and wonder what you are dreaming about.

The fire last summer.

Dad.

Mom.

Or are you dreaming of me?

The thing is, I'm not watching you because I want to. I'm not doing it for me at all. I'm doing it because I can't quite figure it out: What you're thinking. Who you are. What you're capable of.

Shadows move and shift along the walls of our childhood bedroom, and the feeling comes to me as heady as this night. It's overwhelming. Stifling. But I accept it, welcome it inside me, let it seep into all my organs like the slow poison you've become.

Because it doesn't matter.

There are no other options. Whatever you're thinking, whatever you do next, I'll be there too. Just like last summer after the fire.

I'll be with you.

After all, you're my sister.

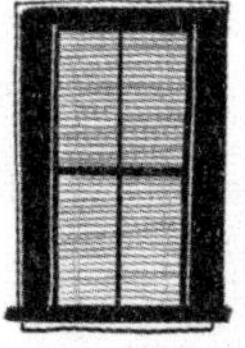

CHAPTER ONE
CASSIE

There is always trash at the Blacktop and never anyone around to claim it. Today it's two aluminum beer cans. One is crushed, and I picture a teenager chugging it and smashing the can against his skull, careless as he tosses it to the dirt.

The blacktop is the field west of our campsite. It backs into the dirt road that leads to the highway and is the entry point of the forty-five-acre campground. The dirt road itself swerves through hundreds more acres of barren woods. It's a surprise the kids still make trips out here at all.

Wayne said it's called the Blacktop because there used to be a day when this entire ten-acre field was covered in tents and bustling with campers. You'd pull in along the dirt road, and the sea of black tent tops would make it look as if someone had tossed a black sheet over the field in its entirety.

Now there are only beer cans and the occasional trespasser. Teenagers shushing each other as they silently close their car doors.

Balking at the dark forest around them, too afraid to go farther into the woods. Giggly and drunk as they lay a blanket in the wet grass and then don't come up for hours.

The sun is setting behind the trees, and the heat on my face almost makes me forget it's winter. Almost makes me forget the gentle ache of hard, frigid dirt beneath my toes and the uncontrollable pull at my back—a yearning for home.

Lenora will be wondering where I am.

I turn in the direction of our cabin when a glint of plastic catches my eye just beneath the overhang of a large rock—the one I sit on most often...my favorite rock—a vape pen. And something about this abandoned piece of trash irks me. The trespassers can have the Blacktop but not this. This is my spot. This is too close.

Somewhere behind me a car door slams, and I tuck the pen in my pocket, keeping hold of the beer cans. There's always trash to be found on the Blacktop, but sometimes there are treasures too. Lighters, coins, and keys. Once I even found a shot glass. A dribble of cold, piss-colored liquid leaks down my hand, but I don't pay it mind.

Need to get back.

To Lenora.

There is no path through the woods that will lead me home. At least not one I can see. The beech trees battle for dominance with the hickories and oaks. Their branches twisted and writhing beneath a sky they will never reach. In the winter they are as naked as the teenagers who stumble out here in the dark. I lay a hand on the tree nearest to me. An American beech. My fingers move across its smooth, polished skin.

The trees might spring up from the same plot of earth and look the same, but if you got closer, you'd find their thumbprint. Their bark. No two are exactly alike. I might know this forest and all the dead things in it well enough now that a clearly marked trail isn't needed. I might know this whole campground better than anyone. Maybe except Wayne.

But sometimes I still touch the trees, if only to remind myself that even the most identical things have thumbprints.

I'm coming out of the woods when our home appears before me. The three cabins and a bathhouse. The cabins are small and square. They're built with wood so dark, it looks wet, and they're pushed so deeply into the trees, they may as well be a part of them.

If they ventured just a bit deeper, the teenagers would see there aren't ghosts out here at all, just people who live like them.

I notice the man right away. He has his cell phone in the air like he'll magically find service six inches above his head. I stop at the base of the hill and spit on the ground near my bare feet. Recognition sets in. "No service out here," I call out to him.

He looks up, clearly startled. I've seen Wayne's nephew before in passing, a tall and gangly man with weirdly rounded cheeks that look out of place on his thin body.

"I always forget." He clears his throat and inches closer. "Didn't mean to sneak up on you."

I want to tell him he didn't sneak up on me, and he couldn't. Wayne's cabin, or what was previously Wayne's cabin before he went and died, sits at the tip of a triangle at the bottom of a long slope through the woods. We call it Cabin One. Mine and Lenora's cabin—Cabin Two—sits at the top. Across from ours is Cabin Three. That's where the guests stay when we have them.

In the summer, when the trees are thick with foliage, you can't see Cabin One at all. But it's winter. The dirt is ice, the trees are skeletons, and even if I hadn't seen the nephew coming, I still heard his car door slam.

"You don't have shoes," Wayne's nephew says. "It's freezing out here." He blows on his hands as if emphasizing how cold he is. Like only his warm breath will save his precious fingers.

"Guess I forgot." But I didn't. I don't like shoes. Even in the winter. Even when I can't feel my toes. My sister's therapist would most likely hypothesize why. Something to do with past trauma. The need to *feel* something.

I believe in ghosts more than therapy. Not that I'd ever tell Lenora that.

"Been meaning to come by," he says, his eyes trailing to the leaking beer cans in my hand. He doesn't ask, and I don't offer. Instead, he takes another step closer. "Thank you for what you did, by the way. Finding my uncle. If you hadn't checked on him, who knows when we would have found him."

I want to clarify I wasn't checking on Wayne a week ago. I'd walked down the hill in search of the firewood Wayne sold me and never delivered. It wasn't unusual for Wayne to disappear for a few days. He does—*did*—that frequently. Got lost in projects. Lost in his own mind. But this was different. There was silence at his cabin. Not his muttering to himself about the government or his hammering on nails inside. Wayne hadn't answered the door at all. I looked in his window and saw him.

Which wasn't necessary, having smelled him from the porch.

The smell of decomposing flesh isn't something you forget. One day I won't remember the expression Wayne made when he talked about politics or puttered around his garden. But I'll never let slip the smell that seeped through the cracks of his front door. I know this from experience.

After all, Wayne isn't the first person I've known to become a corpse.

"Listen," the nephew says when I don't say anything back. "I'm glad to run into you. I was going to walk up anyway. We have someone who's interested in the campground. We've told them about the situation with you and your sister. They said they'd honor Wayne's contract with you. Said you could keep renting your cabin and finish your lease. She should be here in a couple of days once we get everything ironed out."

"You're selling the property?"

His cheeks redden. "I just live so far away. It seemed easiest." The red spreads to his neck like a viral rash. "Anyway, I should get back to packing. It's going to take me the rest of the day to clear his place."

"OK." I maneuver around him, knowing I'm way later than I said I'd be. Lenora must be frantic.

"Wait—"

I stop and glance over my shoulder. But Wayne's nephew isn't looking at me. He's clearly distracted by something that lies ahead.

I know what he sees without looking.

The same thing the teenagers would see if they ever came this far. Maybe the sight would be enough to force them back. To make them never come here again.

"That your sister?" he asks, his eyes shifting back to me.

"Yes."

"She could scare the hell out of someone standing there like that."

The flash of irritation is instant. Makes me think of the first few years after that night. The night that led my sister and me here. The looks. The rogue comments. Especially toward Lenora.

I turn to face him, attempting to block his view of her. "Did you need something?"

"What? Oh, right." He stutters, another flush creeping up his neck. This one might stay forever. "I was just going to thank you again."

"You've already thanked me. There's no need to do it twice." I'm about to walk away when I force myself to pause once more. "I'm sorry for your loss, by the way. If it's any consolation, Wayne once told me he'd rather be dead than living in this godforsaken snowflake pile of garbage we made of America."

The man nods slowly, clearly taken aback. "Uh, thanks."

I leave him there, with his mouth slightly parted and his eyes wide. I turn toward my cabin and see what he sees. Lenora is at the window. As I knew she would be. Like a Halloween decoration long forgotten.

Lenora's brown hair is longer than mine, nearly waist length. She lets it hang in her eyes while mine barely brushes my shoulders. That's the only visible difference between us. We have the same thin lips and blue eyes set just a smidge too far apart.

People say we're as identical as it gets.

We shared a sac and placenta in utero, my sister and I, not just a womb, and that, according to our mother's doctor, is an important distinction. Our dad told us the doctor warned my mother of the dangers surrounding mono-mono twins. One of us would inevitably steal nutrients from the other and grow stronger as the other grew weaker. We were born six weeks early during the hottest summer Alabama had seen in a decade. Me at seven pounds and Lenora at four. Dad said even as infants, we'd cried when separated. Apparently, Lenora didn't hold it against me for trying to kill her in the womb.

That would become our pattern. She'd always forgive me. I'd always let her.

Especially when I didn't deserve it.

Lenora is all frown lines and suspicion when I open the back door. "You've been gone for seventy minutes, Cassie. I was starting to worry. Who was that?"

"Wayne's nephew," I answer as I look at her. Try to see what the nephew saw. A pale girl with a worried face just staring at him through the window. Had a chill rolled down his spine? Had he taken a step back as the unease slipped around his neck and tightened like a noose?

But that man, just like all the others, doesn't see what I see. The years Lenora spent outside. The summers we slathered our teenage selves in baby oil and tried to tan on the back deck even though the willow always blocked the sun. He doesn't see the girl who falls apart at sad movies and who hates hard candies.

He doesn't understand that I'm the reason she's ruined.

That it's my job to protect her.

"What did he want? Damn it, Cassie, could you at least wipe off your feet? You'll track dirt all through the house."

"I'm sorry." But I'm not apologizing for my dirty feet. I'm apologizing for something else. Something far more significant.

Lenora's gaze moves over me. "Everything OK? He's not evicting us, is he?"

And what would we do then, my dear sister, if he were? The question is right there on the tip of my tongue.

Anyway, maybe that would be for the best. An eviction. A reason to leave.

"Came by to tell us he's selling. I wouldn't let us get evicted," I say, scrubbing my bare feet one at a time over the rug, then tossing the cans in our trash. The heat of the cabin is already sending needle pricks to my frozen toes, and the sensation is painful as I walk. It was better when I was outside. When I couldn't feel anything at all.

Our cabin is just as small as it looks: a tiny alcove of a kitchen, a slightly larger living room, two bedrooms, and no bathroom. Hence the bathhouse. I used to take our laundry to a laundromat once every couple of weeks. But when that became too much, I invested in a compact washing machine we had installed. It sits neatly by the counter in the kitchen.

Sometimes, when I feel like the walls are closing in and I can't breathe, I tell myself it's quaint.

And when the urge to run strikes me, I tell myself it's OK as long as I come back.

To Lenora.

"Selling to who? Did he say what's going to happen to us?" she asks, already fidgeting nervously.

"He said the buyer is going to run the place same as Wayne."

"Huh." She breathes out again and turns back to the window, fogging it with her breath. "That was fast."

There isn't snow on the ground in our pocket of Tennessee, only a bitter chill and the eerie sound of the wind. It's four days into December, and the bite in the air teases the first frost. We're days away from keeping our woodburning stove going all day—not just at night.

"It's so sad, isn't it? What happened to Wayne?"

"Yes," I agree.

But I'm only thinking of Lenora. The girl who used to run outside barefoot with me.

Maybe it's all true. Maybe I don't wear shoes because I need to feel. Like some distant part of me has long since been shut off. Maybe being inside this cabin makes it impossible to feel anything except fear and worry, and I need the jagged rocks to cut my feet and the ice to freeze my toes. That's all better than what waits for me here.

The guilt hits me faster than the thought can leave.

Not her fault. None of this is her fault.

I look at my sister—back in place, staring out the window—and think about what Wayne's nephew said. Lenora and I look just alike. Identical, down to the freckle above our lip.

Identical like the trees growing from the cold dirt floor outside at night.

He'd have to look closer to find our thumbprints.

On that night fifteen years ago, Lenora and I walked down a hallway together. But when the door opened, the scene unfolded like a sick feature film.

Lenora closed her eyes.

I only know because mine were open.

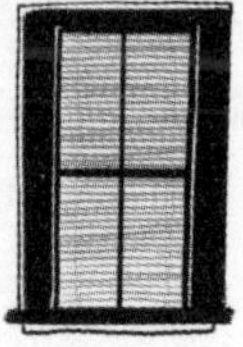

CHAPTER TWO
LENORA

"I'm not afraid to leave my house." My voice is stiff as a wet blanket left out in a winter storm. There's a coin in my hand. A dollar coin my father found when I was a kid. It had been raining, and we were running into the grocery store. He stopped abruptly in the middle of a busy crosswalk, nearly getting plowed down by a minivan in the pouring rain, to pick it up and give it to me. At the time, I tossed it into my jewelry box and forgot all about it.

Then my father was gone, and suddenly it seemed all I had left of him was that coin.

I've carried it with me ever since. Now, fifteen years later, you can't see the face at all. Just the indentation of my thumb. I roll it around my palm and squeeze, but the panicky feeling doesn't leave.

"I never said you were, Lenora." Daphne stares back at me through the screen of my laptop, her hand clenching a pencil and scribbling in her notebook just as every therapist has done since the dawn of time. Luckily, she can't see my hands. "This anxiety you feel about leaving, where do you think it comes from?"

The answer is there, blasting through my mind like fireworks.

Twenty-one, twenty-two, twenty-three—

"Lenora?"

"I don't want to talk about that night." My fingers still, clenched around the ball. I don't have to clarify which night. There is only one.

"We don't have to talk about it. Let's go back further. Before that night."

This is the part where my pulse quickens. Where the blood inside me boils into a thick, mushy soup. The need to squeeze my eyes shut against the images is there. That's what I've always done, isn't it? Closed my eyes when looking became too uncomfortable. When the truth had the power to corrode my insides, looking away was the only way to save myself.

The only memory I can handle is the one right before. The memory of Cassie and me walking down that damned hallway when we should have turned and run the other way.

"Come back, Lenora. I can feel your mind drifting. Are you thinking about it? Have you ever wondered why it is that no matter what we're talking about, it always seems to come back to your mother or father, but we just can't get past this point?"

The thoughts come on their own. I can't block them out. Dad. His kind smile. His calloused hand squeezing mine. His love for car shows and potato chips.

It's not my father who's the problem.

It's my mother. "I don't have the energy for this today." And it's true. But it has nothing to do with me or this topic and everything to do with what's happening today.

My thumb rubs along the face of the coin harder, and my blood begins to loosen. My vision opens and widens or perhaps narrows and closes, depending on how you look at it. I'm not there anymore. Not in that hallway. I'm here. In the cabin with my sister.

And today we have bigger problems.

I fight the urge to look out the window. Surely nothing has changed in the five minutes since I last looked.

"We're almost out of time anyway. Just humor me here. Your anxiety, it all started that night. The more we talk about it, the closer we can get you to going outside."

"I do go outside."

"The bathhouse doesn't count."

"I can go out anytime I want. I choose not to." But it's a lie. I hear it. Daphne hears it too.

Her eyes shift down to her notebook, and she sighs. "I think sometimes we tell ourselves that. Is this about your mother, Lenora? About not knowing where she is?"

It's like she opens a door, and *everything* comes rushing out. The memory of her, my mother, is a shock of black hair against a white sheet hanging out to dry. A burst of red against the darkest night.

I force everything back. The memories. The turmoil. The vomit. Shove it all into a six-foot hole in the ground and bury it. Not today. Can't do this today.

"No one knows where she is. It doesn't matter anyway… I'm happy here with Cassie. We're happy. And I'm working on all the other stuff."

"I know you are. You've come so far, and I know this is difficult to talk about. But maybe we should? Maybe that could help. She's still out there somewhere, isn't she? Is that where your anxiety comes from?"

More words I don't think about. Words I can't think about. They tracked her at one point. There was a sighting of her somewhere in Colorado, then in Oklahoma. Every time a new crime documentary airs or there's a newscast on the anniversary, a flurry of tips come rolling in.

None of them ever lead anywhere.

I stare at the long braids wrapped in an elegant twist on Daphne's head, but I'm thinking of outside. The new owner arriving. The pressure in my chest and all the things I wish I could do to alleviate it.

Daphne must sense my distraction and thankfully closes the notebook. "That's it for today. We'll pick back up next time I see you."

I offer her a quick goodbye, close my laptop, and release a shaky breath. I want to tell her more. The truth. That there's a battle in me. A war waging in the deepest pit of my stomach. The thing I did versus who I am.

Or maybe those are the same thing.

Can you be defined by one moment?

I hold my stomach, pressing my fingers into the soft skin beneath my belly button.

And I'm still there. Standing at the end of that hallway with my eyes closed.

"I think she's here."

My body starts, and my hands come down on the tabletop. "Come on, Cassie. You can't just sneak up on people like that."

Cassie doesn't acknowledge me as she walks past the table to the kitchen window. Today Cassie wears an oversize sweatshirt with a college logo on the front. It's one of at least fifteen in her closet and strewn around her room. A collection of secondhand collegiate apparel from colleges she's never attended. T-shirts that tout nursing or engineering programs. College football mascots and national championships. She's barefoot, of course. That's why I didn't hear her footsteps.

"Someone is definitely there."

Our corner of Maryville, Tennessee, thirty minutes outside Knoxville, is something visitors once considered idyllic. Wayne told us stories of the years this cabin was packed every summer and fall. But we'd never seen it. Most of the time, it just sounded like the ramblings of a man who believed in conspiracy theories and packed his house full of food storage and toilet paper.

But that doesn't mean we don't have them. Visitors. Plenty of them in Cabin Three over the years. Writers on a deadline, couples on weekend getaways, families wanting to unplug for the weekend. I don't know how they find this place, only that they do. The difference between them and us is that they always leave.

Cassie and I stay.

"Come here and look," Cassie says, "and you'll see what I'm seeing. I think that's her."

It's like wading through a vat of mud as I move to stand beside her, inching a little closer to her warmth. There is a thin layer of frost blanketing the maple and pine trees between our cabins. That's what I notice first. The beauty of this place. This is the closest we'll get to snow at least until January. Even then, it's hit-or-miss, but it's enough. Sometimes if I stand close enough to the window, press my hand against the frozen glass, I tell myself I can even feel the breeze cut against my cheeks.

"I don't see anything." But I'm not really looking. My heart is going too fast. I don't want to see the new owner. I just want Wayne to be back. For things to be normal again.

"Look," she exclaims loudly. "That's a car that just pulled in. On the other side of Cabin One."

She's right. The corner of a black vehicle peeks out from the top of the driveway. Something about seeing the car sends my anxiety free-falling. Even more than my earlier conversation with Daphne. I rub the coin in consecutive strokes while counting them out in my head.

The counting helps. It's like moving a pot of water off the stove before it boils over. Keeps all my bullshit inside. Keeps me normal.

Cassie pretends not to notice.

She likes to do that when it comes to me.

When I make it to twenty-one, the door of the black car swings open. A puff of smoke slips out with a woman.

I squeeze the coin tighter.

And tighter.

"Are you OK?" Cassie asks without looking at me.

"I'm fine."

The woman disappears inside the cabin in a flurry of color, too far away for me to identify features, and I step away from the window, busying myself with my laptop.

"Should we introduce ourselves?" Cassie asks. "I'll need to talk to her about rent. By the way, have you seen the car note? I swear I left it on the counter."

Icy-hot fear sluices through me at the thought of speaking to her—a stranger. I hate these parts of myself. The parts that are so cut up and mangled, I can't manage the simplest tasks.

"Haven't seen it."

Cassie moves toward the sink, answering her first question before I get a chance. "She's probably busy today, and I need to cook dinner anyway. Maybe we can drop in tomorrow?" She says "we." Always says it. Always pretending.

"You should do that," I force myself to say. "I've got work to do anyway. It'll probably keep me busy tonight and tomorrow."

She hums under her breath, still not looking at me. "Do you want hamburgers for dinner or chicken?"

There it is. Proof I don't deserve her. Another constant reminder of all the ways I failed her. How much I screw up doesn't matter when I have a sister who's always ready to help me pretend everything is OK. Even though sometimes I wonder if Cassie is pretending or if she genuinely forgets. Like there is a part of her, more dominant than all the more reasonable parts, that cannot see me as poison. Cassie is like that. So honest in her own mind and with herself that she can't picture anyone else any other way. Especially me.

Hamburger or chicken?

A long walk down a short hallway.

Cassie's gasp right before everything went to hell.

All my fault even if Cassie sees it differently. "Hamburger is fine." I say, sliding back into my chair. She bangs around in the kitchen, and I open my laptop to the current manuscript I'm ghostwriting. Counting usually calms me, but counting words—or rather, being reminded that I've yet to break fifty thousand words on a manuscript due in two weeks—has the opposite effect.

"You remember that geriatric dog in our neighborhood?" Cassie asks suddenly. "With the scruffy gray hair. You snuck him in and tried to rescue him."

The memory is so stark and sudden, it takes me a second to process it. To fish it from the depths of my mind beneath the filth and carnage. "He had the mange and worms."

Cassie chuckles. "Mom and Dad were so angry. What were we, eight? Nine?"

"Eight." I want to laugh at the memory, but something stops me. How seriously we hid the animal, claiming we were going to keep him forever without our parents knowing. We didn't make it a single night.

The thing about good memories is they eventually get overwhelmed. Like a giant tarp filling with water until it collapses, leaving everything beneath ruined. My fingers freeze on the laptop, and my stomach drops.

Yes, I remember the old scraggly dog. I also remember what happened after. Cassie is humming to herself, oblivious and in her own perfectly normal world. "The dog died," I whisper.

"Hmm?"

"The dog," I say, louder this time, and I don't know why. I don't know why I have to ruin things. "I killed him."

Her back tenses. "You didn't know he couldn't have grapes, Lenora. It was an accident."

"Do you think the moonshine is what killed Wayne?" I ask, not knowing what's gotten into me. What I expect from her. It's bad enough, the images of the lethargic, vomiting dog. Now there are images of Wayne mixed in. Dead Wayne. I never saw his body, and that's almost worse. I only have my imagination to fill in the gaps.

"I don't know, Lenora."

"He was drinking a lot toward the end. Always out in the woods doing who knows what. I always thought maybe he drank himself to death." I haven't thought about it much. But when the thoughts creep in, it's the only one that makes sense. Someone like Wayne is a pillar. A person untouchable by death or ailment. Honestly, it's hard to picture Wayne dead at all. In my mind, Wayne is coming through the woods with a bundle of firewood or knocking on our door when UPS delivered our packages to his cabin by mistake.

He always lingered, talking about some government conspiracy or another. An election. An outbreak. The good old days before his campsite turned into a ghost town. Yet another thing he blames the government for and not his own loosening grip on reality and his reliance on alcohol. But Cassie and I know the truth. As Wayne ventured deeper into the idiosyncrasies of his mind, the campsite went downhill. His own fault.

But after all he did for us, we put up with his idiosyncrasies gladly, renting out this cabin for pennies. A camping trip that turned into a two-year stint with no end in sight. There was no contract. Just cash exchanged each month and no questions asked.

"Poor Wayne," I mutter mostly to myself. I was comfortable with Wayne. I knew what to expect.

Cassie drops a hunk of red meat onto a pan, and it sizzles loudly. "You act like you were friends or something. We hardly spoke to the man."

"He let us live here, Cassie. That means something." *And you saw his corpse*, I want to add but don't. That should mean something too.

"He'd get drunk at night and stumble around in the dark, mumbling about how our government is planting microchips in our food. Not to mention I'm pretty sure he was racist." Cassie doesn't speak with disdain. There's no judgment. Really there is no feeling at all. Just a simple conveying of information from one person to another. That's how Cassie is. The words that break on other people's tongues slip right off Cassie's. Everyone, she says, should always speak exactly how they feel. But I know better. I know there are some things even Cassie doesn't speak.

"He's dead," I tell her. "You could at least pretend to care."

"It's normal to dub others with sainthood when they die, but some people are intolerable. That's just the way it is." As she says it, she cuts an onion briskly. "Do you remember Aunt Lisa at Dad's funeral, mumbling about how it all must be a mistake? Do you remember how she looked at us?"

The second mention of my family today, and my blood pressure rises.

Think about it, Lenora.

Talk about it, Lenora.

The words I want to say form on my lips and die in the same spot. I'm one of those. The weak ones who can't say the words we're all thinking. Can never quite get them out.

My feet are firmly on the hardwood of the cabin, the room locked in around me, but, hard as I fight it, the world sways like a watercolor painting blending into somewhere else. Another room, in a house in Alabama with a screened in porch. The night so silent except for one solitary noise.

There's the door and the hallway and the sliver of light.

And everything that came after.

Me with my eyes shut tight, willing the scene to change. Please, please change.

Cassie with her hand in mine, tugging, tugging.

Running.

I gather myself. Focus on my sister in this moment. The line across her forehead has gotten deeper over the years. Particularly over the fifteen that have passed since that night.

Too much. Too much for today.

"I should make a cake for dessert, I think." I return to my laptop. Sometimes it is better to not think of such things. Even if Cassie doesn't think so. She gets back to the meat, and I turn back to my work.

But the thoughts linger, one piercing through worst of all, a vision of me standing in that hallway, my hands slick with red. Cassie's high-pitched voice from behind me.

Lenora, what did you do?

And the fear. Burning hotter than the blood on my hands.

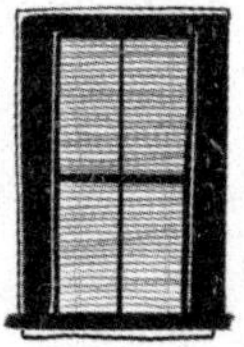

CHAPTER THREE
CASSIE

When I sit in front of the camera, I like to wear their skin. The victims. Slip them on like an evening coat and pretend their lives and mine are the same. I'm not just me anymore. Not just Cassie—a woman who lives in the middle of nowhere, avoiding a sordid past, taking care of her sister.

I get to be *them.*

It didn't use to be that way. I used to focus on the killers for my channel. That's what everyone else did. The ones who took lives were the ones who got clicks and views and blood thrumming with curiosity and awe.

It was Lenora who made me change course. Lenora who asked me one day if I could name three Bundy victims, and I couldn't. Couldn't even remember the name of one. Now I can name them all. It's like there's a file folder in my mind, and I welcome them in.

Pop their eyes out of their head and into mine.

I want to see what they saw. Analyze every part of it.

That perspective is what made my channel grow. The comments on my videos were mostly alike. Telling me how refreshing it is to learn about the victims. To focus on them. To remind ourselves that they are not defined by one single moment. They were *alive* once. People who loved and hurt and lost.

Though, with each case I bury myself in, there is a distinct feeling of guilt. A hidden motive that borders on exploitive.

If I can be them, it means I don't have to be myself.

If I sink deep enough, if I work hard enough, my own memories will quiet. All the ways I went wrong. All the ways I could have done better.

All the ways I allowed my sister to be hurt.

When I record for my channel, I am so much better than Cassie Lowe. As I tell their stories to an internet audience, hundreds of thousands of faceless names, I can feel them come back alive. Sometimes too much and too potently. Like they're the ones finally getting the chance to tell their own story, and they just can't shut up. And I think if I do it enough, it will become my own form of penance.

Except I don't need God to forgive me. I only want to forgive myself.

I begin. "Beatrice Martin left her home at approximately 8:18 in the morning the day she went missing. She was seen on two security cameras. One caught her on the corner of Parks and Court; the other caught her crossing onto Main Street."

But inside my mind, the story goes differently. I visualize it the way Beatrice might have.

Beatrice is feeling well. The sun is out, the breeze is calm, stirring the hair around her face, and she has lunch plans with her sister. This will be a good day.

"The day her life was taken, she wore a jean jacket her brother had passed down to her. Her friends said she rarely left home without it. It was oversize and faded by one too many washes. Over the years, she'd ironed patches onto the back and lapels. Her favorite band names—always an indie band you've never heard of. Song lyrics—indie as well." I chuckle and then sober too quickly.

"You might read that she was last seen outside a twenty-four-seven pharmacy before witnesses saw her getting into a dark SUV. The same one her ex-boyfriend drove. You might read the condition in which they found her body. Or whether she'd been sexually assaulted. These facts are important. But arguably not the most important part of Beatrice Martin. When Beatrice walked into that pharmacy that day, she purchased a bottle of lemonade—her mother told me she was obsessed with the stuff—and a pack of Red Vines. And when she climbed into her ex-boyfriend's car, allegedly, that girl who loved underground bands and the comfort of her brother's well-worn jean jacket never thought that day would be the last day she'd wear it."

The rest of the story unfolds inside my head violently, and I'm unable to stop it even if I wanted to. This is the part of the story I save only for myself. The worst part. But I make myself live it every time. Force myself to picture every aching moment. *Beatrice trusts Josh even when he's angry. He just wants to talk, he says. And she thinks that maybe she owes him that much. Into his car she goes. He drives quickly, acts erratic. Beatrice is afraid, her hands clutching the lapels of her jacket, her face pale. She talks to him quietly and low, like she's speaking to a child. But her voice raises the farther they get from civilization.*

And she's aware in some primal part of her mind, between the feeling of the condensation from the lemonade clenched between her thighs wetting her leggings and the acrid taste of fear in the back of her throat, that this isn't right. Josh isn't right.

Sweat rolling down her face and back. Beatrice doesn't want to die. Please, *she begs. But he doesn't answer. He just stops the car. Makes her get out. They're alone. In the middle of nowhere.* Please, *she tries again. But he doesn't talk. He's crying now. Screaming. Red-faced. "You bitch." Spit flies from his lips. He pulls the trigger. Beatrice falls. Her hands feel the warmth of her own blood before the pain registers. She stares up at the sky and thinks of the lemonade she never had the chance to sip. Thinks of her mother singing to the radio on the way home from work. Her sister waiting for her at that café with the good bread. She doesn't want blood on her jacket but nuzzles deeper into the worn denim anyway. She pictures it's her brother's arms and closes her eyes.*

Sometimes I want to squeeze my eyes shut against the violence. I want to cup my hands to my abdomen as if stopping a pulsing, bleeding wound. Sometimes I don't want to think about any of this at all.

"This is where we're going to pick up next week. Before I sign off, I want to remind you to be respectful in the comments. On this channel, we don't victim blame. If I see any of that with this case, your comment will be deleted. As always everyone, thank you for watching. I will see you next Friday."

I stop recording and sit with my back to the wall where a tapestry hangs behind me. Lenora picked it out. She said the blue-waved design reminded her of the ocean, and it's supposed to be calming. It reminds me of drowning, but I didn't tell her that. That day, she'd hung it with worry in her eyes, as if she knew the effect telling these stories has on me.

I never told her, but the tapestry isn't enough to slow my heart.

To stop the brutal flickering images in my head.

I should start editing my video. Start posting on my social media channels, promoting Beatrice's episode. Send Beatrice's mother a first look at the video like I told her I would. Start doing something. Anything.

But I can't just yet.

I'm still in her head.

The blue sky. The feeling of life slipping away. The feeling of dying. Of knowing that her own death is inevitable. The fear that impales her with ice right before she closes her eyes for what she must know will be the last time.

That's the part I always get stuck on, the moment when they know they're dying. That moment when they know this will be their last breath. What do they think about? Their family. A beautiful memory. Waves lapping at their sand-covered toes. Or are they panicked as they grasp at the ground, at their own clothes, at their murderer? Anything to stay tethered to life, to *stay.*

The recording room is tiny. Just five feet across and eight feet wide, it used to be an alcove in the corner of the living room. I built the wall and soundproofed it myself. Just inside is a tiny desk with a microphone and camera set up and my laptop on a stool with the script running on the screen.

But it began with a video recorded in my car. Me detailing my own story. Not in the way the media wrote about it. I talked about Lenora. Her strength. Our fears. I didn't touch much on the actual crime. The video went viral, and I decided to start my own channel. Seven years later, I have over a million subscribers, several hundred thousand views per video, sponsors, and even a fan base. People who love the way I tell the stories of victims almost as much as they love the fact that I was one too.

Lenora pretends to be OK with it all.

But I don't miss the way she averts her face every time I open that recording room door. The fact she won't watch a video and refuses to edit my scripts when I need a second set of eyes on them. Too busy, she says. On a deadline.

Always an excuse.

Sure, I can name all of Bundy's victims now. I know the most recent missing people. I have Google alerts on dozens of victims' names. I like to think that my channel is different. That what I'm doing is somehow better.

But the truth comes in the queasy roll of my stomach each time I post and wonder if the victim's family or friends will see it. Unlike Beatrice's mother, they don't always participate in interviews or give me their blessing to make the video. Sometimes I wonder if they will think I'm just like all the others picking at their grief like vultures, tucking into their hurt like we're ravenous for it. Hungry for clicks and views and money.

And I wonder, since I'm a victim too, if that makes me a cannibal.

The door to my recording room swings open. Lenora is rolling her coin between her thumb and forefinger so absentmindedly, I don't think she even knows when she's doing it. Her eyes are two buckets of anxiety. "Someone is here."

I glance at the time. It's after ten.

There is no window on our thick wooden front door or even

beside it. These cabins weren't built like modern ones. Open and airy with clear visuals to outside. Cabins Two and Three were built for camping. For economic soundness. There is a woodburning stove, window units for air in the summer, a flimsy screened-in front porch, and an outdoor bathhouse between Cabin Two and Cabin Three. The bathhouse doesn't bother Lenora or me. After all, we're mostly the only ones who use it.

And I secretly like it because it gets Lenora out. The brief steps she takes to the bathhouse twice a day provide the only fresh air she gets.

Knock, knock, knock.

I feel the warmth of Lenora's body as she trails me to the door and hear the click of her nails as she fidgets behind me.

I open the door to reveal the screen and a blurry figure. They're angled back into the shadows. The light from inside doesn't even touch this person's toes.

"Hi, I'm so glad I caught you." The feminine voice is cheerful, and I realize who I'm talking to instantly. Lenora grips the back of my shirt. She must get it too.

The new owner.

The woman smells like artificial cherries, which makes me think of the smoke we saw coming from her car earlier. Not a cigarette. Vape. There was a couple in Cabin Three once with a seventeen-year-old son. He'd stand behind the bathhouse vaping while his parents argued over the charcoal grill. That same artificial fruity scent would come in through our window units. It was summer, and I couldn't close the window no matter how many migraines the scent gave Lenora.

"I saw you next door," the woman continues. "I've been wanting to introduce myself, but I've been so busy. I'm sorry to drop in so late now. Your lights were on, so I figured I'd take my chance."

"I'm Cassie. This is my sister, Lenora."

"Lovely to meet you both." The woman shifts just enough for the shadows to move across her face and for me to make out a few features. A long thin nose. Wide mouth and dark eyes. Her hair is lighter than ours, almost blond, and she wears it short like me.

"Why'd you do it?" I ask curiously. "Buy this place, I mean?"

Lenora's nails dig into my back through the fabric of my shirt.

The woman grins, revealing a row of perfectly straight white teeth. "I just moved to the state. Had a high-stress job back home. Needed a change. It's peaceful out here, isn't it?" Her eyes flick over my shoulder to Lenora and then back to me again. "I didn't know you were twins. You look exactly alike."

"We've been told."

She laughs under her breath, and it all just feels awkward. Meeting living people. I'm not good with warmth and heartbeats. How can I know this woman when I haven't seen her pale arm on a coroner's table? When I can't imagine what she thought of as she died?

"Well, look," she says finally, "I don't want to keep you."

"We've been wanting to speak to you about rent. We usually drop it off the first week of the month."

"About that. Mark gave me all the paperwork he could find. I'll be honest, it's all a bit jumbled. Very disorganized. I've been trying to make sense of it. But there isn't a lease for you all. Do you happen to have a copy for me?"

"We didn't ever sign anything. We just pay Wayne monthly."

"Paid," Lenora corrects, and I'm surprised she even spoke at all considering the way she's trembling behind me.

"Oh. Maybe I'll draw something up then." The woman looks between us once more. "I mean, other than the hair, it's like looking at the same person. It's almost eerie."

"That must be why they've banished us here."

Lenora nudges me. Hard.

"Right." The woman laughs again, as artificial as the cherries on her breath. "I should get going. I've got a lot to unpack still."

"You never told us your name."

"That's right. I didn't. Sorry." Another laugh. Another waft of cherries to the face. "I'm Sarah Hill."

Lenora mumbles, "It was really nice to talk to you, Sarah."

"You too." Another warm smile as she inches toward her vehicle.

"You drove here?"

"It was so dark. I didn't see a walking path."

"There is no path." There are only woods. But surely she isn't afraid of a little jaunt through the trees. It's certainly faster than hopping in a car and using the dirt road to get to our cabin.

She waits a breath as if expecting me to expand further. "Right. Well, perhaps there should be. Nice to meet you both again."

"Is it just you?" I ask, bringing her attention back to me and glancing from Sarah to the car behind her as if expecting someone to be sitting in the passenger seat. A husband, wife, or child waiting impatiently. But it's empty.

"Yes." I can't see her well enough to decipher if she thinks the question is intrusive, but her tone doesn't change. "You know, I like the idea of having you both here though. We can help each other out. You'll let me know if you see something out of the ordinary, and I'll do the same for you. We can take care of one another. We're neighbors now."

"Are you expecting something out of the ordinary?"

This time when she laughs, I cringe, and I know it would be polite to smile, but I can't make myself.

"I hope not."

"Where did you say you were from?"

"Ah, San Antonio."

Lenora pinches the skin on the back of my arm, and to save the few unbruised portions left, I decide to bite back any more questions.

Sarah takes another backward step down the porch stairs. "I'll let you both get back to your evening."

Lenora tells her good night, and when Sarah's taillights fade to pinpricks, she turns to me. "It's like you want us to be on the street. You do understand she controls if we have a place to live or not? Cassie?"

"They were innocent questions."

Lenora's stepped fully back into the cabin now. A dark silhouette with the light from the kitchen encases her in an unearthly glow. Another creepy Halloween vision, my sister.

"She's kind of strange, isn't she?" Lenora says, "The way she kept smiling, I mean."

"I'm sure she's thinking the same thing about us right about now."

Lenora swallows loudly, her fingers folding in and out, her lips moving. Counting. She's counting silently.

"Hey," I whisper. "She seemed nice, and she said we could stay. There's nothing to worry about."

She takes another step into the dark living room, her vision flickering one last time to the spot where Sarah disappeared. There's something there. Something in the look that I recognize. That has me instantly on edge.

"I'm going to bed. 'Night, Cass."

An inky blackness spreads through me, a poisonous film covering me from my scalp to the tips of my toes. I can't explain it, but as I turn off the lights, lock up, and stand just a moment beside Lenora's closed bedroom door, I wonder if Lenora's looking out her window. Down the hill at our new neighbor. Watching her move boxes in and out.

Watching.

I go into my room and make a call.

Two months before the night our lives went to crap, my mother smiled for the first time in weeks. Mother was considered beautiful in the small town where she grew up. She was homecoming queen and a cheerleader. Our father was a quarterback from another school who'd worked his way up to earning everything he had. My father's parents were Brazilian immigrants who taught him the value of hard work. Regardless of what would happen, Mom and Dad truly loved each other once. We grew up watching them show affection: the kisses, the dancing, the touching. It was all there, until one day it wasn't.

Mom said it was Dad's fault, how they reached that point. I wonder, if she were beside me now, if she'd still say the same thing.

"That was amazing, babe." Parker breathes against my neck,

filling my senses with the smell of citrus and mint. The scent pulls me back to reality first. Then the feeling. His calloused hands on my hips. His rough beard against my skin.

Parker. Attentive and giving Parker. Parker who always wants to talk and be with me longer.

I am not in Alabama. Not with my parents. Not a victim looking death in the face. Not stuck in an endless loop of that night. Not wondering what Lenora is doing.

I'm only with Parker.

But when he's with me, over me, in me, my thoughts can never focus. I try and try to feel, but sometimes life is too distracting. And in the back of my brain is Sarah. The way Lenora looked at her.

"Cassie?"

I tuck the sheets against my chest and roll sideways. "Make sure to be quiet when you leave. I don't want Lenora to hear you."

Silence. "Are you serious?"

I don't say anything, and I can't see his face, but I can feel his anger. It's clear in the way he throws the sheet off his body, slaps his feet against the hardwood, jerks his pants on. I sit still and watch where a spider makes its lazy way to the ceiling. How simple the life of a spider must be. How misunderstood.

Parker is still in the room, but he's not moving or making a sound. "I'm sick of this, Cassie. I'm sick of sneaking around. Of leaving in the middle of the night like a dirty secret. You have to tell her about me."

I lose sight of the spider now.

"Cassie, are you listening? Do you know how this feels? You call me at midnight and ask me to come over. Twenty minutes later you're telling me to leave. We haven't even talked."

As his voice rises, my cheeks heat. "Lenora is sleeping. Keep your voice down."

"Really? Your sister? It always comes back to her, doesn't it? Do you think this is healthy, what you two have here? You think this is *normal*?"

The spider is back, making its way down the wall. It stops near the baseboard, and it looks at me with its tiny eyes and little mouth. *Normal,* the spider says with a harsh grin. *What is normal anyway?*

That flicker in Lenora's gaze.

"Are you even listening?"

"Parker?" I roll over to look at him. His dark hair is messy, and his tawny skin gleams in the moonlight creeping in through my parted curtains. He really is a vision, and in another life, he'd be wrapped around me, still cuddled in bed. In another life I'd be this thing, this elusive normal. "You know what this is. I told you from the beginning, I can't offer more than this."

"It's been months. I thought…I thought you'd change your mind by now."

I don't say anything, just stare at the disappointment on his face. Yes, I hate that it's my fault he feels this way. But maybe this is better. Maybe he needs to hate me.

"I'm sorry."

His mouth slackens before he snaps it shut, rips his shirt on, and makes it to my door before turning to face me. "I really cared about you. Clearly, you don't feel the same."

Parker leaves quietly, but I don't relax until his car cranks and headlights shine against my window. When I met the man, he and a few buddies were staying in Cabin Three. The first night they arrived, I invited him in. I've seen him a few times a month since. Each time, Parker seems to expect more and more.

He forgets the first thing I ever said to him. His friends were drinking around the fire, and I sat beside him a little too closely, holding my feet to the flames, enjoying the way the warmth of his body at my side made me forget about the chill to my back. I was curious about him. The strength in his jaw. The way his hands seemed to circle that beer can twice. He'd be a fighter. Someone came at him with a knife, he'd fight. The only way to get a man like him would be to take him by surprise, and that appealed to me.

He caught my eye, and we stared at each other for a long moment before I curled his hand in mine and whispered, "I'm not interested in the dream. I don't want a husband or kids. I don't want to know your favorite sport or where you went to college. I can't give you any of that either. I can only give you one thing if you want it."

He sputtered over his beer, set the can down, and allowed me to lead him inside.

He knew the score before I even knew his name.

The walls of the cabin feel too tight, suddenly. The need to get out of here is stifling.

Careful as to not wake Lenora, I creep down the hall and slip my coat on for once. Too cold to pretend I don't need it. The night air is bitter, but at least there's no wind. I walk down the hill, past Cabin Three.

"Whoa, you're walking too fast."

"Come on, I want to see the waterfall."

"Your sister can't keep up."

Lenora is several feet behind us, picking up rocks as she walks.

Dad grabs my arm, forcing me to stop. To slow down. "Just wait a second."

"But it's so close."

"Hey, I know it's close. We're going to get there. Right now, let's enjoy being here."

The memory is enough to unspool me like yarn. Six-year-old me didn't know that everything good in him would soon be gone, and eventually he would be too. That version of me stands at the lining of the woods and watches me with calculating eyes, still wearing the hiking boots she never had a chance to break in.

Stupid girl, she says.

"Yes," I whisper.

The tear that trickles down my face takes me by surprise. I don't wipe it away as I hang a right and take a U-shaped trail through the woods. A part of me hopes it will freeze on my face and stay there forever. My own teardrop tattoo. A reminder of death. Just not someone else's—my own.

My father's face doesn't leave my mind. Neither does his voice. Or his smile that day on our hike. Until suddenly it's weaving in and out with another image. The fear on Lenora's face that night.

My own shaking voice—

No.

Not going there. It's over. We're safe. We're together. That's all that matters. My fists clench at my sides, and I hold them there stiffly with my eyes closed until the thoughts leave. Something about Sarah. Her coming here. It's brought all this back to the surface for me, and I just need to find a way to shove it all back down.

I open my eyes when I can breathe properly again. I meant to head to the Blacktop. To the rock. Maybe some teenagers would be there, fumbling around in the dark. Stuck in their vortex of happiness and oblivious to me.

But I'm not at the Blacktop. Somehow, I end up here. Cabin One is just through the trees. Every light is off. There is no sign of life at all.

I walk toward Cabin One because I'm not ready to go home.

Because I only want to look.

Because I'm not really doing anything wrong.

It's larger than the other cabins. I've never been inside, but Wayne mentioned once it's a three-bedroom. The day I found Wayne's body, I looked in all his windows because I was curious, and he was too dead to stop me. His kitchen was stacked floor to ceiling with canned food, MREs, and supplies. His living room was littered with boxes, tools, and hunting paraphernalia. That must be why it took two moving trucks and several large men to clear the place out. Lenora swears she saw weaponry as well—bags of guns and a bow. It had been dusk at that point, and we didn't have a clear view through the trees, so she could have been wrong, but I wouldn't doubt it.

Either way, the whole thing makes me uncomfortable now.

The cabin looks the same as it always has. The dark wooden structure is a black mass beneath the shade of the pine trees and in the shadows of the moon. My feet move of their own volition over the brush, closer to the cabin. The curtains aren't pulled, and there's a clear view inside. I know I shouldn't, but I can't stop myself.

My breath comes out heavy as I peer in. The kitchen. A table with some papers neatly stacked on top. A mug beside the sink. A bag of chips rolled closed on the counter. A laptop tucked neatly into a corner. Miscellaneous unpacked boxes.

She is every bit the normal that I'm not.

What did I expect?

There is a dart of movement, and I glance just to the left of the doorway. There. Faintly, I can just see the outline of something. I squint into the dark, cupping my hands around my eyes. No. *Someone.*

Sarah is standing there looking right at me.

I jerk my head to the side, out of view.

I wait there, just like that for several long minutes. The temperature feels like it drops; my fingers go numb, and a cramp travels up my leg. But I don't move. I can't risk moving a single muscle. Sarah is bound to rush outside any moment and demand to know what I'm doing.

I'll tell her the truth, and Lenora will be quite angry when Sarah kicks us out.

I wait, but nothing happens.

Several more minutes pass before I lift my head.

The kitchen is empty. The spot in the doorway is shadowed, and I blink into the darkness, trying to make sense of what I thought I'd seen. Boxes stacked high with cloth draped over them.

I'm losing my mind.

"What are you doing?"

I jump, banging my back into the side of the cabin, a startled gasp slipping from my lips. But it's not Sarah demanding answers—it's a teenage girl.

"Are you some kind of pervert or something?" the girl asks, a sarcastic lilt to her voice. It's night, and I've never seen this girl before in my life, but she doesn't look afraid. If anything, she seems amused.

I hold a finger to my lips and grab her hand, confirming she is real and not a figment of my imagination. I drag her behind us, back toward the woods, back toward my cabin. Away from here. Her hand is warm, and her nails sting as they sink into my palm.

"Hey, what are you doing?" She shakes my hand free and steps away, snatching her hand to her chest like I've burned her.

We make it into the forest now, halfway back to the clearing that leads up the hill. I shoot one more glance toward Cabin One. All is silent. "What are you doing out here?"

"That's a cop-out," she says a little too loudly. "I asked you first, and you're the one looking into windows."

This is the first time I've been close enough to the girl to fully take her in. She's sixteen or seventeen, with waist-length board-straight hair and petite features. Apart from a nose that's slightly large for her face and two front teeth that are just a little crooked. What strikes me the most about her, though, is what she's wearing: a pair of cotton shorts, flip-flops, and a thin hoodie. Her arms are wrapped around herself, and she's shivering.

"What are you doing out here dressed like that?"

"Dude, you're not even wearing shoes. What are you, some kind of stalker with a foot fetish?" Her hair swishes as she says it, and I'm hit with a strong earthy smell.

"No, of course not," I say.

"You were creeping hard."

"I was not being creepy. I was…checking something."

The girl smiles, and it makes her look younger in a way. Faintly, I wonder if she *is* younger than I think. "Yeah, I think that's a solid excuse."

"How old are you, anyway?"

"Old enough to see through your bullshit. Not sure why it matters." The way she curses is like she doesn't do it often. Like a child with a power tool. She doesn't know how to use it, only knows that she wants to, and if she isn't careful, she might hurt herself. She folds her arms, elongates her neck. I recognize the look, the stance. A girl wanting to be older.

"You're not supposed to be out here. It's private property. Why don't you get back to your car, and I won't tell anyone you trespassed."

Her eyes spark. "We're staying here. Camping or whatever. What are *you* doing out here?"

"Camping?" I glance behind her toward Cabin Three. A silver van is in the driveway. How did I miss that? "You rented out Cabin Three?"

"My parents did. We just got in."

But it doesn't make sense. I hadn't heard them. Hadn't seen them. Didn't even know they were coming. Sarah didn't mention it. Wayne always told us before we had guests. "That doesn't explain what you were doing in the woods. You could get lost out here, you know." That's when I identify the smell. "Do your parents know you smoke?"

Her smile falls. "I don't know what you're talking about."

"Your face turns red when you lie. Do your parents know that too?"

"Look, what my parents don't know doesn't hurt them. It's not a big deal anyway. Weed should be legal in all fifty states."

"If you're so sure, why don't we go talk to them about it?"

Her eyes flash, her mouth tightens into a smirk. "I'll tell them what I saw. You looking into that cabin like a perv."

"They won't believe you."

"Let's find out." I can tell by the smile playing on her lips that she knows she has me. It's a real smile that puts her crooked top two teeth on display. "I've never blackmailed someone before. It feels good."

"You shouldn't smoke."

"Give me a break. You adults think you know everything. But I see the six coffees a day my teachers are drinking, my mom's wine after work and margaritas on the weekends. Don't get me started on my dad at the casinos. They've got much bigger problems than me chilling with a joint occasionally. They're hypocrites."

I expected her to fold into my questioning or get mad and huff away. But she did neither. And she's not wrong. I sigh. "You have a point. But it's illegal in Tennessee, so it's still wrong."

"So is looking through people's windows at night, and yet here we both are."

"Right again."

Her eyes narrow sharply like that was the last thing she expected me to say, and she isn't sure if she believes me.

A beam of moonlight slices through tree branches with the ease of a sharpened blade, dividing the light from the dark. The young girl inches back, out of the shadows. Away from me. Clearly not as unaffected as she appears.

"What's your name?" I ask, noting her lips are blue now. But, if I'm right about her, she's too stubborn to retreat first no matter how cold or uncomfortable she is.

"Tilly."

"I'm Cassie." I hold my hand out. She takes it slowly. Her hand is smaller than mine and colder. Her teeth are chattering, and her eyes keep shifting to the mangled trees and darkness surrounding us. Behind me there is rustling. A branch snapping.

"You really should get back inside your cabin."

"Wh-why aren't you wearing shoes?" she stutters.

I glance down at my feet. They're so cold, I can't feel them. "Sometimes I forget."

"But you remembered a coat?"

I glance down at myself and let out a gust of air. "I guess I don't really like shoes. I like to feel free. Feel the dirt. That kind of thing."

"And the shirt. Did you go to Harvard?" She gestures to my T-shirt peeking out of my coat. "That's where my mom went."

"No."

"Why are you wearing it then?"

"A friend went to Harvard." No need to give details. No need to explain that this "friend" is dead, and I never really knew her at all. Just like I don't know any of the victims I cover for my channel—at least while they were alive. But their alma maters are always easy to find.

Her face falls, and she goes to step away from me, but something clearly stops her. "Are you camping here too?"

"We live here."

"We?"

"My sister and I."

"Like live here, live here? Like year-round? This is your home?"

"Yes."

"How though? There's nothing out here at all. What do you guys even do?"

"Look through windows," I say. "Steal things. Kidnap small children. Read lots of Stephen King."

Tilly's lips quirk up. "Is this the point where you drag me into the woods and murder me?"

A door opening.

A flash of red.

My hoarse voice echoing in the night.

I must make a face or a noise or something because Tilly's brows pull together in concern. "You really are a weirdo, aren't you?"

"I think I am sometimes." Parker's words loop in my head. *Do you think this is normal?*

There's something about her though. Something that makes me want to be honest. Maybe it's her youth and innocence. Something that was stripped from Lenora and me at such a young age. Or that she reminds me of Lenora before she was broken. Before the world chewed her up and spit her out.

"Why did you and your family get here in the middle of the night?"

"Super eager to get to the woods, I guess."

"Don't you have school?"

There is the sound of a screen door flapping against a cabin and then a woman calling Tilly's name. Tilly stiffens. "Crap. I've been gone too long. You're not going to say anything, are you?"

I can't explain it. The need to protect her. But I can't fight it either. "No. I won't say anything."

"Good. And I was serious before. I won't tell anyone that you're a creeper either."

"You can. I won't ask you to lie for me."

Her mom calls her name again, but Tilly doesn't move. "If I told, what would you tell her you were doing?"

"The truth."

"Which is?"

"I'm a creep."

"Jeez. You're the weirdest person I've ever met." Tilly laughs as she says it, and then her name is shouted again. She groans. "I should go before she comes looking for me." Tilly takes off through the woods with a sarcastic salute in my direction.

I walk back to the cabin alone on stinging feet. There is no mother calling me home with worry in her voice but, I realize as the cabin comes into view, something far worse.

My sister. Wide awake and standing in the window. Wispy hair parted down the middle, curtaining her face. A white cardigan wrapped over thin shoulders. Waiting on me. Searching for me in the night, and for one second, one brief moment, I consider turning around and running. Going anywhere except that cabin.

Instead, I lift my hand in an apologetic wave and walk toward my sister.

And I can't help but wonder how much she saw.

Or why it seems to matter so much.

"Where were you?" Lenora's voice is calm when I walk in. But there's a tinge of alarm in her tone. The concern of a woman who must have found my bed empty and gotten worried.

"Just on a walk."

"Your feet, Cassie."

I sigh and wipe them on the rug. "Is this good enough for you?"

"If you would just wear shoes—"

"Why are you even up? It's the middle of the night."

Lenora glances away, and guilt spirals through me. "Heard the commotion outside. I checked your room. Saw you weren't there." She chews on her bottom lip and stares pointedly at the wall like she's trying not to cry.

It makes the crust around my heart crack and splinter with regret. "I didn't mean to snap at you."

"It's OK."

She turns to look at me, her glasses slipping down her nose. She only pulls out the giant purple-framed glasses at night. She prefers contacts, same as me. "It's weird, isn't it? That Sarah is running the place as if Wayne never existed at all. He's not even cold yet, and she's already booked a family."

"You saw?" *What else?* I want to ask. *What else did you see?*

"Hard not to. With all that screaming. I saw her daughter come from the woods. Same direction as you."

"I saw her out there," I say casually. "Talked to her. Nice kid. And I'm sure Sarah just took over Wayne's books. They've probably had the reservation for a while." But something Tilly said sticks out to me. A weekend getaway. Maybe it wasn't as planned as I thought, their coming here.

"Still. It would be respectful to wait."

"It's been nearly two weeks, Lenora. By now Wayne's nails and teeth have fallen out, and his body is beginning to liquify. Shall we wait until he's dust to keep living our lives?"

She turns to me in revulsion. "That's disgusting, Cassie. Even for you."

"Do you want the world to stop turning when you die, Lenora?"

"Possibly." She sniffs, doing that thing she does with her nails. The clicky thing. A nervous habit. For the first time, it makes me want to cover my ears or drag my own nails over my face.

I fight the feeling. This is Lenora. She needs her ways to cope just like I do. "We all die," I say, my voice softening. "The world keeps going. No one really cares."

She's quiet for too long, and that should have been my first clue that something is wrong. Her voice is icy when she speaks. "Were you going to tell me?"

The thing about twins, or at least us, is that explaining ourselves is never really needed. I know exactly what Lenora is asking me the moment I see her face.

"It's not a big deal," I tell her.

"You had a man over."

"Don't say it like that."

"Like what?" She looks at me, really looks at me. "I'm happy for you, Cassie. I want you to be happy."

I walk to the sink. Fill a glass with water. "This is why I didn't want to do this."

"Do what? You have a boyfriend? That's great. He sounds like he really likes you. Or at least what you were doing with him."

"I don't want to talk about this."

"What's the problem?" She stands and walks to me. Takes the glass away and places it on the counter. I realize now my hands are trembling, water splashing down my wrist. "This is a good thing, isn't it?"

And it all hits at once. The weight of guilt, feelings, fear, anxiety. It all comes tumbling onto me in that moment. "They loved each other, didn't they? Or did I make that up?"

Lenora pales and drops my hands, knowing at once whom I'm referring to. "I—" her words seem to get lost in the murky night. She takes a step away and leans on the counter. "Mom and Dad were complicated." It must take every ounce of her strength to answer. To talk about this at all.

But I can't stop.

"Parker said this isn't normal. We're not normal. Is it because of our parents? Is it in our DNA? Are we always going to be this way?" I'm spiraling; each question reaches into my stomach and tugs. The walls close in on all sides. This cabin will be my coffin.

In my head, there are Tilly's words and Sarah and bad mothers and all the ways our parents maim us. Everything starts wrapping together, and I think I'm crying.

Lenora spins around and takes in my tears. She hugs me to her, and she smells like safety and freshly fallen rain. "I think we just need some sleep," she says softly into my hair. "That's all."

"Lenora?" I ask quietly. "Do you think that night ruined us forever?"

She doesn't answer me.

Not that she has to.

I already know.

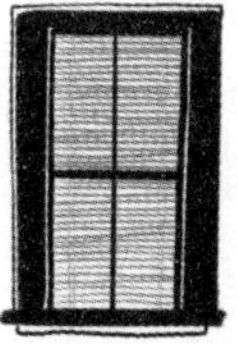

CHAPTER FOUR THEN

The smell hits me first.

It's rich and nauseating. A scent that crawls into your nostrils and sinks its nails into the sensitive flesh there. Unmistakable even in the ruins of Wellesley House. A place I shouldn't be. A place *this* shouldn't be. And if the smell weren't enough to upend me, then the carcass of the dead cat would do the trick. Hunched over and black, with patches of fur scattered on its abused body like an unfinished quilt lying on a pillow of rot and ash.

The most basic question is there. Right there. Burning—no pun intended—incessantly on my tongue. Who did this? Who would do this? But it's almost as if the question is being asked just as a steel door slams. I can't let myself answer it.

Can't even think the answer.

I feel you before I see you. Hear your footsteps creep along the dilapidated ruins of Wellesley House. The miscellaneous walls and framing of what was once a three-story manor. Hear your sharp breath when you notice me. The hitch in your chest as you suck in air, preparing to speak.

"You're not supposed to be here," you say.

"Neither are you."

There's a chuckle. A brush of warmth against my arm as you stand beside me. Together we stare at the dead animal. Neither of us says anything, and I wonder who will break the silence first. I don't have to wonder long.

"Mom will be getting home from work soon."

"Did you do this?" There it is. The words burst out of me as the dam breaks.

"Of course not! Are you serious?" You're appalled. Honestly shocked I'd even insinuate such a thing. The guilt gnaws at me. Maybe I spoke too soon. Jumped to a ridiculous conclusion.

"Who did it then?"

"It must have been another animal." Your voice lowers into a near whisper. "I can't believe you'd think it was me."

Since we were kids, I've admired that about you. Your ability to think on the spot. To smooth over hard situations with delicacy and finesse. Your ability to make me feel like an idiot.

"Another animal? It's been—it's been burned."

"I don't know what to tell you. No one comes out here. It had to have been another animal or a kid playing a prank or something." Your eyes move over the scorched creature and fill with unshed tears. The guilt comes back, mauling me. "Mrs. Rhodes is going to be heartbroken. Who could possibly do something like this?"

Your words ring sincere. The emotion on your face is so real. It reminds me of the nights we used to stay up watching *Survivor*. I never was good at figuring out whom to believe and who was just playing the game. The quiet sets in again. This time I'm the one to break it. "Well, we can't just leave him here."

"Should we bury him?" There is no humor in your eyes, no pity. Only genuine curiosity and care. And I feel horrible for my callousness. For the accusation.

"I'm sorry. After last summer, I can't help—"

"I get it," you interrupt, and there's a glow in your eyes. A sincerity that tells me I'm already forgiven. Just like that. You're always so quick to forgive, even when I don't always understand why I'm being forgiven in the first place. "But I need to know that you know me better. Last summer was one mistake. I'm so much more than that." Your smooth hand grabs my calloused one, and I stare at them, our hands intertwined.

"I'm sorry," I whisper.

You smile sadly. "Come on. We should hurry so Mom doesn't wonder where we are."

"Is it the right thing to bury him? Shouldn't we bring him back to Mrs. Rhodes or at least tell her where he is?"

You get that look that makes me feel so small, so naive. Like there's something I'm missing, and you have all the patience in the world to explain it to me. Sometimes I hate that look, even if it's on the face of the person I love the most. "If we tell Mrs. Rhodes, it will destroy her."

"If we don't, she'll still be destroyed. This cat is like her child."

"But she'll have hope. You understand, don't you?" There's a light in your eyes. A softness in your expression. How could I have misjudged the situation so completely? "There will be a part of her that always believes he's alive somewhere and happy. As opposed to dead and gone. We can give her that much."

"He's in heaven and not roaming the streets starved. Surely knowing that is better than wondering where he is for the rest of her life."

You squeeze my hand. That look is back on your face. I'm the child, and you're the adult. I'm the forgiven, and you're the forgiver. "You really believe all that heaven and hell stuff?"

"Of course I do. Don't you?"

"It isn't comforting," you say, avoiding my question deftly. "Trust me. Mrs. Rhodes would rather think her cat is somewhere real. A place she can visualize. Nothing against heaven, but who has actually seen it to confirm it's what it's cracked up to be?"

"But we don't even have shovels."

Your eyes lighten, and your gaze flashes over my shoulder. "I have an idea."

You lead me to a hole at the edge of the woods. An animal burrow. "How did you know this was here?" I ask. It's about forty feet away from the remains of Wellesley House. Not to mention nearly hidden by brush.

"How have you not noticed it? Now come on. We have to move him."

I follow you back, and we both hesitate in front of the cat. I close my eyes, unable to bear the look of it. Much less the smell. I can't believe this is Aswell, Mrs. Rhodes's prized pet.

"I don't know if I can do this." On cue my stomach turns.

And you're there. Suddenly and completely. Taking my hand. Giving me that look again that reminds me when I fail, you'll always be there to clean up the messes. "I've got this."

You take off your T-shirt, revealing a tank underneath, and ease the body of the stiff cat onto it. We walk together to the hole. You gently lay it inside, and together we cover the entrance with sticks and weeds crudely ripped from the ground.

Once we're done, we stand side by side, staring at the make-shift grave. "Should we say something?" I ask.

"Dearly beloved—" you say instantly, and then your face whips in my direction, your eyes bulging. We both burst into laughter. A bubbling hysterical laugh that doesn't end until we're both wiping under our eyes and bracing ourselves on our knees. "I guess we've always had weddings for our dolls but never funerals. I'm out of practice."

The sun beats down on us mercilessly. The grass and trees look as dry as my mouth feels. But it's good. Being here with you. Remembering dolls. Laughing. Reveling in innocence I thought was stolen last summer. "Can I ask you something?"

You wipe the corners of your eyes, still smiling. "Sure."

"You really don't believe in heaven?"

The happiness doesn't fall away. Instead, you're giving me that look again. The one akin to pity, like you know something I don't. "I believe in you. Us. I believe in laughter. In hope." Your gaze sweeps to the ground. The haphazardly buried cat. "I believe Mom has her own agenda for telling us the other crap. Speaking of Mom."

"I know." I link an arm through yours, and we fall into step together the way we do everything else. In perfect synchronization. Like we practiced it a hundred times before. Maybe, in some ways, we have.

"You come here often? To Wellesley House?"

You glance behind me at the crumbling foundation of what once was one of the grandest homes in town. Last summer hangs over us. The balmy night air. The mosquitos. The smoke. Finally, the mirth leaves your eyes. I regret my question instantly. I never mean to upset you. "Same as you."

We walk home together, and I watch you. The way you carry yourself. The ease with which your head is held high. You have your camera. I didn't notice it before. You must have set it down somewhere inside Wellesley House. Or perhaps it's with you so often, it's become as noticeable as your arm. You carry it most places you go. A little black Polaroid that prints photos instantly.

You're right. You must be right. Maybe not about everything but at least right about what happened to Aswell. Another animal. A kid playing a joke. You're not defined by what happened last summer. I can't judge you for one mistake. That's the antithesis of my own beliefs. I should know better.

Even if I still wake up at night and hear the screaming.

And I want to ask you, ask the question that's festering inside me. I want to ask if you can hear her too. Hear the finality of that mistake. The agony it's brought. How can I ask the one thing you've sworn to me would never come up again? *It's over*, you said that night as you wrapped your arms around me.

You smelled like smoke, and it reminded me of bonfires and childhood. I loved and hated you at the exact same time.

It's over, I tell myself firmly.

Another animal.

A kid playing a prank.

That's all.

And when we make it home and you're fiddling in your pocket for the house key, we both pretend not to hear Mrs. Rhodes on the street calling Aswell's name. We both pretend a lot, you and I.

Only I think, Sister, that you're a little better at it than I am.

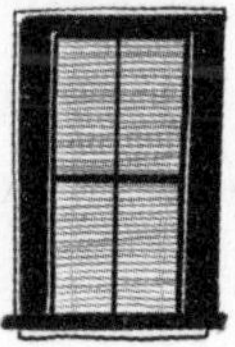

CHAPTER FIVE
LENORA

Cassie would hate this, but I watch her through the window. The girl. I can't help it. She sits on a rocking chair on the porch of Cabin Three, bundled up with a book open on her lap. I noticed her parents first. As Cassie and I ate breakfast in silence and before she retreated to her room, I watched the parents.

A handsome couple. Tall and complementary to each other.

The father messed with some fishing line. The mother helped him set up a hammock. They laughed about something and called out to their daughter, who either didn't hear them or pretended not to.

But there was something stiff about their movements. A feeling of forced togetherness. Something seething beneath the surface. The mother retreated into the cabin, and the father disappeared into the woods with hiking boots and his fishing pole.

Not before stopping on the porch and kneeling in front of his daughter though. He laid a hand on her shoulder. Said something. I watched and imagined, just for a second, it was my own father. In front of me. Whispering to me. Smiling at me.

Breathing.

Just breathing would be enough.

Whatever he said to the girl clearly must have worked because, for the first time all day, she smiled. But she still didn't go with him.

The girl stayed.

She went back to her book, tapping her foot on the porch along with a beat.

Does she have a radio playing? Or is the beat in her head? A song she's humming to herself.

I hum under my breath. Try to match the beat of her foot.

Her hair is long and straight and cradles her face. While she reads, one of her fingers twirls a piece of hair round and round, and I count each time her finger loops. Together we make it to fourteen.

And I do it too with my own hair. Twisting and twisting until the pressure rips at my scalp. I hold it like that for a long moment before releasing. Watch the way she laughs at the pages like she's watching her favorite sitcom. *Free*, I think. *This is what being free looks like.*

I click my fingernails together. In and out. I want my coin, need something to do with my hands, but it's in the other room, and I'm afraid if I look away, this girl will disappear.

Click, click, click.

Cassie says the sound doesn't bother her, but she wouldn't tell me even if it did. She does that sometimes, treats me with kid gloves. Holds me like I'm a delicate baby bird. She must have entered her recording room without me noticing at some point because I hear her in there. The gentle lull of her voice. The rise and fall. She thinks I hate listening to her tell their stories, but really, I just hate that some people have to be the victims.

Suddenly, the girl's head shifts up, and her eyes meet mine through the glass.

I stop moving and humming. For a second, she does too. But then she's on her feet, shaking the blankets off before sauntering toward me and up the grassy hill. The grass should be slippery after the morning frost. The hill is steep. But the girl's steps are unbothered. She doesn't stop until she's right in front of my window. I still haven't moved at all.

"Hi, Cassie," she says, her voice muffled through the glass.

All the words I want to say are lodged in my throat. So I don't speak. Just keep watching her. The rise and fall of her chest. Angry. She's angry with me.

She thinks I'm Cassie.

The girl lays a palm against the window, her fingertips applying pressure that makes them go white. "You like watching people."

I still can't move. It's like I'm paralyzed by some unseen thing. A feeling that stiffens my joints. It drops me back to the last time I felt this way. The last time I couldn't move, but I should have.

She slams her hand against the glass, and I jerk back, my heart ramming against my chest. Behind me, Cassie's recording room goes quiet, and the door opens. "What was that?"

I see it then. The moment the teenager looks between my sister and me, a crease forming between her brow and her mouth opening wide.

I expect Cassie to come to my side. Tell this girl to get lost. But she pushes past me to the door and walks right to her. "What's going on?" She steps outside without firmly closing the door behind her. Their voices sink to quiet murmurs.

"I thought she was you."

"My sister."

The young girl's eyes flash to me. Holds my stare. "She was watching me."

"I'm sorry."

"Why doesn't she come outside to talk for herself?"

This time it's Cassie who looks back, and the expression on her face mutilates me. But I pretend it doesn't. Pretend I'm unfazed as she turns back to the teen. "She gets anxiety going outside. Especially when other people are out."

They sound so familiar with each other.

Like friends.

"Damn." The girl's fingers twitch like she wants to do something with them that she can't. A nervous habit she's fighting back.

It's a feeling I relate to. Common ground that gives me the confidence to inch forward. Open my mouth to say something—

"Bro, this is bizarre."

I look at the girl, and this time when our gazes collide, there is another note swirling among the rebellion and disgust. Curiosity. "Tell her she shouldn't stare. It's rude." And she's gone.

Cassie watches her until she disappears into Cabin Three and is silent when she returns inside, wiping her feet on the mat before I can remind her.

"I'm sorry," I say.

"You can't just stare at Tilly like that, Lenora. It makes her uncomfortable. It would make anyone uncomfortable."

"I know."

"If you know, then why do you do it?"

Because I like to look. I like the way she looks. I like that she is free in all the ways I'm not. But I settle for another weak apology. "I'm sorry, Cassie."

Cassie swallows and nods, her head bobbing. "I thought you were working."

"I was. Just got up to stretch my legs."

She doesn't say anything about my closed laptop on the counter. Or that if she were to touch it, it would be cold.

"Let me just finish up," she says slowly, avoiding my eyes. "I'm almost done. Then I'll make dinner."

I do not look out the window again.

That night we eat to the sounds of Cabin Three's guests laughing around a fire. Someone must pull out a guitar because the melodic strums filter through our walls. I wonder what they look like as their faces dance in the shadows of the flames. Is Tilly—that's what Cassie called her—playing along? Is she leaning into her parents and smiling? A real perfect family moment. Or is it forced? Are her fingers twitching like she wants to be anywhere but there?

I want to look.

I want to *see.*

But I sit still. Spoon scraping the bottom of a tepid bowl of soup. The only sound in the room except for that guitar.

I dip my finger into my pocket for my coin, but it isn't there. My throat tightens.

"I'm going to bed," Cassie says suddenly, not quite meeting my eyes.

The room tilts. My breath catches. I spot my coin on the kitchen counter. I can't remember placing it there, and I fight the urge to lunge for it, not wanting Cassie to see how bothered I am. Instead, I roll my thumbnail into my palm and, with my other hand, gently place my spoon on the table. "Early for you, isn't it?"

"I'm tired."

"She knew you earlier," I say suddenly without meaning to. Without any clear control over the words. They've been plaguing me since Cassie went to her. Since Tilly stormed off. "Tilly. That's her name, right? She thought I was you. She knows you, doesn't she?"

"I told you we ran into each other outside last night."

"You didn't talk to her today?"

Cassie laughs, but the sound is snarky and sets my teeth on edge. "You know I haven't left the cabin. Unless you count my trips to the bathroom, but I'm sure you know I was in there alone since you've been watching Tilly all day." As soon as she says it, her face falls. "Wait, I didn't mean that. I'm sorry. I'm just tired, Lenora."

There are things I want to say, and they push at my lips, begging to come out, but I don't let them. Cassie and I are almost always in perfect sync. But some days, like today, there are things that throw us out of whack. Some days it's my guilt. I'm the reason we're stuck in this cabin after all. Some days it's Cassie's. Some days it's something or someone else entirely.

Like that sarcastic blond.

Cassie came in so aggressively.

You scared her, Lenora.

You shouldn't stare, Lenora.

But I didn't do those things. Not really. Not when I'm still stuck at the end of that hallway. Not when Cassie is the one who left me there. Rage pools inside me until I can swim in it. There are more words I want to say, but I swallow them back, pick up my spoon, and force a smile. "It's OK. It's been a stressful few days."

Daphne is practically screaming in my ear about the importance of communication, but I force her voice away. It's much easier to pretend.

"Good night, Lenora." She stands and shoots me a tight smile. "Leave your plate. I'll clean."

Cassie nods, and when she walks past, her fingers brush my shoulder, trail up to my cheek. "I really am sorry."

"Me too."

"I love you."

"You more."

I stay up another half an hour trying to get some words on the page. I tell myself I'll listen to Cassie. I don't want to give her a reason to be cross with me. But my fingers are dead weights on my keyboard, and my eyes are still burning from earlier.

You're both crazy.

That's when I hear the whispers.

I think I must be imagining them at first before they get louder. Deeper. They don't belong out here in this quiet expanse of woods. The kind of whispering that's closer to yelling than anything else.

I glance sideways toward the window, and my feet move silently across the floor. I slide back into my spot like I'm a missing puzzle piece. Like the way a house settles after an earthquake.

I place a hand on the icy glass and listen.

Their voices.

They're muffled, but the intensity is unmistakable.

I start counting in my head as I watch Tilly and her mother. Two shadowy forms leaning toward each other, closer to our cabin than theirs. As if they don't want the other person in their cabin to hear them. I keep counting. Keep tapping my fingernails together.

Tilly steps closer, brings a finger to her mother's face. I think I hear the word "liar," but I can't be certain.

I make it to one hundred and three as the mother shushes her daughter, steps even closer until they're nose to nose. Two boneless figures fusing together. So close.

I can't look away.

Their voices lower, and I can't pick up a single word. Suddenly the mother's hand reaches out, moves so fast, I almost miss it, and slaps her daughter across the face. She turns around and walks quickly back to Cabin Three without looking back. Tilly doesn't move. Her body is tilted sideways toward me, her hand to her cheek like she's still frozen in disbelief.

And I'm frozen with her. My breath is a handful of cotton in my throat as I count until I lose it. Think about starting over. But I don't know where to start.

My fingernails keep clicking, clicking, clicking, and her eyes tilt up to mine. I don't have time to move. Couldn't even if I wanted to. And we stand there like that. Two strangers in the night. I want to tell her I understand. I want to tell her it'll get better. That mothers misbehave too.

I get it more than anyone.

But then she looks away from me and moves down the hill to the forest.

The nightmare starts the same as it always does. Cassie's sweaty hand clenched around my wrist. Her eyes telling me to be quiet. Our footsteps silent as we pad across the runner. The door to Mom and Dad's room cracked, barely any light leaking out.

Cassie stops just outside the door, pulling me back with worry on her face. We listen to the sound, the one that siphoned us from bed.

Thwack, thwack, thwack.

Cassie's expression asks several questions at once. None I can answer. And there's a moment, right before she opens the door, where I visualize returning to our room and climbing back into bed. Part of me knows whatever is behind this door is abominable, and if I don't actually see it, then it's not real.

But Cassie pushes it open anyway.

And I see only darkness. My hands swing wildly from side to side, searching for my sister. Searching for the warm place where she once stood. But she isn't there. There is only a cold so vibrant, so bitter, my limbs feel brittle and close to snapping clean off. My body gets heavier and heavier.

"Cassie?" Her name is a whimper on my lips.

Then I feel it. An ice-cold fingertip against my forehead. Right at the center.

"No. No, no, no. Please." But I can't move. Can't run. Can't see.

The finger starts moving. Down. Over my nose. My lips. My

chest heaves up and down, in and out, so quickly that I can't count the movements. The finger tilts my head up at the chin. I think my sister's name. Scream it inside my head.

But she's nowhere.

And I'm here.

"Lenora, what did you do?"

I wake up in a pool of sweat, tangled in sheets and sucking in air. It hurts to breathe through this. It hurts to remember. Not because of what I saw but because of what it means. Even now, it can't be true. At least not all of it.

A dream, I tell myself. Only a dream.

A memory.

I swing my legs over the side of the bed and try to breathe. Try to focus on anything else. I reach for my glasses on the bedside table and freeze, looking at my hand. It's covered in dirt. Under my nails, layered over my palm. My wrist.

And I look down. My sheets are marred with brown handprints and smudges.

Mud is smeared everywhere. The bed, the ground, my body. I wait for the image to dissipate like the dream I hope this still is. But it doesn't. Just like I know it won't. Because I'm not dreaming, no matter how much I wish I were.

"No," I choke out, lifting a clump of tangled hair from my shoulder. "Not again."

Worse than the mud are the feelings inside me. A memory just out of my reach. Like an unidentifiable flavor in the back of my throat. Something there, tucked behind a curtain. Something important.

The memory comes chopped and scattered. I gather the pieces.

Try to put them back together. A flash of pale skin. Perfectly white teeth and lips parted in a hesitant smile.

Me running through the woods, branches slapping against my body.

Cold. So cold.

And there is someone else.

A person.

Hunched over and curled in on themselves.

And something else. Something slipping away with the remnants of my hope.

I have to act quickly and quietly. It's not that I don't want Cassie to know I sleepwalked again; it's that I don't want her to worry about it. To worry about me more than she already does.

I'm silent as I slip on my glasses and walk barefoot down the hall. Cass is asleep with the door open. She's not snoring, but she's breathing loudly, curled around her pillow, her face buried. I used to think I hated the way she slept so heavily and noisily. I shared a room with her my entire life, and when cracks of thunder and creaks in the hallway woke me, I was always jealous of her. Her ability to be oblivious to it all. Sometimes now I miss it. The sound of her sleeping beside me. Whenever I awake suffocated by fear from a noise I can't name, a feeling I can't describe, I remember how she would center me. The dichotomy of that sound's normalcy and me standing in the doorway covered in mud is nearly my undoing.

I follow my muddy footprints to the hallway mirror. Dirt-smeared cheeks. Twigs and debris in my hair. It looks like I rolled around on the ground. What happened out there?

Just like that, pieces of a memory come surging back. A pale hand waving. A smile in the darkness. A scream.

No, that's not right.

What can't I remember?

I fight the urge to shut down. But I can't. I can't let Cassie see me like this. I have to move, have to keep going. I throw all my sheets into the washing machine first, then grab my coat, slip on my boots, and walk to the back door. My whole body is trembling, and I haven't even opened it yet. I never go outside at night. Something about the dark, about the shape of the trees. It makes me see things. Makes me remember things.

I ease the door open slowly, feel that first blast of icy air against my cheeks, and take a deep breath of it. Then another. But I'm not like Cassie. The fresh air doesn't calm me. I can still smell leftover bonfire and another type of burning that reminds me of things it shouldn't. A life gone up in flames. The person I no longer am.

I try to click my nails, but my hands won't stop shaking, and a sob slips past my lips. My gaze shifts up and over. The trees are slender shadow people, standing shoulder to shoulder around the property. They smile at me. They beckon me outside.

Tell me it's OK to remember.

"No," I whisper to myself, swiping at the tears on my cheeks. Images ghost through my mind. Someone outside. Running with me. No. Just a dream. "Just trees. Just outside. You have to—you have to—" I take the first step without looking anywhere except at my feet. Then the second and third. The farther I get from the cabin, the more it feels like my organs are being plucked from my body one by one. I'm crying softly.

The bathhouse is placed strategically between Cabins Two and Three. It sits at the point of a triangle on a slight hill. It's a wooden rectangle structure with two toilets and two showers where the water stays hot for no more than fifteen minutes before dropping to Antarctic temperatures in the winter. It is twenty-three steps away. I know because I've counted several times. Every time. "One, two, three..."

I don't look sideways, at the darkness, at the woods.

"...thirteen, fourteen, fifteen..."

I don't wonder what I was doing out there all alone.

"...twenty...twenty-one...twenty-two..."

I don't wonder who was out there with me.

In one hundred and fifty seconds, I am completely clean and shivering and shoving my coat over my violently shaking and wet naked body. Holding my clothes in my hands. Twenty-three steps back. Then it's over. Then I'm done.

I force myself out of the bathhouse.

Don't look at the woods. Don't think of anything.

"...sixteen, seventeen, eighteen..."

Somewhere behind me a branch snaps.

My body goes stiff. Goose bumps cover the back of my neck.

Don't look. It's probably a squirrel. Keep walking. A bird landing on a branch. Another step. *There's nothing wrong. There's nothing ever wrong.*

Another branch cracks.

A person lurking in the dark.

Where was I? How many steps has it been? Another sob catches in my throat.

I ease around to look over my shoulder. The door to Cabin Three is swinging closed as someone walks outside. Tilly or her mother, maybe. The silhouette moves quickly, but they don't notice me.

I'm five steps from the back door now, and I lunge for it. Close it behind me. Rest my back against it as I wait for the adrenaline to stop raging inside me. I deflate slowly and can think of only one other night I've ever been this tired.

And the night is only just getting started.

I get dressed and then start cleaning. I don't know how long it takes to scrub the mud from the hallway, the floor, and the doors, but when I finish, I bring a glass of water to the window. My eyes are heavy; my body is weighted with the pressure of something I can't place. I don't want to carry it, any of it. The weight is too much.

I'm afraid to sleep.

"What are you doing up?"

I spin around to see Cassie yawning from the doorway, wearing only an Ohio State University T-shirt.

"I got thirsty." My voice breaks on the last word, and I sip the water, hoping she doesn't notice. The water has a strong flavor. I roll it on my tongue. Try to place it. It takes a second to realize I'm still tasting dirt.

"Did you go outside?"

"No."

She walks to the fridge and pulls out a string cheese. Instead of peeling it, she takes a bite right off the top. "Did you have a nightmare again?" I don't say anything. I don't want to lie to her, but I don't really want to talk about it either. "Daphne said to write them down in your journal. Did you do that?"

"I just got up for some water, Cassie. Don't make it a big thing."

"Your hair is wet."

"Cassie."

She finishes the last bite of cheese and watches me for a long moment. "In your dream, does it happen the same way?"

"I don't want to talk about this."

"Daphne said it would help you."

"She's not always right, you know," I snap, tightening my fingers on the glass.

I need to get ahold of myself. My body feels close to splitting in two. I start counting in my head.

"She said talking about it is therapy. Talk to me about it."

"I don't know, Cassie," I answer, so tired that my vision starts swimming. "It's us in the hallway. Holding hands. That's how it starts."

"And when I tell you to run?" she asks, her voice barely above a whisper.

"I run."

Cassie opens her mouth like she's going to say something. Then she snaps her teeth together and faces out the window. "So not exactly the way it happened. Are you going to tell me why you're in the middle of the kitchen and dripping wet, Lenora?"

My eyes connect with hers, and neither of us speaks.

I finally identify the weight hanging from me.

It's a secret.

And I know Cassie must have one too.

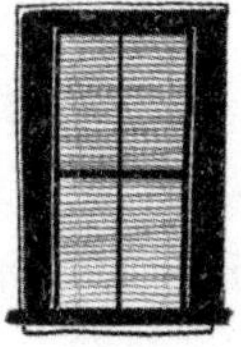

CHAPTER SIX
CASSIE

As soon as my eyes open, I think of Lenora. There is an unshakable pressure on my rib cage. The last time I felt like this was when I awoke that night fifteen years ago. That pressure hadn't ceased, but as years passed, I learned to bear it, carrying my sister's weight, dragging us both just a little further.

This feeling is different.

There is no explanation for it. The sun is shining. I've slept in. Got all my work done yesterday. Why do I feel like I'm forgetting something terribly important? I sit up, look around the room, searching for the source of my anxiety. The black spot on the otherwise good morning.

That's when I hear the shouting.

I slip on a pair of sweatpants and head down the hall. Lenora is already at the window. I don't have a chance to be annoyed before I'm joining her. Seeking the source of the noise and commotion.

"They lost her," Lenora says, her back slightly angled toward me as she says it. Like she's still angry about last night. About the questions I asked her. The ones she never answered.

Your hair is wet, Lenora.

Right this second, it takes too long for her words to sink in. For me to comprehend them. "What are you talking about? Lost who?"

But then I finally make sense of the shouting. The clear terrified shouting of two parents.

"Tilly!"

"Where are you?"

"Tilly!"

The two parents walk around Cabin Three. Tilly's father is cupping his mouth toward the lining of the woods, and her mother is walking briskly out of the bathhouse.

"They've been calling her for a few minutes now," Lenora says quietly.

"I should help them."

"How?"

But I'm already outside.

The air smells of pine trees and wet grass, but when I breathe, the cold hurts. For the first time, not in a good way. I move down the hill, and my foot slides along the grass, slippery from ice not quite melted. I right myself just before I lose balance entirely.

The parents notice me and head in my direction.

"Have you seen her? Have you seen our daughter?" Tilly's mother is almost an exact replica of Tilly. The same eyes and nose. A strong tall build. She's the confident type. The "shows up to the school pickup in full makeup and designer jeans" type. But this morning she is unmoored. Her voice is breathless and desperate.

"She was in her bed last night. But this morning—oh my God, we don't know where she is."

"She was gone when we woke up." Tilly's father is not quite as tall as his wife, but his chest is wide like he's spent his whole life in the gym trying to make up for it. "Have you seen her? Did she walk up to your cabin?"

"No." I swallow thickly, my eyes moving to the woods behind them as if I'll be the one to see her. Hiding behind a tree, a finger over her lips. But there's nothing and no one.

His bloodshot eyes fill with dread as his hands cup the back of his head. "She's never done this before. Never for this long at least. Not like this. Not in the woods."

"Hey," a new voice calls out. Sarah walks toward us hurriedly. Her hair is tucked into a knit hat, and her coat is buttoned to the top. "I just got your message. Has anyone called the police yet?"

This is the first time I've seen Sarah since she introduced herself to Cassie and me two nights ago. I caught glimpses of her carrying empty boxes in and out of Cabin One a couple times, but she's kept to herself. This morning she looks especially frazzled.

Tilly's mother places a hand over her mouth. "No, we've just been looking. She's not here. She's not anywhere."

"We'll find her," Sarah says soothingly, her eyes meeting mine as she pulls Tilly's mother into a hug. I watch the gesture, how it seems so natural for Sarah. Sarah rears back, holding her at arm's length. "I'm sure she just got a little turned around out there. We'll call the police. Get a search and rescue team."

"She likes to smoke marijuana at the Blacktop."

All three of their heads whip toward me, and Sarah's arms fall to her side. "What did you say?" Tilly's mother asks, her voice as frigid as the morning air.

"Your daughter, I caught her out there two nights ago behind Cabin One."

"Behind my place?" Sarah asks, her hands nervously tucking her shoulder-length blonde hair back. Black ink peaks out from her shirtsleeve, and she pulls her sleeve tighter around her wrist.

"You never told us." The father's voice edges into anger. "What the hell do you mean you caught her out there? You didn't say anything."

"What time was this?" Tilly's mother asks, talking over her husband.

"Around one in the morning. Two nights ago. Your first night, I guess."

"She's fifteen." The words are almost an accusation.

I thought she was closer to eighteen, but that's a sorry excuse and not really the point at all. The truth is I wanted to tell her parents about the drugs. It's illegal, and they deserve to know. But I couldn't.

I couldn't do that to Tilly.

Sarah is watching me, the cogs turning in her head. I can see them shifting around in there. I look away, carefully out into the woods, wondering how Tilly got lost. I assumed she'd been at the Blacktop the night she was smoking, which is a fairly simple walk. She'd know it was there because she'd driven past it as they came in.

But why would she go deeper into the woods last night?

The mother points an angry finger at me. "If she's lost out there, this is your fault." The woman breaks into sobs, and the man folds her into his arms almost robotically. There's nothing comforting about the gesture. It looks like he's doing it because he knows he's expected to. While he holds her, he scans the woods, his body tense. Maybe still expecting his daughter to walk right out with her trademark smirk.

But the trees are empty and lonely, and the dirt is as cold as our cheeks and hands.

"What were you doing out there?"

It takes a second for me to understand that Sarah is speaking to me. The crying couple are whispering frantically to one another, and Sarah has taken a step closer.

"Pardon?"

"Behind my cabin two nights ago at one in the morning." Her face melds into one of suspicion. "What were you doing?"

That night comes back in bitter waves.

Do you think this is normal?

Parker's disappointed face.

The need that clawed inside me to get out, to breathe in fresh air, to *be* normal. "I was on a walk," I say finally.

"At one in the morning?"

"Couldn't sleep."

Tilly's mother pulls back, an angry haze slowly filtering over her eyes. "Show us where you saw her. The Blacktop. Take us to the Blacktop."

I do because I must do something. The walk is silent, and when we get there, the field is empty. Not even a beer can in sight. We stand at the perimeter for a long minute before Tilly's father turns away sharply. "I'm calling the police. This is ridiculous."

It happens as we're leaving. As Sarah is talking to Tilly's mother under her breath, both several steps ahead of me, and Tilly's father tries to find service to call 911. It's there that I see the flash of silver catching the early morning sun. Nearly hidden by brush and bramble.

A coin.

The image doesn't connect at first. It's something I see every day, that coin with the face rubbed off. The perfect indentation of Lenora's thumb. Not like it's alien to me. But it being *outside*. Sitting here on dead grass beside my rock. That's what doesn't make sense at all.

The pressure from this morning is back, and harder.

Before I can think too hard about what I'm doing, I slip it into my pocket, standing in one motion. When I turn around, Sarah is looking right at me, an expression on her face that I can't decipher.

My cheeks heat, but I keep my head up as I walk toward her.

"Everything OK?"

"Just thought I saw something," I say and walk past her.

I wear shoes to search, a jacket, and even a wool cap. I listen to a police officer explain the severity of the situation to the volunteers. It's supposed to storm tonight. We need to find Tilly before sunset. They set the ground rules. If you find anything, don't touch it, alert an officer immediately. There are whistles and groups and teams and a helicopter searching overhead. There are divers in the two lakes on the campground. Searching. Everyone is searching.

But we can't say for certain what we're searching for.

A young girl lost in the woods, scared, cold, and all alone. Or a lifeless pale body, facedown in a lake. No one can make up their mind. And all I can think about is that coin. Lenora never goes anywhere without it.

The tightness in my stomach when I'd found it. The meaning of it that's made the pressure in my chest worse.

I think about Tilly too. Because that lively girl I met in the woods can't be missing. It's just not possible.

I stomp through the bramble and trees with strangers, searching for a young girl I don't quite know. When night falls, the campground is canvassed, and the first raindrop falls, I wonder if Tilly would rather be dead.

I watch her, my sister.

I try to remember a time when I knew what Lenora was thinking. Our mother used to tell us about her pregnancy. The doctor didn't know she was even having twins until her twenty-week ultrasound when the tech went pale and fled the room. I think about that sometimes. Which one of us was seen first. Which one of us was anticipated. Which one of us was hiding behind the other. The doctor couldn't say. With identical twins in the same sac, it's hard to tell.

But I know the truth.

Neither of us was hiding. We were just one person the whole time. And I don't know what made us split apart, but whatever it was must have been against nature. Peeling us away from each other against our will, cell by cell, forcefully, sadistically. And I can't help but think we were never meant to be apart.

And maybe the last time I really knew what Lenora was thinking was when she was me.

She moves around the kitchen fluidly, her head swiveling to the window every so often as the volunteers pack up. Like the staff in an elaborate play, they strike the set, leaving our hillside naked and empty. Silent. But I still hear the screaming. I hear Tilly's name over and over, bouncing off the trees with their roots gnarled and writhing against the weight of the secrets they're keeping. There is no evidence of Tilly on the grounds, and I want to pretend life is normal. There is a cabin to clean and work to be done.

But I can only watch Lenora and wonder what I missed.

What she's not saying.

Why she's not saying it.

Lenora catches my eye as she grabs the saltshaker off the table. "It's almost ready." Like my anxiousness is because of hunger. Not because of a girl missing in the woods. Not because Lenora was in those woods that night. Not because her silver dollar—

The thought sends me huddling deeper into my damp coat.

The coin itself is tucked into one of my drawers, and I can hear it rolling around in there all the way from the kitchen. Banging against its enclosure, screaming at me to just let it out. I can hear it chanting a simple truth.

Lenora was in the woods.

Lenora was in the woods.

Lenora was in the woods.

Tilly is still in the woods.

"Do you think Tilly's really lost out there?" Lenora asks, her voice pitched high. "They searched the whole campground, and there's no sign of her. How far could she have gotten?"

My guilt is fierce in that moment. Guilt for my thoughts. I can hear the pain and uncertainty in Lenora's voice, and the urge to comfort her is second nature. I push back my own feelings, my own questions, and try to put on a brave face. "She might have wandered past the fencing into the woods. Maybe she was looking for a road."

My sister glances over her shoulder. There's something insincere about her voice. Like she's not really listening to me. "But why haven't they found her?"

"I don't know."

The pressure is back, and it's loud and heavy. My next words spew out of me. "You were out there. Last night, I mean. You were outside at the bathhouse, weren't you? Did you see anything?" Her being outside is not the question because I already know the answer. Lenora's hair was wet from a shower. Her coin was on that Blacktop. No, it's not a question of whether Lenora was outside last night. The only real questions are about what she was doing out there and what she saw. "Just tell me the truth, Lenora. Whatever it is, I won't be mad."

Her back stiffens, and when she speaks, her voice is low and rough. "Just went to the bathhouse. That's it."

"You were outside?"

Lenora still won't look at me. "Just for a minute."

The confession brings me up short, and I don't really know how I should react. She lied, and we promised each other we wouldn't do that. Not to each other. Never to each other. And she's still doing it.

If it was just the bathhouse, how did her silver dollar get on the Blacktop?

"Why didn't you just tell me that last night?"

"Same reason you didn't tell me about your boyfriend."

I slam a fist onto the table, knocking over a small cup of pens balanced beside Lenora's notebook. Lenora freezes, her fingers going to the counter and clenching around the edges. "It hurt me, Cassie." She says, "It hurt that you lied about him. It hurt that you need him."

"I lied to protect you." Regret slowly fills me all the way up until I'm overflowing with it. "I didn't want you to feel bad. He's nothing to me, Lenora. If he were, I'd have told you. I'm sorry about it. All of it. I hate lying to you."

She turns suddenly, tears in her eyes, a broken look on her face. There it is, I think. Finally. *Tell me. Tell me your secrets.*

"There's something else." The sound of her voice is as jagged as shattered glass. "Something else that happened last night. I think—I think I may have seen her." With that, the glass splinters. "Around the time I was awake. I think I saw Tilly leave her cabin."

"You saw Tilly last night?"

Lenora's eyes flash to the window behind me. "I didn't know if it was her. I only guessed it was. She moved quickly out of the cabin. I thought she was going to the bathroom or something, but she didn't."

"Did you see where she went?"

"Into the woods, I think. It was so dark."

"You should have said something before now. They've been looking for her all day, and you told the cops you didn't see anything."

"I didn't see anything important. Not worth mentioning."

"It could have helped. Anything would help to secure a timeline." Last night. The utter destruction on Lenora's face. Was this after she saw Tilly? After she went to the bathhouse alone in the middle of the night for a shower? After she lied about it?

She doesn't want to tell me the truth, but I'll take it from her anyway. Because she's me and I'm her and we're the same. "This has something to do with the nightmare, doesn't it?"

"No, I don't think—"

"I know what happens when you have that dream, Lenora. Did you wake up outside? Is that what happened?" Memories press against my brain. Memories best kept at bay. It goes against every protective instinct I have to pull them to the surface. To think about all the things my sister did. When I do that, sometimes the bad overwhelms the good. And I hate that feeling. Especially when none of this is her fault.

Because if every bad thing stems from that night, then I'm the catalyst. I'm the one who ran. Who could really blame Lenora for what happened afterward?

Her eyes widen, her hand shooting back to the countertop like she needs the support. No. She's searching for something. Her fingers glide along the counter's surface. I know what she's looking for without asking. It knocks the breath out of me all over again. "I just went to the bathroom. To shower. That's all, Cassie."

Something on the stove is burning, but neither of us moves. "Just a shower," I repeat slowly. "You're sure?"

Lenora's mouth tightens in a line. "I wouldn't lie to you. Not about this."

The logic is on her side. What reason would she have to lie? Even if she were sleepwalking, why wouldn't she just tell me? Sure, there might be a fear of being associated with whatever happened to Tilly. But if she was asleep, then it's all moot anyway.

Forcing myself to take a calming breath, I think of the day before Tilly went missing. The way Lenora watched her out the window. Then I think of her coin on the Blacktop. Now sitting in a dark drawer in my room.

There has to be another explanation for it all. Something I'm not thinking of. Something that doesn't involve Lenora sleepwalking and then lying about it.

The rain surges against the roof, and a streak of lightning breaks across the sky, lighting the room for one brilliant flash. The storm is here. And I wonder if Tilly is out there this second, just as cold as I am.

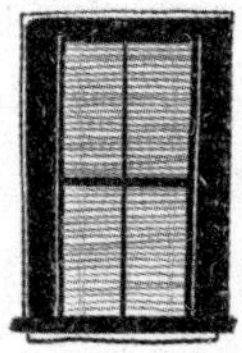

CHAPTER SEVEN
LENORA

The storm riots outside, and I tried counting myself to sleep. Tried to write. Tried to journal. That's what Daphne would want me to do. Get all my thoughts out and organize them distinctly. Get them ready for her to devour so she can tell me all the ways I'm effed up.

None of that worked, and I know I shouldn't do it, but Cassie is asleep. The cabin is dark. The hillside is desperately empty, and I can't think of anything else. I sit up in my bed, leaning back against the headboard, and slide my laptop on my lap.

There's a creak in the hall that has my gaze jumping toward the door. A minute passes, and when nothing happens, I relax back into my pillows. I shouldn't be this nervous. Just because Cassie doesn't like it or understand it doesn't mean I'm doing anything wrong. Besides, this is different from last time.

I think of her face earlier in the kitchen when I looked her in the eye and lied.

I didn't have a choice. Her knowing I was out there that night would only stress her out and make things worse.

My fingers brush the keyboard when—there it is. A gentle sound. A shifting of weight on hardwood. My breath catches, and my eyes flick to the empty doorway. I can hear Cassie's steady breathing from across the hall. No one is here. Just us. It takes several minutes for my heart to slow and panic to ease.

Just the cabin.

The creaks and groans of a too-old structure.

My laptop screen has darkened, and I run my finger along the touch pad, casting my room in a dim glow. It's enough to drive the shadows away. This is about Tilly, and nothing about her being missing makes sense. They searched everywhere in those woods. She wasn't out there. They'd have found her if she were.

A girl like Tilly couldn't be lost, starving, shivering from the cold.

I remember her. The look on her face as she confronted me at the window. The sound of her voice standing up to her mother. The slap reverberating across the hill. I heard it. I saw it. Tilly was hurt that night, and what do hurt, rebellious teenagers do? They run.

How do I tell my sister that I don't think Tilly is in those woods? That Tilly is free. Tilly got away. From her mother, from the ivy that grows out of this hill so quickly, you don't see it until it's wrapped around your ankle, as alive as a boa constrictor.

Tilly isn't in these woods suffering.

She's not stuck on this hillside.

I just need to find her so I know for sure. It only takes a minute until her beautiful bright face smiles at me as if to tell me, *Good job.* As if to say I'm the only one who knows her well enough.

I grab my phone and start with her Instagram. Her pictures and videos get thousands of likes. Her page is carefully curated. There's a soft-color, neutral-toned theme when you look at it as a whole. And I do. I scroll back until the beginning of the year. Read every caption. Analyze every picture.

This is not a girl lost in the woods.

This is a girl who gets away.

Next, I switch to my laptop and find her Facebook, then her Tumblr, then her TikTok. And I watch. Look. Listen. I even laugh at some of her reels. She's so witty. So much more than I thought. Eventually, I switch back to my cell phone, lie on my side, and find her Instagram again. I can't stop. Even as Daphne's voice enters my mind. *You're hyper fixating, Lenora. Why do you think you do this, Lenora? You can't go down this rabbit hole again, Lenora.*

My fingers still over the screen. What am I doing? She's right. I can't do this again. Can't go there—

A video stops me. Makes me sit up. Makes Daphne's voice disappear.

This one is different.

Usually Tilly's with her friends, particularly a redheaded girl whose face reappears a lot. If she's not with them, then she's alone. But in this video, she's neither. Tilly's standing in front of a luxurious pool that reappears on her Instagram often, and in the background is her mother. Phone to her ear, pacing.

Tilly walks around behind her, chuckling under her breath, and then breaks out into a dance, bumping her hip against her mother.

Instead of laughing or even smiling at her daughter, the woman furrows her brows in annoyance before stomping off. Tilly turns the camera back around, rolling her eyes playfully. But I can see something else there. I can see the hurt. The caption on the video is *when your mom is a low-key bitch.*

I pause it, hold her face closer to my own. Look at the edges and lines of her skin. My stomach suddenly hurts as my mind goes to the one place where I never let it. I see my face in Tilly's, and I want to hug her to me. I want to tell her that it's going to be OK. I want to tell her my mother is the same as hers.

Instead, I hold the phone tight to my chest, and I think of a different reality. One where, like Tilly, I ran too.

I'm clean when I wake. That should be enough, but it isn't. My phone is dead, and I put it to charge before rubbing my hands up and down my arms and over my legs just to make sure. To confirm the gritty feeling on my body is only a memory. The mud slick against my skin. The twigs and leaves in my hair. The dirt beneath my fingernails. The taste of the earth coating my tongue like those powder-candy pouches Cassie and I used to inhale.

The sun beams through my window. I must have forgotten to close the curtains before bed, and I have a clear shot of a cloudless blue sky. You'd never know a storm raged nearly the entire night.

Though it's barely seven in the morning, there are people outside. Their voices are muffled through the cabin's walls. If I were to get up and look, I'd probably see the white tent and the hillside sprinkled with volunteers. I'd see Tilly's parents huddling together, mugs clenched in trembling hands as they wait for any news or direction. Even her mother. Out there, playing the part.

Pretending she isn't what drove her daughter to run.

There's an intimacy between Tilly and me. One formed last night as I spent hours becoming her friend online. It might be presumptuous or naive, but I feel like I know her. I *care* about her.

I roll over to face the wall. There's a painting of the sun that Cassie got me for our birthday one year ago. She knew the artist and had it made just for me. Usually, I love looking at it. Usually, it makes me feel better.

But today, the streaks of yellow remind me of Tilly's hair at the beach when she went this past summer. The caption was *vitamin sea.*

The last time I went to the beach was when Cassie and I were almost seven. Our mother hated to sweat and swore she'd never take us back. She kept that promise.

There's a quick rap on the door, and I flip around to see Cassie. "Morning," she says, her eyes scanning over my body. I know what she's doing. What she's looking for. The same thing I checked for this morning. Evidence that I went outside last night.

"I'm clean."

"I didn't say anything."

"You didn't have to." I sit up, swing my legs over the bed, and stretch.

She takes a step back from the doorway, her hands falling to her side restlessly. "I'm probably going to join the search again today. I think they've got new dogs out there."

"The dogs couldn't pick up her scent yesterday. Why would they try again after that storm?"

"They're a different type of dog, Lenora." Cassie averts her eyes, and I read between the lines. Cadaver dogs. It would be a sickening thought if I didn't know the truth. Tilly isn't out there, and she definitely isn't dead.

Tilly is free.

My heart stutters with jealousy.

Cassie makes a humming noise. "Your nails. You're doing that thing again."

I stop. "I'm just stressed. I'll talk it out with Daphne."

"You can talk to me."

I don't say anything, and she moves closer. The bed sinks with her weight, pressing her hip into me, and the proximity is an instant hit of calmness. A feeling of solidarity. I want to sink into her until we're the same person, but I know it won't work.

Cassie has a theory that we were the same person in our mother's womb until some unseen force broke us apart. But I don't buy in to that. In my eyes, Cassie and I were always separate. She was the thriving one. The one our parents looked at with smiles on their faces. She was the one they wanted and planned for. I was always the one behind Cassie. So dim that no one could see me past her shine. The one without a purpose. So small, I was whisked to the NICU as soon as I was born.

Never quite belonging in the world I managed to sneak into.

She sits back on her haunches, the crease between her eyebrows not going away. "I love you, Lenora."

She means it. Cassie has always meant it even when no one else has. Even when she shouldn't. And when I did that horrible thing and the regret and guilt began their fight for dominance in my brain, she refused to stop loving me. But I always wonder where her line is.

What I would have to do to make the love stop.

"You more," I whisper just as a dog starts barking.

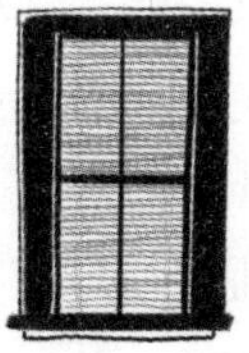

CHAPTER EIGHT
CASSIE

The air is cold, and the ground is muddy. I'm not wearing shoes, but not on purpose this time. I ran outside too fast to think. I get a few strange looks, but no one says anything. Everyone is too consumed by the sound of the dog somewhere in the forest.

No longer are there fresh faces, optimistic for Tilly's future. The people stuck on this hill grimace as they walk purposefully in and out of the white tent.

Girl or body. Girl or body. Girl or body. What will she be?

"You forgot something."

I glance sideways at Sarah, still preoccupied by the sound. By the flurry of activity at the tent. "Pardon?"

"Your shoes?"

My toes curl instinctually into the soggy ground. "Yeah."

"You're not cold?"

"Sometimes."

She lets out a steady breath that sends a tuft of her hair flying into the air before settling back into place. "Been cleaning the bathroom. There's so much mud tracked in. Paper towels on the ground. Messy toilets." I don't speak right away, and she lets out another breath. "Anyway, I need to make a run to the store for toilet paper. There's a Walmart near here, isn't there?"

"Straight shot on the interstate. Exit four. Do you hear that?"

"What, the dog? It's a good thing, right?"

Then there's silence. It seems to creep over the entire hillside at once. A chill shoots through me, directly into my lungs.

"You think they found her?"

I don't answer right away. Just watch as several people head purposefully from the tent to the lining of the trees.

"Probably found something of hers," Sarah murmurs. "If you ask me, I think she ran away."

I don't answer, still watching the lining of the woods.

Sarah hoists a caddy full of cleaning products farther up her arm. "Don't you think? She's a teenager. If she were lost, they would have found her yesterday. Their grid search covered the campground."

"But what about the miles of woods around the property?"

"Why would she have gone around the fence line even if she were lost?"

"Maybe she was trying to find the road," I say, repeating what I told Lenora. But it doesn't sound right. Who would cross the fence? She'd have no idea what was out there.

"I mean, don't get me wrong. I hope they find the girl. I just think it's going to be in a few days, and she's going to be at her boyfriend's house or something."

I don't get a chance to speak before the commotion really starts. Officers jogging out of the tent. Voices coming through walkies, too low for me to catch. I look back at Sarah, whose eyes are so wide, it would be comical if the circumstances were different.

"Did you hear what they said?"

She shakes her head, and I don't wait for more. I take off after them.

I naturally know where they're going. Can't explain it or the intense feeling mounting inside me as we get closer to the Blacktop. I'm pushing through the final tree line when a big, burly cop stops me. His arm shoots out, blocking me before I can make it into the clearing. "Whoa, you can't go through here."

But his words are pressure points in my ears as I look past his shoulder. A huddle of cops circle around something on the ground about thirty yards from my rock. The ground is covered with strewn tree branches from last night's storm, partially obstructing my view.

But I can just make out a slender pale arm.

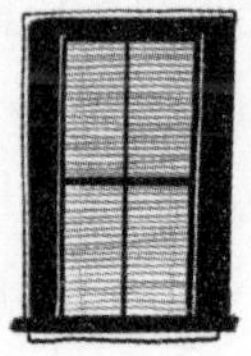

CHAPTER NINE
LENORA

I'm in the hallway of our childhood home.

Cassie holds my hand tightly and draws a finger to her lips with the other.

Or maybe she looks curiously to the door, beckoning me forward.

But wait, that's not right.

Our steps fall together, in line with each other, but we're walking like we don't want to take another step.

And that noise.

Where is it coming from?

Thwack, thwack, thwack.

It isn't too loud or too overbearing. There is no obvious sign that something is wrong. No sirens. No screaming. Just a thumping sound that doesn't belong.

Thwack. Thwack. Thwack.

Awareness creeps over me. I want to go back to our room. I want to climb into bed and cover myself and wake to the sun.

At the door, Cassie holds a hand up to me, and she reaches for the door, but I grab her arm, stopping her before she can touch it. I shake my head.

But Cassie doesn't listen. She never listens.

The door creaks open, and a sliver of light slowly becomes as blinding as the lights in an operating room. I wish it were just the brightness making me cover my eyes.

Cassie's voice is a hammer breaking me out of my quickly crashing reality. "Run," she says. And I do. I run.

But I know that's not quite right either.

"Lenora? Are you still with me?" Daphne's voice seems to be coming from the other end of the long hallway.

I shake my head of the thoughts, the memories, and I search for her in the haze, allowing her to untangle me.

Daphne looks disappointed. "You can't focus today. You're stressed," she says. "With everything going on, you'd have to be. A girl is missing. What does that mean to you, Lenora? How does that make you feel?"

My fingernails click at my sides, and reflexively I reach into my pocket for my coin. It isn't there. Another thing that's slipped away from me. Another thing I can't remember. The memories come back, poking and prodding at my brain. I squeeze my eyes shut.

"Your mind is racing."

My eyes flutter open, and I focus on something tangible. The light streaking across the table from the window behind me. The smell of cinnamon from the oatmeal I hurriedly made and scarfed down before jumping on this call.

"Tell me what you're thinking."

"I think she got away when I never could." My fingers stop

moving, my whole body shuddering with the pain of admitting the words out loud. Earlier, the dogs barked, and Cassie ran outside with foreboding on her face. But I stayed behind and avoided the window.

I didn't know what those dogs were barking at, but it wasn't Tilly.

"Good, Lenora. That's a normal feeling. You feel stuck. There. In the cabin with your sister."

"That's not it."

"You don't have to be there."

But she doesn't know. She doesn't know about what happened that night. After the noises, after opening that door. She doesn't know that coming here wasn't a choice. It was the only way we could save ourselves.

"Is this about your mother, Lenora? Are you afraid?"

"No." My teeth knock together on the word.

"She is out there somewhere while you're stuck in this cabin with your sister. Now there's a girl who has gone missing. Someone who may have run away or may be lost in the woods. Either way, she's accomplished something you haven't. She got away when you couldn't. But don't you think that isn't fair? You're not giving yourself enough credit. You did get out of there, Lenora. You've made progress."

She's right, of course. But there is so much more to escaping than leaving. I might have managed to walk out the door that night, but I left something behind. Something that will tether me there forever.

"Cassie told me once that childhood trauma is sticky," I say, my voice low and shaky. "She says it will embed itself into your DNA, sink its teeth in, and change you. She says it can make you physically sick in adulthood. How can I get away, Daphne? How is it possible when I carry evidence of that night around in my blood?"

"It's not about erasing all evidence of your past. It's about learning to accept and cope with what happened to you. You'll always have that weight, Lenora. But it doesn't have to be so heavy. I know you still feel trapped. That is especially difficult after you and Cassie fought so hard the way you did. Then you see this teenager, leaving the campsite, disobeying her parents."

"You don't even know her."

Daphne doesn't react. Her eyes stay level and focused. Her lips carefully press together. "Tell me about her."

There are flashes of Tilly's face. All still shots from her photos. The sound of her voice through the window. Her angry shadow in the darkness as she argues with her mother. "She's complicated," I answer hesitantly. "Brave. Not afraid to speak her mind."

"Those are things you want for yourself."

"That's not a question."

"Should it be?" She quirks her head. "Tell me, is that all? It seems like there's more you're not saying. How important is she to you, Lenora?"

"I don't know her that well." But the voice in my head argues.

Don't you?

I know her laugh. The side of her face she favors in photos. The way she twists her hair as she reads. The way she isn't afraid to call someone out or stand up for herself. Her relationship with her mother.

I know her.

I wish to be more like her.

Tilly's face and memories and choices are twisting around my own memories, encapsulating them until somewhere deep down, a connection forms between us. A bridge linking us even if she got away before realizing it.

"I think that's time," I say to Daphne without looking at her directly.

There's a long pause before she speaks.

"It'll be a few days before our next session. Will you be OK?"

"Of course." This time I look at her. I peel a page back from Tilly's book, and I straighten my spine. "Thank you, Daphne. I don't tell you that enough."

"No need to thank me, Lenora." The worry doesn't leave her eyes.

After Daphne goes, I stare at the darkened screen, not quite ready to move. There is work I should be doing. A word count I need to hit. But it's like I just spent the past hour siphoning out my life force.

Everything feels so heavy and wrong.

The door opens, and with it, cool air creeps inside. Goose bumps break out on my skin. Cassie is perfectly still in the empty doorway, even as her disturbed gaze clashes with mine. The look on her face makes me stiffen. Makes my stomach recoil.

"They found something at the Blacktop." The anxiety coursing through me is instant, but it's unfounded. They couldn't have found anything important. Nothing worthy of putting that look on Cassie's face.

"It's Tilly," Cassie says. "She's dead."

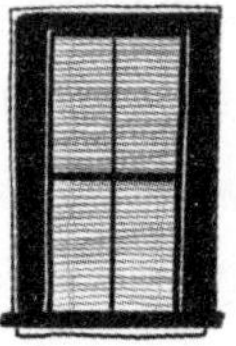

CHAPTER TEN
THEN

The bugs are biting this evening. I swat mosquitos away every few seconds, and somehow, I'm still covered in bites. I should go inside. I need to go inside, but I can't pull myself away.

Our home sits in the cul-de-sac of a neighborhood that might have been considered quaint at one time. But somewhere along the way, the quaintness gave way to peeling paint, a lack of yard maintenance, and double locks on the doors.

I'm on the front-porch steps, leaning against the railing and watching the road. The smell of BBQ wafts toward me with the sound of a new Weezer song that will undoubtedly be stuck in my head for the rest of the day. Our neighbors must be having a party, and judging by the sounds, it's just getting started. Dusk settles in, thickening an already-insufferable humidity, and I can't fight my irritation.

You should be here with me.

Intermittently scratching mosquito bites and lifting the hair off our necks because we're too lazy to walk inside for bug spray and elastics. Suffering through our neighbor's radio station choices and the smell of food we won't be invited over to have. Not after Mom had words with them three months ago over the loud music. *Satanic music*, she ranted, while peering out the kitchen window. *Clearly, they're trying to drag all of us to hell with them.*

You should be here, and I'm antsy that you're not. After our last conversation, after finding Aswell, there's been a cloud over me. I'm determined not to define you by your past mistakes, but at the same time, how can I protect you if I don't expect the worst?

So here I am. Waiting for you to come home, Sister.

As minutes tick away, the antsy feeling grows stronger. If Mom beats you home, we'll both be in trouble. She's been taking on more shifts at the hospital since Dad left. More shifts mean less of her. Seems like a winning situation for everyone. But it also means when she is home, she prefers silence and solitude. She prefers us to be in place, acting the part. Even though she doesn't bother pretending much anymore herself unless someone is around to see.

And you're not here.

There's the sound of a car making its way up the street, and I hold my breath.

I release it when I see it isn't Mom's green Taurus rolling and shaking to a stop in front of the house. It's a sporty black car I don't recognize.

I swat another mosquito, and blood splatters on my thigh and hand. I wipe it on my jean shorts without looking just as the back door opens. Loud music spills out with you. Fall Out Boy. Something about going down swinging, and I know you think it's nonsense. You hate rock.

And I think that's it. You'll get out, slam the door, and come to me. I'll ask where you've been, and you'll have a suitable answer. We might salvage this afternoon after all. But another leg steps out after you. A leg connected to a person I've never seen before.

A girl.

You both wave to the driver of the car, who peels away. My heart pounds in my chest as I think of the last time I saw you with a girl. What that led to. It's not about her or the fact you've made a new friend. It's that I don't know if you can handle this.

The girl is taller than us both. She's pretty, with long blond hair and a big-toothed grin. Her hair sits in curly spirals on her shoulders, layered with multicolored feathers and beads.

Neither of you sees me.

You laugh at something. Lift your hand, tug on a curl. You laugh again. Then the new girl steps away. Hoists her bag over her shoulder tightly. And waves as she goes left down the street.

I can't read your expression as you walk toward my place on the porch. But I clearly see the exact moment you notice me and stop in your tracks.

"You're late," I say, unable to hide the vulnerability creeping into my voice.

"Not that late."

"Where've you been?"

"Out with friends." You push past me to the door but don't move to open it.

I stand and face you. "Who was that girl?"

"Nobody."

"Nobody?" I ask past dry lips. "Of course she's nobody. Of

course you'd say that. Do you hear yourself? Do you expect me to believe that?"

"It's not your business."

This time the anger nearly knocks me off my feet. I look at you. Really look at you. The gentle wave to your long brown hair. The glint that usually lingers in your eyes but is gone in this moment. You are killing me, and you don't even care.

"It can't happen again," I say. "You understand, don't you?"

Your head drops with your voice, and I hate that I've caused you pain. "You're never going to let me forget it, are you?"

"I'm just trying to protect you here."

"I don't need it." You don't say it in a rude way. It's more matter-of-fact. "I just need you to trust me again."

I'm scrambling for words when another car suddenly pulls into the driveway in one fluid motion that sends the brakes squealing. You lift your head and look back just as the car door flies open, and the man steps out.

The smile on your face is instant, and you jog toward him. "Dad." You say his name fervently. "Dad, you're back."

I don't smile. Don't move an inch. I can't. I merely follow you. Watch you lunge from the front porch into him.

Our father catches you in his skinny arms, and I try not to wince. He's lost so much weight. His cheeks are sunken, his eyes shadowed. Even from this distance, the changes in him are so apparent, it makes me uneasy.

It's not because I'm worried about him. That bridge burned a long time ago.

His arms are still wrapped around you. I haven't missed this man at all, but you have. The parts of me that are hard and splintered are the same parts of you that are gooey and soft. Mom used to tell us if someone hurts us, the Christian thing to do is turn the other cheek, and I think that's what you're doing.

But I don't think getting into heaven is worth it.

"'Course, I'm back." He sets you down and looks up at me, holding his arms open as if to say there is room for one more.

I don't move from my spot on the porch. He thinks it's because I haven't forgiven him, only that's not true either. I don't trust him. Not with your heart. Not after what happened last time he ripped it from your chest, and I was left to deal with your corpse and our mother's.

Slowly, his arms lower.

"Does Mom know you're here?" I ask.

His mouth tightens, and he kicks his door shut. "I don't have to tell your mama everything. This is my house too, you know."

"She told you not to come back this time."

"You gonna keep being her parrot, doll? Or you gonna get me a drink?"

There's something to know about Dad. He makes your eyes light up. He reminds you of being a little girl and learning to ride your bike. He is all things good and patient. At the same time, he's none of those things, and you don't see it.

His metamorphosis began with a back injury and Vicodin. It ended with him nearly coding on the living room floor with a needle still in his arm.

We were twelve at the time, and I still remember the taste of the blood in my mouth from when I bit my tongue while watching it. I remember the way you rushed to him, clinging to his chest.

And I remember every day afterward. The highs and lows. The jobs he couldn't hold down. All the times he promised "Never again." and "I've really changed." The way his voice gets rough when he drinks. The way he looks at me in bewilderment like he's still expecting to see a little girl, but I'm not anymore. As if the world stopped spinning the day he popped that first pill.

And you, you're just a breakable egg. Dad cracks you without remorse over and over. You let him, and I can't stop it.

I listen as he and you talk at the kitchen table while I start on dinner. He's back. Says all the same things again. Says why this time is different. The fury echoes through me, and I can't fight it. I grab a knife from the holder. Imagine swinging it.

Would he bleed the same blood as you and me? Or is his blood tainted? Watered down by cheap vodka and heroin?

I tilt to the left only a little, my eyes shifting to him. He's looking at me too. Those eyes. So much like yours and mine. Pieces of him are in us both. It makes me twist in knots. Dad watches me quizzically before his eyes shift down to the knife. I let it go. Let out a breath. He's not worth it. He never has been.

"Get me one more, will you?" he says, waving an empty Coke can.

"I got it, Dad." You jump up to do his bidding like an eager kid. It's a weird juxtaposition to your usual demeanor. Your typical casual resistance to household rules. The way you jut your chin in defiance when Mom asks you to do something. It all melts away when our father opens his mouth.

I frown. Work out in my mind how long we'll have. I give it a month tops before he's gone and you're back to normal. Though the length of time never matters. Each time he leaves, it gets harder and harder.

You're happier now than I've seen you in a while, but I know the crash is inevitable.

It's what you looked like earlier when the girl outside laughed at something you'd said. The happiness on your face. What happened last summer started out with one of your smiles too. Suddenly it feels like everything is slipping out of my control. Like I'm losing you even though you're right here.

I turn back to the counter, brace myself on it.

Does the girl know how many times your heart has been broken and sewn back up? Does she know I'm always the one holding the needle? Last summer washes back over me, every moment that led to the climax, and I can't help but feel like this is all déjà vu.

Dad is here. Dad will be gone. You will be sad. Another girl will be hurt.

The key turns in the front door, and the atmosphere in the room shifts. You look lazily toward the entryway. I'd think you were relaxed if I didn't know you so well. You're tense. Prepared for battle. Even as you desperately attempt to appear otherwise.

Dad doesn't move from his spot except to lean farther back. The front door opens, and Mom comes in, her arms full of grocery bags and still wearing her scrubs. She stops at the door, her eyes on our father.

Dad grins at her lazily.

"What are you doing here?"

"This is my house, last I checked."

Her lips curl, and she glances at my sister and me. "You going to help with these?"

We go to her and each grab a bag. Start unloading the groceries without a word. But I don't miss the tension in the room as Mom's gaze keeps shooting to our father.

"Don't look at me like that," he says to her, slowly standing from his chair.

"I told you not to come back," she says.

His face darkens, and he steps toward her. "Why don't we discuss this later?" But the way he says it, the pitch to his voice. This isn't a question at all, and Mom seems to notice.

She turns away from him to us. "Wash up. Then we'll have dinner."

You and I go to our bathroom with the double sink upstairs. Our bathroom, like our bedroom, is decorated in your photos. Tiny square Polaroids taped to the mirror. A picture of me brushing my teeth with a frothy smile. One of us making a silly face in the mirror. A crumpled towel by your bare feet, your toes curling into the rug.

Photos that probably mean nothing to most people but mean everything to me. Each one represents you. A peek inside your mind. That's something I don't get often.

We wash our hands in silence. But I can't stop looking at you. Your face is expressionless. How are you so calm right now? What are you thinking of?

Our father? That girl?

I don't know which is worse.

There's a flash in my head of me grabbing the blond girl with the feathers in her head. Shaking her until she agrees to stop seeing you. Stop tempting you. Until she confirms what I know to be true. It doesn't matter how many times she makes you laugh. I'll always know you best.

"Hey," I say as you turn the water off. "Can we talk?"

"Mom doesn't have to be so cold to him." Your mouth is in a tight line, your eyes not quite meeting mine. I sigh. You would be thinking of our father. The little girl in you will never stop running eagerly to the door whenever he knocks. Doesn't matter what he does to us.

"You know how he is."

"He's clean." You toss the hand towel into a crumpled heap on the ground. I make a note to pick it up before Mom sees. I'd do it now, but it might irk you more. "He told me he's clean. It's different this time. She doesn't even give him a chance. She never gives him a chance, and neither do you."

Your shoulder brushes mine as you walk past me.

Dinner is unremarkable and silent. Dad makes jokes. Slurps spaghetti loudly. Our mother doesn't even look at him. When it's over, he tells us he will take care of the dishes, and Mom goes upstairs without another word.

"Why don't you girls watch some TV?"

And we do. Or at least we pretend to. A rerun of *Lost* plays, but I can't stop thinking of the girl and Dad. And wondering what you're thinking about while your eyes are glued to the screen.

Dad finishes and turns the lights off. He tells us good night. Kisses each of us on the head and goes upstairs.

We stay curled on the couch, and that's how I fall asleep.

I don't know what wakes me, only that suddenly my eyes are open, the TV is flickering, and I'm all alone on the couch.

It takes a second to sit up, to orient myself. There is an empty spot at my feet. A quilt tossed to the side carelessly. You must have gone to bed, but it's strange you didn't wake me. I make it to the top of the stairs and almost turn into our bedroom when I see a figure at the end of the hallway.

I blink and rub my eyes, but the vision doesn't change. You're standing there. Just standing. So close to the door, it's like you're trying to see through it. It doesn't make sense what you're doing. At least, not until I hear it.

The noises coming from our parents' bedroom.

I cringe. Clearly they made up.

There is an expression of pure disgust on your face. The floor creaks beneath me, and your eyes flicker up.

I don't say anything, don't move or react. Only I can't control my eyes, and I'm not sure if you can see them in the dark, but if you can, then you see them softening.

"I heard something from downstairs," you whisper, taking a step away from the door. "I was just making sure everything was OK."

"It *does* sound like Mom is getting murdered."

You smile, your shoulders relaxing. The sounds in the room quiet, and you draw a finger to your lips.

I nod in understanding, and you walk past me into our bedroom. I'm not tired anymore. I go into the bathroom. Brush and floss my teeth slowly. Slip out of my pants until I'm just in my T-shirt. Then I hit the light and swing open the door.

There's someone standing in the hall.

Not you this time. Mom.

She's wearing Dad's shirt, and I want to say something about it. Ask her if it was proper for a good Christian woman to do what she just did with a man she'd claimed to be done with. I can't say it, though, because it wouldn't matter. When my mother was baptized, she was reborn a hypocrite.

Her eyes narrow into slits. "What are you doing up?"

"I fell asleep on the couch. I'm just getting up here."

She looks over my shoulder. "What have I said about picking your stuff up?"

On the ground is the towel you left on the floor before dinner. I snatch it quickly and smooth it out on the counter. "I'm sorry. I didn't mean to."

Her jaw pops in and out slowly before she nods toward my room.

I slink past her. "'Night, Mom."

She doesn't say anything, but I feel her eyes on me until I close the door.

When I get to the room, you're lying in bed perfectly still, but you're not asleep. I walk past my twin mattress to yours and pull the covers back before sliding in behind you. We haven't curled up in the same bed together since we were kids, and the comfort of it, the warmth, it's everything I didn't know I was missing.

"I wasn't standing there long," you say suddenly. "The noises woke me up. I just wanted to see what was going on."

"It doesn't matter."

"Did Mom come out? I heard her in the hallway."

"Yeah, I talked to her for a second."

"She's so fake. Being so hard on him, then spreading her legs like none of it matters. Going to church every Sunday like she's better than him when all it takes is one apology for her to forget every single one of her morals."

I don't say anything for a moment too long. Mom has always struck me as a hopeless type. Not necessarily forgiving. But so desperate to fit in, to be what she thinks she should be, that she'll do anything or sacrifice anything to get it.

"You don't agree?"

"You know I do," I reply and clear my throat. "That girl earlier, the one I saw you with outside." Your body stiffens almost instantly. It's almost enough to make me stop. Almost. "Who is she really? I've never seen her before."

"She's new. She'll be at our school this fall."

"How'd you meet?"

"The park with some friends." You're silent for another minute. "She's like me. Doesn't talk a lot. Her parents are sketchy. She understands."

"Understands you?"

"Yeah."

"And I don't?"

"That's not what I'm saying. It's just nice sometimes. To have a friend."

I think you say things that hurt me on purpose just to see my reaction. I swallow, trying to stop myself from giving you one. It's stupid. I should be happy for you. Of course you need a friend. Of course that's good for you. But when my eyes shut, I only see the flames. Hear you explaining what happened while I pretend it makes sense.

I only see what I did to help you. Me. No one else. And really, isn't that what friendship is? Everything we are.

I tell you I get it. I tell you I understand, but inside, I am mangled chaos as I try to work it out in my brain. How can you need anyone else when all I've ever needed was you?

I lick my lips. "What are we going to do about Dad?"

There's no answer, and when I turn to look at you, you're already asleep. You don't have to say it because I already know. Dad will take care of himself. You will do something you shouldn't.

And then I'll do something even worse.

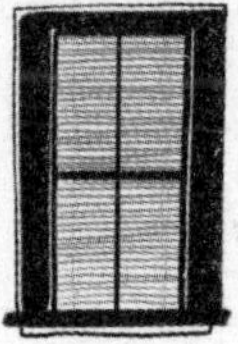

CHAPTER ELEVEN
LENORA

She's dead.

The words won't stop running through my head, and they still don't make sense. I tap my finger against my thigh and count. Not stopping until I hit a thousand. But it's not good enough. Nothing can stop the feeling of my bones trying to break free from my skin.

The memories crawl all over me, oozing into my nose, mouth, and eyes until they're all I can smell and feel and see. Waking up covered in filth and debris. Someone else in the woods with me. Translucent skin in the moonlight. An inhuman figure.

No.

A dream. It was all a dream. I was sleepwalking, and no one was out there with me. They couldn't have been.

But someone was.

One person at least.

Tilly.

Cassie dissolves her nervous energy into cleaning. Tinkering in the kitchen and on her laptop. Her face was severe as she delivered the news, and it remains that way even now. Different from when she found Wayne. That day she walked calmly into the kitchen, completely straight-faced. *Wayne's dead*, she told me, and I nearly choked on my orange juice. Cassie poured herself a bowl of cereal before calling the police department. She spoke to them around a mouthful of Lucky Charms.

It's very clear that I'm not like Cassie. She's able to channel her confusion and concern into being productive. I don't compartmentalize. I hyperfocus. And I can't even pretend to focus on anything other than her words.

It's Tilly. She's dead.

But what happened to her?

How did Tilly go from a person with a beating heart to a body on the ground?

An accident? Did she get lost, get attacked by an animal?

There it is. The tug on my brain. The feeling that I'm missing something.

"It's been hours, Lenora. Why don't you eat lunch?" There's a tremor in Cassie's voice, a glitch in her apathetic demeanor. Proof that even as she stares at her laptop, she may not be as focused on her work as she wants me to believe.

I don't answer. Don't move. I stay at the window. Watch the police trek in and out of the woods. Watch the twitches and groans of Cabin Three. Picture Tilly's mother running from the tent into the cabin screaming. Holding her middle like she's holding every single one of her organs inside her. She hasn't come out since, and there's something unbelievable about it. The way she spoke to Tilly the night she went missing, the way she hit her. She doesn't actually care about her daughter. She can't.

"Lenora?" Cassie's whisper is a cry behind me. A prayer in the dark. I know she's worried. I know she sees my turmoil and is desperately trying to understand it.

But how can I tell her that I'm afraid? How can I tell her that it feels like I'm watching my body from the third person, and sometimes I don't know what's real or what isn't? How can I say I'm a good person? I know I am. Even when I don't feel like it.

As much as I want to, I can't mask my feelings. Not for Cassie.

"What did she look like?" I ask.

"What?" Cassie's eyes search the side of my face. Worried. So worried, and it's my fault.

"Tilly. You said you saw her. What did she look like? I mean, how did—how did they miss her? She was at the Blacktop." Maybe she was alive the night she went missing. Maybe I did see her walking out of her cabin that night, and she did get lost. But something happened to her that next day. Right when she was on her way back.

The theory doesn't quite make sense to me.

"She wasn't there yesterday. She couldn't have been."

"So what? She was lost in the woods, wandering around, finally made it back to camp and fell over and died?"

"I don't know." Cassie watches me the way someone might watch a car crash. "I didn't get a good look at her."

"What did you see exactly?" My voice is uncharacteristically desperate as I grab my sister's arm. "Surely you saw something."

"You're hurting me."

I let go, place a hand on the windowsill to steady myself. "I'm sorry." And I am. I'm so sorry. I just don't know what for. Not yet.

Cassie's expression hardens. "I need to know you can handle this."

"Of course."

"If it's too much, all this, first Wayne, then Tilly, if this is too hard, then it's OK. It's OK to be hurt, Lenora."

"I just want to know what happened."

"I don't think you need to hear any of this."

"Please, Cassie."

"I only saw her arm," Cassie says abruptly. "She was lying on the ground. That's all I know."

Her arm. Pale. Colorless. Without the rush of pumping blood. No more holding a book or posting on social media. Useless. Dead.

The memory comes fast and hard and nearly takes me off my feet. Branches snapping against my face, my breath heavy as I sprint through the woods. Running. Toward or away, I can't tell, only that running is my only option.

There's someone with me.

A person in the woods.

But it's all so blurry.

And I'm so tired.

The knock is abrupt enough to shake me from my thoughts.

Cassie and I stiffen and look over her shoulder. Two people stand behind the screen door, a man and a woman.

Cassie's expression turns grim. "That would be the detectives," she says. "I'm sure they have a lot of questions for us."

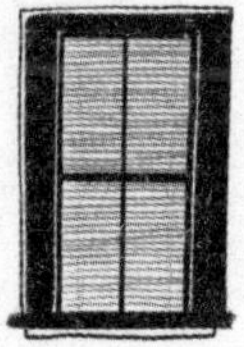

CHAPTER TWELVE

CASSIE

I'm thinking of Tilly. Of her hand. How it came to rest there, spread on the ground like a crumpled newspaper with the rest of her. She hadn't been there the day before. It just isn't possible. I'm thinking of all the questions everyone else is.

How did she get there?

How did she die?

Was it painful? Quick? Did she look someone in the eye as her life drained slowly like a clogged sink?

But I'm also thinking of something else. The look on Sarah's face when I walked back up the hill grimly. Her face crumbled, and she audibly gasped. Devastation sank into her as swiftly as a knife. You didn't have to know the kid to be utterly gutted.

Then I compare that to my sister's face. Most wouldn't notice. They wouldn't see past the shock. The tremble in her lips. But I know the subtleties of her every expression. The way her eyes avoid mine and her jaw clenches—it tells me something different.

When the detectives introduce themselves as Detective Eubanks and Detective Harrison, I wonder if Tilly was alive when she hit the ground. If she got one more glimpse of the sky before her eyes closed, or if they were closed when she fell. The itch crawls over me. The urging in my gut to get in her head. To imagine her death. But it seems morbid. Wrong somehow. I wasn't friends with Tilly, but I knew her. I liked her.

She's alive in my head even now.

Lenora still won't meet my eyes.

Eubanks, a stiff woman with board-straight black hair in a loose ponytail at the nape of her neck, lets her eyes roam the room, roam my sister and me like she thinks she'll find the answers tattooed on our skin.

Detective Harrison is more relaxed. He has a stain on the breast of his button-down that makes me picture him hunched over his desk eating a hot dog when the call came in. He'd have had a fleeting moment of annoyance about the dead girl who'd been found before he scarfed down the last bite, a glob of ketchup falling out that he'd swipe up with his finger and dab at during the whole drive.

An odd pairing.

I lead them to the living room. Eubanks and Harrison take the couch. Lenora sinks into the recliner, and I sit on the arm. The living area is quite small with my sound booth squeezed into the corner. Between the couch and chair and booth and all of us, there doesn't seem to be enough oxygen in the room.

We're so close to the detectives that Lenora's sock-clad feet nearly brush Harrison's loafers. I act like the confined and crowded space isn't bothering me. Like I'm focused on them. Focused on anything other than the sound of Lenora's fingernails clicking against one another or the vision of Tilly in those woods. Her life seeping away as I slept soundly.

And where was Lenora while I was sleeping and Tilly was dying?

There is a look of awe on Detective Eubanks's face as she gazes between Lenora and me. "You two look exactly alike."

"That happens with twins sometimes," I say dryly.

"That must have been fun growing up. Switching places. *The Parent Trap* and all that." She smiles, and I'd almost believe it if I didn't know better. If I didn't know how these investigations work.

Even so, the mention of our childhood catches me off guard. When I think of my past, it all comes back to one night. The night Dad died. But there are years of memories that came before. Millions of them I could sit and sift through if I wanted. Some are decent. Most hurt too much to remember.

"How did she die?" I ask, looking between Eubanks and Harrison. The need to know burns inside me. "You introduced yourselves as homicide detectives."

Their eyes flash with surprise. "We're in the preliminary stages of our investigation here. Not much to tell. Only, based off certain facts, we feel the need to ask a few questions. See if you can help clear some things up about two nights ago when Tilly Meadows went into the woods."

"I was asleep."

"Her parents mentioned that one of you, Cassie, right?" She motions to me, and I nod, curious how she got it right on the first try. What did Tilly's parents tell them about me? "You saw her a few nights before smoking marijuana in the woods."

"Yes."

"What night and time was this?"

"Around one in the morning."

"Do you go outside at night often?"

"Sometimes."

Harrison jots something down in his notebook, but Eubanks doesn't lose focus. "What did she and you talk about that night?"

"Nothing really. I think we both surprised each other."

"You don't remember anything specific?"

"No. We only spoke a few minutes before her mother called her back inside."

"Let's shift to two nights ago. Were you up or out of the cabin that night?"

I shake my head and feel Lenora tense. Her hand moves to my leg, and her nails sink in.

Eubanks follows the gesture. "What about you? Lenora, right?"

Lenora clears her throat. "Yes. And yes, I stepped into the bathhouse that night."

"Can you tell us what happened?"

"I went to the bathhouse around one or one thirty." She wraps her hands together on her lap, bouncing her knee harshly.

"How long were you out there?"

"Maybe a few minutes."

She clearly has both detectives' attention now. Lenora's nails twist into my skin, and I lay a hand over hers. Slip her curled fingers into mine. I want to convey to her everything I'm feeling. Whatever this is, whatever happened, we'll get through it. Eubanks tracks the motion before looking back at my sister. "When you were out there, did you see or hear anything unusual?"

"I didn't hear anything. To be honest I try not to look at anything when I'm outside at night. The woods, they can be scary."

"So, you walked back to your cabin without looking at the cabin the Meadows were staying in at all?"

Lenora's face floods with red. "That's not what I'm saying. Just that I wasn't trying to see anything."

"Did you see something, Lenora?" Detective Eubanks shifts closer. "You can tell us. Whatever it is. However unimportant it feels, please tell us."

"I think..." Lenora pauses. "I think I might have seen Tilly leave her cabin."

"You saw her leave that night? This was right after you left the bathhouse, when you were on your way back to the cabin?"

"Yes. It was just a figure moving quickly in the dark. I couldn't tell who it was at first. But the next day, when I realized Tilly was missing, I figured it out."

"And she was alone? When you saw her, she was alone?"

"Yes."

"What direction was she headed?"

"It was too dark to see. She came out and turned left. It looked like she was going straight into the woods, but I didn't stay and check."

"Good," Eubanks breathes. "This is all really good, Lenora. Was she holding anything when you saw her? A backpack? A flashlight? Anything like that?"

"I couldn't tell. I don't think so."

The detectives ask a few more follow-up questions and have Lenora go through the whole story one more time. Detective Eubanks sits back, looking between Lenora and me. "Is that it? You didn't see anything else out of the ordinary?"

Lenora hesitates, and it's like everyone in the room takes a breath. Eubanks looks at her. Waits.

"There is one thing." Lenora's voice is a breath above a whisper. "The night Tilly went missing, I saw Tilly and her mother get in a fight."

I try to place the memory, try and figure out what she's talking about, but I have no idea.

Eubanks asks, "A fight? Can you explain to us exactly what you saw?"

"It was dark, so I couldn't see clearly, and they were too far away to really hear. I just know Karen slapped her daughter."

"And what did Tilly do when she was hit?"

Lenora's lips tremble. "I don't know. She took it, I guess."

"Did she look angry?"

"I don't know," Lenora says, and I can already hear the impending crash of her falling apart, like her words are the warning crack right before a building crumbles. "I really don't."

Eubanks turns to me. "Did you see this happen?"

I shake my head and swallow a fresh wave of anxiety. "This is the first time I'm hearing about this."

Lenora turns to look at me, but I don't meet her eyes.

They ask Lenora some more questions. Questions about Karen and Tilly's relationship. Lenora can't answer them, or maybe she just chooses not to. Either way, she sits nearly silent, fiddling with her fingers in her lap. Eventually, the detectives stand together, slapping their notebooks closed.

"Thank you both for your cooperation and time. Will you give us a call if you think of anything else?" Harrison extends a business card, which I pocket when it's clear Lenora isn't reaching for it.

The detectives walk straight down the hill to Cabin Three.

"Why didn't you tell me about their fight, Lenora?" I ask quietly as we stand side-by-side, staring out the window. It's still crawling with police. Their muddy footprints will probably remain on this hill long after they're gone.

"I didn't think it was important."

"Her mother hit her the night she went missing. Of course it's important."

Through the woods there are two officers holding something. I tense when I realize. A gurney. A long zipped black bag on top. Lenora notices it the same time I do, her face paling and breath coming out in an exhausted rush.

A second passes before I speak. "We all die," I say, and it's supposed to make her feel better. But her teeth snap together, and she turns away.

"Yes," she says. "But not like this."

It's not until she's gone that I finally place the look on her face, and my heart feels like it might pump right out of my chest.

Guilt.

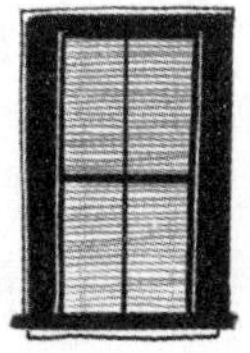

CHAPTER THIRTEEN
LENORA

I sometimes count the branches on the trees, and as careful as I am, I get a new number every time. I tried to think of numbers when the detectives were here, and it reminded me of being a kid. Second grade. The first year Cassie and I weren't in the same class. Somehow, I ended up sitting with my teacher during recess every day as she questioned me.

What's wrong with you?

You can't act this way just because you miss her.

You mustn't scream at other children, Lenora.

I counted the gray hairs sprouting from her chin and cheeks until my steady gaze and silence antagonized her even more. She didn't understand that sometimes I don't always have the tightest control of my emotions or actions. She didn't understand me. I've learned that most people don't. Not even Cassie. But at least Cassie loves me anyway.

My fingers thread too tightly around a broom I'm doing a crap job of using, and I continue to stare blankly at the tree branches. Afraid to let go. Afraid to be still.

Afraid of what I might think of if I do. I want to be calm, but nothing is working. Not when I keep going back to the night Tilly went missing. Not when I can't make sense of the memory of it.

Not when there are others trying to make sense of it.

As I think of the detectives, my hands go sweaty. Slick on the rough wooden handle. The sun is close to setting, and Cassie is pacing like it isn't obvious she's driving herself crazy watching me. It's like she's afraid to do anything else, and I don't know how that makes me feel.

The screen door to Cabin Three suddenly opens, and the detectives step out. They walk around to the back of Cabin Three where the road loops, but before they round the corner, Eubanks glances back sharply. Her eyes meet mine over the expanse and glass separating us. It reminds me of two nights ago. Of seeing Tilly and her mother. The way Tilly looked at me afterward.

The detective finally lifts her hand in a wave.

I wave back and they're gone.

"That's enough." It's Cassie's voice. Cassie's angry voice. "You've been sweeping the same spot for ten minutes. I know you have work to do. Hell, anything to do. Just *do* something."

"Cassie—"

"No, don't. I can be worried about you. I'm allowed to worry, Lenora."

"I know."

"The way you're acting, it's like—" She stops suddenly, and the thing is, she doesn't have to finish. I know what she's going to say. I always know what she's going to say. Like the day my teacher finally called my mother, and she chastised me for acting out at school. Cassie slipped her hand over mine in the back seat and squeezed my hand rhythmically on the drive home. One, two, three… She did it the whole way as if she knew I couldn't think of the words our mother was saying. When Mom angrily climbed out of the car at home, Cassie looked at me without letting go of my hand. I knew what she was going to say and that it contrasted with what she felt.

"You can't keep getting in trouble."

"I just want to be in your class."

"I know."

"Your teacher is nicer and prettier. The girls treat you better, and…you're there." When I finally meet my sister's eyes, she smiles sadly.

"Yes, but Jamar is also in my class, and he always takes the markers I want to use. Peter sits right in front of me, and every day after lunch, he asks me to pull his finger, and when I don't, he farts anyway!" I'm giggling now, and her grip on my hand tightens. "I'm being serious. If you don't believe that the grass isn't always greener on the other side, then we can switch tomorrow, and you can go to class for me. I'll be on my best behavior for you. Maybe even earn you a best-behavior sticker for once!"

"That wouldn't work."

"Sure it would." Her eyes twinkle. "Either way, it would be a cool story to tell. What do you say?"

"OK."

"OK?"

"OK, I know I need to act better in class." She knows I'm not brave or stupid enough to switch places.

She grins and pulls me in for a hug just as our mother opens the door and waves us inside. Cassie pulls back to look at me. "Don't forget that it doesn't matter where we are. You and me, we're together no matter what."

Cassie slams the broom against the counter, and it clatters to the ground. She doesn't look at it or flinch. "Look at me, Lenora. Look at me and tell me there's nothing else. There's nothing else you're holding back."

I intake a breath sharply, feel my heart gallop, my blood quicken.

"Tell. Me."

"No." I emphasize the word. Say it deliberately and slowly. "No," I say again and again and again.

"You showered that night. You were out there. You won't stop watching their cabin. Is this about Tilly? Is she—"

"No," I say again. "Listen to me, Cassie, I was out there that night. Just like I told the detectives. For five minutes. I took a shower. I saw her shadow. That's it. That's all there is to the story." The lie hurts. It's a pain that reminds me of being a kid. The sting of my knee scraping against pavement or cutting my thumb on a piece of construction paper. Subtle. A pain that won't kill me but will remind me it's there all day.

"So how come you weren't honest about it? Why didn't you just tell me all this that night? And the fight between Tilly and her mother, why wouldn't you mention that sooner?"

I don't get a chance to answer before the beating on the back door starts. Cassie swings it open without checking.

Tilly's mother and father are there, and his head swivels between me and my sister as if trying to decide who is who. "I need to know which one of you saw my daughter that night."

His wife grabs his hand. "This isn't how we should do this, Rob."

He pulls his hand free and steps forward, forcing Cassie to step back into the room. He's so close, I can smell him. Mildewy and sweaty like he hasn't showered in days. His eyes are bloodshot, and his shirt is crumpled and wet. Worse than that is the pure fury on his face. "One of you saw her that night. And I want you to tell me what you saw. I want you to tell me the truth for once. Not that shit you told the detectives."

Cassie angles herself in front of me, her arm acting as a buffer as if she senses that this man is on the edge. "She told the police everything she saw."

His eyes shift to me. "You should have told us when you saw my fifteen-year-old daughter sneak out! You should have woken us, and this wouldn't have happened. She'd still be here."

I can't see Cassie's face, but I hear the tremor in her voice, the anger. "Look, we're sorry about what happened. But you need to leave. You can't be here like this."

He looks past Cassie to me, spit flying from his mouth with each word. "What else did you see that night? What aren't you telling us?"

"Rob." The tug on her husband's arm is stronger now, more desperate. "Let's just go. You're not thinking rationally. Please don't do this." There is anger on her face too, but it's more contained. More overshadowed by intense sadness.

"Don't you get it?" he demands, his voice rising with every word, snapping me back to now. To this moment. "Someone murdered her. Someone murdered our baby, and she—" He swings a fist in my direction, looming over my sister with a face so tortured that it makes me think this man might kill someone. "She was outside. She could have stopped everything. Now, what else happened, what else did you see?"

"Maybe you should ask your wife," I say before I can stop myself. Before I can think better of it. The room goes silent. "Wait, I didn't mean to say—"

"What the hell does that mean?"

But the woman, Tilly's mother, is watching me closely. "I knew I saw you in that window that night."

"You were yelling. You were angry at something. You hit her." There's a hand dipping inside me, squeezing my insides until they're pulverized while I desperately try to recollect everything I saw. What it meant. For some reason, I can't lift my head or look them in the eye.

"You have no idea what you're talking about," she says, her lips curling into a sneer. But I see through it. Anyone would. Anger isn't a good substitute for guilt because, most often, anger is its predecessor. I would know. "My daughter told me about you. How you were watching her like some kind of pervert. Maybe my husband is right. Maybe you do know more than you're saying. Maybe you're more than a sick, twisted little stalker."

"That's enough." When Cassie says it, she presses a hand against the woman's chest, forcing her to crash into her husband. They both stumble back. "Get out."

"Not until she answers us."

"Lenora," Cassie says. "Just step away a minute."

But I couldn't even if I wanted to. Couldn't move. Not with Tilly's mother's words hanging over me like a guillotine. Not with wet palms and a sickness spreading in me.

The broom is still in my hand, and another vision is born. One where I swing it until something cracks. Until everything stops. Until she admits what she did.

My hands tighten.

Cassie steps closer to them, her arms out like she's herding wild animals. "I'll ask you nicely one more time to get out. I know you're mourning. I know you're hurt, and we're sincerely sorry. But what you're doing right now, these accusations, they won't bring Tilly back."

"I think you're the ones making accusations," Karen snaps, taking a step toward my sister. "Why would my daughter leave in the middle of the night anyway? It was freezing and dark. I know her. She wouldn't have gone alone." Her attention swings back to me. "There's something you're not telling me."

"I think she told you everything," Cassie says, her voice no longer kind. "I think we know Tilly had every reason to want to get away from you."

The slap echoes across the room, and I'm too shocked to move. Too shocked to do anything except stare at the counter. There are crumbs scattered across it from breakfast. With all of Cassie's puttering around and cleaning, she didn't wipe it.

The broom clatters to the ground.

Tilly's father has a hold of his wife, pulling her back. She keeps her gaze on my sister as he hauls her over the threshold.

Cassie closes and locks the door, then lowers herself onto the nearest chair. There's something cold in my hands, and I realize I must have grabbed the peas. I hold the package to her face. There's a bruise already forming.

Cassie's face and Tilly's morph together in my mind. The night Karen slapped her daughter. This moment. It all feeds together.

"Steady," I murmur. "It's OK." Suddenly, my eyes are filling with tears, and my face is hot. There's another knock on the door. A gentle one. Sarah is standing there, rubbing her hands together. Nose red like she's been out for a while. When I look back at Cassie, she seems to understand what I'm asking and nods for me to open the door.

"I heard the commotion from my porch. By the time I made it up the hill, I saw Karen and Robert leaving. What happened?" Sarah lingers in the doorway wearing a thick coat and dirty hiking boots like she put them to use with the search party out in the woods.

"Isn't it obvious?" Cassie's voice is dry. "I'm trying to warm up this bag of peas with my cheek."

"Did you get hit? Did—did they *hit* you?"

"Karen did. Funny, the name is fitting, isn't it?"

Sarah's hands twitch at her side, and mine do too, like neither of us knows what to do with them. It's too late for any useful reaction from either of us. I step closer to Cassie. Dig into my pocket for my coin.

It isn't there.

I haven't seen it for days.

And it's all too much. Too overwhelming. The white noise in my brain blurs in and out to Sarah's voice. She speaks quietly but assuredly. "They've been like this all day. Hysterical. I don't know what could have made her do this though. Not that it's your fault, but did you say something?"

No, I think without saying. *No. Cassie didn't do anything. It was my fault. All my fault.*

They don't warn you about this in school. They warn you about the men in vans offering treats to get you inside. They warn you of drug use and STDs. But no one ever warned me about the dangers of my own thoughts. No one ever told me that there could come a time when trusting myself would be difficult and hating myself would be easy.

What to do when the monster is you.

"Lenora saw Tilly the night she disappeared, and they found out about it." Cassie doesn't mention what I said. What I saw. The fight between mother and daughter that clearly struck a nerve. Cassie doesn't throw me to the wolves in the same way I did her. After all, Tilly's parents came for me. But somehow it was Cassie who took a hit.

And I stood to the side, too afraid to move.

Like always.

I walk to the counter. Fill a glass with water and hand it to Cassie. Her eyes show gratitude. They show sorrow. There is no anger or resentment. Like a loyal dog. So very Cassie. Sarah looks between us once more confused, her gaze landing on my sister.

"I'm Cassie."

"Oh." Sarah's forehead wrinkles. "I thought so, with your short hair, but…"

"If you're wondering why I'm the one who got slapped when they came up here angry at my sister, I guess we could attribute it to my talent with words."

"It doesn't matter. This wasn't your fault. Either of you. Regardless of what you saw. It isn't your fault." Sarah scans our cabin, landing on the recording booth through the doorway. "What is that?"

"Soundproofed room. I record in there."

"Ah," she says. "The YouTube videos."

Cassie glances at her sharply. "You've seen them?"

"I'm a fan of true crime. I recognized you the first time I met you." Sarah stops herself, the weight of the past few days seemingly crushing her at once. I always thought Sarah was a few years older than Cassie and me. Now it seems much more than that. "That's morbid, isn't it? For me to call myself a fan of true crime after this happens."

Cassie's head is tilted, her eyes on Sarah. Something about her face seizes my attention. Makes me pause. Cassie is looking at her with an air of affability. An almost camaraderie. I touch a hand to my sister's arm. She grabs it absentmindedly but doesn't look away from Sarah. "Not morbid. I know what you mean."

"Are you going to tell this story on your channel?"

"I don't know."

"Let me know if you do. I don't think I want to watch it." Sarah tucks her hands back into her pockets and shivers. "Anyway, I should check on Mr. and Mrs. Meadows. See how much longer they're planning on staying. You sure you're OK? Both of you?"

"Where were you that night?" I ask sharply.

Just like earlier, the room drops into an icy silence. Cassie finally looks away from Sarah to stare at me with confusion. "What?"

"I'm asking where she was two nights ago when Tilly went into the woods." My body is tense and on guard. It's like I'm talking outside myself. Like I'm watching my body, my actions, from somewhere at a safe distance, and I have no control over what I say.

Sarah's nose crinkles. She pulls her beanie tighter over her ears. "I was in my cabin. Asleep."

"Lenora, maybe you should go lie down—"

"It's a valid question. The detectives came here treating us like criminals. Then Mr. and Mrs. Meadows came and did the same. What about her? Did anyone ask her where she was?"

Surprisingly, there is no anger from either woman. There is something much worse. Sarah's lips draw together. A show of pity. Cassie grabs my hand. Squeezes once, twice, three times.

One, two, three.

One, two, three.

The anger fizzles. And I'm tired. So very tired.

I take a breath and another. "I'm sorry," I whisper. "I don't know what's gotten into me."

"That's OK." Sarah smiles like someone would at a contrite child. "I think we're all on edge here."

"We need to be careful around Karen. I don't think we can trust her."

"I think it's time for bed." My sister's voice is soft.

"I'm sorry, Cassie."

"Shhh..."

Cassie and Sarah murmur to each other. Hurried words I don't bother trying to hear. I head for my bedroom.

I don't mean to be a liar.

I don't mean to be—what did Karen call me? A sick, twisted little stalker. And I'm not. I just can't let it go. I went to my room. Attempted to sleep. Tossed and turned. Desperately wanting to be unconscious. But I couldn't let Tilly go. My mind wouldn't rest. Daphne would have given me some sort of psychological load-of-crap explanation for my behavior. Something about seeing myself in Tilly. Seeing my mother in Karen.

But that's not it either.

I'm unraveling. Hell, I almost did when Sarah was here. I don't have a problem with Sarah. No gut instinct about her. It feels like in the movies when the bad guy is chasing someone, and the soon-to-be victim is running through a house, turning behind them every so often to toss a lamp, box, or plate at their pursuer. That's me. I'm constantly running from this feeling I can't name, tossing anything at anyone. Doing anything I can to protect myself. And absolutely none of it is working. But it's not all in my head. Karen slapped her daughter, then my sister. I saw the emptiness in her eyes. How instinctually she embraces her own brutality. The way she and her husband interact. It all makes me feel like I'm missing something.

It makes me curious to know if someone had noticed the same thing about my family once. An indescribable wrongness.

And if they did, if they said something, could things have been different?

I'm curled into my sheets, my laptop perched on my thighs. It's after midnight, and I've found myself here again. Tilly's social media. It's harder to be here now than the first day. Not just because I know she's dead but because everyone else does too. Her parents have posted to all her channels a quick, impersonal message:

Our beautiful daughter, Matilda Nicole Meadows, has gained her wings. We ask for privacy at this time as we focus on grieving our daughter and attempting to understand the circumstances of her untimely death. Thank you.

Karen and Robert Meadows

It seems that all ten thousand of her followers are in the comments in different degrees of shock. I read through them. Most are as impersonal as Karen and Robert's statement. It makes me cringe.

I'll miss you forever

Not Tilly. Not this queen. Help Jesus.

Fly high angel

Watch over us always

Clearly, none of these people knew Tilly. They didn't know the books she read or her favorite breakfast or if she even believed in God. They didn't know her voice when she was upset or the secrets she kept, and I might not know everything either, but I know enough.

Enough not to comment something stupid and generic.

Enough to know Tilly had more substance than that.

I also know one of her secrets. Her relationship with her mother. The reason they went camping in the first place. It all had to come back to Karen. I shift gears and search Karen's name. A local news article comes up reporting Tilly's death. It's repetitive, with nothing new to add. Under that is Karen's Facebook account. Private except for her last post. The same message she posted to her daughter's social media page. Like her daughter, the status is full of generic comments and has been shared hundreds of times.

Next, I search a site Cassie told me about once. A background-checking app that scours public resources for information on people and compiles it together. Cassie uses it for case research. After logging in with Cassie's information, her email and the password she's had for everything since she was sixteen years old, I search Karen's name. There are too many hits to wade through. I need some other type of identifier. I backtrack to

Tilly's Facebook and do a screen search for "Happy Birthday." There are several hits this time, and it takes a second to find the one I'm looking for.

Happy 40th Birthday, Mom! Don't worry, you don't look a day over 25!

The post is from several years back on April 16. It takes a second to load, do the math, and then try it all together with Karen's name. Then, miraculously, there's a hit. But the screen is mostly empty. Just Karen's address and her job. A paralegal at some law firm near Tampa, Florida.

I'm just about to type in Robert's name when I see movement from the corner of my eye and slide the warm laptop onto the bed. My knees ache and creak as I walk to the window. Press a hand to the cold glass. There is no wind tonight. Not even a breeze. The shadowed trees look as if someone pressed pause on them. Like the whole forest is lying in wait.

What did I see?

I scan the woods. The cabin. Nothing. There isn't—

There.

Down the grassy hill, to the left of Cabin Three, there is a shadow. A lump at the base of the tree. Did the searchers leave something? A bundled tent? Some sort of crumpled tarp?

I stare at the shape harder, but it only makes my vision swim. Darkness so thick, I'd need a machete to penetrate it. There's a feeling that comes with staring directly into it. A prickly feeling traveling up my spine that tells me something is staring back.

A loud thud, and my heart takes off.

Robert Meadows storms out of Cabin Three with a suitcase in his hand. It's too dark to make out his expression, but there's fury in his movements. His car cranks; the headlights beam and reflect on the cabin.

Karen steps outside, her face gaunt beneath the glow of light only for a moment before his headlights disappear in a squeal of rubber on gravel and Karen is lit only by a flickering light through her cracked cabin door.

I stay still.

Not even breathing.

Suddenly she turns, and her gaze clashes with mine.

Neither of us move for several seconds too long before she turns back toward the cabin, slamming the door and taking the light with her.

My breathing comes out raspy and shallow as I look over the cabin and—

I stop.

Blink but the scene doesn't change.

Whatever was there, huddled or abandoned at the base of that tree, is gone now.

My hands shake as I close my curtains.

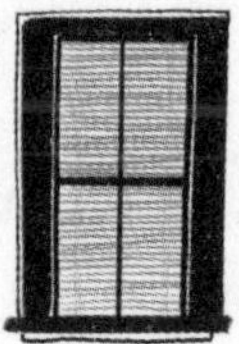

CHAPTER FOURTEEN
CASSIE

The cabin feels different. The whole property does. There's a shift in the air. A tangible difference that the discovery of Tilly's body brought. I work on research. Force myself to watch a documentary for a case I'm covering next month.

But my mind constantly slips back to Tilly.

I try to think of her like the other victims I come in contact with while doing my job. Try to picture what she saw in her last moments. Try to imagine her fear. But I can't. Something prevents me from fully visualizing it.

An image I desperately want to shake.

Lenora.

She's still locked in her room. I checked on her once this morning, and she told me she has a lot of writing to do. I haven't bothered her again, but that hasn't stopped me from walking down the hallway to her bedroom door. Leaning against it. Pressing a hand against the wood and wishing I knew the words to say to her.

But what is there to say?

A girl's body was found on our property.

My sister was outside the night she died.

The urge hits me. The need to run. To go anywhere as long as it takes me from this cabin.

I want to yank her door open, to demand she talk to me. To demand she tell me the truth. But my questions get distorted on my tongue, and I walk away each time before I can even touch the handle.

This day feels anything but normal. Maybe it's the pulsing blood in my cheek. A steady staccato to remind me of yesterday, the hit I took. Maybe it's the emptiness of the hillside. No cops. No volunteers. No Tilly. Just me and my sister.

Somehow in the end, it's always just me and Lenora.

It should make me happy. This is what we wanted when we came here.

But I feel strange. The things that felt so liberating suddenly feel constricting.

I walk to the window. Expecting to see gray clouds or the first drops of rain. But the sky is bright and blue. No shadows to be cast on this day. Hundreds of blackbirds pepper the trees. They cling to branches, their beady black eyes roaming the forest floor.

It's the only sign of life out here at all.

I don't know if Karen and Robert are still here, but their car is gone, and I haven't seen either of them all day.

I think I see a curtain twitch at Cabin Three, and I'm tempted to walk down. Press my face to the glass and look. Would I see them clinging to each other, grieving their daughter? Would they be arguing, growing in separate directions as the chasm divides them further? It seems death has one of two effects on couples, but I know better. There's really only one. Even the ones who stay together, who claim the tragedy mended something else that was broken, aren't really happy. They're just too afraid to stop pretending. When the sun finally sets outside and the black birds have scattered along the hillside, I intend to lie in bed. To not think of Tilly or Lenora or anything.

But when I stop at the end of the hallway and stare at Lenora's still-closed bedroom door, the thought of lying in my own bed is stifling. It doesn't help that I'm wearing the Harvard T-shirt. Not on purpose. My fingers sank into the worn fabric, and I slipped it on before thinking better of it.

It made me think of Tilly.

What did Tilly say that night we met? Her mother went to Harvard. Now Tilly won't have a chance to go anywhere at all. So I'm wearing it for her like the other victims I talk about on my channel.

That's the thought that makes the decision for me. That sends me barreling for the door, eager for night air and mud splatter on ankles and calves.

I am a bullet in the forest. Insignificant as long as I avoid contact with any living thing. No coat. No shoes. No flashlight. Only foggy breath and the scratch of branches against my skin as the moon guides me to where I need to go. I breathe in pine needles and forest air and move past Cabin Three, without approaching it. Even as my fingers twitch at the thought of peeking inside. The birds are behind me, flapping their wings, and perhaps they're screaming. But most likely I wouldn't be able to recognize the sound if they were.

I head straight for the Blacktop. Tell myself it's because it's my favorite spot to think, to jot things down in my notebook while I mull over a case. But when I see the yellow crime scene tape fluttering in the wind and the breath leaves my body, I know what I'm really searching for.

The spot where Tilly's body was found is several yards from my rock.

Every one of those cops would have driven down the dirt road that passes by the Blacktop just to reach camp. Yet no one saw her. The morning after Tilly went missing, when I took the Meadows and Sarah out here, Tilly wasn't here then. I sink to the ground, dig my fingers into the dirt, and stare at it.

And I can't help but imagine.

Tilly running through the woods. Lost, scared, Tilly running and crying. But what was she running from? And what caught her? How did she end up here?

The image in my mind shifts and morphs into something unrecognizable and blurry.

Tilly on the cold dirt floor gasping for air, staring up at a starless night. In the back of her head, behind the panic, behind the disbelief, is the hope. The hope that someone will hear. Someone will save her. The hope that when her eyes close, they will open again. They do. Once more. But there's another image. Another person. Swimming in front of Tilly's vision. "I'm sorry," they say. "It shouldn't have turned out like this."

The person's face comes in and out of focus until I see with perfect clarity. See exactly what Tilly saw. I see myself.

My eyes squeeze shut, and I will the images away. Watch as they explode into inky-black shards and disperse themselves to any other place apart from my head. I can't think of Tilly like that.

Can't think of what she saw.

A branch snaps somewhere at the edge of the Blacktop. I jolt to my feet, taking a second for my eyes to adjust to the darkness. The trees come into focus. A large pine just near the dirt road that leads to the entrance of the campsite. The night is silent. I don't even hear the birds anymore.

But something is wrong.

The vision doesn't make sense. The twisted form at the base of the tree. At first, I think it's some kind of animal curled into the hollow. A fox or rabbit. But the proportions aren't right. This thing is bigger. I keep my gaze trained on the shadowy black mass. Feel sweat pool at the base of my spine even as my body temperature drops. I can't tell if I'm shaking from the cold or something else.

Then it moves.

Slowly the figure unfolds, a pale arm sliding out of the hole, then a leg. Aberrant and crude. Not an animal. Not human.

I stumble back onto cold dirt, a sharp pain digging into my heel. But I can't look away. Can't run. I stand in place, urging the image away. It isn't real. This can't be real.

There is a burst of sound. A descending black cloud. The flock of blackbirds, hundreds of them, swooping low overhead. This time I fall back, whimpering as my tailbone slams into the frozen ground.

And I'm up again, swiveling back toward the tree. Toward the person. The thing. But it's empty now. No one is there, and I can't help but wonder if there ever was.

The birds have landed and scattered themselves across the Blacktop. They watch me wearily as if I'm the interloper. As if whoever or whatever I saw is as much a part of their surroundings as the trees, and I'm the one who doesn't belong.

I'm all alone.

As if to punctuate the thought, the wind howls, sending the last shred of crime scene tape fluttering in the breeze. The last bit of evidence that anyone else was ever here at all.

I walk back to the cabin slowly. Because I'm tired. Because I'm deflated. And because my foot leaves a trail of blood behind me. I guess I stepped on glass when I panicked at the shadows.

I'm focused on getting home and the hot pain in my frozen foot, so I almost miss the music. Low folksy music coming from Cabin One. Sarah's cabin. I stop and listen. Hear someone stepping over brambles. Picture something crawling toward me on all fours. My pulse picks up.

"Cassie?" Sarah's voice carries the lilt of a question. Like she's unsure of who I am even though we both know Lenora never leaves. Who else would it be?

I release a breath. Feel the blood in my body slow. It's just Sarah. "Yeah," I say, turning away from her cabin to face her.

Sarah's arms are full of firewood, and she looks perplexed to see me. "What are you doing here?" She glances at my feet. Probably noticing the way I'm distributing my weight. "Your foot. What happened?"

"I didn't mean to just pop up on you like this. I was on my way home, and I heard the music."

"Sorry, I can turn it down."

"No, it's fine I was just...checking it out." I rock back on my heels and wince.

"And your foot?"

"Stepped on something." I can't tell her the truth—my mind is so plagued by nightmares that I'm dragging them into reality. I let a tree, some shadows, and a flock of birds get to me.

She walks forward, brushing past me, her shoulder grazing mine. "Come with me."

And I follow because I don't know what else to do. I'm still not ready to go home. She leads me to the porch, which is strangely warm. She has an extension cord pulled through her cracked door with a speaker and an electric heater plugged in. I plop in front of it, wincing at the smear of blood left on the first couple of steps.

There's a key sticking out of the door, and she seems to notice it at the same time as me. "Oh, shoot. Meant to put that back." She grabs it and walks down the steps to lean under them. She slides it onto some ledge under the porch, then winks at me. "It's a spare. I lock myself out at least once a week. Hold on, I'll get that bandage."

Sarah comes back out. Arms empty of firewood, she tosses me a black hand towel. I press the towel against my stinging foot and notice a little aluminum box in her other hand. At first glance, it looks like one of those lunch boxes Lenora and I used as kids. It brings back a strong memory. Like the blackest coffee, just a taste overwhelms my palate. That's how memories from before that night are. Lenora and me on the first day of second grade. I don't know why the lunch box conjures this memory. It isn't even the happiest one. That was the year things started going downhill. Even before that night.

Lenora, skittish and hesitant to step into the world, put kids off, while I seemed to have the opposite impact. They were drawn to the blunt way I spoke to teachers and the stories I'd tell. Lenora was different. She reacted emotionally to the slightest inconvenience. She'd scream when she was angry. Scream when she was sad. Scream when she was happy. Other kids didn't understand her.

That first day was the first we'd been placed in different classes. Lenora was sitting alone at the lunch table, looking like she'd been crying.

In my assigned seat, two tables away, I watched the boy next to her jut an elbow into her side. It sent me to my feet, but I wasn't fast enough. As soon as the boy turned, Lenora gripped the back of his head and slammed his face against the table.

"Cassie?" Sarah is staring at me questioningly.

I wrench my gaze from the lunch box. From the memory. "Sorry about the blood." I gesture to the foot-sized smear on the wood.

"Don't worry about the blood. I'm planning on staining the deck anyway." She sits with a sigh, cross-legged beside me. "Now, are you going to really tell me what happened to your foot?"

"Do you prefer being outside?" I ask, motioning to the heater. "It's much warmer in the cabins."

She looks at me for a long moment. "I like the woods. They're peaceful. The cabin can feel small, so I prefer to take my work out here."

"What do you do?"

"Right now?" She laughs. "Run a haunted campsite apparently. Though my lawyer says the deaths here might actually bring in more clientele if I market it right."

"The blood on the porch shouldn't hurt then."

Sarah snorts out another laugh, passing me the box. "Sorry, this is all I have. There are some alcohol swabs and a bandage at least."

"Thanks."

"I'm thinking of expanding, you know. Least I was before everything with Tilly." The artificial cherry scent is strong as she takes the vape from her pocket and lifts it to her lips. The smoke tickles my face when she blows it out. For the first time since meeting Sarah, the thought hits me that I don't really know her.

"Expanding?"

She offers the vape to me.

"No thanks. There are a thousand ways I'd rather die."

She laughs again, and I'm realizing she does that a lot. But it isn't a fake laugh. It's one of those like I've surprised her. Which must not be too hard to do. "I want to bring RVs back to the field at the entrance."

"The Blacktop?"

She nods, gesturing widely with her hands as she talks. "Was thinking of getting that field open again and another cleared out. Maybe the one near the lake. Figured one could be for tents and the other I could dig for RV hookups."

"Dig?" The chilled sweat on my back feels sticky all of a sudden. I picture men with shovels digging on the Blacktop. By my rock. It feels like more of an invasion than I can take. Like bringing that compacted dirt to the surface would hollow me out at the same time.

"Just some sewage hookups. Though there are a couple down there already." She takes another drag before blowing the smoke out slowly and motioning to my foot. "You may want to clean that."

I pull the towel back and flinch as the blood makes it stick and sting. It's hard to tell the depth of the cut. But it doesn't appear that long, and it isn't pulsing blood anymore at least.

I pick up the silver box and open it. It reminds me of the drawer in the kitchen with a little bit of everything inside. There are batteries, bandages, ChapStick, a tampon, and a handful of cotton balls. There's one alcohol pad, which I rip open with my teeth and wipe over the cut, clearing the blood away.

"Not bad." Sarah whistles. "What were you doing out there anyway? You can just toss it in the box. I'll get it out."

I throw the soiled wipe in and grab a bandage. My gaze lingers on the silver box.

The bang of that boy's head against the table.

"Is everything OK?" Sarah asks.

"The box just reminded me of something."

"You're staring at it hard."

"Has something ever brought back a memory for you so visceral that it feels like you're living it again?" The rough wood of Sarah's porch digs into my thighs, and my foot still aches, but I'm not as planted in the moment as I'd like to be. It still feels like I'm teetering between now and a dream.

"A good memory or bad one?"

The empty look in Lenora's eyes when the boy started screaming. "Just a memory."

"What were you doing outside so late, Cassie?"

I busy myself with neatening the contents of the box. Folding the bloodied wipe.

Stalling. I'm stalling.

"You wanted to see it, didn't you?" Her voice is barely a whisper now. "Where they found her?"

Our eyes connect. "You been down there?"

"After the cops left, sure. I needed to check out the damage."

"What do you think?"

"What do you mean, what do I think? I think it's all a mess. Something like this would happen to me—" She stops herself with a wince. "I don't mean it like that. Poor Tilly. And her parents. I know I sound selfish. I just mean, I haven't even been here two weeks, and someone gets…whatever happened to her." She cuts herself off with another pull on the vape and then gestures to me. "What about you? You're the true-crime expert, aren't you? What do you think?"

"I agree," I answer. "It's a mess. It's all a mess." Lenora that night with her wet hair. Lenora promising me she was telling me the truth. Lenora lying to my face.

And that damned coin.

"How were they?" I ask suddenly. Don't even know why I care, but I do. "Tilly's parents. I haven't seen them since Karen slapped the hell out of me."

Sarah chokes out a laugh. "I really shouldn't laugh. I know it's not funny."

"It's fine. Least it wasn't her husband who hit me. That would have required more than a bag of peas."

Sarah's smile falls away. "I still can't believe they did that. But maybe it shouldn't surprise me so much."

"Why shouldn't it?"

She leans forward conspiratorially. "Wouldn't this be where you'd go to kill someone? To hide a body?" She motions to the vast woods around us. "If they'd come here for that, then surely, they wouldn't have any issues with other types of violence."

"You think her parents did this?" There is a shakiness in my voice that we both pretend not to notice.

"You should know this. It's true crime 101." Her lips settle delicately over the vape, and I watch as she inhales, the relaxation on her face as the smoke funnels out of her mouth.

"You think Karen and Robert brought her here to kill her?" The thought sends my brain spiraling. Falling down, down, down. What if Lenora was just in the bathroom that night and the coin was a fluke, and everything was OK in our world again? The parents. Of course.

"Had to have been one of them, right?" Sarah shrugs. "Some hitchhiker at the right place at the right time, possibly. But it's always the parents."

I smooth the bandage over my foot carefully. Reaching into the box for another to place over it long ways. My fingers settle over something thin and papery. I pull it out. Ticket stubs. Sarah isn't looking at me. She's staring blankly toward the woods, and I don't even think about it. Don't even consider my choices before I'm slipping them into my pocket and grabbing another bandage. She won't even miss them. Won't notice they're gone.

A memento of this moment will surely mean more to me than those stubs do to her.

Sarah looks at me right as I pull my fingers free. "What about you? What are your thoughts? You gathering content for a video?"

"I don't know." I toss the trash back in the box and close it. "I don't know if I want to make a video on this one." The guilt hits me out of nowhere. Tilly deserves awareness. She deserves for people to know her name. To know she was brave and sarcastic and liked to read. She's more than a body in the woods, and I know that. But these are *my* woods. *Our* woods.

People would ask questions. They'd speculate online. Dig into my past and Lenora's.

No.

No, I couldn't do that. Tilly is already dead. It's best to minimize the tragedy there.

The pain in my chest is intrinsic. Diseased fingers crawling through my body, infecting everything they touch. I don't recognize myself. I try to think of their names. The victims. I think of the promises I made to them even as my channel started profiting and rising in popularity. I'd put them first. It was about them.

But how could I put them before Lenora?

They're dead, and she's breathing.

"Missed opportunity."

I wince at Sarah's choice of words and look up and see them. The victims. The ones who died. They stand in the woods, lining the trees. Only they're not the people they were in life. Not in the way I like to remember them. Some have bullet holes, knives sticking from their sides, lacerations around their neck. Some are soaking wet, water plastering hair to their blank faces.

They tell me with their eyes what I already know.

When we start talking about them like this, they become a commodity in death. The more brutally they died, the more they're worth.

My breath catches when I see Tilly. She's mostly in the shadows. I can't see her body well or her face, but I know it's her. I know her long matted hair. The slender curve to her pale neck. But she's not herself.

Her eyes are empty.

Death has objectified her.

I wrap my arms around my middle.

Sarah lays the vape on the step beside her. "You done?"

I nod in her direction, then look back to the woods.

There are only trees.

She closes the box, placing it on her lap and folding the towel over it. Sarah must notice something in my face. The crack splintering me, pulling me in two separate directions. "I'm being insensitive. I promise I'm not trying to be. It's just always the case, you know? Parents are always killing their kids or spouses." She looks at my face and grimaces. "And I'm being insensitive again."

I don't know what she means at first until it clicks. She knows about my family. Of course, she does. If she's familiar with my YouTube channel, then she knows how I got my start. My very first video. "You're apologizing because of what happened to me?"

"It's not a touchy subject for you?"

I stare off into the forest without answering. There's nothing there but the trees.

There never was.

"You don't have to answer that. I'm just on a roll tonight." She stands, holding the box and towel in her arms. "You want a drink? I've got wine and soda."

"No." I stand, careful to keep the weight off my injured foot. "I should get back to my sister." I turn toward the steps, but her voice stops me.

"Cassie?"

"Yes?"

"Why don't you wear shoes?"

I walk backward toward the woods, toward a single dot of light that's my cabin. "I guess I really like feeling the dirt on my skin. Why do you work outside?"

She smiles. "Guess I like it too."

The cabin is quiet when I return, and Lenora is asleep at the kitchen table. It's the first time she's been out of her room all day. She must have snuck out after I left. Now, though, she's snoring, her cheek pressed to the smooth wood. I almost don't want to disturb her, not when she's peaceful like this. I brush a finger over her warm cheek, tucking a strand of hair behind her ear.

When she's like this, my thoughts seem ridiculous. The imagery that painted my brain with violence at the Blacktop. Dead people in the woods. Lenora hurting Tilly.

All of it is so preposterous.

This girl. My sister. She wouldn't hurt anyone. The idea, in this moment, watching her like this, is absurd.

But someone hurt Tilly.

Karen and Robert were here that night. They had ample opportunity. They might have even had a motive. But what if Sarah was wrong? What if someone else is to blame?

A person we're running from.

A person who finally caught up to us.

Tilly stumbling through the woods. Falling to the ground. A branch snapping. Looking up. A face I recognize. One that looks like Lenora and me but also different. Older. A face we haven't seen in fifteen years. Every good and bad thing we do always seems to come back to her.

Our mother.

Even if she's not here, it's her fault anyway.

I think of Lenora, small and shy. Huddled into herself at that lunch table. The fierce protective instinct I've had over her since before either of us can remember. It's an instinct that comes from the worst place. A hypocritical place. After all, I was the first person to ever hurt Lenora. The first to nearly kill her.

In the womb. Stealing her nutrients and oxygen. Growing while she shrank.

I sigh and move her laptop out of the way so I can wake her. If she keeps lying like this her neck will cramp. But as I jostle the computer, the screen lights up.

At first, I don't realize what exactly I'm looking at.

I don't want to.

But I can't pretend. Can't unsee it.

Tilly smiles at me. Her social media. It's like a boulder is dropped inside me, and I sway on my feet. I can't fight it now. I must know. I scroll through the timeline, then start clicking through Lenora's other open tabs. More of Tilly's accounts. News articles. And another article with the headline *Signs of Abuse in Teens.*

My fingers tremble as I slide the cursor to her history.

A wave of trepidation settles in my stomach.

She's visited these pages every day.

"What are you doing?"

I tense, my fingers frozen on the keys.

"Cassie? Why are you on my laptop?"

"What is this?" I step away and slide the screen toward her. Watch her rub her bleary eyes and blink against the brightness. Watch the blood desert her cheeks, and I wonder if I touched them now if they'd still feel warm.

"I just wanted to check a few things out."

"A few things? There are seven open tabs, and your search history, Lenora." The images come violently. Lenora doing something terrible. My mother's face. Lenora's. My own.

We're all connected because of that night. "You went through my history?"

"All your social media accounts are fake. Want to explain that? Why you're on Tilly's page using fake names?"

Lenora snaps her laptop closed, but it's too late. There's no point.

"It's worse than I thought," I say.

"No, it's not like that. Look, I didn't want to bring it up. Not like this, but there are some things you should know. Some things I haven't told you."

The coin our father gave her and how it got into those woods.

Her obsession with Tilly.

The *lies.*

"The night Tilly disappeared, I mentioned I heard Tilly and her mother get in a fight, an argument." Lenora's voice rises desperately like I'm sand between her fingers, and she's trying to catch me before I fall away. "Well, what if it was more than that? It was intense, Cassie. She hit Tilly, and we saw the way she hit you. She's impulsive. No self-control—"

"What are you implying?"

"Last night, Rob and Karen Meadows got into a fight. I know because I saw him storm out and leave. He took his stuff. I think—I think there's more to Karen and Tilly's relationship. Something that might have given her a reason to want her daughter dead. Or maybe it was an accident. Another fight that spiraled out of control."

They got into it last night? I hadn't heard anything. It explained where their vehicle went. But where has Karen been all day? Locked in Cabin Three all alone? Sarah's words rock through my mind. It's always the parents. True crime 101, Sarah called it.

None of this information helps the ocean waves roaring in my stomach. I rub my eyes with the heels of my hands. "What are you doing, Lenora? Why are you researching this?"

Lenora stands, her eyes holding mine. "I'm here. All the time. I've seen things through that window. And sometimes they mean something. It can't be a coincidence that Karen and Tilly got into a fight the night before she was killed. Or that he left her. Why would you leave your wife here after something like that happens? Why would you leave her alone?"

"Lenora—"

"No, don't say my name like that. Like I've lost it. I haven't. I'm not telling this to the police or shouting it from the rooftops. I'm just trying to learn more. There's nothing wrong with that." She cuts herself off, breathing heavily, waiting for me to argue back. Ready for combat.

"Tilly is already dead. Who are you trying to save?"

"And what if someone had done it for us?" Her voice cracks. "What if someone noticed how wrong everything was in our family? What could have happened then?"

I look at her and notice how tired she looks. How manic. "Have you been sleeping?"

"Not this, Cassie."

"You want me to answer you? You want me to tell you the truth? What if what? What if someone had noticed something in our family that could have changed things? Lenora, there wasn't anything to notice."

"Our mother—"

"There weren't signs."

She shakes her head, her brows furrowing. "No, she was acting different. She was horrible to us."

"She wasn't, Lenora." My voice softens. "You're remembering it incorrectly."

"No, I can't be. I know what I remember. I know what's real."

Reality is a fickle thing. My reality is of a mother who wasn't unkind. She yelled sometimes and could be slightly aloof, but she wasn't a bad mom.

Not until that night.

And does one choice cancel out all others? Did opening that door at the end of the hall fully erase every good thing, soft touch, sweet smile, whispered song?

Should it?

Lenora is trembling.

"You're doing it again, aren't you?" I take a step closer and can feel her body heat.

"This isn't the same thing." She looks away too quickly, and all my fears are confirmed.

"The last time you did this, you remember how it turned out? We had to move, Lenora. You accused our neighbor of cheating on his wife. You were obsessed with him. You thought you knew stuff, but you didn't. You were wrong."

"That isn't—it isn't like that."

But the memories come back, fighting against all the others. Waking in the night to find her out of bed, the front door open.

Her pacing by the window, refusing to leave the house, watching our neighbors. Her hair greasy, her teeth unbrushed.

She lost herself. She let go of all the good inside and became this obsessive, angry person. Then she ruined everything for the second time. And it's me. It's always me who must gather her broken pieces and put them back together. But each time I do, she looks slightly different. Like I put something in the wrong place, and it doesn't quite fit.

I dragged us out here to this cabin. I thought it would be good for her. I thought if it was just me and Lenora, then everything would be OK. She would be OK. But I made a mistake.

"You start hyper focusing and fixating," I say. "You did it to them. To Toby and his wife. You almost ruined their marriage. You almost got arrested. You do it with Mom. Now you're doing it to Tilly."

I remember the night Lenora rushed into our neighbor's home. Confronted them. Luckily, I was home. I got her back inside our house. But I couldn't talk Toby out of calling the police. "I thought moving out here, away from people, away from neighbors, I thought it would be good for you. I thought you needed this to heal."

"It is." Her voice is shaky, desperate. "I'm happy here. Therapy is helping me. This isn't the same as last time. I know that was wrong. I know a lot of that was me. In my head or whatever. I get it. But this is different. I know what I saw. Karen *hit* you, Cassie. For what? For saying something rude? She's shown her character to all of us, not just to me. This isn't me inferring or guessing—it's about what we saw with our own eyes."

"What's your plan?" I ask her quietly, barely finding the energy to form the words. I'm tired. Down to my bones. It makes me heavy, jittery. I can't do this again. I can't keep doing this. "Where do you go from here?"

"I just want to make sure. Make sure I don't miss anything. She's staying here. I need to make sure she isn't dangerous."

"And what? If you find something, you're going to tell the police?"

She steps back, tears forming in her eyes. "You think this is all in my head."

The vexation is instant. It's overwhelming all other feelings. Overriding them until I throw my hands in the air in exasperation. "We've been here before. I was with you when everything blew up in our last neighborhood. Everyone thought you were unhinged, Lenora, except me. Never me. What did I do? I scooped you up. I took you here. A weekend away. And I saw how good it was for you, for us. So I talked to Wayne. I begged him to let us stay here. And it felt right, didn't it? It felt better."

"It is better."

"But you're doing it again." Maybe I was wrong. Maybe Lenora hasn't changed over the years. She's not two different people—one good and one not. She's one person. And every time I put her back together, it's not that the pieces aren't fitting; it's more that I don't like the picture she makes.

"I'm not."

I shake my head. "I know you were out there that night, Lenora."

"I was. I went to the bathroom. I told you that."

"No." I shake my head, my lips pulling together in disappointment. Without a word I go straight to my room, open my bottom drawer, and dig out the coin. Lenora is in the same spot when I make it back to the kitchen and toss it at her.

When she catches it, her mouth falls open. "How did you get that?"

"I found it. On the Blacktop. The morning after Tilly first went missing."

"No." Lenora shakes her head. "That's not possible."

"Just admit it!" I dig my hands into my hair and pull at the roots. I can't even feel it. "Admit you were out there that night. Admit you were on the Blacktop."

"I don't know." Her voice is strangled. "OK, I don't know. I was asleep. I don't remember any of it."

There is silence. The heavy kind. The kind you can reach out and touch. Neither one of us seems capable of breaking it. I release my hair. Take a step back. Then another.

Finally, Lenora looks away and takes in a ragged breath. "What does that mean for me, Cassie? That I don't remember it."

I want to speak. Want to do what is natural to me. Comfort my sister. Love her. Whisk her away to safety. Even if that means saving her from herself. But the words elude me, and I'm so damned tired. "You were sleepwalking."

"Yes. I woke up covered in dirt. I know I was out there, in those woods. But I have no memory of it. No idea what I could have—" She cuts herself off. Her teeth snap together at the same time. Like she can't bear to say it.

That's OK because I can't bear to hear it.

There are things I should say. Ways I could try to mend her. Reassure her. But the words won't come. "I'm so tired, Lenora."

She looks away toward the window. Her eyes dimming, her face shuttering. "You said it yourself, there were no signs. Mom didn't do anything before that night."

"No." I lift a finger to her, taking a step closer. "I won't allow you to go down that road. Just let me think. Give me time to think about this. We'll figure it out. OK?"

"Coming here to this campground. Hiding away like this. It never made any sense. How can we run from something inherent to us? It doesn't matter where we go or how long we hide, our DNA won't change."

I can't take it. Can't take the images. Lenora standing over Tilly. Lenora running back to the cabin covered in blood.

No, no, no.

"Why does this sound like a confession?"

"I can't confess to something I don't remember. But I know, Cass, I know there's *something* to remember."

I grab her shoulders. Shake her. Once. Twice. "No. You're not her, Lenora. What happened that night wasn't your fault. You're not responsible. Same with Tilly. You happened to be in those woods that night, but that's it. You were asleep. There's no reason you would have hurt Tilly. No reason you would have wanted to. Now stop saying it."

Tears seep from Lenora's eyes, but she doesn't speak.

"Listen to me," I tell her. Then I force myself to take a breath. "You're too close to this. On Tilly's social media, watching her parents—you have to stop it. You have to let the police do their job, and you have to focus on yourself. Keeping yourself healthy. You can't spiral again. Not like this. Not now."

"I know."

"Promise me. Promise me you'll let all this go." I stress the words to her. Urge her to understand that I'm not capable of fixing this situation yet. I need more time. Need her to keep it together just a little longer.

"I promise, Cassie."

And I don't release her. Instead, I pull her into my chest, hold her tight, close my eyes, and breathe her in. My sister.

Memories flutter through my brain. A lifetime of them, all with her. Every moment. The good, the scary, and the blisteringly painful. Most of our lives, I've lived with one universal truth: I know my sister as well as I know myself.

I know her goodness.

And now, in this moment, my shoulder wet with her tears, I repeat that over and over.

I know Lenora.

She wouldn't hurt anyone.

But the words are hollow even in my head, where the sound of that boy's head slamming against the lunch table still reverberates. I guess Lenora isn't the only one who lies.

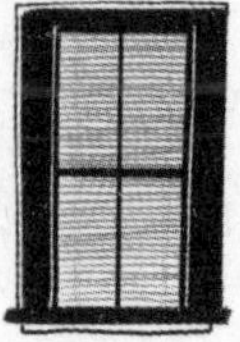

CHAPTER FIFTEEN
THEN

When my eyes open in the morning, you're asleep next to me. I don't want to get out of bed at first. I don't want to leave you. Not when you feel so safe here, so at peace.

I should feel better. Dad is back. You're making friends. Things are changing. Maybe everything before now has only been a fluke. This new version of reality tempts me to latch on. A reality where Dad is healthy. Mom isn't so bitter. You're happy.

But last summer tugs at me like a little kid on their mother's sleeve, annoying and incessant even as I swat it away.

A pan clatters downstairs. Someone is up. After an evening shift, Mom usually sleeps until midday. Same as you. That leaves one person.

It takes the maximum amount of effort to crawl from bed. But I do. I get ready, careful not to wake you. When I make it to the doorway of the kitchen, I pause. Mom hung a crucifix above the door several months ago. A ten-inch black cross with a skinny and bleeding Jesus hanging from it. So realistic, I expect stray drops of blood to roll down and plop on my forehead. She said she bought it to remind us of our forgiveness. That every good Christian family should keep Christ in the center of the home. But I know she hung it as a warning.

Here's what happens to sinners in this house.

And it seems especially ironic that taking a step through this doorway in this moment feels a lot like entering hell.

I'm right. Dad is in the kitchen when I come down. I blink against the image of him now and try to make sense of it. He's standing at the counter, flipping pancakes like he's died and woken up as Martha Stewart. It's fitting that she got out of prison last year.

Everyone has secrets and flaws.

But not everyone gets caught.

He's changed. That's what you said last night, isn't it? And there must be some truth to it because I haven't seen this: him up before noon, *cooking* of all things. Haven't seen it since we were kids.

The floor creaks beneath my sticky, slip-resistant shoes, and he glances at me over his shoulder. "Morning, doll."

"Don't call me that."

He only smiles and turns back to his task. "You'll always be my baby doll."

I roll my eyes and ignore him, grabbing a can of Coke from the fridge and a granola bar from the cabinet.

"I'm making breakfast," he tells me pointedly, and it's like I'm the one who died this time, except I've woken up in a sitcom. He seems so normal. So sober.

"In a hurry."

I'm almost away, almost fully out the door, but he stops me.

"Wait a second."

"I've got to get to the diner. My shift starts at eight."

"I know what you're thinking," he says quietly, almost shamefully, and it takes a second for his words to sink in. It's way too early for this. "I know you've heard this before from me. But it's different this time. I'm different. I've talked to your sister about it, and I wanted you to hear it from me. I want you to know that I'm going to be a whole new dad this time."

There's a rush of emotion applying pressure behind my eyes, and I bite my lip until I can force it back. Slowly, the yearning and sadness change to something else. Something angry and dark. I want to throw something. To bash my head against the wall. Bash his head against the wall. Because after he left last summer, that's when it all fell apart. That's when you did what you did.

"I love you girls. And I've worked it out with your mom. She's agreed to give it a go again. So I need you to know that. I'm here to stay."

"Sure, Dad," I say sarcastically before I can stop myself. It's weird. How much I dream of him saying these words and meaning them. But every time he does, I can't let go of my rage. I see the hurt on his face, and it's a spike through my gut. Yet I can't react differently. I can't pretend or perform. "How long will it last this time? One month? Two?"

"Look, you have every right to be angry—"

"No." I shake my head slowly. "I have every right to be furious. You ruined them after you left last summer, and I was the one who had to fix everything." The sight of you sobbing yourself to sleep.

The way Mom looked at us both like we're the reason he left. Like we're the reason her perfect life fell apart. All of it. The pain. The suffering. The mistakes. It leads back to him. I let out a deep, gusty breath. "It doesn't matter. Forget I said anything."

He flicks my ponytail. "Surely, you can't be mad at me forever."

Tears sting my eyes, but I fight them away, refusing to let him see. Refusing to let him know he's made me feel anything at all. I want to scream at him. To beg him to tell me who he is and what he has done with my father.

"I really am in a hurry."

"I mean it. You can't be mad at me forever. You'll see."

I don't acknowledge him, don't respond, and I can only hope that works as answer enough.

I used to be mad that I was forced to get a summer job and you weren't. It's not that Mom didn't ask you to work too; it's that you simply didn't. I went out and applied. You chose not to.

It's like when we were kids, and you would throw tantrums over the slightest thing. Cry and scream and kick your feet for hours. Mom would attempt to punish you. Time-out. Spankings. But nothing would work. You didn't seem to care about any of it.

Of course, I brought up the unfairness of the job situation. Mom only got annoyed. Said as long as you were contributing to the household, she didn't care how you did it. But she said that to save face. We both know the truth. She can't actually make you do anything, and she's too embarrassed to try.

Every time you obey her, it's because you have your reasons for doing it. Never just because our mother told you to.

Today, though, I'm just thankful for a reason to get out of that house. I like my job anyway. I like talking to people and interacting with them. Even as I spill an entire breakfast tray on my uniform and mess up several orders with my distractions, I'm grateful to be anywhere if it means I'm not home.

It's nearing the end of my shift, and the lunch rush is slowing down. This is the part where I typically start my side work. But the bell over the door dings, and I turn to the door, menus in hand, stopping and smiling when I see it's you with your bag thrown over your shoulder and camera hanging from a strap around your neck. You came to visit me. You must have wanted to get out of our house too.

The smile falls away.

You're not alone.

The elation sours quickly. It's her again. The girl with the feathers. She's even prettier today than she was yesterday. Her skin glows without a drop of makeup. Her eyes sparkle with a giddiness that can't be faked. I don't want to approach. Don't want to speak to you at all. I don't want to do anything but stare. You're with her again, and it shouldn't bother me. Not after our conversation last night. You were honest. You told me what she means to you as a friend.

You assured me I have nothing to fear.

But here she is, right in front of me, and all those words go out the window. The feathers in her hair seem more colorful today. So does she. Like a rainbow sprouting out of asphalt. And the way you look at her, it's like you see it too.

I walk toward the table carefully. I'm fragile. I feel so fragile, and there's nothing I can do about it. "Hello," I say stiffly. "Drinks?"

You chuckle, and your friend looks between us, wary at first, until she must sense your ease and smiles.

"My sister," you tell her.

She looks between us again. "Yeah, I kind of noticed."

When you look at me, there is an emotion in your eyes I recognize. Annoyance. Like you're mad at me for not playing along.

"Drinks?" I ask again, all too aware of the coffee stain on my apron and the ketchup on my shoes. I don't want to be here. Don't want to bring this girl anything. It's bad enough when anyone from school comes in, and I have to serve them like I don't sit behind them in French watching dandruff flake onto their shoulders. That's its own hell, but *her.*

"This is Monica," you say, your eyes narrowing. "Figured we'd stop in and say hi. Told her this place has the best sweet tea. She's never been here before." You're doing it again. Trying to hurt me. I'm aware of it, and it makes my job easier.

I maintain my smile. "Hi, Monica."

"It's nice to meet you," Monica says excitedly. Totally overcompensating. Pretending I don't smell like a deep fryer so I won't do something to her food most likely. When you leave she'll probably giggle about how cute it is that I work here, when we both know she doesn't mean it. "I've heard so much about you."

And I want to strangle her.

Pick her up off the ground by the neck.

Slam her into table four's all-day breakfast special.

The thought catches me off guard. Disturbs me even. But it's true. I want to take a saltshaker and pound it into her head until you can't tell the difference between those red feathers and her hair.

But it's not her fault. None of this is. I just need to let her know it's better if she leaves. Better if she forgets she ever met you. Better for all of us. Especially her.

"That's cool. So, two sweet teas?"

"To go, please."

I spin around toward the counter. It's been a busy day, but the brunch café is mostly deserted. The other two servers working have three tables between them and are sitting at the bar rolling silverware.

I'm pouring the drinks when one calls out to me. "That must be your sister."

I look up at her, not quite reacting. "Wonder what gave it away."

Then I'm turning my back, on them, on the whispers coming from your table. It's a twist. One quick movement before I slide out from behind the bar. But it's long enough for me to spit in Monica's drink and swirl it around with the straw.

You go quiet when I drop the drinks off, sliding Monica's toward her first. You watch the motion, your eyes narrowed into slits. Before I can do or say anything else, you've swapped yours and Monica's and taken a huge sip.

There's a smug smile on your face when you stand, the Styrofoam cup in your hand. "Thank you," you say. "Here." You drop a five on the table. "We've got places to be."

This time, I can't help but say anything. I can't fight the anxiety coursing through me. Swapping the cups was one thing. But that comment, that was your checkmate, and you know it. "What time will you be home?"

"Curfew." You laugh again like you can't imagine why I'm asking.

"It's just, with Dad being back—"

"I told you I'd be home by curfew."

An awkward silence ensues. A standoff where I hold your eyes and you hold mine. Neither one of us is willing to give in.

Monica holds her cup with both hands and stands, clearly confused. You take her arm and start leading her to the door. "It was nice to meet you," she calls over her shoulder, and my heart is in my throat. The stench of Monica's flowery perfume lingers even after the glass door swings shut behind you.

I walk home that afternoon alone.

I should be thinking of how much my shoes pinch my feet or the fact I hardly made any money today. But I can't stop thinking of Monica and you. I can't stop wondering what you're doing with her. Why you'd leave me home alone knowing Dad is back.

It's all so familiar, and I can feel us teetering to the edge of a waterfall as I claw and fight against the current back to shore. But I won't make it alone. Not unless you're swimming with me.

That night you don't make curfew.

Mom is working, and Dad is out with some buddies. When Mom calls from her shift to check in, it surprises me. She doesn't usually check on us. I tell her Dad is out with friends and you're asleep. She tells me to take out the trash. I listen and agree.

When midnight rolls around, I finally hear you. Scraping at the base of the window I left open. Sliding in feetfirst and smelling like alcohol and something else. Something flowery. I smelled it earlier when Monica stood.

You don't notice me right away as you fall onto your bed. A moment passes before you glance in my direction, and a husky laugh slips out. "You look like a creeper right now," you say, placing your camera on the nightstand. The urge hits me to grab it. To see what photos you've taken tonight. Which moments were so potent, you wanted to remember them forever.

"You're late."

Another laugh, and I hate it. I hate when you laugh at me. Laugh when I'm worried like this. "You're acting like Mom."

"I covered for you, by the way. Told Mom you were home. You're lucky she's on the night shift for the rest of the week."

You roll in bed to face me, and I notice the mascara stains under your eyes. Your lipstick is smudged. "Are you mad at me?"

I hold your gaze, wait for the anger to come, the anger I was nursing all day, but it doesn't. It just dissipates. "I was."

"I told you, you don't have to worry."

I look away from you. Stare at your bookcase across the room. They say you can tell a lot about a person by what they read. I've never known anyone with a more imbalanced taste in books. There's something from every genre on that shelf, and I have a theory that you read so widely because you don't really know who you are, or else you're too afraid to find out. "You brought her in today on purpose. You know I don't like her."

"I just wanted you to meet her." You sit up. "If you gave her a chance, you'd like her as much as I do."

"I'm scared."

"Don't be." Your voice is soft and comforting. You cross the room to me, sit down, and stroke my hair. "I told you this is different. It's not like last summer. She's safe."

"I'm not worried about her." That's a lie. My worry is exactly why I hate her.

"I'm safe too."

I turn my head, catching your eyes. "I can't keep covering for you." The words slip out before I can filter them. "Mom thinks you were here sleeping. I had to lie to her. I can't keep doing this all on my own. What's going to happen when he leaves again? What's going to happen when it all falls apart?"

"You really think that, don't you?" you murmur so softly. *Here it is*, I think. *The gentle part of you. My favorite part.* Every time you're callous, I remind myself of your inner layers. That I just need something sharp to scrape the dead skin away until I get to the real you, baby smooth underneath. "You think it's all going to implode again."

"How can it not? What will Mom do when Dad leaves? You know how she gets. You know how she's been lately."

You stand and pace to my desk, running a finger over the surface. "I'm not afraid of her."

"That's because she lets you do whatever you want."

There's a beat of silence, and I think I may have pissed you off. But your expression is contemplative. Not angry.

"What are you thinking?"

"What if we just did it?" you say, your back to me.

"Did what?"

"Killed them."

I shake my head, my brain rattling around, trying to decipher the meaning of your words. "Kill them? What are you saying?"

You turn around with clenched teeth, and you're somewhere else, I can tell. Thinking of something else. "You're right. That's crazy." You go to your side of the room, your bed. Flop heavily on the edge. "I can't believe I even said that. Wow, I must be really tired."

But I've been tired, and I've never thought about murdering our parents. I guess my expression says it all.

You start laughing loudly to yourself, muffling the sound with your inner arm. "Look at your face. Your eyes are bugging out of your head. I didn't mean it. Chillax. It was a joke."

Faintly, there's the sound of a car door slamming. Footsteps. The front door opening and closing. Your laughter levels off, and we both listen to the sound of Dad walking up the stairs to his room.

"Are you still overreacting over there?"

The blood rushes back to my limbs. "You really didn't mean it?"

"I mean, who in the hell do you think I am?" You laugh again. "I've never hurt anyone." But the words aren't true. Not even a little bit. Like you're thinking it too, you add, "Not like that. Not on purpose."

I slide under the covers and pull them to my chin. There's this feeling of a ticking clock hanging over my head. I don't know what will happen when the alarm sounds.

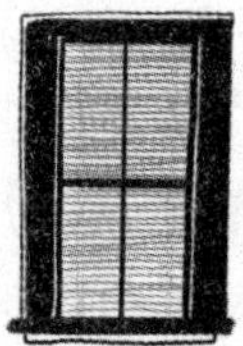

CHAPTER SIXTEEN
CASSIE

I call him because it feels like something is thrashing beneath my skin, and I don't know how to let it out. I don't know how I'm supposed to keep holding everything together. Not when it feels like everything is falling apart.

He answers on the fifth ring. "I told you I can't do this anymore."

"I need you."

"Not like this, Cass."

"Please."

There's silence on the other end before Parker sighs.

Parker comes, and I take, and I ask myself if this is all that's needed to make a monster. A person ignorant, oblivious, concerned with only their self-gratification.

I think of my earlier conversation with Lenora.

My thoughts about her.

What she's capable of.

But what if I turn that lens on myself? Examine myself like I do her. What will I find? Who is the real monster out of us two?

When it's over, when Parker is on his side next to me and snoring, I stare up at the ceiling, trying to identify who I really am and if any of it really matters. The feeling that comes over me is instant.

I'm dirty. Unclean. Like kudzu is growing over me, spreading its earthy tentacles into every crevice of me until I'm nothing but the ground it springs from. I don't know what time it is, only know it's late. But I can't slip in the Harvard T-shirt. Can't crawl back into my bed beside this snoring man and pretend any of this is OK.

Can't sleep when I'm this dirty.

I grab my shower bag and head toward the door, careful to close it behind me.

The cold air stings my face, and there's a crisp slick of ice over the grassy hill. It makes me regret wearing my shower shoes even if they provide a little protection from the elements.

I steal a glance at Cabin Three. The lights are off. I think at first Karen must be sleeping. But then I see the tracks of mud leading into the bathhouse. Both stalls are firmly closed; however, one is occupied. A pair of red sneakers is the only visible part of whoever is in there. Karen. I saw her wearing the shoes before.

I don't know the exact time, but it has to be late. Way too late for bathroom breaks. She probably didn't expect anyone to come in here, and a part of me considers leaving. Going back to my cabin, lying down in my bed beside Parker and being normal for once.

"I'm sorry," I croak. The last thing I should be doing is speaking to her. The words simply fall out. "About your daughter. About what I said." Her feet don't move, and she doesn't say a word.

The showers are next to each other at the end of the room, and I force myself to walk to them. Karen needs space. She doesn't trust me or Lenora.

I don't blame her.

I understand what Sarah said. *It's always the parents.* It's an easy thing to assume. But without any other evidence, she's just a grieving mother, and it makes my heart sink to think differently. To presume she's guilty when I don't have all the facts. Not that I want them.

I just want this to be over.

For Lenora to be herself again.

Whoever that is.

The shower is a slab of tile about four feet across with a flimsy cloth curtain that can never touch both sides of the wall at the same time. Which means I can always see out just a sliver.

I flip the shower on as hot as it will go and strip, ignoring the goose bumps breaking out across my flesh. I jump into the water quickly and shake until the chill is chased away and I'm breathing in steam. This heat is almost enough to thaw the deepest and coldest parts of me. The place where my fear grows and freezes, there to stay forever, and if I let it, a place where Lenora and I will stay forever too. Buried and sinking.

I don't see Karen, but I hear the toilet flush. Her stall door slamming shut. The sink turning on.

I close my eyes and let myself go into that frigid dark place. Tilly is there, breathing heavily, her eyes scanning the darkness of the woods. Rain pelting her tiny body. Fear. Cold. So much cold. And hunger. Sadness. She sinks to the ground inside the crevice of a tree and closes her eyes, shaking relentlessly. Maybe she's thinking of her mother and father. A good memory between them, a time she felt truly loved. Maybe that would be enough to keep her warm just a little while longer.

Then another image assaults me. Lenora leaving the cabin, creeping down the hill, running into the woods, branches snapping against her arms and face, her bare feet slapping the cold hard ground.

Did she go into the woods and come straight back? Had something or someone startled her awake and she just reacted?

Maybe there was a terrible accident, and she's afraid to tell me.

There it is. A beam of light. A rational explanation. Maybe something awful happened that night, but it wasn't on purpose. Lenora was sleepwalking. She could have done something and woken up frightened and confused.

That could mean she wasn't lying when she said she doesn't know what happened. She doesn't know. She only knows it involves her somehow.

But then something darker occurs to me.

Suddenly, the movie reel plays again. Lenora's eyes opening. Tilly nudging her. *Hey, you OK?*

Lenora's hands shooting out, reaching for her neck, squeezing, squeezing, squeezing—

I press my eyes closed with my fingers, pinching the delicate skin there until it hurts. *Stop it. Think anything except this. It's not real. It's not real. It's not real.*

I double over until my head clears, until I find the energy to stand up straight. But the water is too hot, and my head is too cloudy.

I let out a labored breath and open my eyes.

The darkness doesn't leave.

I blink a few times, and it still takes a second to register.

The lights are off.

"Hello?" I say, popping my head out of the curtain. The sink is no longer running either. "I'm in here. Karen?" When there's no answer, I groan. "You've got to be kidding me."

I yank my towel off the hook, and careful not to slip, I half jog, half walk to the door. My hairs stand on end as the cold surrounds me. Luckily, I'm familiar enough with the room to know exactly where the light switch is, and it only takes a few seconds to slap it on.

I pause in front of the stalls. Both are empty.

Karen must have hit the lights on the way out without thinking.

Or maybe she *was* thinking when she did it.

Again, can't really blame her.

I jog back to my steamy shower, my whole body shaking as I dive under the hot water. A nasty feeling develops in my stomach as I bathe quickly before the hot water is gone. I'm working the soap out of my hair when the lights flicker off once again.

This time I freeze, my hands on my head and suds seeping down my back, not moving or breathing. I rinse the soap off my hands and pull the curtain back. "Hello?"

There's no sound. No movement.

No Karen.

Not quite as quickly as last time, I grab my damp towel and cross the wet and muddy floor, grateful I wore flip-flops, or else I'd be slipping all over the place. When the lights are on again, I crack the door and look out both ways. The cold is almost painful.

But there's nobody lingering. No light on in Cabin Three. No Karen or Sarah or Parker. I glance into both stalls once more and pull the curtain from the other shower back. But there's no one there. I'm alone.

I feel weird, untethered. It's the feeling of taking a sleeping pill and then staying awake for too long afterward. I finish rinsing beneath water that's getting less hot with each passing second and decide to skip conditioner and body wash. I'm just pulling on my robe when the lights turn off again.

My breath releases like a balloon slowly leaking air.

I don't move or blink.

Maybe the light bulb is faulty. That has to be it.

I pull the shower curtain back and step out. My eyes widen and adjust to the darkness before I attempt to walk across the slick floor in the pitch black. That's when something creaks about five feet in front of me.

"Is someone—"

But the words die on my tongue.

At the end of the room, between the light switch and the door, is the outline of a person.

"Karen?" I hate the way my voice shakes. The way the goose bumps spread over my entire body. "This isn't funny."

No movement.

"I apologized for what I said, and I meant it. I'm so sorry about your daughter." I start to twitch, fear crawling up my spine. "Just turn the light on, and we can talk."

But she doesn't.

Somehow the darkness gets thicker. I can taste it on my tongue as the seconds tick.

"Karen, please."

She inches back toward the door, slipping out before it's fully opened. Without thinking, I cross the room after her, lunging outside, spinning in every direction, searching wildly. My flip-flop gets caught on something and rips off my foot. I don't try to find it or mend it even as my foot sinks into the mushy grass.

I head toward Cabin Three. Wet and with one bare foot seeping into the ice-cold muddy ground. I'm shivering harder than I ever have before. Forcefully. Sickly.

The lights are out in the cabin, and even as I knock relentlessly, no one comes to the door.

A weird, unsettling weight crashes into me. I walk toward the window and cup my eyes, trying to peek through the sliver of closed curtain, but I can't see anything.

I turn back around and stumble over something on the porch, barely catching myself on the railing before I trip.

A pair of dirty red sneakers lie on their sides.

Parker is in the kitchen when I open the back door. He has bedhead, and his keys dangle from his hands. "Hey, where'd you go?"

I hold a finger to my lips and glance toward the hallway. "You shouldn't be in here. I thought you were sleeping."

"I was looking for you."

"You might wake Lenora."

"Are you serious?" He looks me up and down in confusion. "Why are you wearing that?" He motions to the robe I'm clasping together with one white-knuckle fist.

My mouth feels oddly dry as I swallow. "Were you just in the bathhouse?"

"What? No. Why?"

Maybe I should question him. Maybe someone else might. But there was something about the person in the bathhouse that was feminine. Their skinny limbs. The way, even though I couldn't see their eyes, they seemed to watch me in the dark. Something else too. A sense of familiarity between us. Like the shadow I saw on the Blacktop. What if that wasn't my imagination?

What if it was something worse?

"No reason. Look, it's been a long day, Parker. You should go. Before Lenora wakes."

He nods, not quite meeting my eyes. "Right, OK."

"Thank you for coming—"

"You're thanking me? Seriously?"

"Parker—"

"Good night, Cassie."

He goes, and I don't regret it, but I still feel like a monster. No amount of water or soap can wash that feeling away.

I lie in bed that night and think of Tilly. Except it isn't Tilly alone in the woods, curled in a ball and forced to brave the elements. There's someone with her. A tall, thin shadow of a woman with too-long arms and a grotesque smile. And for reasons not belonging to the wind, rain, or cold, Tilly is terrified.

And I am too.

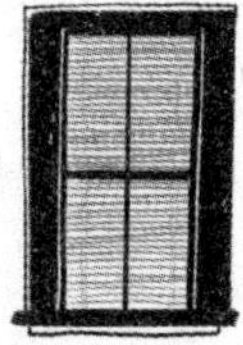

CHAPTER SEVENTEEN
LENORA

I click my fingernails in and out, in and out. Daphne is talking, but I can't pay attention. All I can think of is the coin Cassie grabbed from her room. My coin that's been missing for days. The fear on Cassie's face as she confronted me. As she brought up one of my lowest moments. As she made me promise to let this go.

To let Tilly go.

My brain is fuzzy and itchy. I want to stick my fingers in my ears and touch it, wiggle it around. Maybe after it's adjusted, it will be normal.

"Lenora." Daphne lowers her pen. "I've lost you again. I've been doing that a lot lately."

"I'm just stressed."

"They still haven't solved it, have they? The girl who died near you. They don't know what happened."

The itch gets stronger. It tells me to go to the window. To rip all the skeletons from the closets and splay them like it's a macabre museum. Is Karen out there today? Is she watching me? Waiting to see what I'll do next? I can't resist leaning forward, glancing toward Cabin Three. Their curtains are closed. I sigh and lean back in my seat at the kitchen table.

"No," I say.

"Does that make you nervous? That it's unresolved."

"I don't know." Movement from the corner of my eye. I turn my head, just enough to glance sideways. The curtains have parted.

My breath catches.

In Cabin Three, someone is standing with their back to the window, completely still. I can only look at first. Stare at the person. Blond hair. Long and straight. Their body oddly hunched.

Tilly.

I jerk to my feet, the chair toppling backward.

From somewhere in the room, a voice calls to me, but I can't listen or focus on anything but Tilly. Slowly, ever so slowly, she begins to turn at the neck. Her hair smothers her mouth and face, sticking to her skin in weblike strings as she twists at an unnatural angle. Turning, turning—

I close my eyes and try to go somewhere else. But where can you go when the worst parts live inside your head?

Thin, brittle branches pinching my skin like newborn fingernails.

The silhouette of a person under the moon.

Glacial fear sluicing through my veins.

Daphne's voice breaks through the static in my head. "Just breathe, Lenora. Breathe."

I try until I do. I breathe in and out, counting each breath. But the image doesn't leave my head. It only grows stronger, and my imagination fills in the blanks. Tilly's back to me. Head turned in my direction. Skin becoming more discolored until it slides off, falling to the ground in patches.

She's dead.

It's not possible.

"I can see you're afraid right now, Lenora."

I rub my temples. Dig my fingers into my head.

"I know you saw something. Can you open your eyes?"

Run, Lenora!

"Open your eyes."

The room comes into focus. Daphne's concerned face on the screen. I force myself to look. To seek out Cabin Three even as every cell in my body screams at me not to.

No one is there.

But the curtains are opened.

Someone must have opened them.

"Lenora, talk to me."

"I saw something in Karen's cabin. It looked like..." But I couldn't tell her who it looked like without her worrying about me even more. "Someone was standing there. They were just facing the other direction."

"You said it's Karen's cabin." Daphne is using her most soothing voice. "Did you see her?"

"No." The puttylike image morphs and shifts. "I mean, I don't know. I don't think it was her."

"Who else could it have been?"

"I don't know," I answer weakly.

"Can we discuss an alternative?"

"The alternative being that I didn't see anything at all?"

"Like maybe you thought you saw something. Light and shadows can be responsible for all kinds of tricks."

"No." I shake my head. There was someone standing there. They turned their head in my direction. Blond hair. Slender body. Tilly. "No. She was there. Someone was standing right there."

"Who, Lenora?"

"Karen. It had to have been Karen. She's messing with me. Trying to get back at me."

"Get back at you for what?"

When I don't say anything right away, Daphne continues.

"Let's look at this from another angle. There are other things in your life that are unresolved, aren't there? We don't know where your mother is. Does that make you nervous?"

This time I don't control my reaction. My hands clench; my eyes squeeze shut. "I don't really think about it."

"I know you don't like to. But maybe that's why this case, this girl, is causing you so much distress? Maybe you see yourself in her. Have you found yourself seeking out similarities, Lenora? Have you found ways to connect yourself to her life?"

My teeth grind together. "It's not like that."

"That's what happened last time. With your neighbor and his wife. You thought her husband was cheating. You saw yourself in her. You saw what you thought was someone taking advantage of another person. You grew to hate him, didn't you? That hate festered in you. But it wasn't real, Lenora. It was fabricated."

Like all the other dark things in my mind, I don't usually think of what happened at our last home in Chattanooga. It was a fresh start. Cassie was just getting into YouTube, and I had so many freelance writing jobs, I could barely keep up. We did well.

We were happy. But then I started noticing things. Found myself staying up late to watch my neighbors from the window. Found my anxiety skyrocketing as I wondered what went on behind their closed doors. What secrets they held.

His name was Toby. His young wife reminded me of my sister. As perfect as they seemed, it couldn't be true. I knew from personal experience that when it came to secrets, we all had them.

"Lenora, you hated him because of a narrative in your mind, do you remember? You had narratives about all your neighbors. None of the things you thought you knew were true. Especially with him."

The night it all came to a head was explosive. Embarrassing. Cruel. I tried to get her, my friend and neighbor, to leave him and run away. To see the signs I knew were there. I thought I could trust her, and she would trust me. But that night, when I saw her stepping out of her car, I ran over, and she acted confused. I didn't have much time and had to explain everything before he got home.

I told her about what I'd seen. The way he'd linger in his car, always on the phone. The one time I'd caught him tucking his shirt into his pants. Checking his neck in the rearview mirror. These were all classic signs of infidelity. I still remember the look on her face. The silence after I stopped talking and she wrenched her arm from my hands like I was the enemy. Like I had done something wrong.

Then his car pulled in behind us.

"Lenora, talk to me." Daphne's voice is calm and coaxing. "Do you think your need to identify with victims is because you feel like you are one?"

“I am a victim. That’s true.” I know it, and yet I’m squirming. Resisting the label like I don’t deserve it. If you hurt someone really badly, can you be a victim too?

“Yes, but you’re also a survivor. Your trust was broken by your own mother, a woman whose sole job was to protect you from this world. But she didn’t, did she? Now you find yourself wondering what other people are hiding, what other people are capable of because of that hurt. Isn’t that right, Lenora?”

“Yes.”

“But that’s one person. Not everyone is like her.”

“Yes,” I say. “You’re right.” And I can’t help it. I look again at the window. Daphne is saying something, her voice a soothing murmur that fades into a gentle hum.

The curtains in Cabin Three are closed.

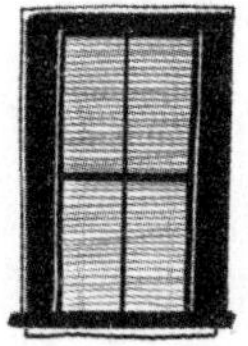

CHAPTER EIGHTEEN
CASSIE

I am outside again. Feet slapping over frozen ground. Inhaling winter air as bitter as liquid nitrogen. It's a little after nine, and Lenora has been in her room for hours. I can't help but think I missed something. After Lenora's session with Daphne, she acted strange and retreated to her room like something was bothering her.

I wanted to ask, felt an irrepressible need to know.

But something stopped me.

What if I didn't really want to know? What if allowing her to tell me would just exacerbate all that she was feeling? In that same vein, what if I didn't have the strength to pretend any longer?

The pain forms in my gut and builds outward until my whole body is throbbing. It takes physical effort to know my sister is hurting and not jump at the slightest chance to help her. Because what does helping her mean? Probably that I shouldn't enable her any longer.

And it goes against my very nature.

There's a light on in Cabin Three. A flutter of movement shadowed behind the curtain. I haven't seen Karen properly since our encounter in the bathhouse. Can't say I want to. I don't know what that was about or why she'd do it.

If she did it.

But who else?

Another truth I'm not ready or willing to face. What if there was another person out that night? And what if I loved them? What would that mean for me if Karen was just a grieving mother and the real monster resided even closer?

I move into a jog, ignoring the pain in my feet. More uncomfortable than usual. Fitting that it matches the pain everywhere else. I should head to the Blacktop. Try to use my privacy and this time to clear my head. But it's like my legs have a mind of their own, and I'm moving in the opposite direction. Weaving through the woods to a familiar front porch.

Sarah sees me the moment I break through the trees. "Cassie? Is everything all right?" She's on a wooden rocker. The same heater with an extension cord is at her feet. There's a steaming mug in her hands, a blanket over her lap, and a look of concern on her face. All these are things I'm immediately drawn to.

"I just needed some air."

She nods to the front step and nudges the heater so it will be aimed in my direction, and I sit. Neither of us jumps into conversation right away. It's another thing I like about Sarah. A commonality I've found pleasantly surprising in her.

"I love my sister." The words escape as a thief would. Under the cover of darkness and at risk of completely upending their life. I wrap my arms around myself but not from the cold.

"I know."

"We've always only had each other. When things were scary or hard or complicated, there was always just me and her." I hesitate. "But I don't know what's happening now. It feels like things are changing."

"Change isn't always bad."

"But this change is."

Her chair stops its rhythmic squeaking, and she slides down to sit beside me. Drapes the blanket over my lap as well. I'm not cold, and the fabric is scratchy even through my leggings, but there's comfort in the act itself. "Why do you think that?" she asks.

"Because we've always done things a certain way. If I mess things up, if I change it, it isn't fair to her."

"At what cost will you stay the same, Cassie?" I shift to look at her and find her staring at me. "If change is what you need, then it's only natural to give in to it. We all change and grow. You can't resist it just because there's comfort in the known."

"You don't get it."

"So help me understand."

The massive trees no longer seem like a cage blocking me in but a barrier between Lenora and me. A canyon of separation that makes the air squeeze into my lungs just a little easier. "Do you have a sister?" When she doesn't answer right away, I look at her. Devastation is the only word that seems adequate to describe her expression. "I'm sorry. You don't have to answer."

"I do. Did. I mean, I have a sister, but she passed away. When I was young. Cancer. It all happened so quickly." She lifts the sleeve of her shirt to show me the black ink on her wrist. Two hearts interwoven together. She traces the image with her right index finger.

"I'm so sorry."

She shakes her head, her eyes full of unshed tears and vulnerability. Gives the tattoo one more long look before pulling her sleeve down. "No, don't be. I love to talk about her. Even if it still hurts. Pain's good, right? Reminds you that you loved someone well enough."

"I must sound so selfish to you right now." Looking at Sarah, I feel that way. Regardless of anything Lenora has done or will ever do, if anything happened to her—

I can't bear to finish the thought. But it just leaves me more confused. This. Being here with her all the time. A vortex of her and me. This may not be working, but being without her altogether would be worse, wouldn't it?

"Not selfish. If you broke your leg and I was terminally ill, I wouldn't say to you to just be glad you're still alive. I'd say I'm sorry for your pain." She bumps me with her shoulder. "I'm sorry you're struggling with Lenora. For what it's worth, I think your relationship is nice."

"Not codependent? Creepy? Weird?"

Sarah looks at me with humor in her eyes. "Can't it be all those things?"

For the first time all day, I laugh. And it feels good. Like rubbing aloe on a sunburn. I'm not healed, but at least in this moment, I'm not thinking of the ache.

"You know, you're a lot better of a neighbor than Wayne. I know we're supposed to speak kindly of the dead, but he was pretty much abominable."

Sarah snorts another laugh and doubles over. "I'll never get used to your honesty."

"It's true. He was one of those end-of-the-world planners. There was always a conspiracy. A government cover-up. It was exhausting."

Sarah's laughter fades away, and she rubs her temples. "Well, if I start losing my mind, you can't resent me for it." I give her a curious look, and she sighs. "It's just everything. I never signed up for this, you know? A girl was killed on the property. Her mother is refusing to leave."

"Karen is refusing to leave?"

"Says she won't go until she has answers. I've had to cancel another stay at the last minute and got a one-star review online for doing it."

I glance toward Karen's cabin. The light is off. "Why don't you ask Karen to leave?"

"I can't do that. She's grieving."

"Last I talked to you, you thought she was a murderer."

Sarah draws her bottom lip between her teeth. Suddenly the atmosphere between us shifts. "If not her, then who?" The aloe is gone. Instead, someone has poured boiling water over my skin, and I can feel it burning and bubbling. "Karen told me she doesn't even know how Tilly died. The police haven't given her a cause of death. They say it's guilt knowledge."

I make a sound low in my throat. I can't imagine your kid dying and then not even knowing how it happened. Not knowing who did it.

If not her, then who?

"It has to be Karen, right? There's no one else here but us."

She makes a face so quickly, I don't think she means for me to see it. But I do. And I understand it instantly. No one else here but me, Sarah...and Lenora.

"It could be someone else. A stranger."

"Could be."

"Or maybe someone we know," I continue. Sarah doesn't say anything. Just brings her mug to her lips without taking a sip. The light turns on in Karen's cabin, and I wonder what she's doing right this second.

I stand abruptly. "I should get back before Lenora wakes up and gets worried."

Sarah nods in understanding but calls out to me just as I make it to the bottom of the porch. "Cassie?" I stop. "I understand what it's like to love someone the way you love Lenora. Even if loving them hurts. If you ever want to talk again, I'm here."

Of course she does. Regardless of how I'm feeling, nothing could be more painful than loving the dead.

My throat is tight. I nod because I'm not capable of saying anything else. Then I walk back through the trees and up the hill. Back to my sister.

And for some reason I can't name, I feel guilty.

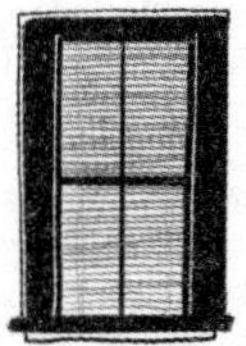

CHAPTER NINETEEN
LENORA

I wake up suddenly expecting sunshine and morning. Expecting to be covered in remnants of outside. But I'm clean, and it's still the middle of the night. Moonlight slashes across my bedroom, lighting even the darkest corners. My curtains are parted.

I don't remember leaving them that way.

I groan and stretch out across my bed. The last thing I remember is retreating to my room and spending the evening in here. Thinking about the person I saw in Cabin Three's window and about my conversation with Daphne. All evening it felt like I was desperately trying to hold myself together as something unraveled within me.

None of this is about my mother. I hardly think of the woman at all. I know what Cassie says. She likes to point out the good in her and thinks that night was some sort of isolated incident. A mental breakdown or whatever. But Cassie isn't remembering the buildup. The way Mom checked out and wanted nothing to do with us leading up to what she did. Whatever person raised us, she was long gone months before that night.

And I certainly don't care that I don't know where she is.

Or where she went at all.

I check my phone—barely one in the morning.

I sit up and reach for my glasses, figuring sleep might be a distant dream at this point. My hand slides along the side table. They're not there. I shine the light from my phone screen along the ground in case they had fallen.

Nothing.

This isn't right. Something about this isn't right. I inch the covers back and slide out of bed, heading toward my door.

The curtains.

My glasses.

Someone was in here. No, not someone. Cassie. It had to have been Cassie. But why would she take my glasses? I open the door and stop so suddenly, I have to touch the wall to steady myself. Then I blink to make sure what I'm looking at is real.

A glowing red light at the end of the hall.

I squint into the blurry darkness, hoping it's enough to salvage my eyesight. Cassie's camera is on the tripod, flashing the light that it's recording.

The dread is so visceral as it courses through me, it might as well be winter rain. I'm soaked and shaking.

There's a pull right at my navel. The gentle tug of curiosity that leads me forward. I remember reading once in some article about out-of-body experiences. Everyone who had one described it like you're watching your body from a distance. That's how it feels. Only I'm not just watching. My hands are tied behind my back, and I'm writhing against restraints, begging myself to stop.

Go back to bed.

Don't take one single step forward.

Sometimes it's better not to know.

I don't listen, and I reason with myself that maybe it was all an accident. Cassie might have gotten tired while she was recording and left it out. There has to be some digestible explanation.

Unless.

What if she wanted to catch me sleepwalking?

When I'm close enough to touch it, I turn it to me. Stop the recording. Go to the video. I'll see Cassie walking away. Worried Cassie, just trying to protect me. An accident or act of love. Then the video starts playing, and it's not reasonable. It doesn't make sense at all.

I drop it on the ground and scream.

The screaming must wake my sister because suddenly she's beside me, holding my face, coaxing me off some invisible ledge.

"Just breathe. Breathe, Lenora."

It goes like that.

Her whispered words in the dark and me slowly falling, falling, falling back into my skin. And I tell her the truth. The unavoidable truth.

"Someone was in the cabin."

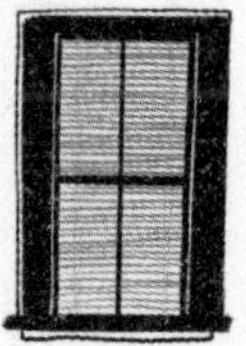

CHAPTER TWENTY
CASSIE

I sit across from my sister at the kitchen table. She's leaning forward, her hair curtaining her face, her fingers threading together. In and out like she's nervous and uncomfortable.

All this is a step up from her hysteria.

The memory of the past hour plays over and over in my head. The utter devastation on her face. The panic. Her fear was real. At least, real to her.

But is it *real?*

I hate these thoughts. They peck at my brain like pigeons, and they're conveying to me a truth I'm finding increasingly more difficult to deny.

Something is terribly wrong with my sister.

I think of the cocoon of warmth and understanding of Sarah's front porch. Hate myself for wanting it.

The camera sits directly in front of me. The screen black. My fingers trembled as I held the power button down to shut it off. As

I pushed it away from me because I couldn't look at it a moment longer.

"Lenora." I say her name softly. She doesn't look up, but her fingernails start moving together. Doing that weird clicking thing she always does. "We need to talk about that video."

"What's there to talk about? You don't believe me." Her words are marred with hurt.

I didn't say as much. Not yet. But hearing her say it burns. Not because the words are untrue but because they are. "It's not that I don't believe you."

"You saw it." Her face tilts up, her eyes swelling with tears. "You saw her. Walking down the hallway. Wearing my robe."

I hadn't expected anger. But it's here, pressing into my chest. The suddenness of it is painful, and I don't want to be angry at Lenora, but I watched the same video she did. I saw the dark and blurry figure turn quickly wearing Lenora's robe, walk down the hallway to Lenora's room, and shut the door behind her.

The video had been dark, but I could tell the person was a woman.

Wearing my sister's robe.

Wearing her glasses.

Other than that, I couldn't make out any other identifying features. It was too dark, quick, and unfocused.

What intruder does that? What intruder records themselves and then retreats to an occupied room? And how had none of that woken Lenora? It doesn't make any sense.

Or maybe it does.

The pressure intensifies. I clench my fist under the table and take a deep breath. "The doors were locked. No one has been in here. And they went in your room. How do you explain that? How do you explain not waking up?"

"I don't know—"

"Lenora." There's a quiver to my voice now. It's not anger anymore—it's disappointment. "Think about it. Just think about this for a second. What if it was you?"

"You think I'm lying?"

"No. Sleepwalking. You've done it many times."

"I've never done that. Set up a camera like that—I wouldn't."

"And who would?" The question is sharp on my tongue.

"It had to be Karen."

The light is off in Karen's cabin. I checked right after I got Lenora settled. Not that it means anything. Still, it doesn't feel right. Sarah's words from earlier are heavy. Karen's unwillingness to leave. Surely, if she hurt her daughter, she'd cut her losses and move on. What reason would she have to stay?

I shake my head and reach across the table for Lenora's hand, but she slides it back. "Why would Karen do this? How does that make any sense at all?" She doesn't answer, and I press her further. "Just think about this for a minute. I know Karen has acted strange. I know that more than anyone. But what could she have gained from this? Isn't it more logical that it was you on the recording sleepwalking again?"

"Karen was down there earlier at her window. I think she's messing with me. I think she knows we suspect her, and she's trying to make it seem like *I'm* crazy."

"Lenora—"

"Just listen to me for once!" A gasp of air, mine or hers, it doesn't matter. We both catch our breath as Lenora's jaw ticks with rage. "If I were anyone else, would you believe me?"

There's an inflection to her question. One I don't really want to dissect, but I can't help it. "You think I think badly of you?"

Her eyes connect with mine. "Don't you?"

My teeth grind together, and the thoughts attack me. All the ones I've held back. Visions of Lenora running through the woods. Her pale hands around Tilly's throat. The memory of that night fifteen years ago. The night everything changed. It all comes back to her.

My sister.

To be afraid for someone you love is one thing. But to be afraid *of* them is another entirely. And to feel both is all-consuming.

Lenora slides back from the table and stands, avoiding my eyes. "I'm going to bed."

"Wait." I stand too, but I don't try to reach for her again. I can't. The chasm that separated us earlier is back. I brought it with me, and it feels like this time it might be here to stay. "I'll order cameras. Some that stay on inside and out. I'll order them if it'll make you feel better."

She's quiet for a moment before her eyes catch mine again. "You can do whatever you want, Cassie."

And I think she's disappointed too.

Her door clicks closed and the sound of her lock turning echoes through the hall.

I drop my head in my hands and groan, rolling my face to the side.

There's someone standing at the window.

I react reflexively, wrenching myself to my feet and stumbling back. My heart hammers wildly and then slowly levels out.

There's no one there.

My chest deflates. Here and gone in one instant. Or maybe never really there at all.

I walk to the window and place a shaking hand against the glass. This winter hasn't been harsh. Not in a physical sense, at least. No snow yet. Barely any ice or frost. The bathhouse sits at the base of the hill, a tiny light illuminating the closed wooden door, and it doesn't look like winter outside. Like cracking the door will blast you with freezing air. It just looks like nighttime.

The look of it, like the rest of my thoughts, is deceiving.

There's no one out here.

There never was.

I'm jumpy and consumed with worry for my sister.

That has to be it.

There's another flash of movement, and I look at Cabin Three. Someone is on the front porch. The rocking chair lurches back and forth, and Karen Meadows stares blankly in my direction.

That night fifteen years ago flashes in my head. A glint of silver. A river of red. Everything Lenora and I did after.

Neither Karen nor I look away.

Until I back away and close the curtains.

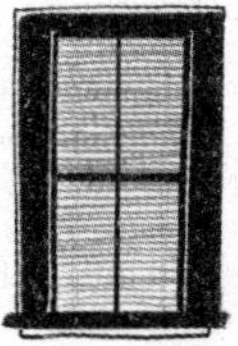

CHAPTER TWENTY-ONE
LENORA

Falling into obsession for me is a lot like falling in love. I've never loved another person before. Not romantically, at least. But I've thought about it. The free-falling. The desperate grasping at the walls, clawing at the floor, struggling not to let yourself go, but in an instant losing yourself entirely. That's how I feel. Like my entire self is gone. And if not gone, then at least different. I'm different, and I don't know what it means.

There was no falling in love with Cassie. The love was just there. Like it was woven into our DNA without giving us a choice. There was no choosing, only accepting it for what it was. But as Cassie avoided my eyes after our discussion, I felt as if I didn't know what was in her head. And that makes me feel like I'm losing my mind.

My legs are tangled in sheets, but my head is spinning too quickly for me to fall asleep. Every little noise in the hallway has me flinching.

I can't stop thinking of my sister.

All the things we didn't talk about. The longer the silence, the more I fester.

It's nearly sunrise, and I haven't been able to fall asleep. Just tossed and turned while waiting for the sun. Waiting for whoever broke in to come back and finish the job. Just as I think I'm getting close, just as unconsciousness seems within reach, I hear something.

With the tips of my fingers, I gently push the covers off my legs and creep to the door, pressing my ear against it.

Whispers.

"Shhh…she's sleeping…"

"You wanted me here…"

"Come in."

The click of a door. I climb back into bed and pull the covers over my head. But sleep doesn't come. And I should feel alone, but I don't. Instead, there is another feeling altogether. A worse feeling. One that whispers in my ear as it traces a rough fingertip over my cheek; I'm no longer alone even though I should be. It's coming home to your empty apartment and finding the TV on when you know you left it off. It's hearing a creak in your attic when you know you're the only one in your house. It's ice injected directly into your veins, eyes crawling along your skin, someone watching you through a window you cannot see out of.

A kid in bed as their closet door slowly, ever so slowly, eases open.

But none of these things are happening, and they all are. Why does reality matter if it all seems so real anyway?

I want to close my curtains, but I sink deeper into the mattress, hiding from some unseen thing. Just before sunrise, when my stiff body feels as if I've been in a gym for hours and my eyes are heavy with sleep that never came, I hear footsteps creeping down the hallway once more.

And nothing feels right. Nothing feels right at all.

"I told Sarah and Karen about the break-in," Cassie says from her spot on her knees in front of the cabinet. She's going through our expired food and making a grocery list. I'm working on a manuscript. We deserve Oscars, the pair of us. I nearly convince myself it's just another day.

But then I remember someone broke into our cabin, Karen is behaving erratically, Tilly was murdered, and I cannot remember what happened the night she died.

I don't know if it's better to connect those dots or leave them suspended on the canvas like some knockoff van Gogh painting.

Oh, and Cassie has a boyfriend.

Daphne's voice is in my head. Her soothing tone asking why this bothers me so much. The boyfriend thing. But it's not the fact she has a boyfriend but the fact she *lied* about it.

"Did you hear me?"

I blink at Cassie, but the sun is too bright. My head is too foggy. "You told them about last night?"

"I had to. You think someone broke into our cabin." The way she says it, the pitch to her voice. She didn't believe me last night, and she still doesn't believe me now.

"Why would you tell them if you think it was me on the video?"

"I'm just covering my bases." Cassie stands in the middle of the kitchen, her arms full of cans. "If we bought cameras, Sarah should get some too. Anyway, they thanked me for letting them know."

"You spoke with Karen?"

She looks away. "No, Sarah told her."

The way she says her name. Sarah. I can't put my finger on why I don't like it.

"Anyway"—Cassie deposits the cans in a box—"I'm getting rid of this and going to the grocery store. We're out of everything. Why don't you come with me this time?"

My Word document is open in front of me, and the words swivel in and out. I can't figure out where I left off. "I can't. You know I can't."

"Lenora," she says, "I don't want to leave you here after last night. Please. You can sit in the car." I see through her. My sister isn't worried for me. She's worried about what I'll do. Like I'm a child who requires supervision.

I think of my options. The two evils. Be here or go. How can both options be equally terrifying? Sometimes I think of my future. I try to visualize and imagine what it might look like, and every time, all I can see is this damned cabin.

To leave means to acknowledge the rest of the world exists. It means to cut myself out of the skin of this campsite like a cancer and slide under a microscope. But I don't know who will be looking. I don't know what they will see.

But if I stay…

Another image. Me old and gray. Cassie's silver hair falling in tangles to her crusted and dirty feet. Tree roots and wisteria wrapped around our bony bodies, slowly driving us into the ground. *You'll like it here*, they say. *You'll never leave again.*

"I can't." Do I sound as insecure as I feel? "I have so much work to do. You go."

She watches me for a long moment. "Will you be OK here alone?"

"I always am."

She nods, glances toward the window and back. "I should be back before the sun sets. Lenora?"

"Yes?"

"Why did you meet with Daphne again today? You've already met this week."

"Daphne thought an extra session would benefit me."

"Are you OK?"

"I'm fine."

She nods quickly, her gaze going back to the open refrigerator. I pretend not to notice the way she shifts and moves things around, tossing items into the donation pile and recycling. The silence between us stretches like a tumultuous ocean.

A silence that started last night.

"Cassie?"

"Yes?"

"You've been acting different."

Finally, she faces me, wearing a forced-looking smile. "I've just been stressed. I should get going if I'm going to be back before dark." But there's something behind her smile. Something she isn't saying.

I wonder if her boyfriend will meet her in town. If her bimonthly grocery store trips are just a cover for something else.

More secrets between us. Her face. This person. My sister. I thought I knew her as well as myself. Maybe I don't really know her at all.

And clearly, she doesn't know me.

"Just be careful," I say.

She goes to her room and returns with her keys and a wallet. Loads her arms with the boxes and hesitates by the doorway. "You sure you're OK?"

"Just tired."

"I'll go ahead and bring dinner back too. That way neither of us has to cook."

"Chinese?"

"If you want."

It's my turn to pretend now. As Cassie slips on her shoes. As Cassie walks out the door and closes it behind her. It's my turn to pretend I'm not falling apart. But there's no one here to pretend for, and I'm not fooling myself.

Something wakes me.

The first thing I notice is the night is pitch-black, and Cassie still isn't back.

A tingle of awareness spreads over my body. The sofa squeaks as I sit up, and that seems to be the only sound in the world. Sunset was an hour ago, and I don't remember falling asleep with the lights off, but I must have.

I clear my throat. "Cassie?"

The silence is my only answer. Cassie really isn't back. This isn't abnormal. The nearest Walmart is an hour away. That's why she only makes the trip twice a month. I reach for my phone on the arm of the couch, but my hand slides over cool fabric.

It's not there.

I feel around the cushion and beside my legs.

Creak.

My body stiffens, and the awareness is stronger now. A feeling like I'm not really alone. My movements are jerky and sloppy as I stand and fumble along the wall for the light switch. It only takes a moment to find it and flick it, but nothing happens.

The power is out.

"Damn it..." I mutter, scanning the room, willing it to come into focus. Slowly it does. The light from the moon filters in, and I blink a couple of times before kneeling by the couch, sliding my hand along the floor.

Where the hell is my phone?

It's OK, I tell myself. *Cassie should be here any minute.*

This cabin just makes noises sometimes.

I'm OK.

I close my eyes and start counting. "One, two, three—"

And I hear it.

The sound of a door clicking closed.

Something ice-cold lodges in the base of my throat.

There's someone in the house.

No.

No. I'm alone. I locked the door when Cassie left. No one could have gotten in or out. Not without waking me up.

"Four, five, six—" I stand on knees that protest and walk sideways with my back to the wall, until I'm able to see down the hallway. It looks like Cassie's door is open and mine is shut. Carefully

I inch forward. I instinctively reach for my phone again and am reminded that it's missing. I close my eyes. Make it to fifty-seven before I open them and start moving. My feet creak as I walk, and each noise makes me flinch, makes my heart race.

There's no one in the house.

There's no one in the house.

There's no one in the house.

I look in Cassie's room first, scanning it quickly like ripping off an adhesive bandage. Unkempt bed. Clothes in a bundle on the floor. A collection of trinkets on her chest of drawers.

The room looks just as Cassie left it.

My breath of relief doesn't come.

I turn on my heel to face my bedroom door.

My closed bedroom door.

But I left it open, didn't I?

No. I couldn't have. It's clearly shut. Cassie wouldn't have shut it. At least, she never has before.

That means I closed it.

I reach for the door now, fully ready to thrust it open like I did Cassie's. But something makes my whole body freeze.

A sound.

A rustling. What you might hear if someone pulls the covers back from a bed. It reminds me of being a kid. My dad standing over me and tucking the sheets around me until I couldn't move.

I press my ear to the door.

There is only silence, and I try to convince myself I only imagined the noise, but my door is closed, and the lights are out, and nothing makes sense.

Still facing the hallway, I walk backward to the kitchen and pull a knife from the holder. A large, finely sharpened knife that Cassie uses to chop raw vegetables. I count my steps back to the room, stumbling and skipping a number. Then forgetting where I was and what I was doing.

I'm sweating, my heart racing.

When I stand facing my door, a strange feeling comes over me. An urging. *Get away. Do not open this door.* I want to listen, to run. But where will I go? How can you run when you're trapped inside?

Anyway, I know how this plays out. I've been here before.

I never run.

I always open the door.

A palm on the door handle.

Knife in the air.

In one motion, I turn the handle. Push. And wrench the door open.

There's a moment of complete stillness.

Then someone rams into me, and we tangle in the hallway floor, all twisted limbs and chaos. The knife slides from my fingers and is somewhere beside my head. I cry out as the person takes my shoulders and slams me into the ground hard. "What did you do? What did you do to her?"

My breath is choked, my breathing uneven. I couldn't answer if I wanted to, but I can see. Karen leaning over me, pure hatred on her face.

"What did you do?"

I can't speak. The words are mangled on my tongue. My whole body is shutting down. There is no fight. No flight. Just me left to *feel.*

"I know it was you. I know it was you who hurt her. Just tell me why. Just tell me what you did." Her words squeak out as though her throat is caked with rust.

They also bring something back to the surface. A feeling in the woods that night. A taste on my tongue. A vision in the dark. Tears leak sideways out of my eyes as I stare up at this woman. This grieving, pained woman. Nothing makes sense. Nothing I thought before makes any sense.

What did I do?

"Please," she whispers, and her grip on my shoulders loosens. "You have to finally tell the truth. I know it was you. I know you keep coming into my cabin."

"I—"

There's a click somewhere behind me, and Karen freezes, her gaze slowly shifting up. I can't see, but I hear my sister's voice. "Get off her."

Karen lifts her hands in the air and stands. I heave and roll sideways onto all fours, scrambling away until my back hits the wall.

Karen's body trembles and tears start falling. "This wasn't supposed to happen like this. I didn't mean—I thought you weren't home. I was just looking—" Her sobs keep cutting off her words, making her difficult to understand.

I slowly stand, still leaning into the wall, watching Karen fall apart.

Cassie, still holding our rifle, calls the police.

Two uniformed cops, as well as Detective Harrison and Eubanks, show up to make the arrest. Sarah walks up the hill and speaks quietly with my sister. I watch their body language. My adrenaline has crashed, and I feel as though I've been in a car accident, but nothing is more uncomfortable than watching Cassie and Sarah.

There's a familiarity between them. I can't figure out how it happened or when. But each time they look at me, their heads pressed together, concern etched onto their faces, I feel just a little more alone.

The words and people all seem blurry.

Sarah squeezes Cassie's arm.

Nothing will make sense until Cassie and I are back in the cabin together.

I stand at the door. One foot in and one out. But I can't make myself fully go inside. Not when Cassie is out here with these flashing red and blue lights. "Cassie." My voice breaks, and she must hear it, how close I am to stepping off the ledge.

"It's OK. It's fine." She comes to me and smooths back my hair. "You were right. You've been right the whole time. And I'm the one who should be sorry. I am. Sorry. So sorry, Lenora."

But something doesn't feel right. Being right doesn't feel *right*. It hadn't in that moment with Karen. Not with her weight on me. Heavier than her hundred and thirty pounds. Not with her eyes searching my face.

Certainly not with Sarah watching my sister and me now. Shooting me a half smile like she actually cares. I step closer to Cassie until I can't see Sarah at all, and she can't see me.

"I don't understand," I whisper. "They arrested her."

"It's what you knew all along."

Yet that interaction with Karen contradicted everything I thought I knew. Karen wasn't the callous mother from the video. The one who slapped her daughter. She was a mother at her breaking point, hopelessly searching for the truth.

A truth she thought I knew.

And they're there. The answers Karen wants. All the answers are in the night Tilly went missing. The feeling of running through the woods. Another person with me. Smiling at me.

The face of this person is blurry. It's been blurry. But like a pixelated image, it slowly clicks into focus, and I see Tilly.

My stomach turns.

Why do I see Tilly?

The images come faster now. Tilly running. Me—me, what? Me *chasing*?

I shake my head, try to shake them away.

"Lenora?" There's concern dripping from Cassie's voice as thickly as regret. "What's wrong? It's OK. You're safe now."

But I'm not safe. Nothing about this memory is safe. My eyes meet my sister's, and she must see something in them because she flinches. "I don't know what's real anymore," I whisper. "The way she looked at me. It's like she knew something. Like she thought—"

"This." She takes my hand and places it over her heart. "This is real. Just count with me. You're safe. I promise you're safe now."

I jerk away, trembling, panicking. Feeling like I'm seconds away from deserting my own body. Leaving it behind in the dust. This is the part of my anxiety that no one understands. The distrust in myself. But I don't have to lie to myself or anyone else. Not anymore. "That night. There was someone out there with me. I think it was Tilly. I think I saw her that night—"

"Stop it." Cassie's voice is sharp and cold. It pierces me, and her hand on my wrist tightens.

"I can't tell what's real or which memories my mind just filled in. I don't—I don't know what I did that night, Cassie. And maybe Karen does. Maybe that's why she came in here. Maybe she knows—"

"I said stop it!" Cassie grabs my shoulders now, holds them tightly. "You're panicking because you're scared. I know you, Lenora. You wouldn't do anything. You wouldn't hurt anyone."

But there's the night fifteen years ago.

The awful night that didn't make sense then just as it doesn't now. The only thing I know based off that night is that Cassie is wrong. I would hurt someone. I have.

"That's not true. We both know that's not true."

Cassie only shakes her head. "None of it matters. Because I *know* you. You get that? I know you, Lenora. Better than you know yourself. Karen broke in. She was looking for evidence, she said. She wanted to find proof you or I hurt her daughter. She saw my car leave and didn't know you were in the house. She waited till dark and broke in through the back door. Didn't see you on the couch. She was arrested. You didn't do anything wrong."

"And if I did? What then?"

She doesn't answer, but she doesn't have to because I already know. We both do.

The ocean roars in my ears. Can't think. Can't fathom this. "She thinks I hurt Tilly. That's why she was here. You understand, don't you?" I *need* my sister to understand. I'm not a bad person, and I may have done a bad thing, but it doesn't mean I want to get away with it. Not if it means carrying this weight with me for the rest of my life.

Not if this cabin is a prison anyway.

"We don't know the truth. None of us does, except maybe Karen." There is silence between us, and Cassie sighs. "And it doesn't matter. The police have her now."

"You never answered me." My voice is a guttural whisper. "What will you do if it's me? If I did something terrible?"

"I don't have to answer that, Lenora."

"Because I know?"

"Because your secrets are mine and mine are yours," Cassie says, pulling away from me. Hurt cracks her face like the San Andreas fault, and it's my secrets that burden her. She'll take them to the grave if I let her, even if it means becoming a person she was never meant to be.

My brutally honest and sacrificing sister.

Lying for me.

Dying with me.

Us together, two beacons of lies and suffering just waiting for the day this hillside caves in and swallows our cabin whole with us still inside.

"You don't have to be this person, Cass. Not for me."

Her eyes are flames, burning with the truth that lives and dies with us. "I've already done it once before."

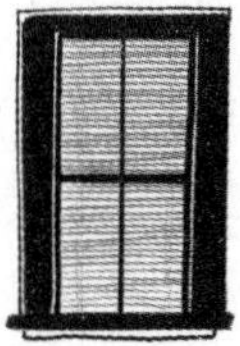

CHAPTER TWENTY-TWO
THEN

An overweight middle-aged white man with sweat dripping from his underarms, Pastor Smith is as boring as his name. I watch the sweat trickle down his neck into his collar and imagine it's his skin peeling back from his body.

It's an absurd thought, but it's distracting enough to make me laugh.

Distracting enough to make me forget your words three nights ago. Your joke about killing our parents. It still makes my stomach roll even now.

How could you say that?

You must notice the look on my face because you nudge me with an elbow. I nudge you back a little harder. It leads us to linking our arms together. Mother looks past you at me, her eyes narrow. I wonder if she cares what God thinks or if it's just about the women in the first row.

We're in the middle near the back. Behind all the perfect families.

Women in wrinkle-free dresses singing about bathing in His blood, men in khakis pretending their wives didn't drag them out of bed this morning, and children avoiding eye contact with the pastor so they don't get asked to come to the front to worship. These perfect Christians, ignorant to their own fallacies, have never accepted us. Not my father's drug problem. Not my mother's willingness to be a single mother or her decision to always take him back.

They judged every part of our family the moment we passed through these doors the first time, and it only got worse after our dad left and Mom dragged us here alone. They whispered under their breath "poor dears" and "bless their hearts" like that made up for the awful things said in between the endearments. Of course, after last summer, even the pity stopped. I think Mom only keeps coming out of sheer stubbornness alone. It can't possibly be because she believes any of it.

If you pray enough, God will help you, Mom says when she's on one of her tangents. *But if he'd just help in the first place*, I think but never say to her, *we wouldn't need to pray so much.*

The white church is the kind of old that niche vintage stores try to replicate. The wooden pews are ramrod straight, the walkways are narrow, it smells like dust and decay, and the people here are all posers, pretending being here is their choice. Not the secret to their oppression.

The choir sings of Jesus and God, and I can't help but wonder if this is even real, or maybe life is one giant pyramid scheme, and Jesus and God, if they're there, are perhaps sitting at the top of the triangle watching the insufferable people below them hurt and judge in the name of Christianity all the while they're collecting souls.

"What are you thinking so hard about?" you whisper between barely parted lips. Mom glances at you with a warning on her face. You snap your lips closed and face forward. We will all be as close to perfect as possible under her watch. Even you. We haven't talked about what happened the other night. What you said. I almost brought it up twice, but each time the words didn't come.

You were joking. I know you were joking. You would never hurt anyone purposely, especially our parents. But after you said it, I can't help but watch you. Stare while you scarf down your cereal or watch your shows on the carpet in front of the living room TV. I look at you and wonder what you're thinking. What you're capable of.

That's when I feel eyes on me.

You're facing forward, mouthing the words to a song. No one should be paying me any mind, but the eerie feeling doesn't leave.

It only takes a second of searching to see where the feeling is coming from. Across the aisle and a row kitty-corner behind us. The breath is knocked completely out of me as my eyes connect with Joan Wellesley's.

Now the only skin peeling from a body is my own. She's doing it to me, peeling me layer by layer with only her gaze, and it hurts. It hurts to remember what happened last summer.

It's shocking to see her.

And it isn't just her staring. There's a shift in the air. An imbalance. Not everyone knows the details of what happened last summer, but there are rumors. Rumors that make the women in this room tut their tongues and shake their heads.

Don't know what those girls did, they murmur to one another, *but they did something. Something is not quite right with that family.*

The rumors died a little after the police cleared us, but they'll pick up again no doubt with Joan being back.

She's not supposed to be here. She's supposed to be with a relative in Florida. Not here. She *can't* be here.

But she is, and so are the burns on the left side of her face. The uneven red skin perpetually puckered, forever blistered. Her hair is perfectly coiled and styled in blond ringlets; her outfit is designer, and her makeup is immaculate. But I can't see past the scars.

Can't hear anything except her screaming.

I lurch forward in my seat, pretending she's not searing holes straight through me.

"What's wrong?" you whisper from the corner of your mouth, glancing over your shoulder at Joan before facing the front again. Your expression of trepidation matches mine, but you don't say anything. You stay facing forward, and I don't know if it's for Mom's benefit or your own.

I don't look back again because I know what I'll see. Joan's eyes blazing into mine like she's watching someone burn at the stake.

She knows.

The thought is abrupt and sharp. It slices into my very bones.

She knows.

But she can't.

Her stare burns for the next hour, and with that feeling comes the reminder of that night. Finally, I work up the nerve to turn around again, but the seat Joan occupied is empty. She's not anywhere to be seen.

I don't know what makes me do it, but I stand.

Mom grabs my wrist.

"I need the bathroom." I pull away from her, knowing I'll pay for this later. Mom doesn't argue, just as I know she won't. She won't do anything to make a scene in public.

When she lets go, the white ring she leaves around my wrist pulses as the blood flows back into place. I move through the row, careful to keep my head down and walk out the double back doors. No one looks twice at me as I slink away. Not because I don't attract attention leaving in the middle of a service but because I'm not worthy of it.

The foyer is empty too. Joan must have left.

The relief is so severe, my knees nearly buckle.

The women's bathroom is tucked into a corner of the foyer. Inside are two stalls. I head straight for the first one and sit heavily on the toilet seat, letting my head fall into my hands. I need a minute to myself. To compose myself.

The expression on Joan's face.

The *hatred.*

The feeling of her gaze on my neck is like the tip of a blade.

Why is she here?

Why did she come back?

There is shuffling in the stall next door, and it makes me tense. I hadn't realized anyone else was in here. I was too preoccupied with thoughts of Joan. Of Wellesley House.

Of the terrible, horrible thing.

The toilet flushes next to me, and a woman steps out to wash her hands.

But all I'm really aware of are the flames. The screams. The feeling of horror. The hotness of the night. Sweat coating my body, my upper lip. And you, my sister, running toward me.

I wipe under my eyes, dragging my fingers up and through my hair, pulling on the roots. The pain is enough to rip the images from my hand, and I rock back and forth until they're gone. Until I shoot up, unable to think of anything else except getting out of this church.

I'm distracted when I stagger out of the stall, and I don't see the person standing stock-still in front of the mirror until it's too late, and my eyes connect with Joan's. I can't speak, even though the words beat against my lips. I can't walk, even though I yearn to be anywhere but here. And it's like she knows it. Like she knows the upheaval inside of me is more prominent than blood, and it pleases her.

This is the first time I've been alone with Joan since what happened last summer.

"You think it helps?" she asks, the first to break the silence. She looks away from the mirror and turns to face me. The puckered skin on the left side of her lip causes her mouth to droop. It makes me uncomfortable, not because of the burn itself but because of how it got there. She and Kate were always the prettiest in school. The richest. The meanest. With parents who loved them the most. Things like this don't happen to girls like her. Joan tilts her head toward me. "Do you really believe coming to church is enough to absolve you?"

I don't say anything.

"Look at me," she says. "The least you can do is look at what you did. Maybe your sister—"

"Don't," I cut her off, my voice harder than my spine when I spin toward her.

"I know it was her. I *saw* her."

"No. We didn't—she didn't do anything." I'm careful with my words, careful with my memories of that night. "The police know it. Your parents know it. We were at home."

The words are pungent on my tongue.

The door to the bathroom is flung open, and two loud elderly women walk in, going straight for the stalls. Church must have let out. That's when I see you. Catching the door before it closes, peeking inside. You don't look at Joan. "We're leaving," you say coolly.

I don't give Joan another glance, but I hear her whispered words before the door closes behind us: "You know what you did."

You grab my hand and tug me toward the exit doors where the congregation is lining up to shake Pastor Smith's hand on their way out. Mother stands near him, her face unreadable. But her fury is there. Tamped back just beneath the surface of her skin. She's careful not to let it show.

"What was that?" you whisper right before we get to her.

I only shake my head, not trusting myself to speak. I'm still caught in the flames. The feeling of dread unspooling inside me. The fear.

"Hey." You stop me with a jerk of my arm. "What did she say to you?"

I look away. Bite my lip. Fight the tears clinging to my lashes. "She said she saw you. That it was your fault." I don't add the other part. I saw too. I saw much more than I should have. More than I ever wanted. I don't know if following you that night was the best or worst choice I ever made. I got to save you, even if it broke me to do it.

"It was an accident," you tell me, shaking your head. "I told you. None of it was supposed to happen. The fire wasn't supposed to spread like that. Joan's hurt because she lost her sister. She's going to say those things, but it's OK. We know the truth."

"Yes," I say. "The truth." You disappearing behind the house. The flames. The screams. The surprise on your face when you saw me.

"Accident. You know I wouldn't have done that on purpose."

"But Kate," I say. "I always thought—I mean, she wasn't always very nice to you." The memories of Joan's sister are fresh. The ways she used to respond to you on the bus, so snippy and sarcastic. Her laughter when you walked past.

"You think I killed her on purpose because she was rude to me sometimes?" The way you ask so incredulously makes me feel silly.

"No, that's not what I'm saying."

"I think that's exactly what you're saying." Your brows pull down, and you take a small step back. "I don't know what I have to do to prove to you it was an accident. I never in a million years thought I'd have to prove anything." The first tear falls down your cheek. Lonely but not for long. "What do I have to do or say to convince you I'm a good person? What more do you want from me?"

"I'm sorry."

You wipe your cheeks. Hold the tip of your fingers to your eyes. I look around us and notice a few stares. Two girls our age whispering behind their hands. "We shouldn't do this here," I say, trying to grab your hand, but you don't let me.

"Why not? What does it matter what they think when my own sister thinks so little of me?"

"Please, you know that's not how I feel. I didn't mean that."

"Girls!" Our mother's hiss echoes across the foyer, and we both turn toward her on instinct. She's enraged. Practically seething.

I've broken several rules today, and I know I'm going to pay for it later. But the thought doesn't bother me as much as your anger.

You push past, and I fall into step behind, trying to get straight in my head everything I want to say to you. I just need you to understand that I'm not judging you. It's not about what you did or why. I just want to protect you. That's all I care about.

We're the last to leave, and Pastor Smith is watching us with a saccharine smile. "That was a lovely sermon." Mother's voice drips with honey.

"Well, thank you. It's surely the one God intended for you all to hear today." He dabs at his upper lip with the back of his sleeve, and his eyes pass over you and me. "You sure have a beautiful family."

You say something. Something that makes him laugh, and his gaze lingers just a little too long on your chest, his eyes roving up and down like you're a shiny piece of jewelry. Even after I cause you to break down, you're still in perfect control. Like all the times Kate was mean to you on the bus. It never seemed to bother you as much as it did me. Like you knew something we didn't. I always thought you were confident and aware of your own self-worth even when she wasn't. I didn't know how hard you took her words. Not until it was too late, and Kate was already gone.

Pastor Smith's gaze settles on me next, and the pressure of our moment with him is ending, and all I can think about is how gross he is. How much of a hypocrite he is. The way his nervous wife averts her eyes when his hands linger on a woman for too long.

Then there's Joan and Kate and how I feel like a pressure cooker.

Pastor Smith tilts my chin up. "Smile, sweetheart."

His words bust me right open, and all my anger is exposed like organs in a slit-open chest. "I thought only sinners are supposed to sweat in church, Pastor Smith."

Before my words even seem to register on his face, Mom has a hold of me. "I'm so sorry, Pastor. Don't know what's gotten into her. Excuse us."

And she's dragging me toward our green beater. I stumble behind, barely keeping up, barely staying on my feet. She shoves me into the back seat and slams the door.

"The hell is that about?" Dad asks, his tie undone and a cigarette hanging out of his mouth. He must have left the service soon after I did. He drops the cigarette out the window before Mom makes it around the car.

"You shouldn't have said that." Your voice is quiet as you slide in and shut your door. You're worried about me even after what I said. It makes my chest swell with hope.

Dad looks between us as Mom's door flies open.

"Did you see the way he was holding—"

She doesn't let me finish. The first slap catches me off guard. It shouldn't, but it does. It's the second slap that I brace myself for. The third that I revel in. The fourth that cuts my cheek.

With my head whipped sideways, my cheeks hot and bruised, and a warm trickle of blood creeping down my jaw, Mom turns forward in the driver's seat and slams her fists against the wheel and screams.

We three watch her break down like an erupting volcano. Eventually, she flips the driver's side mirror down and pats her eyes with a crumpled napkin she pulled from the console. When she's done, she tosses it at me. "Clean yourself up."

Dad's eyes are wide, but he doesn't say anything.

I press the napkin to my cheek, and it comes away red.

The car pulls away, and I see Joan Wellesley standing in front of the faded white church, watching us.

My anger boils over, bubbling all around me.

And it hurts.

My eyes meet yours, and in them I see exactly what Joan accused me of trying to find. Absolution. Something passes in this moment, unfolding between us. A mutual understanding.

For the first time in my life, I feel like I can honestly kill someone.

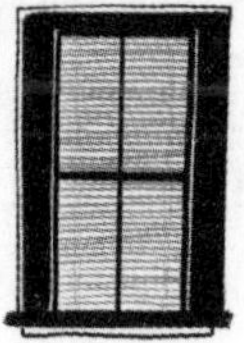

CHAPTER TWENTY-THREE
LENORA

I try to focus on it, the memory.

It comes in pulsing, hot flashes. My feet covering wet grass and broken bramble. Trees flanking me on all sides like soldiers standing at attention. And there—just between the branches—someone is standing. Thin and willowy. Feminine. Awareness creeps in. Recognition.

That's when I wake up.

The moment I try to analyze the dream or memory is always when I lose it. Reality converges with my mind, and I'm left wondering what's real and what's not.

The morning sun is bright and warming. I'm tangled in sheets and drenched in sweat. It's a new day. I should feel safe. But I only feel discombobulated. Uncomfortable in the light.

I lurch out of bed and put my contacts in first. They've been sitting in solution for too long and burn as they go in. I try blinking away the discomfort, and when they start watering, I press the heels of my hands into my eyes. I still haven't found my glasses. Karen must have taken them at some point. Though I can't imagine a reason why. I picture her trying them on. Wearing them like in the video, as if doing so would make her see what I see.

Was I wearing my glasses the night Tilly died?

Cassie is waiting by the window when I get to the kitchen. Maybe I should tell her about my missing glasses. But when she looks at me, her eyes are too wide and worried. Something is wrong.

"What is it?" I ask.

Then I turn my head and notice someone else in the room. Sarah sits at our kitchen table with a travel mug clenched in one hand and a vape in the other. She's watching me hesitantly. Unlike my sister, there isn't worry. More like a wariness. A woman afraid of…of what? Me?

The scene is so absurd, I almost think it's my contact lenses playing tricks on me. I blink against the lingering burn, but Sarah doesn't disappear. The look on her face makes my chest and neck get hot. She brings the vape pen to her lips and inhales. When she pulls it back, smoke swirling from her lips in a gray cloud, the room smells too sweet. Artificial. Cassie doesn't seem to notice at all.

A migraine forms at my temples.

"What's she doing here?" I don't mean to ask so abrasively. But I'm taken off guard, and she's watching me too closely, and my eyes are still stinging.

"They've been here all morning," Cassie says, pointing to the window.

They? Confused, I follow her gaze. There's a stream of people walking in and out of Cabin Three. Police. I recognize Detective Harrison on the porch staring at his phone.

"What are they doing?"

"They got a warrant." Sarah delivers the news like someone might comment on the weather. But there is a hint of satisfaction. An "I knew it all along" vibe. It makes me relax beneath the weight of her stare just a little. "They're searching Karen's cabin. I don't know what happened, but I think they believe she killed her daughter."

It stalls me. Makes my breath catch. And it shouldn't because I thought it first. I thought it from the beginning. But then I remember Karen's eyes when she broke in. Her plea to me.

I remember Tilly's face in the dark.

"Why do they think that?"

"Physical evidence," Sarah answers and takes a sip from her mug. "I overheard a cop talking outside. I don't know what they found, but it sounds like they think they've got her."

Cassie lays a hand on my arm, and I startle. Still so jumpy. Even more than before. Karen was *arrested*. "Why don't you eat?"

"In a minute." I move to the window, numbly. Watching them walk in and out with various items bagged and collected in their hands.

Cassie's footsteps fall away, and she and Sarah speak quietly together in hushed voices. Eventually, Sarah walks back to her own cabin, and Cassie disappears into the recording booth. But I stay by the window.

They bring bag after bag out of that cabin. Evidence. I should feel better now. Better after having answers.

But I only feel worse.

Dinner that night is garlic butter noodles and bread made by me. I bring Cassie a bowl. She's sitting up in bed staring at her computer screen. She acted like she didn't want to be in the kitchen. Didn't want to see what's going on outside the window. Her Harvard T-shirt is wrinkly, and there's a stain near the collar. She's worn it one too many times in a row.

"You want me to throw that in the wash?" I ask her.

She looks up blankly, and I can tell she didn't even hear me. "Are they gone?"

"Just left." I sit on the edge of the bed and pass her the bowl.

She holds the bowl but doesn't reach for the fork. "I just don't know how I missed this. I thought after she broke in that it could be possible. But I didn't think—I mean, I thought she loved Tilly. She acted like she did. They arrested her, Lenora. It means they have something solid."

"We don't know if she actually did anything." I play with a piece of loose thread on her comforter. "You know how this works. Their investigation could reveal nothing."

"But you knew, didn't you?" Cassie tilts her head at me. "You heard their fight. You saw how strange she acted. You knew, Lenora, and I'm sorry I doubted you." Doubted me. Is that what she calls it?

"You don't have to apologize." I say the words sincerely. An apology is never what I wanted from my sister. Yes, I wanted her to believe me. To not think the worst of me even as I saw the worst in myself. But seeing the regret and pain on her face now makes up for all that. I can't stand Cassie hurting. Especially for my sake.

Especially when the truth still feels so far out of reach.

"No, I do. I thought—well, I don't even know what I thought. But it wasn't this. And I'm sorry." There's something else on Cassie's face. Relief.

"Is that why you didn't tell me about him?" I ask. "You didn't trust me?"

"Who?"

"The man I heard in our cabin. Your boyfriend."

She looks away, her jaw ticking. "I told you he's not my boyfriend. He's not important."

"Then why did you call him?" I ask, my voice rising uneasily. "Why did you reach out to him when you needed someone? I needed you, Cassie. Tilly was murdered. Karen has been watching us for days. She broke in and attacked me. I needed you, and it just feels like through all this, you never needed me."

"I needed a distraction. That's it. Sometimes I need to think of anything else. This—" She gestures between us. "It's starting to hurt, Lenora."

"Because you didn't trust me. What did you think? What did you think of me?"

"You were unraveling. You were sleepwalking again and obsessed with Tilly. You were so afraid of that night. And I know you. I know you wouldn't hurt anyone, but you were unconscious. And it was all too much for me. I just needed to think of something else."

"You thought I was a murderer. Some kind of serial killer." There. I say it. I actually say it, but the satisfying feeling doesn't last long because I never wanted to be right. Not about this.

"No." Cassie shakes her head, shoves the noodles to her side, and sits up on her knees to face me. "Never. That's not it. That's never it."

I close my eyes.

Our footsteps were a dream, echoing down the hallway. Emphasizing the violent sounds coming from our parents' room.

Thwack, thwack, thwack.

Cassie's sweaty hand in mine. One last moment to brace ourselves before opening the door. One last moment before our lives changed forever.

But I closed my eyes.

And when I did that, I didn't just shut out the violence and trauma. I shut out Cassie. She told me to run, and I didn't listen because somehow I felt safer like that. Eyes closed. Ignorant.

She ran and I stayed, and we've paid for it ever since.

We're still paying for it.

Because I'm still clenching my eyes closed.

"Lenora?" Cassie grabs my hands in hers. "Please, don't be upset. I'm sorry. Please. I'm sorry. I'm so sorry." I let her hug me. Let her tears wet my shoulder. Feel it drip down. Feel her security.

"I love you," I tell her.

"I was just scared," she whispers against my neck. "I'm sorry I doubted you."

"What you said last night, about my secrets being yours. Did you mean it?"

She pulls back, looks at me. "Doesn't matter. There are no secrets. It was Karen. Not you. You wouldn't." She brushes my hair back from my face and sighs. "I knew you wouldn't."

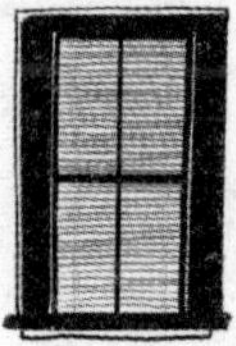

CHAPTER TWENTY-FOUR
CASSIE

It's always good to have resolution. With each of the cases I cover for my channel, the unsolved ones are always the hardest to swallow. But there's something about a case like this...a mother killing her own daughter. It almost seems worse. Like the humanity within us would rather not know.

But also better somehow.

Better than what the truth could have been.

There are no reasons for the visions to still haunt me. It's over. It was Karen, and it's over. I should feel safe to sleep, but I don't. I should be happy. Karen is most likely in jail, but I can't let myself relax. Not when I missed so much. Not when I denied so much of what was right in front of me.

Lenora practically shouted it from the roof, and I ignored her. Made excuses. Told her she was being paranoid.

It makes me want to vomit.

It's late. Not sure how late. I don't check, but I climb out of bed anyway. I'm restless, and my body aches.

I can't explain it, but there's a need to know. To prove to my subconscious that it really wasn't Lenora. That it was Karen, and it's been her the whole time.

I get out of bed. No coat. No shoes. Slip outside. Inhale the crisp night air. There are no cops. No one else on this hill except my sister, and that's a relief I haven't experienced since the Meadows family came here that night. I didn't know I needed this privacy. Craved it. And with each step away from our own cabin, I feel even lighter.

The trees jut from the earth like teeth in a smiling mouth, and I want them to chew me up and swallow me. To welcome me back properly. There are no birds. No animals. Just me walking swiftly over crunching leaves.

I head toward the Blacktop. The grass shimmers like lake water beneath the mostly full moon, and my rock urges me forward. But there's another urging. Another itch I know I shouldn't scratch.

I stop beneath the canopy of trees, not quite stepping into the clearing, and I inch backward just a little bit at a time. In an attempt to convince myself this wasn't the plan all along.

I don't go to the Blacktop.

I pivot to Cabin Three, and every step toward it is as natural as breathing. Getting inside is easy. The door is unlocked. I push the door open with an ominous, slow creak, and the first thing I notice is the smell.

The scent of rot coming from the kitchen. A pan on the stove with something discolored in it that's clearly been there a while. There are flies and gnats flying around a bowl of black bananas. Dirty dishes stacked high in the sink. Half-empty cans of beans and corn.

I can't believe Karen has been living here.

I tug my shirt over my nose and turn away.

There's a woodburning stove, a quaint family room that connects to a kitchen, and a hallway that must lead to the bedrooms. All of it is trashed. The police must have opened and uncovered every single drawer without putting a single item back.

Pillows hanging off the couch, kitchen cabinets all opened, empty hangers on the ground of an open closet, and a hole in the wall beside the back door. Like they thought the very walls held secrets.

Then I think of another reason for the hole. Karen yelling at her daughter. Rage consuming her. Clenched fists. A young woman's scream.

Tilly most likely wasn't killed where her body was found. Which means this very room could be a crime scene. Did it happen on the couch, her mother's hands around her neck? In the kitchen, a pool of red seeping out from a gaping head wound, spreading over the floor like a fallen can of paint?

I take a step, and my foot squeaks loudly on the hardwood. I shouldn't. I'm not supposed to be here. But I can't help it.

I just need to see for myself.

The hallway is dark; the moonlight through the window barely makes a dent. I consider running back to my cabin for a flashlight, but my fear of disturbing Lenora is too great.

And I can't miss this opportunity. I don't know when I'll get it again.

I peer into the first room. A queen-size bed pushed against the wall, checkered curtains covering the window. It's stale in here too, almost musty. Like my laundry when I forget about it in the washer.

How could this have been so different only a few days ago? Images of the little family of three sleeping, cooking dinner over a fire, playing games together—it doesn't match this scene. This cold, empty place. There's an unopened candy bar near the corner of the room. I pick it up and slip it in my pocket. I do the same with an abandoned pearl earring.

No one would miss these things. Most likely, I'm just helping Sarah anyway. She already mentioned needing to call a cleaner for this place.

Then I hear it.

A footstep creaking on hardwood.

I swing around, heartbeat in my throat, and for just a second, I picture Tilly. Sarcastic expression, her hair pushed over her shoulder, blowing smoke from between barely parted lips. *Look at you, being a stalker. Again.*

But, of course, Tilly isn't here.

Tilly will never be anywhere.

I swallow and peer into the hallway now. There are no windows, and at the end of the hallway, there's a shape forming in the darkness. Probably a piece of furniture pushed against the wall. A laundry hamper. I blink, but my eyes don't adjust. "Hello?"

The shape in the dark doesn't move, and I breathe out. It's all getting to me. Lenora's words. Karen. I think about checking the last room, but an overwhelming feeling stops me. One I can't explain at all. But one that is clear. It tells me not to go back there. Not to step down this pitch-black hallway. Images flash in my head. Tilly as a corpse, crawling over the hardwood, reaching for me. Her skin swarming with maggots, her hair falling out in thick clumps. Dead.

That's the smell. Death and decay. It reminds me of finding Wayne. I can't believe Karen's been living in this darkness all alone.

The silence is too heavy now. A thick blanket might as well be spread over me, muffling all my senses. Making them untrustworthy.

Suddenly there's a twitch in the dark.

Movement.

I squint.

The black mass almost looks like a person standing there.

"Cassie?" A hand on my shoulder. I jump and twist around. Sarah is behind me. "Hey, just me," she says, her arms going to the air as if I'm holding a gun.

I turn my wild gaze back toward the hallway.

There's nothing.

No shape in the dark.

No movement.

An empty hallway.

"What are you looking at?"

"Nothing." I breathe out unsteadily and turn back to her. "You scared me."

"Sorry. I was outside burning boxes and saw you go in. You're not supposed to be in here."

"I just wanted to look."

She motions for me to follow her, and I don't look back at the hallway, but it feels like someone is right on my heels, breathing down my neck as I follow Sarah out. I have to physically stop myself from running down the porch steps. It's an unnatural feeling for me. One I'm not familiar with. I love the night and the dark and being alone. But something about that cabin.

The feeling inside it.

It was more than darkness.

And I don't want to go back.

I inhale deeply once off the porch and several feet away. Catch the faintest hint of smoke. Sure enough, I see the glowing red of a fire behind Cabin One. The black clouds curl up between the trees.

"I don't know what's in there. You probably shouldn't go in again until I have it cleaned." Sarah is wearing jeans and an oversize sweatshirt tonight. The sleeves are so long, they cover her hands, and she's shivering.

"You're cold?"

"You should be too." She motions toward the fire in the distance. "You want to walk with me?"

I agree, though I'm not sure why. I should get back to the cabin. Lenora will be upset if she wakes up and I'm not there. But there's something about the vulnerability in Sarah's tone that has me falling into step beside her.

And the thought of going back inside any cabin makes my stomach tense. *A little longer*, I think. *Just a little longer, and then I'll go back.*

The sounds of our feet crunching over bramble is the only noise until we get to the fire. Hear the snaps and crackles. The wave of heat slams me in the face, but the discomfort is satisfying. I step closer.

"How was it in there?" she asks, resuming her spot beside the fire. Warming her hands before bending down to pick up a box from a dwindling stack. She throws it in, sending up a flurry of sparks and ash. These must be her leftover moving boxes. It's weird thinking about how little I've known Sarah. She's been here for such a short time that she's still dealing with moving boxes.

Yet the ease with which I can be with her is reminiscent of a much longer relationship.

"I can't believe Karen has been living like that."

Her eyes flash to Cabin Three over my shoulder, her expression tight. "Did you find anything? Inside the cabin."

"It smells strange in there."

"I noticed." There's something about her voice, about the way she's watching me. A question on the edge of her tongue.

"You want to know why I was in there?"

She looks surprised for only a moment before nodding.

"I guess I was curious."

"It's sad, isn't it?" she says with a shake of her head. "What happened to that girl. She was only a kid. And her mother. I know I said the comment about the parents, but I didn't really think. It's messed up to hear it, you know?"

"She broke into my house and attacked my sister. Doesn't get more messed up than that."

"Makes you second guess all the soccer moms driving around in those vans." Sarah looks back to Cabin Three, her gaze lingering over a window. I wonder if she sees shapes in the shadows too, or are they just for me? Sarah looks back at me and clears her throat. "I've canceled all reservations through January. There were only two anyway. That'll give me time to clean. You all time to… heal. I still don't get it. It's one thing after another since buying this place."

My body feels too warm, and beads of sweat trickle down my chest. But I stay put.

"Can I ask you something?" she asks, throwing in the final box. "You said something earlier, when Tilly first went missing.

You mentioned you saw Tilly at my cabin a couple of nights before. I just wondered—what were you doing out there so late?"

She's watching me in that way again.

I shift my weight between my feet.

And I don't know what makes me say it, but I chalk it up to how tired I am of sneaking around in the dark. Of lying. Of pretending.

Your secrets are mine.

"I was curious about you. So I looked in your window," I tell her. The flames flickering between us cast a fluid light over her surprised face. "That night, Tilly caught me. That's why I didn't tell her parents about the joint."

Several emotions cross her face, too fast to read. But it's her response that surprises me. "Did you find what you were looking for inside my cabin?"

No disgust after I admit to looking in. No anger or even fear.

Without her constant feeding of it, the fire begins to dim. Glowing red sparks and flaky black ash dance like confetti. I try to remember that moment. The moment I ducked and waited with my heart in my throat after thinking I'd gotten caught. She's been open to me, so I want to give her my most honest answer. "I thought I saw you. Thought you caught me. Everything else looked normal though."

"Why did you look in my windows?"

"I told you I was curious about you."

"Curiosity, huh?" She's trying to figure me out, and she can't. That bothers her. I can tell.

"I don't know." I hold her gaze for a long moment before dropping it, looking away. "I don't know what I'm saying. Maybe this place is making all of us crazy. Maybe that night I really saw Wayne's ghost," I say.

It takes a long few seconds before Sarah responds. "I've never really believed in ghosts before coming here."

"You believe in them now?"

"Maybe not the cartoonish figures clad in sheets. Or even transparent apparitions. But I believe in being haunted." The way she looks at me and then turns her head to the right. Eyes on Cabin Two.

"What are you trying to say?"

Her lips tighten into a line.

"I've been honest with you," I press.

"You and your sister," she says, "you're both haunted, aren't you? Why else would you be here?"

"You know what happened to us. You're familiar with our story."

"Why won't your sister leave the cabin? Obviously, she can. She'll walk to the bathhouse. What's stopping her?"

Lenora in the woods. Her coin on the Blacktop. Lenora running to the cabin. Showering. Washing her clothes. Not telling anyone.

Lenora leaves when she has to.

"Cassie? You don't have to answer."

"Complex post-traumatic stress disorder. Anxiety. There are probably lots of words for it."

Sarah seems to process this. "Because of what happened when you were young."

"Yes."

"Your sister," Sarah says, "she's healthy, isn't she? Apart from her struggles."

"Are you asking or insinuating?"

"No. Just wondering. You have to be the most interesting people I've ever met." Looking at Sarah's face now, I notice the lack of judgment or fear. She's not trying to get away from me, shrinking from my traits that send others running.

She simply wants to understand.

The pieces of her click into place. A woman with no friends or family nearby. A woman who lost her sibling young. Who seeks connection. Who looks at Lenora and me not with shrewdness but with envy. "I know you said your sister passed from cancer. Do you have any other family?"

"Dead." She looks back at me with wounded eyes. The loneliness is there again, and maybe it always will be. "My parents died when I was young. I have a maternal grandmother in Florida, but I haven't seen or heard from her in years."

Sarah is alone in the world, and that thought unlocks something within me. Makes me want to scoop her up. To comfort her.

I'm not familiar with any of these feelings.

Caring for another person who isn't Lenora.

Not since I was a kid.

Before that night.

The power is electric, running on a line between the two of us. I hold her stare, feel the shift in the atmosphere. The kinship between us. I want to tell her I understand. I want to tell her she's done well for herself regardless of her past. I want to let her know it will be OK.

But the thing is, I don't even know if I believe those things.

I don't belong in this fuzzy world of feelings. I don't need a friend. Don't deserve one. Look at Lenora—she can't leave the house.

She's prone to panic attacks and consistently misremembers pivotal moments in her life. And then there's me. Me with my inability to have a relationship or wear a pair of damned shoes. Me enabling my sister with no plans to stop. It's how I punish myself. These ugly parts of me feel permanent. Maybe it doesn't get better. And maybe the best thing for Sarah is to stay far away from Lenora and me.

"I'm sorry," I whisper. "I know what it's like to lose the people closest to you."

"You're lucky you have her, you know." She glances up the sloping hill toward our dark cabin. "You're lucky you have someone to suffer with."

"I know." The wilderness surrounding our campsite is expansive, a place where someone could run. Could keep secrets. But not here, in this moment. As I look into Sarah's eyes, I realize I don't want secrets anymore anyway.

I just want to feel OK.

"Can I ask you something else?" She doesn't wait for my answer. "Don't you think it's ironic that after what you've been through you picked a career in true crime? Do you think exploiting other people's trauma helps you avoid your own?"

"I don't see it as exploitation. I don't treat anyone, their life or death, the way the world treated me and Lenora."

"And how was that?"

"What?" Her question brings me up short.

"How did the world treat you?"

It's difficult to remember those years on purpose. Difficult to go back even in my own mind. "Like we were damaged goods after our father died. Like we did something wrong. Like everyone would get infected just by associating with us."

Sarah glances down, a muscle in her jaw tightening. "I can relate. When my sister was sick, it was the same way. They felt sorry for us, sure. But mostly they didn't want to be around us. Too close to death. Too depressing, I guess."

By now the fire is crumpling logs, glowing embers, and soot. The temperature drops, and it's like a dousing of cold water. I take a step back, my heel digging into a rock.

There.

The cold.

The pain.

I need to remind myself of what my life is now. Not this warmth and comfort and friendship. Sarah was wrong before. I'm not haunted by ghosts. I am the ghost.

She must sense something in my answers. My need for space. The itch to retreat to my cabin, and maybe she has that itch too. That's why we're both here, isn't it? An abandoned campsite. No neighbors. Now we have each other, but sometimes even that is too much.

Sarah smiles tightly and steps away. "I should let you go. It's late."

"If you need help cleaning out Cabin Two, just let me know."

She nods slowly, though her expression isn't decipherable, and I wonder if I did something to offend her, though I'm unsure why I care either way.

I don't say goodbye, just slink into the woods. I don't slow down until I'm through them and into the clearing at the base of our hill. When I glance back, Sarah is gone.

I let out a shaky breath and turn to Cabin One, stopping suddenly. There's someone in the window. Except it isn't a ghost or apparition or a figment of my imagination. It's Lenora standing in the dark. In a too-big T-shirt and nearly concealed by shadows, she's watching me with a completely blank expression.

I wonder how much she saw.

And, mostly, I wonder why it matters.

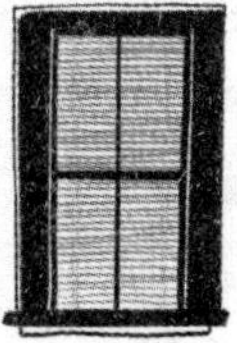

CHAPTER TWENTY-FIVE
THEN

I hear you before I see you. There should be comfort in this. In you finding me. In knowing that even when I'm drifting, you will always bring me back.

It's after midnight, and the kind of dark outside is the kind that can only exist in a starless atmosphere. A blackness I imagine only astronauts are truly familiar with. A blackness that matches the bruises on my cheek. "You shouldn't be here."

"Are you OK?" I can hear your footsteps over the rough terrain of Wellesley House. I wonder how you found me here. Why I came here at all. Especially after today. "I heard you. I wanted to check on you sooner, but Mom was up late. I covered for you. Told her you were in bed."

"How did you know I was here?"

"You weren't home. Where else would you go?" You're holding your camera, and I almost wish you'd lift it and steal a picture of me. That something about this moment might be something you want to remember.

But your arms fall to your side.

Everything feels so bleak.

"I just needed to get out of there. I just needed to breathe."

The flashes of the past few hours beat against my skull. Mom slapping my face in the car. The silent drive home. The way she wouldn't even look at me when she climbed out. Slammed the door.

I couldn't make myself go inside that house.

I didn't want you to see me like this, but clearly, I failed at protecting you again. Because you're here, and your face is crumpling as you look at the bruises on mine. Proof Mom went too far this time.

"She's never done this before. Not like this," you say. But I want to correct you. She's never done this to *you* before. This is her cycle. She shuts down and pulls away until I piss her off, and then it's as if everything explodes out of her all at once.

What's worse is afterward, she seems to regret it.

Like she doesn't understand why she cared enough to get angry in the first place.

I watch you. Watch your fear and disgust and turmoil.

There's a distracted glint in your eye. Something you want to say.

"What are you thinking?" I ask.

"Do you think they've ruined us?"

"What?" Your question takes me off guard.

"I keep thinking about us as babies," you say. "Even little girls. We were…good."

"You're still good."

Something breaks behind your eyes. "It doesn't always feel that way."

"Last summer was an accident."

"It's not even about that." You stop with a shake of your head. "Just forget it."

"Please." I step toward you. Lay a hand on your arm. "Please talk to me."

"I feel worthless." The tears fall from your eyes one by one, and I can't move or breathe. "Why are they like that? Why are our parents like this? It's all their fault, isn't it? All their fault that we are the way we are? They made us this way. They ruined us—"

I tug you forward to me. Wrap my arms around your shoulders. "No. They could never. They don't have that kind of power."

"You know I didn't mean to do it. I don't want to be like this. I don't want to be like them."

My body goes cold, and I pull back to look at you.

My perfect sister.

My perfectly screwed-up sister.

Just like me.

And it doesn't matter what we've done. It only matters that we're trying to be better. "We get to decide who we are," I say fervently. "Me and you. Not them. Their DNA inside us isn't as important as who we want to be. All the bad things that they are will end with us."

Your hands tremble when you pull away. "What if we could get away from them?"

The joke pops back in my head. Killing our parents. "You're not talking about doing something bad to them again—"

"I told you I didn't mean that." Your eyes narrow, irritation seeping into your gaze. "But wouldn't our lives be so much easier if they weren't here?"

I don't say anything right away. Just stare at your face and try to determine how serious you're being. You're unreadable. Like you're waiting for my reaction before you show anything at all.

I breathe out slowly. "It won't be like this forever. We just need to get through the next few years."

"Yeah, OK." Your face twitches, and you clear your throat. "We should get home. It's late."

My stomach drops, and I can't help but feel like I've said something wrong.

We walk home in the dark together. Not speaking. Too much was said. Too much to think about. You must be as lost in thought as me. Distracted. So much so that we walk right into it without warning.

We don't notice all the lights in the house are off, except one.

The cracked front door.

The ghostly silence.

We don't notice until we walk in, and then it's all there is. There's a feeling in the house. A tangible feeling that something is wrong. I step in front of you, push my hand against your chest to stay ahead of you. Keep you back.

An unidentifiable noise comes from the kitchen. A sliver of light slips out from beneath the door.

Someone is up.

I hold a finger to my lips and motion to the stairs. Whoever it is, if we can just make it up the stairs, we'll be fine. No one has to know we were out. But you don't listen. Your eyes are on the kitchen door, and you push past me, opening it with one motion.

I nearly stumble into you when you stop suddenly.

Dad is on the floor in front of the kitchen table. His chair is toppled, and beer is spilled all around him.

"Dad, are you OK?" You rush to his side. Grab his hand. Attempt to help him up, but I don't move. Just stare at the open can of beer.

There's a slur in his words when he says, "I'm fine."

He chuckles and belches as you help him into another chair, and I take in the room. The empty cans scattered on the table. His bloodshot eyes. "You said you were done," I say.

When he looks at me, his eyes are unfocused. He steadies himself on the table once again. "It's a couple drinks. Completely harmless. Don't be a bitch about it like your mother. I won't get lectured by my own kid."

I catch your eye across the room, and you just shake your head at me.

No. I can't do this. I won't. If he wants to ruin himself and this family, he can. But I won't stick around to watch. I turn to walk out, and Dad calls to me. "Where are you going?"

Ignoring him is easy.

Leaving you in there with him isn't.

But I manage to make it to my room, make it to my bed, before I lose it completely. I don't move even when I hear the bedroom door open and your footsteps creep toward me. I know it's you, just like I know when it's raining outside my window. It's natural. I can sense you.

You sit on the edge of the bed and stroke my hair back. "It's just a few drinks. At least it isn't the drugs."

"You know how it starts. You know he always says he has it under control, but he doesn't." My gaze must be sharper than I intend because you wince. "And he's not the only one without control. Anytime he drinks someone gets hurt." We both know I'm not just talking about us and Mom.

Kate. Joan.

Monica.

You don't say anything. But you don't move either. We sit together like that until my eyelids get heavy. Until I fall asleep.

Something wakes me.

I slide off my bed, unsure of how much time has passed. My jeans are too tight, and I'm covered in sweat. A migraine pulses behind my eyes. But there's a bigger worry. A bigger fear.

I push my door open silently and look out into the hall.

Someone is crying.

From our parents' room. I press an ear to their door. Mom is working. Earlier, she left in a rush when she picked up a shift last-minute. But the cries aren't feminine anyway. It's Dad.

I stumble back and look for you. The need inside me to just lay eyes on you is impossible to squelch. I make my way downstairs. Into the kitchen first. Maybe you got up for a drink of water or a snack. But it's empty and dark and still cluttered with mess and beer cans. The living room is empty too.

I'm just about to go check upstairs again when I hear the squeak of the porch swing. See your shadow outside, staring across the street at Mrs. Rhodes's house.

The relief is instant.

You don't see me at first, or at least you don't act like it. I close the door silently behind me and move to join you. "What are you doing out here?" Something is wrong. You still avoid my eyes, but there's just enough light from the moon and streetlights for me to see you've been crying. There's a Polaroid in your hand. Facedown so I can't see it. You tuck it under your thigh and still refuse to look at me.

I don't speak. Not at first. I join you on the swing. Pull your body against mine. There is something happening that I don't understand. I want to ask, but I can't.

Finally, you break the silence. "Do you think Mrs. Rhodes will ever stop looking for her cat?"

"She loves him."

"Would anyone ever look for us like that?"

I don't have an answer for you. Mostly because I don't think they would. If we were gone, Mom might call the cops, but eventually we'd become a memory, and she wouldn't mind. And we could be gone for months before Dad even noticed.

"I want him dead," you whisper. Your change in subject confuses me, and the impact of what you're saying makes the tiny hairs on my arms stick straight up.

"You don't mean that."

"I want them both to die."

My only response is to hold you tighter. "You're upset."

"I could do it myself. You wouldn't have to do anything."

I grab your shoulders, turn you to look at me. "What happened? Why are you saying these things?"

Your eyes fill with tears. They fall one by one, and I want to rub them away. To make sure you never cry again.

"Please," I beg. "What happened to you?"

"You know." Your voice breaks. "God, you know, don't you? Don't make me say it."

Dad's sobs roll through my head. Beat against the walls there.

When someone says something so sickening and disastrous, something with the power to alter life as you know it, the natural inclination is to resist. I try to. But the words attack, and I feel close to throwing up. I pitch forward on the swing. Brace my hands on my thighs.

A cold sweat breaks out across my forehead, and I swallow again and again to keep from being sick.

"How long?" I choke out. I don't want to know. But I have to.

"Two years."

I groan and cover my eyes. He's been doing this to you for years? He's *hurt* you for years? While I've what? While I've *slept*? The thought is impossible. It's impossible to comprehend.

"You're disgusted with me."

I whip my head toward you quickly. "No. Not with you. Never you. Him. I'm disgusted with him."

"It's the same thing at this point, isn't it? After what he did, I'm nothing now."

I choke back my repulsion and anger and focus on you. "You are everything." You look at me with surprise. "Do you have any idea how strong you are? How brave?"

"I do what he says every time. I don't try and fight back. I still give him chances. Still believe him when he says he's going to stop. I'm delusional enough to think he's magically going to turn back into the dad I always thought he was. That isn't brave. That's weakness."

"You're his child. He's supposed to protect you, and it's hardwired into your DNA to let him. That isn't your fault. Look at me. None of this is your fault. Tell me you understand."

"I can't—"

"Tell me you know he didn't ruin you." Your gaze drops, and I take your chin and gently tilt it up. "Tell me you know he's weak. He's the monster. And nothing he or anyone else ever does to you will define who you are."

"It's the drugs that make him do it."

"No." My body quivers with rage. I don't know if it's because of what you said or the fact you're still defending him in the first place. "That's offensive to every person in this world who uses drugs. Drugs don't make you do that. They may lower his inhibitions enough to act. But those thoughts and desires are there. It's not the drug's fault or yours or anyone else's. Nothing can make you do that to your own daughter except your own depravity."

You nod and wipe your eyes. "I'm sorry. I just haven't had anyone say these things to me before."

"Why didn't you tell me? That's not your fault either. But I just want to know. Is it something I did? Did you not trust me?"

"No." You shake your head and wrap your shaking hands together in your lap. "Mom is always talking about sinners and sexual sins. You remember when we started our periods? She talked to us for hours about the...urgings of the flesh. I thought if you knew, you'd see me differently. You believe everything she says."

I lay a hand over yours and try to process this from your perspective. How vulnerable you must be. How scared. "I'm so sorry you've carried this alone. I want you to know that nothing could ever make me see you differently." I pull you to me as tightly as you can go. "If God didn't want you because of something our father did, then I wouldn't want to go to heaven anyway."

"There's another sin I've been thinking about." Your whisper is hot against my neck, and I lean back to look at you. "I don't think I'll ever feel safe as long as they're alive."

"We can run away," I tell you quickly. "We don't have to wait until we're eighteen. We can go tomorrow. We can go anywhere you want."

"That won't be good enough. I'll always wonder when he'll find me. I'll never be able to heal."

I let out a breath and really think of your words. I'm angry, yes. But am I angry enough to kill?

"You understand they deserve to die. For what he did. She knows, and she doesn't stop it." You lean in, lowering your voice. "If we do this, I'll finally be able to move on. Justice will finally be paid."

"We could call the cops."

"You know that doesn't work out for girls. Look, if we don't take care of this properly, he's just going to do it to someone else, and she's going to let him."

There it is.

That's the statement that gets me.

I still feel like I have the stomach flu, my head is pounding, and I can't think past the static in my ears. But I still know we have an obligation to make sure no one ever gets hurt at his hands again.

"God asks his servants to kill people all the time," you say. "You'll help me, won't you?" The way you say it. You're God and I'm Abraham—encouraged to make an unconscionable sacrifice. It feels especially important now, my answer to you.

I'm helpless as I watch you. As you wait for an answer. As the answer comes, and you know it without me even saying it.

Anything for you, I think.

Even that.

It's not until after we're both in bed that I remember the photo you hid from me.

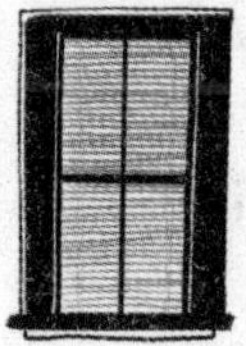

CHAPTER TWENTY-SIX
LENORA

The climax is over. This is the falling action. When things should start working for my benefit. When things should start looking up. Karen is gone. Finally, I feel safe again, and that should mean something. Whatever happened that night, I can let it go.

It doesn't mean anything.

Cassie is vacuuming the living room rug and hallway like she wields the power to erase the remnants of the past few weeks. Like scrubbing the baseboards, vacuuming a couple of rugs, and opening some windows is the key to a literal fresh start. I should be writing, but my eyes keep drifting toward the window. There's nothing to see, and I can't explain where my nerves are coming from.

I click my nails in and out.

Tell myself I'm safe. It's over. We're all alone.

But then I think of seeing Cassie and Sarah last night. Cassie and Sarah by the fire. Cassie and Sarah whispering to each other with a familiarity that made my chest concave.

When the noise of the vacuum disappears into Cassie's bedroom, I stand and walk to the window. Just to stretch my legs. Just to take one little look.

My eyes go straight for Sarah's cabin. She's sitting on a front-porch step, typing away on her laptop. Her blond hair curls around her face, and she reminds me of Tilly. I watch the way she pushes the tendrils back. The way she crosses and uncrosses her legs. We're too far away for me to make out anything else specific, but there's comfort in just watching.

She places a hand on her cheek.

I raise a hand to mine.

"Lenora?"

I spin, and Cassie is in the doorway watching me. "What are you doing? I called your name, like, three times."

"Sorry, I wasn't paying attention."

Her eyes flit to the window, then back to me. "What are you looking at?"

"I thought I saw a deer. But it was gone too fast."

She nods, looking over my shoulder once more. "Can you help me move my chest of drawers? I want to vacuum behind it."

She leads the way to her bedroom, and we each take a side of the chest of drawers. "Ready?" she asks.

I nod, and we lift together. The thing barely budges.

"What if we took the drawers out?" Before she can answer, I get on my knees in front of the bottom drawer and pull.

"Wait," Cassie says. "Don't."

But she isn't fast enough.

I see it.

I see everything.

"What is this?" I ask, staring down at the contents of the drawer. It's like a junk drawer. Small toys, a set of keys, a guitar pic, vape pens, an unopened tampon, bracelets. I sit back and look at Cassie. "Whose stuff is this?"

"It's mine." She tries to push past me, to close the drawer, but I hold up a hand and keep my position.

"Cassie." There's a quiver in my lip, in my voice. "Where did this come from?"

"It's just stuff I found, Lenora. Leave it."

"Found?"

"Yes, people leave stuff here all the time. At the Blacktop. In the bathhouse. It's not a big deal."

There's a white square of paper near the bottom. A faded ticket stub for a movie I don't recognize. I pick it up and unfold it. Something else flutters to the ground. A photo.

"I didn't know that was in there," Cassie says anxiously. "I thought it was just the ticket."

I pick up the photo, recognizing the person in it immediately. "Why do you have a picture of Sarah?"

"I told you, I thought it was just the ticket stub. I wouldn't have taken one of her photos."

"How did you even get this?"

Her cheeks darken. "No, it's not what you think. It was in a box with other junk. I just—I didn't think she'd miss it."

"You were at her house?"

"Yes. It's not a big deal."

"And you stole a picture of her as a child?" I stand to face her, to try to understand her. This is my sister who donates our expired cans and buys groceries the same time every month like clockwork. The woman I know as predictable and honest begins to waver in and out. I picture her sneaking around the campground at night. Taking things that aren't hers. Finding value in the discarded remains of other people's junk. Then lying about it. Hiding it like a dirty habit.

It doesn't sound like my sister at all, and that scares me.

Because if Cassie can do that and I have no idea, what else could she do? She's nervously tugging on her sleeves now. "Don't say it like that, Lenora. It's just a picture. A school photo. All this is just crap. No one cares."

A collector of trash. It would be funny if it weren't so damned ironic. Did it start after that night? Is it some incessant need inside her to find value in the maltreated and forgotten? Is it her way of sticking it to the world? Their trash, her treasure.

"So why do you do it?" I ask desperately, feeling like a boulder rolling toward an answer I don't really want to hear. "Why do you care? Why do you keep this stuff?"

"Because it's abandoned," she says, her chest heaving. "They left it like trash. Or treat it like trash. Whatever. It doesn't hurt anyone."

"Cassie—"

"No, you don't get to look at me like that. You of all people. *You*, Lenora? Staring out that window again because you never seem to learn your lesson. Too afraid to walk outside. You? No, you don't get to judge me."

I jerk back in surprise, not quite recognizing her in this moment. I sneer. "At least I'm trying to get help. I do therapy. I try every day to get better. You just act like you're doing nothing wrong at all. But you're collecting things. Collecting what other people throw away. Is that what you've done with me too?"

"Don't psychoanalyze me."

"You act like you're so normal. Like I'm the messed-up one. But it's not true, is it?" Saying it is like a pipe bursting. All the things I thought were my fault. The pain and guilt from our childhood and what happened that night when Cassie somehow stayed herself. All the ways I've felt guilty for holding Cassie back. When it hasn't been me at all. It's been her. She's the one who found the cabin. Who proposed our stay here. I'm the ticket stub shoved into the drawer.

"You think I believe I'm normal? I live in the wilderness with my agoraphobic sister. You think this is normal? I should have a family, a life, a career, children. Something. I should have something more than *this*." She waves around us. Her tiny room. This cabin. Me. She should have more than that.

I breathe out heavily. "You think I don't want those things? You think I want you here if you don't want to be here?"

"You think I can leave?" She steps toward me when she says it. Until we're chest to chest. "You think I can leave you?" A beat passes. A breath between us.

"That never stopped you before."

"Do you remember what happened the last time I tried?"

"We're adults now, and she's not here. They're gone. You don't have to protect me, Cassie."

She laughs, and it's as hollow as I feel. "She may not be here, but she isn't gone. If she were actually gone, then I would have a choice. We're tangled, you and I. Don't you see that? Two roots of the same tree, fused together, forced to grow in the world's shittiest conditions."

"You think I chose this?" With that question comes an influx of memories. Cassie and me playing at the end of the cul-de-sac. Making milkshakes in our kitchen. Playing Rock, Paper, Scissors on the school bus. Crying. Laughing. Loving. Escaping.

After that night, we stuck together because it was what we always did. What we were supposed to do. The days turned into months and into years. This whole time, as I worked aggressively through therapy, I never forsook the possibility of everything Cassie mentioned. In my mind, we would have careers one day. Maybe families. Each have a partner and kids.

We'd buy houses nearby. Barbeque on the weekends. Take relaxing day trips to the beach. Those were all possibilities. And the mounting panic inside me comes from one thing. One truth. My hope always rode on Cassie. If she could escape that night not completely messed up, then I could get better. I could work through my triggers and memories. We could get out of here one day. But it seems like with every day that passes, we become worse than before. Tilly is dead. Someone killed her. Someone who's still out there.

I don't remember that night.

Cassie is hiding things.

The images and hopes and dreams chip away piece by piece until they're scattered around us, and I'm looking at my sister and thinking that maybe there isn't hope. Maybe we're both too far gone.

There is a memory. Our smiling mother glancing at us through the interior rearview mirror. Sun too hot on my bare arm. Windows down and whipping the hair around our faces.

The best gift I ever gave you girls was each other, she said more to herself than to us. Like she was still convincing herself our births weren't a mistake. There was a purpose for the pain bigger than all three of us.

"It doesn't matter," Cassie says weakly. She looks as broken as me, and the part of me that's always wanted to protect her bares its teeth. The two conflicting sides are at war.

Clearly, she's struggling too. She doesn't want to hurt me. But sometimes hurt is inevitable. She takes the photo from my hand and slips it into her pocket. Her gaze clashes with mine. "It really doesn't matter what you wanted or what I wanted. It's still your fault we're here."

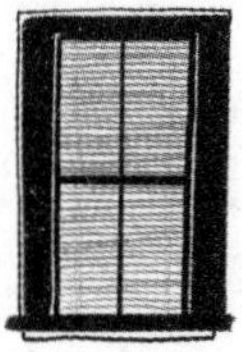

CHAPTER TWENTY-SEVEN
THEN

I tell myself I feel lighter after our conversation on the porch. Under the tent of darkness and the gentle humming of cars from the highway when you told me your deepest desire. Even our neighbors weren't outside or playing music. It was just me and you.

I said yes, and it all made sense.

I wanted it to make sense.

I should feel weighed down and plagued by what he has done to you. By what I've *let* him do to you thanks to my own ignorance. But all this is a blip. It has to be. Our roads are converging into a new path, and on it I'll help you heal. I'll help you get therapy. We'll get through this together.

We'll kill them.

My heart sprints each time I think it. It's absurd is what it is. Inconceivable. It would be different if you'd only mentioned it the one time and called it a joke. But yesterday you weren't joking, and I tossed under my sheets all night plagued by the choice.

They deserve to die. They don't. Like a kid prying the petals from a flower one after another, my answer changed each time another petal hit the ground. They deserve to die. They don't. They deserve to die. They don't.

This morning, I choose not to think of it.

Dad is gone in the morning. No note. Makes me wonder if there's always been a meaning behind his disappearances. Every time he's fled in the night, and we've woken to an empty house with discarded cans or needles on the coffee table, was this the reason behind it?

Each time Mom angrily shouted at us to clean, were you cowering beneath the weight of violence endured at the hands meant to cherish you most?

They deserve to die.

No mess in the kitchen. Mom doesn't say a word either. She sips her coffee at the table, staring out the back window. When she hears me behind her, she glances back, something shuttering in her expression, and it's the first time I notice it, the emptiness behind her eyes.

Has it always been there?

Or did Dad put it there just like he did you?

How much does she know?

I clear my throat. "Mom."

No reaction. No acknowledgment on her face.

"Did Dad leave? Is he gone?"

She holds the coffee to her mouth and looks away from me. Back to the window. "It's nothing new. Same as he always does." Astonishingly there isn't anger in her tone. Just disappointment. She clears her throat. "There are bagels in the cabinet."

I'm not hungry, but I feel like I should make one just because she says it. Mom doesn't mother often. If that's even what you'd call this. Pathetic, really. That I cling so fully to every crumb of attention she tosses at my feet.

I picture you and me on either side of her bed. The glint of silver in the darkening night.

I wince. Spread some peanut butter on the bagel in silence. Walk to the doorway and look at my mother. Her hunched shoulders. The sickly pallor to her skin. The rumpled scrubs. "I'm sorry," I say, not really knowing what I'm apologizing for. Thinking of killing her. Our father leaving. The way she seems to age double every year.

She glances at me sharply in surprise.

In this moment, I can't imagine actually going through with any of it. Killing our mother? There has to be another way.

I walk to the restaurant unable to stop myself from imagining how it would happen.

Our mother screaming.

The two of us on her.

Hurting her.

I close my eyes. Physically jolt against the images. I feel weak for it. Knowing how she's hurt me, and he's hurt you, and they've hurt us. Because it's all the same, isn't it? When one of us is hurt, we both are. You're me and I'm you.

I'm weak because I couldn't protect you.

Even weaker because I can't give you what you want now.

But there is another way. A way we both could get what we want. A way I could protect you, and we'd never have to see our parents again.

We could run away.

You were angry last night. You want our parents dead just like half the other teens in America. Sometimes I even feel the same way. But I know you. I know you don't mean it. You wouldn't be able to go through with it. I just need to get you away from them. Then everything will be better. After I get my last paycheck on Friday, we're taking off. And we won't ever have to see either of our parents again. They'll be dead to us in every sense of the word.

My shift goes by quickly without any hiccups, and the newfound hope doesn't leave me. The feeling of freedom is at my fingertips, and it tastes so sweet already. I just need to explain the plan to you. Promise you that I will protect you. That I'm capable of keeping you safe in a world where our parents exist. I run home, my slip-resistant shoes sticking to the pavement with every slap of my feet to the ground. I didn't even take the time to change.

I just need to get to you.

I cross the road to our home, and the feeling deserts me for the first time all day. I stop cold at the edge of the driveway. At the sight of you beside *her*. You're both laughing.

Gone is the crying girl you were last night.

The agony in your eyes as we shared secrets that could destroy us both.

You're someone else with her.

And my stomach plummets.

I should have expected this. Of course, you needed to say goodbye to her. But if that's the case, why do you and Monica appear so happy?

I stand there for another minute before you finally walk away toward our front door. You go inside like nothing is wrong, like you're perfectly content still. Monica is heading down the street.

The door closes behind you, and I call out to her. "Hey!"

Monica turns quickly, her brows pulled together, relaxing only when she notices me. "Oh, hi."

"My sister mentioned you were coming to our school next year."

She seems surprised I'm talking to her, but her face instantly shifts into a warm smile. "Yeah, I am." That hair is piled on top of her head today, the feathers tucked in so there are little streaks of color woven in. She must think she's such a cool girl.

"Where do you live?"

"Uh." She glances from me to the front door, her smile slipping. "The group home two blocks over."

I can't help but smile. It all makes sense now. Why you're so obsessed with her. She's a lost little doll without a family. You've always found value in things others might find worthless.

There is instant relief that comes with this assessment. This girl is a stage. You'll be over her soon enough. I work to control my expression. Monica is watching me warily, her eyes flicking to our house like she hopes you will walk out any second to save her from me. "You don't have parents?" I ask.

Her mouth parts on a breath. She only shakes her head. No wonder you were so drawn to her. I sigh. "I figured as much. My sister told me. That's why she likes you. Thinks you understand what it's like to have a messed-up life."

She doesn't say anything, and I take a step closer. "Look, she's not going to say this because she probably doesn't want to hurt you, but we're leaving."

"Your family is moving?"

"No. Just us. On Friday. I don't know what she's been telling you about how she feels, but it's important you let her go without a fuss. You understand that, don't you? She needs a clean break."

Monica steps away from me. "She didn't tell me."

"And she wouldn't. She doesn't want to hurt you. But you've got to let her go. Make it easier on her. That is, if you're really her friend."

"Did something happen? I mean, is everything OK?"

I give her a long look, curling my top lip. "I think if she wanted you to know the answer to that, then she would have told you."

The girl looks away sharply and nods with tears quickly filling her eyes.

"Maybe you don't know her as well as you think."

And she's gone without another word or look, walking briskly down the street. I hope it's the last time I ever have to see her.

For her sake and mine.

When I finally go inside, you're in the kitchen making a peanut butter sandwich. You look at me, then look away quickly, almost like you're embarrassed. The thought is silly. Nothing about last night should be embarrassing for you. Learning your truth, developing a plan to escape it—it was honestly the best night of my life.

"I moved the luggage out of the garage," I say.

You keep chewing, but your gaze moves to me. "For what?"

"To pack. We should go ahead and get started on it. Figure out what we're taking." I glance behind me at the door. Mom isn't home, and Dad shouldn't be, but still.

You swallow, and there's a glob of peanut butter at the corner of your mouth. You don't wipe it away. You're motionless.

"You remember what we talked about last night? Just me and you." It feels weird having this discussion in the daylight while you nibble on a sandwich like we're talking about the weather.

You avert your eyes and chew softly, a strange expression covering your face. "I don't remember our conversation going like that."

"That's what we need to talk about," I say, crossing the room to you. "This plan will be better. There's less risk. More opportunity. We'll still never have to see them again."

"I don't know." You wipe your face, still averting your eyes.

"You don't know what? Are you scared? Is that what this is about?"

"What about money? A place to live? If…they're no longer alive, then we could get money for it. Life insurance. It would help us start our new life."

"We're practically adults. We'll get jobs. We'll figure it out."

You set the sandwich down. Swipe at your mouth again with the back of your hand. You move too quickly and nervously. "You told me you would be there for me. You said you would help me."

"It is. I am," I say, crossing the room to you. "Don't you get it? If we do what you're asking, our lives could be over. It could be the one thing that breaks us apart forever."

"It's what I *want*." There's a bite to your voice. A tone that has me flinching backward. And your face. There's an expression there I've never seen before.

A seething anger.

It's like you realize it all at once and look away a little too quickly. "Sorry. I didn't mean to snap. I just thought we had a plan.

I was feeling relief because I thought you were finally going to help me, and I wouldn't have to face him alone anymore."

Of course. Of course, you reacted that way. Here I am, changing the plans when you're so afraid. I can't help but tell you what you want to hear. "Just let me think about it? Please? And you think about my idea. I'm not saying no, but let's just think on everything."

You nod, take another bite of your sandwich, and say around a full mouth, "The insurance money would help. I know Mom is covered."

I feel sick.

"I'm going to think about it," I say numbly.

And you smile. A smile that lights your entire face. It makes my nausea ease. How could something feel so wrong when it makes you look like that?

"I knew you would be there for me. I knew you wouldn't abandon me again."

"I never meant to abandon you in the first place."

You brush past me as you walk toward the door.

But there's one thing I haven't asked. One thing burning a hole on my tongue. "It isn't her, is it? The reason you don't want to run away? That girl? You think you can take our parents out of the equation and stay here. For her."

You don't answer.

You don't even look back at me.

Mom takes an extra shift, and Dad doesn't come home. I'm alone and a bundle of nerves because you're gone too.

It's after midnight, and your bed is empty. It feels like my body is thrumming with electricity. I can't concentrate on anything except wondering where you are. If you're with her.

And if you are, what does that mean?

Because it feels like you're stepping over a line. You're choosing her when you should be choosing us, and that destroys me more than your confession last night.

I pace the room.

Moving because I can't sit still. Can't just wait for you like this is OK.

Back and forth. Back and forth. Until I can't take it anymore. I slam a fist onto your mattress. And another. I keep going until I am flailing limbs, heavy breaths, and silent screams.

She deserves to die.

She doesn't.

More petals fluttering to the ground. More choices to be made.

The mattress slides, and I bear down on both my fists, trying desperately to get ahold of myself. You could be home any minute. I can't let you see me like this.

I lean back to pull away, and that's when I see it. Where the mattress has shifted at the corner, something paperlike sticks out. I reach for it. Ease it out.

The bugs finally stop.

My blood congeals.

Heart splinters.

A photo of Kate Wellesley. Not one I've ever seen before. Not when they dedicated that billboard to her. Not when the school made that slideshow that we all had to sit in the auditorium to watch. Not even one from the funeral. It's a picture of Kate through her bedroom window. The bedroom window of Wellesley House, back when it was the proudest house in town. Her head is down, her pen poised in her hand as she sits at her desk.

I don't want to. Everything in me screams against it, but I push the mattress farther off the box spring.

And there are more. So many more.

Kate walking home with headphones on and her hair blowing in the wind. Kate's profile on the bus. Kate kissing her boyfriend in the front seat of his car. Kate sunbathing in her front yard.

Then I stop, and my stomach recoils.

Not Kate.

Monica. Monica with her feathered hair. Monica laughing as she waits at the bus stop. Monica grinning with her tongue out. Some of these photos, it's clear Monica is posing and well aware of the camera aimed at her. But some are like the ones of Kate. Pictures where Monica doesn't seem to be aware of the camera at all.

You've been lying to me. About everything.

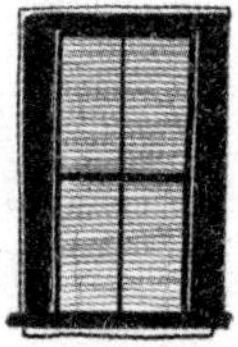

CHAPTER TWENTY-EIGHT
CASSIE

The memory keeps me awake, the guilt like a cloying perfume tickling the back of my nostrils. Draining down my throat. I stare up at the ceiling, my whole body coiled tightly. No feeling in my clenched hands. The memory plays out, and every moment is a reminder of how I failed.

That night it all went wrong.

A few hours ago, when I threw it back in Lenora's face, it was like I literally slapped her. But we both know my words aren't true. It isn't her fault we're here. It's mine. It's all mine because I'm the one who wasn't there.

I didn't mean to leave her that night.

Run! Footsteps. A scream for help. A glance back over my shoulder. Scared. So scared. Forward. Get out. Get out. Get out.

I roll over and press my face into the pillow and scream as loudly as I can. Until the muffled noise carries through the room and my throat is raw. I scream because she's right.

I did leave her.

And I have spent the past fifteen years trying to pretend I didn't. That's where my guilt lives and breathes. A swampy area in my head that I like to pretend doesn't exist. My phone rings from the bedside table, and my fingers are as numb as my brain when I answer without looking.

"Is this Cassie?"

I sit up a little straighter, recognizing the voice right away. "Detective Eubanks?"

"Listen," she says quickly and succinctly. "This is a courtesy call for you and your sister. Karen Meadows has been released."

I hold the phone tighter to my ear. "I thought she was arrested."

There's a long pause. "It didn't stick. The district attorney general made the call. It's out of my hands. There's just not enough evidence to charge. But if you both still want to press charges for breaking and entering—"

I hang up numbly. Stare at my phone. Feel my heart hammering all the way up my throat.

Then I dial his number on instinct.

Because I don't want to think of anything else.

Not right now.

His answer is quick and breathy. "I can't do this tonight," he says. There's someone in the background. Music. It makes my heart yearn. I should be there with him. Dancing and laughing. But I'm here, slowly suffocating to death.

"I'm sorry. I know you don't want to hear it, but I am." I think of Lenora. Of Parker's question: *You think this is normal?* "I can't do this anymore. I just—I need a break."

"Cassie—"

"I know this isn't fair to you. But I need you. I want to be different, Parker. I can't keep living this way."

There's a moment of silence before he sighs. "I'm on my way."

He meets me in my darkness, and our bodies wage a war against each other, but when it's all said and done, I still hate myself. Because he's not who I'm at war with. He's not who I want to fight, and he must know it.

We lie side by side. I'm sweaty and stiff under the sheets, being careful not to touch him. I don't know how to do this. The after. The nonphysical part of connection. Should I roll over and lay my head on his chest when all I want to do is run? Should I tighten the sheets around us both when I'm so warm, I want to peel off my own skin?

"I can tell there's something wrong, Cassie. You're different."

"Is it because I apologized?" I ask, but I'm partly stalling. I'm different because I haven't asked him to leave yet, and I don't know what I'm trying to prove.

He rolls over without tucking the sheet around him. Bare. In front of me like there's nothing to hide. I pull the sheet up to my chin, and I don't face him. Instead, I stare up at the ceiling fan. It's not on. Why didn't I turn it on?

Suddenly, there is nothing I want more than air. A jog outside. Maybe Sarah will be on her porch. She'll invite me to sit. And I'll talk to her. I'll finally be able to breathe.

"Is something wrong with your sister?"

"No."

"I can tell something happened, Cassie. You called me over here. *Talk* to me. Please."

"Did you know that in 1970, there was a dolphin in captivity?" I roll sideways to look at him, and the action seems to surprise him. He tucks a strand of my hair behind my ear, and I force myself to stay in place, to not pull back. "A beloved dolphin who liked being around people and other dolphins but was moved to a different tank where she was alone. She grew more depressed every day. One day she sank to the bottom of the tank and refused to surface. She died, and I've spent every day wondering if she knew she wanted to die or...or if she was simply tired of swimming."

"Cassie—"

"I'm fine." I lean forward and kiss his cheek. It causes my sheet to slip, and I yank it back up. Tighter. Everything feels awkward and mechanical, like I'm just a little girl playing dress-up. His stubble is rough and longer than usual, and it reminds me of my father.

And I hate that thought.

"Thank you for coming. Really." He sits up, and I place a hand on his arm. "No, wait. I told you this is different. I want you to stay."

He slides back down, and I lay my head on his chest.

I try to think of the rough hair scraping my cheek or the sound of his heart against my ear. I hold him tight and wish to myself that it will be enough.

When I open my eyes next, the room is filled with smoke.

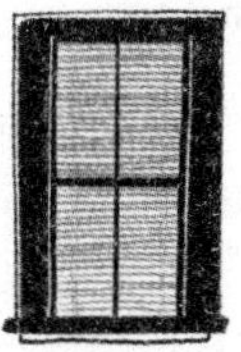

CHAPTER TWENTY-NINE
LENORA

Cassie's hand is in mine as we walk down the long hallway. To Mom's room. We ignore the weird noises. The weird feeling in our stomachs. And I say "we" because I know Cassie feels it too. It's been like that since we were kids. She was me. I was her. We were the same.

A ray of light shines from the crack of the door, and I tug on her hand.

She ignores me, or maybe she doesn't feel me at all, and she stops. Looks at me, a grin on her face. "Go on," she says.

But I shake my head. This isn't right, and I tell her as much. Tell her this isn't how the memory goes. We're supposed to walk to the door together. We face it together. Always.

She backs away slowly, her hands in the air. "Not this. This is all you, Lenora. This is all your fault. My hands are clean."

"No, wait. Please don't leave me." But my voice is weak; my legs won't move to follow her even as the panic builds.

She gives me one last mischievous look over her shoulder and disappears down the stairs. I'm alone in the hall.

I steel myself, turn back toward my parents' bedroom, know what I have to do next.

But it's different now. The door is open. And there's something on the ground. Leaking toward me. Slimy, red.

Blood.

It surrounds me quickly, pooling around my feet. I scream, grab for the wall, but my hands are slick, and I leave a sliding red handprint.

"Cassie!" I scream her name. Somewhere downstairs, I hear her laughing.

I blink away the remnants of sleep as the darkness releases its grip on me. My environment doesn't make sense at first. The cold. The pain in my feet. The deep-rooted confusion.

I'm in the woods.

The disorientation nearly knocks me off-balance. I sway against it and the cold, my bare feet curling into the hard dirt. The pads of my toes are raw, like I've been walking for a while. I'm wearing the T-shirt and leggings I fell asleep in and nothing else. The icy air creeps around me, burrowing into my skin.

How did I get here? Where *is* here? I turn in circles, trying to gather my bearings, trying to make sense of where I am. There's no path or marked trail. At least none that I can see. I'm not wearing glasses or contacts.

I know I must be on the campsite somewhere, but the world is a blurry landscape engulfing me.

"Cassie?" I try and call my sister's name. My voice is rough and low, and I can't seem to get it higher. The panic swells like an ocean wave pounding against the shore. I push it back, swim through it, dive into it—anything not to drown in its depths. "Cassie?" I call again, louder now.

There's a rustle behind me, and I whirl around, squinting into the black forest. The shapes are meaningless, and my skin crawls with vulnerability. I can't see anything. I know what should be there. Willowy trees and naked spindly branches. An animal, maybe. But there's something else. A light.

I rub my eyes.

No, not a light. A fire.

I take off running.

The closer I get, the more my surroundings come together. The bathhouse. Cabin Three. I don't stop and dwell. I don't try to make sense of anything else. I run. Up, up, up the hill. Until the heat is an oven door opening on my face.

And then I stop.

Just a single second to take in the vibrant orange and blazing reds. Our home burning. I scream. So loudly. So agonizingly loudly. I can't take this. I can't take any of this. Cassie is inside that cabin.

Movement to my left.

Just beside our burning cabin.

A person standing in a mist of smoke and shadow. I squint in the dark but can't make out any features. Is it Cassie? Has she gotten out? I step toward them, lift my hand in a wave. Hope builds inside me. She's made it out. She's safe.

But the person sinks backward into the thick forest. I look from where they ran and back to the cabin. That couldn't have been her. She wouldn't have left me. Which means Cassie is still inside.

My sister.

There is no more thinking or observing or stopping. There is only action. Running around the side of the cabin. Everything is too blurry for me to understand the severity of the flames. I only know that whatever time I have left to get Cassie out, it's slipping away.

Something crashes through the window. A person rolling onto their back on the grass and coughing. A man. He sees me, sits up. "Cassie?"

"She's not with you?"

I can't make out his face, but his coughs are loud and wretched, and the glass from the window is embedded in his arm.

"I thought—She wasn't in bed. I thought she got out."

"You thought she got out, or you know she's out?"

He coughs again, a deep hacking sound. "I don't know."

I want to scream again. I want to collapse and rock and scream. But there isn't time. Cassie might still be in there.

"Hey." He wheezes, trying to sit up. "You can't go in there."

But I don't listen.

I slide over the broken glass, ignoring the slices and the pinches. I pull my shirt over my mouth and squint. It's impossible to see. Impossible to breathe. "Cassie—" But I'm coughing. I can't get the words out.

I slide inside, get on my hands and knees. The room is completely full of smoke. Something crashes outside the door like the house is falling around us. I want to call my sister's name, but I can't. I can't breathe at all. My body sways side to side. But I keep moving forward. Just a little more—there.

I bump into something hot and soft and solid.

The coughs can't be stopped, and my chest heaves as I feel for her. As I place my hands on her chest and feel for breaths. Yes. Movement. There is no celebration. There is only me, trying to stay low, as I slide my arms under her. I can't see behind me. Can't figure out where I came from or where the window is.

So I keep pulling. Inch by inch.

I'm swaying again, stumbling. We're both on the ground, a tangle of limbs and tears. I can't even say her name. I try to take a breath, but it all feels like too much.

There's a voice I faintly recognize. A flash of light.

I force myself up again. Grab my sister, my hands tangled in her hair as I pull. Back, back, back. Toward the light.

"There they are."

Hands on me.

"No," I say and heave Cassie up. "Take her."

That's all I can say. All I can think.

Suddenly the world is too heavy, and I fall.

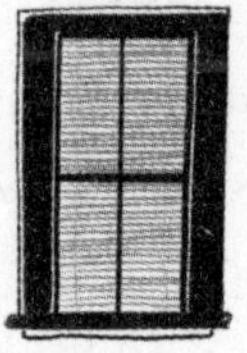

CHAPTER THIRTY

CASSIE

Someone is shoving a curling iron down my throat. That's my first thought as my eyes flutter open and the world falls into place around me. A world I don't recognize. A room I don't recognize. I blink blurrily.

Feel a warm hand in mine.

"You're awake." A hoarse whisper. Relief fills me as the memories come falling back. Waking in a smoky room. Rolling off my bed, dragging pants on, with one thought on my mind: *I have to get my sister out.* That's the last thing I remember. The panic squeezing my insides that was worse than the smoke, than the pain I'm in now.

I squeeze her hand. "You're alive."

We're in a hospital room. It's gray and small, and I'm uncomfortable. Something is in my nose. An IV is in my wrist. But the relief nearly cripples me. Lenora is here. She's in an old T-shirt that smells like a bonfire, and she's dirty, from her matted hair to the dirt under her nails and on her jaw.

"We're alive."

"I woke up and tried to get to you." I swallow past the roughness in my throat. "But the smoke was too thick. I couldn't see." I blink at her in disbelief. "You're here, Lenora. You're out of the cabin."

She shushes me, tears wetting her lashes. "Here." Like always, she seems to know exactly what I need. She hands me a cup of water with a long straw and places the straw to my lips. I drink the water in one go, and I'm still thirsty, but I need answers more.

"You're here," I say again, shaking my head in confusion. "You left the cabin."

"There is no cabin, Cassie." Lenora's voice is small, tortured. She's putting on a brave face, but I can sense the wariness in her. The vulnerability. "It's gone. Everything's gone. But you. You're my home. Where you go, I go." She means it literally, but there's also another meaning there. One only I will understand. Because last night we were both willing to die with each other.

"How?" I clear my throat. "How did we get out? What happened?" Then another thought. "Parker. He was there. He was with me—"

"He's fine," Lenora says. "He was here, actually. He left an hour ago. Stayed all night. He wasn't injured. Managed to crawl out a window. He doesn't have a phone anymore, but he told me he'll be back."

I sit back. Reach for her hand again.

And she tells me the rest.

She woke up in the woods. Sleepwalking. I can't even be upset about it. It saved both our lives. She saw the light from the cabin and ran toward it. Without being able to see well, she managed to find my bedroom window when Parker busted out of it. She went in and found me. Got me back to the window, and Sarah and Parker pulled us the rest of the way out.

"I woke up here too." She says, "A few hours of monitoring and oxygen, and I was fine. You inhaled smoke for much longer, and they wanted to keep you overnight."

"You haven't left?"

"I couldn't."

I hold my wrist up with the IV.

"Fluids and antibiotics. To prevent infection," she clarifies.

The reality of the situation hits me, and it's hard to swallow. We lost everything. We almost died. "The fire," I ask. "What caused it?"

Lenora looks down and away, an odd expression crossing her face. "They found accelerant at the cabin. The detectives think someone set the fire on purpose. Whoever did it must have dismantled the fire alarms first."

"Someone wanted to kill us."

"The detectives want to talk to us. I haven't yet. I was waiting on you."

I nod and attempt to take it all in. Let it absorb. But she's making another face. "What is it, Lenora?"

She breathes out heavily. "I think I saw them. I think I saw the person who started the fire."

Lenora is right. Parker comes back. He's showered and fully dressed. It's strange seeing him somewhere outside my cabin. A cabin that no longer exists.

"Hey," he says, coming to my side as soon as he sees my eyes are open.

I lift a finger to my lips, then wince. He follows my gaze to where Lenora is curled up on an uncomfortable-looking chair. She's only just fallen asleep. I can't make myself do the same.

He stands stiffly like he isn't sure whether to touch me or what to say. "You're awake."

"Yeah."

"I'm sorry." Parker kneels, leaning into my bed. "When I woke, you weren't in the bed. I thought you'd gotten out. There was smoke everywhere. I couldn't see you—"

"Parker," I cut him off, my voice low and raspy. It's been a few hours since I woke up, but my voice still hasn't fully come back. I still taste the smoke in my throat. I think for as long as I live, I'll associate that taste with fear. "It's OK. I'm just glad you made it. I don't know what happened."

But in some ways, I do. Lenora confirmed it. Someone had set the fire on purpose. She said she'd seen someone running from the cabin into the woods and thought it was me at first.

Someone was there.

Someone did this.

And I didn't tell Lenora what I know. That Karen was released last night.

Parker looks down, his eyes shifting to Lenora for only a second, then back to me again. There's something he isn't saying.

"What's wrong?"

"I was in your kitchen last night, Cassie. After you went to sleep. I saw her leave. Your sister."

"What?"

"She walked right past me."

"She was sleepwalking. She does that sometimes."

His brows furrow; his voice lowers as he leans closer. "You don't think that's strange?"

"I don't know what you're trying to say."

"You don't think it's strange that the one time I stay the night, someone lights your house on fire? And on that night, your sister happens to have gotten out?"

I bristle, angry at first that he'd even suggest…whatever it is he's suggesting. "Are you insinuating my sister set the fire? If that's true, why would she risk her life going back in to save me?"

"What if she never meant for you to die? What if she just wanted to send you a message?"

Lenora stirs, and we both freeze. I feel dirty. Not just from the soot and sweat layering my body. But from his words. My thoughts. Visions of my sister sneaking out of my house at night. Leaving on purpose. Pouring accelerant. Lighting a match.

No.

She wouldn't.

"She saw someone," I whisper. "She told me. Besides, where would she have even gotten the accelerant?"

"There was no one else out there, Cassie. No one except me, your landlord, and your sister."

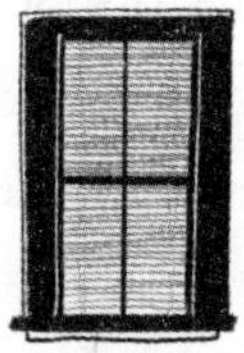

CHAPTER THIRTY-ONE
LENORA

The view is different here.

Looking out the window of Cabin Three and staring up at the burnt rubble that used to be our home. Seeing the world through a different lens. A lens where someone is trying to kill us, and by some other power—or maybe by our own—Cassie and I did it again. We survived.

I squeeze my hands together and count.

Make it to two hundred and fifty, but it doesn't help. Nothing helps the sinking feeling inside me. I just keep drifting deeper and deeper into some unseen abyss. The panic. The fear. The nerves. I can't control the feeling of spiraling. The feeling that I've had ever since waking in those woods and knowing something was terribly wrong.

Sarah and Cassie speak in hushed voices on the porch. Sarah picked us up from the hospital as soon as we were discharged. The first thing she did was make a stop at our eye doctor to pick up a pair of contacts for each of us, and when we made it here, she told us she cleaned the place up, and we're free to stay as long as it takes.

But there's something behind her eyes. A fear. And I don't know where it comes from, only that I've seen it in Cassie's eyes too. When I woke from a nap that had turned into a deep sleep. I saw her sitting alone, staring at me.

She said she was fine when I prodded, but I can't help but feel like I'm missing something.

They've been careful around me. Careful not to talk about what's actually happening. The fact someone tried to kill us. Anytime I try to bring it up, there's a subject change. I kept waiting for the detectives to show up, but Cassie said she asked them to wait a couple of days and give us time to recoup.

I think that's where my anxiety comes from.

The waiting.

Then there's the matter of the figure in the woods. The person I saw leaving the cabin. Who was it? Who would do something like this? Cassie and I don't really talk to anyone. Unless you count her nearly one million subscribers. But even they don't know where we live.

The sick feeling in my chest is thick and suffocating. A wad of mucous that I can't cough up. My fingertips are raw, and my nails are wearing down.

Too much is up in the air.

I turn and look for Cassie. She's in the same spot by the door, and it's the only sight that calms me. Reminds me I'm not floating away or dead. Cassie and I survived. It's what we do best, and we can do it again. Cassie catches my eye. Holds it.

And I breathe.

I just try to breathe.

"Lenora?" she calls. "I'm going to run to the store with Sarah for groceries and toiletries. You want to come?"

I've been out. Out of my cabin for the longest I've been since I moved in. I'm still out. But can't go any farther. The thought makes me tremble. Can't leave. The hospital nearly undid me. It took every ounce of my strength to stay there, and I think it was only Cassie being there that gave me that strength.

I could do anything for her.

I shake my head at her now. Look away. I'm too tired. I just need a minute. "I'm good here. I should wash the clothes we were wearing so they're ready for us." Sarah gave us some of her clothes, pants I have to roll up and a sweatshirt that's nearly to my knees, but the clothes Cassie and I were wearing the night of the fire still smell of smoke and are currently in a plastic bag by the door.

"Why don't you come, and we'll drop them off at the laundromat?"

"That's OK."

"You'll have to do it by hand. There's no washing machine in this cabin."

"I can handle it, Cassie."

She looks disappointed. Hesitant even. "We don't have phones. What if I need to get ahold of you?"

"I'm right here. I'll lock the doors."

"I can hang back," Sarah says quickly, padding over to us barefoot. Her shoes are discarded by the door, and I can't help but wonder when she became so comfortable around us. "How about I cook dinner? I'll bring it over later. Have it ready for you guys."

"You don't have to do that," Cassie starts, but Sarah waves her off.

"We'll be here. You go do what you need to do."

Cassie nods, holding her gaze like they're exchanging some unspoken message. She looks back at me one more time. "Are you good?"

My mouth is dry, and I'm suddenly tired. So tired. "Yes." But I'm lying. I'm anything but good. And I can't figure out why Sarah and Cassie are so afraid to leave me alone.

I stay by the window until dusk. Until daylight fades and night creeps in. I'm aware of Sarah in her cabin. The light coming from it. The feeling of not quite being alone. But Cassie still isn't back, and my heart won't slow down.

As the sun sinks and the cabin is streaked with shadows, I think of that night. And Tilly. I think of her last day here. Where she slept. Where she ate. Something about the thoughts prevents me from going deeper into the cabin. I don't want to explore it, don't want to *know*. I just want to go home.

It makes my breath catch.

What is home?

Where is it?

When I used to close my eyes and think of home, I'd see the house we grew up in. The house in our old neighborhood. And then the cabin.

Now I just see Cassie.

I stay by the window until Sarah walks over with a casserole dish and a giant bowl. She smiles when I open the door, but it slowly drops from her face when she glances at the plastic bag at her feet. Notices my chair by the window. "Have you been sitting here this whole time?"

For some reason, I feel the need to explain myself. "I guess I lost track of time," I mumble.

She nods a little too energetically. Makes me curious if she's taking notes. Listing every weird thing I do to tell my sister as soon as she walks through the door. "It's chicken casserole. I'll set it up on the table. Cassie not back yet?"

"No."

She's silent as she peels the aluminum foil off the top of the dish and does the same to a salad bowl. Placing them on the table, then walking to the cabinet for dishes and silverware. There's an awkward silence. One that screams at me that I don't really know Sarah.

Least not in the way Cassie does.

Sarah is looking at me expectantly.

"I'm sorry. Did you say something?"

"I just said it's lucky you were outside."

Sarah places the plates down and looks at me. "Last night, I mean. You were able to come back and save your sister. That's lucky."

"Yeah, I guess."

"Cassie said you were sleepwalking."

"I've done it since I was a kid."

"Fascinating."

"I've always hated it." Among many other things about myself.

"But it saved both of your lives. That should count for something, right?" Sarah's smile is genuine. Just like earlier when she offered to hang back with me; she seemed like she really cared. It's strange to have that come from someone who isn't my sister. Sarah moves around the kitchen, oblivious to my thoughts. Her hair is in a messy bun, but one of those that look good, with wisps that frame your face. Not the kind Cassie or I wear when we go too long without washing our hair. Her hands are long and thin. They hold cups. Pour drinks. Gently open the refrigerator.

There's a shake to her movements.

A tremble.

"You're scared of something," I say. "You and my sister. You didn't want me to be alone."

She stops across the kitchen, braces herself on the countertop restlessly. "It's not that we're scared. We're worried. After the fire and with Karen out—"

"Wait, what do you mean out? Like, out of jail?" This must be what a flight-or-fight response feels like. My gaze sweeps to the window. It's too dark to see much, but that's fine. I don't need to see. Not when I can picture it so clearly. Karen out there. Watching. Waiting.

Sarah freezes and pales. "I'm sorry. Shit. I shouldn't have said that."

She walks closer, lifts her hands like she might hug me, but then lets them flop back to her side. She sighs. "Cassie wanted to tell you later. She didn't want to overwhelm you. Karen's charges have been dropped."

"So, she was out? Last night, she wasn't locked up?"

Sarah shakes her head slowly, and the meaning behind that omission hits. Karen wasn't incarcerated when someone set our cabin on fire. I think of the blurry figure I saw. The person leaving our cabin and running into the woods.

Karen.

It had to have been Karen.

Suddenly the back door swings open, and it's Cassie coming in with her arms full of bags. "A little help?"

I move on autopilot at her request, but my mind is furiously racing. Karen was here. Karen wants to hurt us. Karen could be here right now.

Cassie brings the bags in, and I unload clothing, toiletries, groceries. I work silently and deliberately. Every time Sarah steps outside with Cassie, I feel like they're talking about more things they don't want me to hear. Of course they are. Sarah pretty much confirmed it. She knew Karen was out, and so did Cassie, but they both made a conscious effort not to tell me.

Cassie shows me the laptops she bought so we don't get too behind on our work while we wait for the insurance money to come through. She explains there's a weak signal, but we can use Sarah's Wi-Fi in the meantime. When everything is out of the car and unpacked as best it can be, the three of us sit around the kitchen table to eat.

I don't say a word.

Sarah and Cassie speak quietly to each other. The logistics of our stay here. What the next few days will look like as they continue to investigate the fire. I barely touch my food and eventually leave them to sit on the couch. Sarah shoots me several concerned looks over dinner, which Cassie doesn't seem to notice.

When Sarah finally leaves, my sister locks the door behind her. Yawning, Cassie glances back at me. Perhaps just now remembering I'm here. "I'm going to try and sleep. You need the laptop for anything? Sarah tried it. It does work off her Wi-Fi, but only when you're sitting in the kitchen."

"No."

The ease on her face stutters like she's thinking something she doesn't want to say. "Hey, are you OK?"

My teeth clench and grind as I bite back several snarky comments.

"Lenora?"

"I'm fine."

"Have you even gone to the bathroom since we got here?"

"You're monitoring me now?"

"Lenora." Her voice cracks. "I'm just worried about you. You came to the hospital, and I thought—"

"You thought I'd magically be all good now? Like the past two years were just me playing pretend?"

"I just didn't think there was a reason to be afraid anymore."

"Because Karen is in jail, right?"

She leans back abruptly, her eyes narrowed. I see the moment it dawns on her. The reason behind my mood. My contempt in this moment. "You know."

"You weren't going to tell me that Karen was released?" I ask, standing to face her. "You didn't think that was important?"

"I didn't want to stress you out even more than you are."

"That's not your call to make." I want to stomp my foot. To scream the words. To beg her to tell me why she's doing this. Why she thinks I can't handle this. When did Cassie become our mother?

She takes a step closer, her arms lifted in that way you do when you're facing an armed cop. "What I said before that fire? About how us being here is your fault. I didn't mean it. We almost died. And look at you. You're basically catatonic."

"That's *right* we almost died. We almost died because someone tried to kill us. And I can't stop thinking about it. I can't focus on anything else."

"That's what I wanted to protect you from."

"You can't protect me forever. You know that, don't you?"

She looks away, grabs a dish on the counter, and drops it in the sink loudly. "I don't know what you're talking about."

"She was released." The words seem almost crazed on my tongue as I go to her, stopping only when I feel her body heat. This close, I don't have to yell. I speak low, and she hears every word. She feels the anger and shock and fear shaking my body. She has to. "She didn't kill her daughter, Cassie. So, who did?"

Cassie stiffens. Several beats of silence pass. "You never did the laundry."

I snatch the plastic bag full of our clothing by the door and flop it on the counter by the sink.

"Lenora, it's late—"

"You can't have it both ways." I glare at her. "You can't treat me like a child. Lie to me. Keep secrets from me. All in the name of protection. And then get upset when I don't do the laundry."

"It's not about the laundry. Lenora, just stop." She grabs my arm, and I jerk away from her grip.

"Then what is it about?" I tug at my hair, past the point of exasperation. "Why are you being like this with me? What aren't you saying?"

Cassie bites her lip, and for a second, I think she's going to tell me what she's thinking. Finally going to make things right between us again.

But she steps away. Backing up until she gets to the doorway. "I'm just tired."

"Yeah, OK."

"You don't have to wash those tonight." When I don't say anything, she sighs loudly. "Look, we'll talk in the morning. I just—I need some time, OK?"

I nod without looking up. Her footsteps retreat down the hall, and I hear a door close.

I'm too tired to hand-wash anything. I still run the hot water and plug the sink. I can at least let them soak. When I untie the plastic bag, I'm hit with the scent of fire. The smell brings me right back there. Running into that burning cabin. Suffocating with every step forward. It makes my pulse jump and my breath catch. I cough past phantom smoke, clench my fingers around the clothing.

I'm not strong enough for this.

I can't do this.

Something crinkles.

I'm holding Cassie's pants. The ones she was wearing when I pulled her out. The same ones she had on earlier that day. My finger catches something in the pocket. I slide the item out, recognizing it instantly.

The photo. The one I found. The one Cassie had stolen. A childhood picture of Sarah.

I'll probably never see my coin again. But this damned photo made it.

"Lenora?"

I freeze, holding the picture under the pants so she doesn't see. "Yes?" I answer without turning.

"I never asked you which room you wanted."

"Doesn't matter."

She doesn't move or say anything for a long moment before

clearing her throat like she's still clearing the smoke away too. "Parker says he saw you last night. Said you walked past him right before the fire started."

"What?" This time I do turn around, but I keep the pants behind me. She looks nervous standing there with an oversize T-shirt swallowing her whole.

"He said it was strange that you'd left right before the fire started. I told him you were sleepwalking. What if…what if you do more than walk in your sleep, Lenora?"

There it is. The reason behind her fears. The suspicion clouding her eyes. The reason she and Sarah are working so hard to make sure I'm not alone. "You believe that." It isn't a question, and we both know it. There's a faint ringing in my ears. "Are we really doing this again? You think I set that fire?" But the room tilts. Me running through the woods. The night Tilly died. The night the fire was set. There are memories there. Almost close enough for me to grasp. Something I'm missing.

Something I did.

"You know I would love you either way."

I inhale sharply. "Even if I tried to kill us both?"

"You *saved* us."

"But what if it's my fault we needed saving in the first place?" With that, I'm plucked from the safe confines of what I thought was reality and dropped somewhere else. A place where I can't trust myself or my memories. A cold, dark place.

"In that cabin, when you were searching for me, when you went back in for me, did you think you were going to die?" she asks, and I hear her faintly like she's calling down to me from the top of a well.

"Yes."

"How did it feel?"

"Lonely," I say.

Silence.

"I was looking for you, you know. That's why I rolled off that bed and left Parker. I just wanted you. Whatever version of you there was. You think it mattered then? When I woke to smoke and flames, the only thing that mattered was reaching you."

"I didn't set that fire. I'm not our mother." These words have to be true. I close my eyes against the pain on Cassie's face. And I see the door opening slowly. Our mother leaning over the bed, a knife in her hand. Our father's lifeless broken body beneath her. I open my eyes. See my sister. "I'm not evil like her."

"She wasn't evil."

I shake my head, my mouth trembling, barely able to form the words. "She killed our father. Could have killed us too if we didn't get away."

Cassie watches me in a way that has me shifting uncomfortably. "Why do you remember her like that?"

"Like what?"

"As this evil monster. Dad hurt her first. It's not an excuse. There is no excuse for what she did. But it wasn't as simple as you tell it. They got into a huge fight that night. They'd been arguing for months. Screaming at each other all night. She snapped. But that doesn't mean she ever planned to hurt us."

The memories run together and converge. A blowout fight between them in our living room. Our mother screaming and clawing at him like a rabid animal.

How could you do this? How could you do this to our family?

His apathetic demeanor. The chill in his voice when he walked upstairs. The way she wouldn't look at us when she followed him.

"No," I say, silent tears falling. "She treated us badly, Cassie. She hated us. She killed him, and then she just left us."

She smiles, and it's watery and sad. "That's not how I remember it. We all make mistakes, Lenora."

My mother's face twists in and out with Tilly's. I stumble back, bracing myself on the counter. Cassie takes a step forward, reaches for me, but I lift a hand. "I just need a minute. Please."

She nods. Bites down hard on her lip. As much as she clearly wants to keep pushing, I know she won't. Cassie doesn't do that. She doesn't pry or force or demand. Cassie mostly just helps me pretend. "I'm going to bed," she says. "You should too."

"Good night."

"'Night, Lenora."

I stay put until the sounds in her room go quiet. Then I go to the kitchen table and sit in the spot Sarah sat at during our dinner.

The photo of Sarah is still clenched in my now-sweaty palm. It's ironic somehow that we lost everything in that fire except for the clothes on our backs and this picture. I couldn't even guess as to why Cassie kept it in the first place. I smooth it out, my fingers lingering on her cheeks. She was a round-faced kid with hair a shade lighter than it is now. Eyes bluer. In the photo she's smiling, but it doesn't reach those eyes. She's missing the childlike wonderment most kids carry around with them.

From my vantage point, I can't see her cabin, but I know she's over there, moving quietly about. She was truly concerned for us. Seemed to trust us. To be eager to help us. How would she feel if she knew Cassie took this? If she caught me looking at it right now?

Maybe she wouldn't care at all. She's like us, Sarah is. That must be why Cassie is so drawn to her.

Cassie's room is silent now, and my mind is whirring. I'm jumpy and twitchy. Too wired to sleep. Too scared to look at myself and to really think about Cassie and my conversation.

I just can't help myself as I slide Cassie's laptop toward me. Just can't help myself as I look Sarah Hill up using her own Wi-Fi. Surely, that's some kind of betrayal of trust.

I start by logging into all my social media accounts. The name and picture aren't mine, and Cassie might judge me for that. But it isn't because I want to hide. It isn't because I'm ashamed of myself. Only that I thrive in anonymity. Sliding in and out of profiles and never wondering who is seeing me. There's a thrill that comes with it.

I type her name into the search bar. Sarah Hill. There are hundreds of hits, and it takes a second of scrolling to realize none of these profiles are her. I try a different social media next and get similar results. Backing out, I type her name in a search engine along with Tennessee. There are more hits. But none are of her.

I think back to the day we first met. Where did she say she was from? The memory is right there, so close that I can almost touch it. But I can't remember. Somewhere in Texas, I think.

Either way, if she were in my area, her profile should have come up in my search. But there has to be a reason why it didn't. There's no way a woman living alone who is as friendly as Sarah doesn't have social media.

I sit back in the chair, glancing sideways into the darkness that rests outside the kitchen window. I feel a pang in my heart when I look at where our cabin used to be. It takes my breath away. Sucks it right out of me. This is all wrong regardless. Me sitting here, searching Sarah in the middle of the night. What would Cassie think if she caught me? What other lies would she believe about me? I'm more disappointed in myself than she ever could be.

I almost close the laptop. Almost get up, walk to Cassie, tell her I'm sorry. Tell her I want to change. But the itch doesn't stop. The clawing need.

I'm just not strong enough.

And this photo won't leave me alone. I lift it to the webcam and try to focus it enough for a clear picture. Once it's taken, I upload it to a search engine and run a reverse image search, expecting nothing, really.

Then the screen loads.

And I realize I'm no longer the only liar.

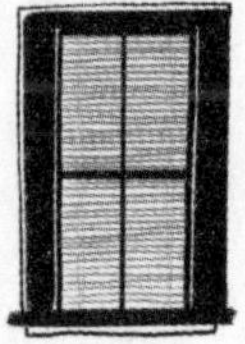

CHAPTER THIRTY-TWO
CASSIE

Lenora's bed is undisturbed. It's the first thing I notice when I stumble, blurry-eyed, out of my room. I feel better physically. My chest still aches when I breathe too deeply, and my throat is raw, but somehow the memory of what happened hurts more than my body.

And my argument with Lenora last night hurts worst of all.

Maybe it wasn't an argument. Not really. But we'd never spoken of that night in so many words. And to hear how Lenora described it, described our mother. Somehow, in Lenora's eyes, she'd become this unrecognizable person. But I remember her clearly. I remember the long car rides when we all sang to the radio. I remember the burnt toast and laughter over Saturday-morning cartoons. I remember the fights. The way Mom shut down after an especially bad one with Dad.

I don't ever remember feeling afraid of her.

She worked too much, especially toward the end. Our parents would fight too much. Mom would spend nights locked in her room crying over our dad. But she was never the evil person Lenora makes her out to be.

I think of Parker's words. The trouble on his face when he told me something wasn't right. That I need to be careful. His warning lingers. I hate myself for considering them. For rolling around in bed all night, trying to decipher the truth from the lies. Lenora wouldn't set that fire.

But who else would? Karen? Sarah?

It all just seems so unlikely.

Now she's not in bed, and it looks like it hasn't been used at all. It's morning. Early, but morning still. She must be here somewhere. I pad silently down the hall, the swell of fear in my body easing only when I see her at the kitchen table. The laptop is open in front of her, and her head is craned sideways, staring out the window.

"Have you talked to Daphne yet?"

She doesn't look at me, but I expect her to be angry at my abrupt question. Expect her to accuse me of not trusting her. Of micromanaging her life. Maybe I wish she would. Anything is better than this silence.

"Lenora?"

"I found something."

Her voice. My veins turn to ice.

"It's about Sarah." Her eyes are red as if she hasn't closed them all night, and maybe she hasn't. "I think—she's not who she says she is."

"What are you talking about?"

Lenora turns the screen of the computer around so I can see. "This picture. The one you took from her. There was a hit online."

"How do you even have that?"

"It was in your pants pocket."

"And why would you look her up?"

"Stop." Lenora grinds her teeth desperately. "Just let me finish. Just listen to me."

I close my mouth, fight the urge to sit down and place my head in my hands. It never stops. Lenora never stops, and I don't know if I can go through this again. If I can keep her from going over the edge this time. "Go ahead."

"Sarah Hill doesn't exist." Her voice curves upward, coming to life with every word. "But the girl in this picture does. Her name is Sandra Wells, and she's been missing for fifteen years."

It takes a second for me to focus on the screen. "What is this?" I breathe.

"An article. Published over a decade ago. I'll save you the trouble of reading. Sandra Wells was taken from her home the night someone killed her whole family. Everyone except her dad, who wasn't home."

"Lenora—"

"Just look at the photo. That's her. That's Sarah. The nose. The face. It's her."

She's right. There's no denying it. The dimpled smile, the large teeth. The only difference is the age. Sarah would have been a teenager when this photo was taken. And I can't help but think of a conversation I had with Sarah. She told me her sister was dead.

"I can't find anything else on her," Lenora says excitedly, on the brink of an immense discovery. "There is no Sarah Hill online. After Sandra Wells disappeared, that's it. Everything is gone. She doesn't exist."

I find myself walking toward the kitchen. Filling a cup with water, but I don't drink. My hand is shaking too badly. Sarah lied to me. It hurts because she's the first person I've trusted in years. Then there's Lenora's obsession. The way she thinks this discovery means something.

I don't know which is worse.

"Cassie, I know this is a lot. I know it changes things."

"What does it change?" I ask, exasperated.

"She's clearly lying." Lenora says frantically. "Who knows what else she's hiding?"

"What does that even mean?" I set the glass on the counter, fold my hands together. "What else could she be hiding?"

"You don't get it." Lenora tugs on her hair. Points toward Cabin One through the window. "You don't think it's weird that she's a missing person? That she has no online profiles, and suddenly Tilly is dead—"

"Damn it, Lenora," I say, and Lenora freezes. Her hands flop to her sides. Her eyes shift to the floor. I rein myself in. Take a breath. "I'm sorry. It's just—it was Karen. Karen killed her daughter. Even the police think so. The DA let her off. A lot of people get away with stuff because of a lack of evidence."

"But what if I was wrong?" she murmurs without looking at me. "What if we've been wrong all along?"

"And what reason would Sarah have to kill Tilly? She went missing as a teen. She's hiding from that, sure. But she's under no obligation to be completely honest with us. We certainly haven't been with her."

"She's a missing person."

"But what makes her a murderer?"

Her head snaps up, her eyes blazing. "Why are you defending her? She's a liar! She's lied to our faces, to everyone. Who knows what she's capable of?"

"And we're not?" The words slip out before I can stop them. "We're not liars too?"

"That's different."

"Why were you looking her up anyway?"

Lenora looks away. Back to the window.

"It was the same with Tilly, wasn't it?" I ask quietly. "And our neighbors back home? You just can't help yourself, can you?"

"No, that's not it. I was curious. I just wanted to know her."

"But some things deserve to be private." I drag both hands through my hair. "You understand that?"

Lenora looks down, and I hate myself. I can see the hurt on her face. The hurt I caused. The pain.

"Look, I'm sorry." I sigh. "I just want you to be well. I want this to all be over. Why can't you just let it be over?"

"What truth are you running from, Cassie?"

My breath rushes out, and I can't say words. At least none that would help because I can't face the answer to her question myself. It all comes back to that night. Lenora made a choice, and so did I. Both had permanent consequences. Sometimes when I lie awake at night, I think of that night and how my choice affected hers. How different things might have been had I chosen differently.

"I just wish you'd stop digging into this," I say. "There's no reason for it. It's not good for you."

"Because you're afraid to know more, aren't you? You're afraid of what you'll find?"

I close my eyes. Think of Lenora out in those woods. Lenora walking past Parker the night she told me she was sleepwalking. Lenora with a can of gasoline. With a knife. "Please" is all I manage to say.

"I'm trying." Her voice is as splintered as mine. As desperate. "I just want to know more. Just a little more, and I'll be able to move on. I'll be able to leave it behind us, Cassie."

I glance out the window. Sarah's car is gone, and I know what I'm about to do is wrong, but I don't have another choice. She's given me no other choice. "You're so convinced she's not who she says. Then I'll look. I'll look, Lenora. And if there's something in her cabin, some nefarious sign that she's running around killing people and starting fires, then we'll know. OK?"

"You can't just go in—"

"But when it's over, when it's all done, you have to promise me you'll let this go. Promise me it's behind us."

Lenora's eyes don't waver from mine.

"I can't lose you too," I say.

"I promise, Cassie."

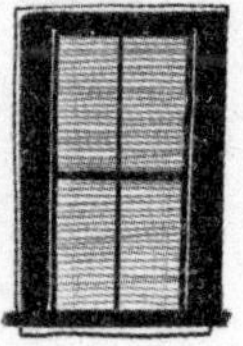

CHAPTER THIRTY-THREE
THEN

It's the middle of the night when you finally crawl through our open bedroom window, and I'm up waiting for you. Even if I didn't want to be, even if I wanted to sleep, I know I wouldn't be able to. You smell like something sweet. Perfume and something else. Probably weed. As exhausted as I am, the anger overpowers all other feelings. You lied to me. You keep lying to me.

Everyone is a liar in this house, and I've spent our whole lives pretending we were different. Pretending you were different. But you aren't. You're just like our parents.

I see that now.

I notice the exact moment you see me and the upturned mattress with the photos I left splayed out. Your secrets put on show. You're upset. Your face pinches, your eyes swinging from me to the pictures and back again. "You went through my stuff?"

I stagger to my feet, and you finish climbing into the room, closing the window firmly behind you. The whole time you watch me with an unreadable expression. Anger just peeking through your eyes.

It's fitting that you're angry with me after everything you've done. After every lie you've told.

I hold the pictures up. "What is this?"

"Those are private." You reach for them, but I stumble back, holding them just out of reach.

"Pictures of Kate. And that—that girl. Monica."

"If you knew, why did you ask?" You snatch the photos and tuck them into place, sliding the mattress back. "You can't go through my stuff."

"I didn't do it on purpose. I just found it." My mouth goes dry as I watch you calmly lie across your bed like nothing is wrong. Like I didn't find photos of a dead girl under there. And somehow it's all twisted. I'm the kid caught with my hand in the cookie jar. You're calm and at ease. I'm the one who did something wrong. After all, I shouldn't have been looking anyway.

"You're not even going to try to explain?" I ask, desperately trying to scrape for the upper hand. I didn't do anything wrong.

"What's there to explain? I like taking pictures, and Monica is my friend. She wants to be a model."

"What about Kate? She wasn't your friend."

There it is. Your eyes flash with a reaction. "Kate and I were complicated."

"Not that complicated. She hated you. She made fun of you. She talked about you to her friends."

"No." You sit up, a sneer on your lips. "No, it wasn't like that."

"Why do you have so many pictures of her?"

"She liked it. She knew I was taking them."

I shake my head, brace myself on my own bed before sinking onto it. "You said it was an accident. You said the fire was just supposed to be a prank." I think back to your face that night. The devastation and ruin when you whispered over and over it was an accident.

"It was." Your face shifts into sadness. Tears springing to your eyes. "You think just because I have so many photos of Kate, suddenly I killed her on purpose?"

"No, that's not it," I say, feeling my irritation give way to guilt. "That's not what I mean. You just made it seem like you didn't know her. She wasn't very nice to you on the bus or whatever. You said it was supposed to be a prank, but the house went up too quickly, and you couldn't help her. Clearly, there's more to the story. More to your relationship." I fold my arms over my chest, trying to stand my ground. I haven't done anything wrong. So why is there a bead of sweat rolling down my back? Why is the hurt on your face making me frantic? "I just need to know more. You have to tell me more about what happened the night Kate died."

"All that's true." You swing your legs over the side to face me, swiping at your face. "We were complicated. Friends sometimes. She had this whole thing about appearances. She cared what people thought about her."

"You were friends?" The words hurt my teeth to even say. Because they're clearly true, and you never told me. "Why didn't you say that?"

"I didn't think it mattered. Besides, she didn't like me advertising it."

"She didn't want to be seen with the druggy's daughter?"

You wince like it hurts you even now. "Something like that. It doesn't matter anyway. I walked over there that night to hang out. She wouldn't talk to me. I only intended to start a small fire in the yard to get her attention. Things just happened so fast. It was a mistake. Living with the guilt of that mistake is torturous enough without you thinking I did it on purpose."

I watch your face. Every twitch of your features. Every emotion. I try and remember what I know to be true about that night. Following you from bed. How I watched you approach Wellesley House. The way you disappeared from my sight. The rise of the flames. "What about Monica?"

"What about her?"

"She's still your friend?"

"Still?" Your teeth snap together suddenly as something seems to dawn on you. "You were the reason she was acting so weird tonight. You said something to her."

"Nothing she didn't need to know."

"What did you say?" Another step closer. "Why are you suddenly obsessed with my life?"

I look you in the eyes. "I told her the truth. Told her we're leaving."

Another emotion rolls across your face, annoyance. "You shouldn't have done that."

"It's the truth. Besides, you're getting too close to her. You need the space."

You're in my face now, leaning closer, your hands on either side of me. "You think I'm going to hurt her like I did Kate?" There it is. A flicker of something I've never seen on you before. I'm not scared, but maybe I should be.

It takes a second to form the words and make myself say them. "No, that's not it."

"Who are you really trying to protect here?" The darkness in your eyes, I realize, is not the presence of something dark but the absence of light. Like all the good has been sucked out of you, and you're hollow.

"You," I whisper. "Always you." For the first time in our lives, I feel something akin to fear. An uneasiness as your hands creep up my shoulders. Press into my neck.

I close my eyes.

There's only a moment of pressure before you back away, flick my hair like it's a joke. I look at you, and your eyes are back. You're back.

I hold still. My body going stiff.

Of all things, I think of that cat. Aswell. Mrs. Rhodes's cat. The missing posters are still up, their corners peeling, and damaged by water. Sometimes Mrs. Rhodes will sit on her porch rocking chair with tears on her cheeks, worrying over an animal that has long since ceased to exist.

Her cat is buried with the rest of your secrets.

I used to think they could all find peace together. Now I'm not so sure.

"I thought more about what you said," you say carefully. "About running away."

My heart softens, and with it every other part of my body. This is you. *You.* You're fragile. You've been through so much. Of course, there are aspects of your life I don't understand. Of course, that doesn't mean I don't know you.

But the look on your eyes when you walked toward me. It was like I didn't know you at all.

"You're going to come with me?" I ask.

You nod, and the weight of the night leaves me. This. This is all I need. To get you away from this town, from our secrets, from our father and that girl. If I just get you away, then everything will be OK. It doesn't matter where we go. Somewhere safe. Quiet. Somewhere where we can be alone. Just the two of us. If we can just get out of here, I can save us both.

"Friday," you whisper, and it sends a spike of adrenaline through me. Two more days.

"Just wait for me to pick up my check, and we're gone. Hey"—I touch your arm—"I will protect you. I'll take care of everything. But this, these pictures, they can't come with us. This has to stop."

"They're just pictures. They don't mean anything."

"I know. But if we do this, then it's just me and you. We have to leave everything behind. A clean break."

"What about Mom and Dad?" The way you ask it, it's almost as if you're testing me. Like there's an answer you're wanting me to say. "Won't they look for us?"

"I don't care." I say, "We'll hide forever. Somewhere far away."

"Me and you," you agree, and it's enough. Enough for me to forget this whole night. Forget the deep foreboding that tells me Friday won't come.

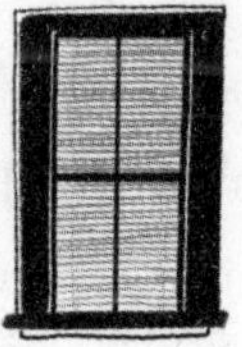

CHAPTER THIRTY-FOUR
LENORA

Cassie's face reveals nothing. I can't tell if she's angry with me. Upset with me. Afraid of me. I can't tell at all, and not knowing is what hurts the most. It's something I'm not used to.

My chest is cracking open, and everything inside is spilling out. Right at my sister's feet. Cassie pulls something from a drawer, oblivious to it. "You ready?"

"Are you sure she'll be gone for a while?" My fingernails click in and out, but it isn't good enough. I want the comfort of the silver dollar. The one with the groove of my thumb worn in. I need something to center me.

Cassie is going to break into Sarah's cabin.

And I'll only be helpless to watch.

"That's what these are for." She hands me a walkie-talkie. "I got this last night to communicate with you better on the property. I figured, with everything that's been going on… Anyway, if you're at the back door, you can see most of her driveway. Just let me know if you see her car coming."

"How will you get in?"

"I've seen her use a spare. Here, test it out."

I press the button, say hello. It immediately comes through on her walkie.

"Good." She swallows, shoots me one more long look. "You OK?"

How can I not be? How can I claim to be anything else when she's the one about to break the law? For me. Always for me. "I'm good."

She walks out, and the nerves are tiny needles digging into every surface of my skin.

From my angle, there's Sarah's driveway and both sides of the cabin. I watch Cassie grab something from beneath the front-porch steps. She walks directly toward the door, and it opens.

"OK." Her voice crackles over the walkie-talkie. "I'm in."

"Just hurry."

"It smells…clean in here."

I press the button. "You sound surprised. I thought you'd been there before."

"Not inside." Her voice is coated with static. "Just on the front porch."

How many times did they sit together on that porch like best friends while I sat alone in my room? And why does that bother me so much?

There's movement near the tree line.

I press closer to the glass.

"Oh, no." Cassie groans.

My hand holding the walkie shakes. "What? Cassie? What is it?"

Silence.

"Cassie?"

"This is bad. This is really bad." Cassie's voice is a harsh whisper. "Her bookshelf is color coded and alphabetized. You were right, Lenora. She's evil."

I press the button to mute Cassie's laughter and take a step away from the window to catch my breath. "That's not funny."

"I think it was."

Another couple of minutes pass in silence. There's no more movement anywhere, but the nerves start getting harder to ignore. I click the button and hear the static instantly. "How much longer?"

"Almost—" Her voice cuts out abruptly.

I wait a beat. When it doesn't crackle to life, I try again. "Cassie?"

"Shhh..." Her voice is low.

"Not going to work again."

"Shut up."

I freeze. Something about her tone this time. My pulse picks up; my body tenses.

A crackle of white noise and then my sister's terrified voice. "I think I hear something."

More silence. A whole minute of it. I'm staring at Cabin One, my body coiled too tight. "Cassie, are you there?"

"I think someone is in here with me."

The hairs on my arms rise.

I want to hold down the button again and call her name until she talks to me, but I'm frozen. Can't move. Can barely breathe.

Sarah's car isn't in the driveway. We watched her leave. But what if Karen was in there?

I scan the woods. The driveway. The door. *Come on, Cassie. Come on. Talk to me.*

A wave of static. "Lenora?"

"What?" I grip the walkie tighter. "What is it, Cassie?"

There's a brief silence, a little too long, before her voice comes through, and my whole body relaxes. "She left the TV on." A chuckle. "I'm losing it. OK, give me a second. I'm almost done."

I'm both relieved and annoyed. "My anxiety is through the roof. Just come back. Hurry."

"There's nothing in the living room or kitchen. Going into the bedrooms."

"Just come back, Cassie." I don't know if I can take any more.

"I'm almost done. We've already broken in. I might as well finish the job."

Fifteen of the longest minutes of my life go by before I say anything else. "Come on. You've been in there forever." I keep the walkie to my mouth, keep my eyes focused ahead, trying not to think of the what-ifs. What if she finds something? What if she doesn't? What if I go to prison for the rest of my life because the police think I lost my mind just like my mother?

What if I have?

"Cassie?" I say again, more frantically this time. A minute passes, and I tamp back my panic and hold the Talk button. "Cassie, this is ridiculous. Just talk to me." More silence. "Cassie?"

Then I see a flash of black through the trees as Sarah's car rumbles up the driveway. My heart free-falls. "She's here. Do you hear me? Sarah is here. You have to get out of there. Cassie!"

It's a horror movie playing out before my eyes. Sarah's car parking. Sarah walking toward the front door. I don't even try to hide myself from my spot near the back door. The only thing that seems to matter is getting Cassie out of that cabin. "Cassie! Get out. Get out now!"

Sarah fumbles with her keys, pushes the front door open, and walks in.

I drop my hands to my sides and stare wide-eyed at the cabin. Cassie never made it out.

The door behind me opens, and I whirl around.

Cassie.

She's here.

I finally breathe, watching as she closes the door softly behind her and wipes her feet.

"How did you get out? I didn't see you." It still feels like there's not enough oxygen in the room. Like my heart may never go back to normal.

Cassie's breathing heavily too. It's clear I'm not the only one affected. "Back door. I'll have to put the key back later."

"How did you even know that key was there?"

She shrugs, walking past me into the kitchen. "I've seen her use it before. She apparently locks herself out a lot. It's a spare. What?" She stops to look at me. "You're still freaking out, aren't you?"

"I was worried. You said someone was in there with you and just went quiet."

"I couldn't talk. It all happened so quickly. I had to see what I heard, Lenora." Her voice softens. "Hey, I'm OK." She approaches me slowly. "You know there's nothing in that cabin, right? Everything was normal. I don't know why she changed her identity. I don't know who she is. Frankly, I don't care. And what we just did, it can't happen again."

"There had to be something."

"An open romance on her bedside table. A prescription for Adderall. Old Halloween candy in a jar. Some half-burned candles. A journal with two entries. Neither one interesting. Is that enough for you, Lenora? Shall I list everything in that cabin that doesn't matter?" she says, clearly frustrated.

"You didn't have to do it," I say, under my breath. "If you were going to be this angry about it, you didn't have to do it. I never asked you to."

"I'm not angry." She shakes her head in what looks like exasperation. "I'm tired. I'm so damned tired. But whatever you're doing, whatever you think you know about Sarah, it has to stop, OK? You can't keep doing this. Karen was arrested for Tilly. Whatever secrets Sarah has, she deserves to keep them. You promised me you'd let this go."

I don't say anything. Just turn around to the window by the back door, fighting the tears assaulting the back of my eyes.

"You can't keep doing this," Cassie says. "I don't know how much more I can take."

I want to tell her the same thing. I can't take any more either. I want to ask her if she thinks I like being this way. If she thinks this is what I want. Because I don't and it isn't. The way she feels inside our cabin, that's how I feel inside my own skin. Like it's all just a little too tight and breathing is a task.

There's a shift in the curtains in Cabin One. My breath catches when I see her. The person standing in the window of Sarah's cabin. A blurry image. Shadowed. Sarah. I don't know if I just caught her looking at me or if she caught me looking at her.

Who is the voyeur here?

She lifts her hand in a wave. I wave back.

"Lenora?" Cassie says, her voice pleading. "I need to know this is going to stop. I need to know I can trust you. I can't do this again. I can't watch you do this again. I won't be able to be a part of it."

"What does that mean?" I turn to look at her. The fear blankets me with the mere thought of Cassie leaving. Of me finally driving her away for good.

She looks away sharply. "Just promise me that it's over."

"Sure. OK, Cassie. It's over."

She doesn't look convinced.

"It looks like it's going to rain," I say, looking back at the window. Sarah is no longer there. Thunder shakes the sky just as it opens and bleeds all over our cabin.

The storm wakes me before the sun.

And I can't explain the instant feeling of dread that takes over, only that it makes me claw at my chest like someone is sitting on me, and I have to get them off. I push myself up to my elbows and look around.

The room is blurry, lit by an overcast light that only the dawn after a storm can bring.

The panicky feeling gets stronger because of my own lack of sight. I lost my glasses before the fire, and I'm still waiting on another pair to come. Contacts. I need to put my contacts in.

But I can't move. Can't relax back into sleep. Can't think about anything other than my own hopelessness. The disappointment in Cassie's eyes when she told me good night. All the ways I've screwed up.

Now it's morning, and nothing feels better at all.

The urge hits me so strongly, I can't even attempt to fight it. The need to see my sister. Lay eyes on her. I pull the sheets back and press my heels into the cold wood. When I was little, I never let my feet down beside the bed, too afraid someone was hiding under there, waiting to grab me and drag me under. But as an adult, I learned that the monsters under your bed are the least of your concerns, and in the light of day, it all just seems so silly. Even here. In Cabin Three.

The cabin is loud with noises. Rain drizzling down like from a faucet that's been turned off but still dripping. Leaves stick to the windows, plastered with the morning frost.

It must have been quite a storm last night, and I didn't hear anything. I slept. Really slept. And clearly, I stayed in my bed the entire night.

I go to the chest of drawers first and slip in my contacts, not bothering with the solution and blinking against the sudden burn. My eyes water as I stumble into the hall. It's quiet. Cassie's door is closed. That makes me pause. She doesn't usually sleep with it closed.

She must be angrier than I thought.

She could be in there doing research or ordering new equipment. She'd want to stay busy even with our limited resources. She most likely only closed the door to not disturb me. Or maybe there's another reason. She could have done it last night, turning the lock too. Scared. Not of Karen or Sarah or some unseen entity—scared of me. Because I know the truth. I knew even as she broke into Sarah's cabin that she didn't believe Sarah hurt Tilly.

It's always been about me.

Her need to protect me. Even from myself.

Prove me wrong and put me quietly back into place.

And maybe that look will still be on her face when I peek my head in. Just as upset with me in the light of day as she was last night. My hand lingers over her door handle, and there is no whisper of caution that rolls up and down my body. No chills or premonition. That's why, when I open the door, the scene is so confusing.

Cassie is not sitting up in bed, her eyes glued to the laptop. She's not curled on her side snoring.

Cassie is not in the room at all.

Night falls at the campground. I've always liked the night as much as I fear it. There is something about the darkness here. How thick it is. Different from any other place I've ever lived.

The signal of another day gone.

I sit with my back to the kitchen, my eyes searching the void around me. Each tree. The cabin. The bathhouse. Back again. Movement in Sarah's cabin. The trees. Only the wind. And back again. I tell myself that if I keep waiting, Cassie will come home eventually. Even as my eyelids fall together with the force of a magnet, even as my back grows stiff, and I start swaying on my feet, I stay put.

All day I was in this exact spot. And Cassie never showed.

My back aches, and I keep watch, and I'm starving, and I hate everything about this.

Her car is gone.

I can't even think about what that means.

Cassie left. She really left. Guess I broke one too many promises.

My gaze roams to the abandoned box on the table. The cameras that arrived today. Security methods Cassie ordered before the fire. Back when she thought the biggest threat was coming from the outside. Not knowing she'd be gone before they arrived.

The rage catches me off guard. Cassie gets to leave while I'm stuck here. She can run from that night while I'm forced to relive it every day of my life. Walking down the hallway. Cassie running. Leaving me. Always leaving me.

Tilly running.

A scream in the dark.

What did I see?

What did I do?

The memories overwhelm all my other senses, and I shove the box off the table, scattering its contents across the floor. I shatter a glass cup, stand, and flip my chair over.

I keep going until the kitchen is destroyed, and I'm destroyed with it. Cassie is gone. She left me even after she promised she never would again.

My hand flies to my chest, and I clench it there, digging my fingernails into my skin like I can dig to my heart. Cradle it. Salvage what's left.

Then I hear it. The echo. The sound of white noise coming from an abandoned walkie that somehow got kicked under the kitchen table. I lunge for it, jerk the walkie up, and hold it to my ear. There is nothing.

"Cassie? Is that you?"

I release the side button and wait. Then I hear it again. A flash of sound, like she's pressing the Talk button but not speaking. I hold the walkie tight, tears forming in my eyes and falling down my cheeks. I've cried so much today that it burns like acid trails all the way into my soaked shirt. "I knew you were here. I knew you wouldn't leave forever. Cassie, where are you? Cassie?"

There is a long, quiet nothing.

My pulse jumps into my throat, and a cold sweat breaks out across my neck. "Please. Please, Cassie. Talk to me." I jolt to my feet and press a hand to the table to keep myself upright as I search the woods. Maybe she's out there, and she got hurt. Maybe she needs me.

But her car is gone.

I reach for the door handle but can't make myself turn it at first. Can't make myself step outside. There is movement out the window. I squint into the darkness, get closer to the glass. It looks like—

A figure standing at the edge of the woods. Beside the lining of trees. A person. "Cassie?"

I don't move. Neither do they.

Another moment passes between us before they turn back into the woods. Then suddenly the door is open, and I'm sliding on the closest pair of shoes and running outside. For Cassie. Anything for Cassie. I stumble forward into the lining of trees. The bramble and leaves rustle under me as I run toward her. That and my ragged breathing are the only sounds.

"Cassie?" My voice is barely above a whisper as I spin in the woods. She was here. She was just here.

Another flash of movement to my left. I turn in that direction.

Branches snap in my face, and I do my best to shove them away. Anxiety surges inside me, but I fight it back. Keep going. Keep moving. Can't go back to the cabin. There's nothing for me there except darkness. I need my sister. I have to find her.

I fall, my palms slap the ground, and the breath knocks out of my chest.

A branch snaps directly in front of me. There is a ray of moonlight peeking in through the trees. Just enough to highlight a pair of familiar shoes. A long, slender, and pale leg. A white T-shirt with *UCLA* printed on the front. "Cassie?" It's both her and not her. Faces blending and pulling.

Pale skin.

A smile.

A whispered sentence: "Help me, Lenora."

I put my hands over my ears and scream.

The forest is silent when I'm found. A pair of hands cups my cheeks and holds me steady. Someone is speaking, calling my name. Up, up, up. I walk forward toward a familiar cabin. Into the warmth. "Just breathe, Lenora."

I try to, but breathing feels a lot like screaming.

Sarah's movements are graceful as she moves around her kitchen. Puts the tea kettle on the stove. Opens her fridge. I stare blankly at her, trying to get my bearings. Trying to make sense of what is going on. "How did I get in here?" My voice is scratchy, like it hasn't been used in a while. Or else was used too much.

She eyes me over her shoulder. "I helped you inside. I would have walked you back, but my place was closer, and I wasn't sure if you would make it."

"How did you find me?"

She pulls a knife from a stand and admires it for a second before she starts slicing what looks like chocolate. "I heard you screaming. Thought you were your sister at first. Not used to seeing you outside, I guess. You nearly scared me to death out there." Sarah turns sharply, holding out a plate. "Here. It's fudge. I made it yesterday. It'll help your blood sugar."

I eye the neat little squares of chocolate and tentatively take one and bring it to my lips.

Sarah pulls one off the plate and pops it into her mouth. "The tea will be done in a few minutes. It's lavender herbal tea. My own recipe. It'll help you calm down."

As she says it, it's like I can feel the weight of my body coming down all at once. A fiery crash of adrenaline and energy. I don't know how I'm staying upright. I pop the fudge in my mouth and chew gingerly. It's good. Creamy and rich. But it's all I can stomach. "I had a panic attack," I tell her.

She turns back to the kettle and pours two mugs. "Here." She passes me one, and I smell it. Lavender and something else. A comforting note of vanilla. I take a sip as she holds the other between her hands. "How are you feeling now? I can call your sister to get you, or I can walk you back."

My fingers tighten on the mug, and the pain is instant. Oh, God. Cassie.

That's the moment I finally take in my surroundings. Cassie was in here just the day before. I was in this place only once, when Wayne was alive. It was before we officially moved in, and it smelled like tobacco and firewood. The counters and tables were cluttered with various tools and trinkets, with boxes stacked to the ceiling. Sarah keeps a very different living space. Neat and orderly—everything has its place, down to the mug hanging from a hook by the sink.

The order is comforting.

And Cassie was right; it does smell clean. Like lemons.

Sarah runs her palms down her jeans like her hands are sweating. "What's wrong, Lenora? What were you doing outside?"

"I was looking for my sister." I place the mug down, but my hands are trembling so violently, liquid sloshes out, wetting my hand and the table.

"She isn't at the cabin?"

"No."

"But why would she be in the woods? Did she not tell you where she was going?"

"I don't know where she is. She was gone when I woke up this morning. The car is gone too."

Sarah's face contorts into genuine concern. "That doesn't sound like her. Is that why you had that panic attack outside? Because you couldn't find her?"

"I saw her. Well, I saw someone. They were in the woods. They were wearing Cassie's clothes."

"You saw someone outside?" Her body tenses and pivots toward the window.

"I don't know."

Sarah's whole demeanor shifts when she looks back at me. "You're not making sense."

A sob hitches in my chest, but I swallow it. I can't lose it. Not right now. Not in front of Sarah.

"Lenora, you're scaring me."

"I'm scaring myself." My eyes collide with hers. "I can't trust myself. I don't know what's going on. I don't know what's real."

"You said the car was gone. Cassie had to have taken it somewhere. I'm sure she'll be back. That's real. OK? We can trust that. It's Cassie. She'll be back, and I'm sure she'll have a perfectly fine explanation."

"Who did I see in the woods?"

She stops. Another glance toward the forest, and her expression darkens. "Maybe there was someone. People come out here sometimes. That's what Cassie told me once. You could have seen someone who walked too far into the woods and then got scared and ran. What if—" She stops. "There is another alternative. What if you were asleep again?"

"You think I was sleepwalking?"

"You've done it before. Maybe you thought you saw someone because you were dreaming."

"No," I say resolutely. "I wasn't asleep."

The floor creaks in the living room.

Sarah doesn't move.

"Is someone else here?"

"What?"

"You didn't hear that?" I ask, glancing toward the doorway. The moonlit living room.

I think someone is in here with me.

A feeling settles over me. Like someone is watching me. Someone I don't see.

"The floor creaked, I guess. This cabin is always making noises. Are you sure you're OK?" Her voice comes from the end of a long tunnel.

I stumble to my feet and wipe my hands on the end of my shirt.

"Where are you going?"

But I'm moving to the living room, twisting around. Picturing my sister. On the couch. On the chair. Standing near the door. Here, I think. She has to be here.

Maybe Cassie came here because she wanted some space from me.

Maybe Sarah is lying about this too.

"Lenora?" Sarah is regarding me from the doorway like I'm an animal. Like I'm the threat. Is that what Cassie was thinking when she walked out the door of our cabin? Finally giving in to the need to get as far away from me as possible.

I stand on shaky knees. There is a couch with a crumpled blanket hanging half off it. An empty mug with the remnants of coffee around the edge. But there's no Cassie. There is no Cassie, and I want to crumble.

"You think you understand her that well?" I ask, my voice hoarse and pathetic.

"What?"

"My sister. You think you know her. You said she wouldn't leave me. Like you know her well enough to know that." It all flashes back.

The moments I've seen Cassie laughing with Sarah. Whispering with Sarah. Keeping secrets between the two of them. My skin heats.

"She wouldn't. I don't have to be her best friend to know that about her." Sarah's eyes still flit around the room. From me to the door. From me and back to the hallway. I wonder if she's planning escape routes. "She loves you." Her words are empty.

I look away to a far point in the corner of the room. This time I can't fight the tears, can't stop them. "You're wrong, you know. She left me before. She left me, and it ruined everything."

The night is a bark of thunder in my mind. A memory I can't drown, no matter how long I hold it underwater. Finding our mother over our father's body. Cassie's voice screaming at me to run. Me wanting to listen to her. Wanting desperately to move my legs. But something stopped me. I was riveted in place.

I should have run.

Sarah doesn't say anything. She doesn't move or speak. She maintains her spot in the doorway, her arms crossed protectively around herself. "I'm sorry," she whispers.

"I know who you are, Sarah." The air in the room shifts. Grows thicker. "We're all liars, aren't we? Not just Cassie and me. You're a liar too."

She steps back like I've shoved her. "I don't know what you're talking about."

"Yes, you do, Sandra," I tell her, and she flinches. The pain crossing her face is so severe, I almost feel bad for causing it. "Cassie found a picture of you. I searched it online when I got curious. I found your missing-person poster."

Her face falls, tightens. "You can't say anything. You can't tell anyone."

"I'm not planning to."

"You don't understand." She steps toward me, her eyes flashing toward the door like she's waiting for someone to burst through it. "They can't find me."

"You're running from someone."

"Aren't we all?" she asks breathlessly. "Wouldn't you have to be to live here? Your mother, she's alive, isn't she? Is that who you're hiding from?"

"I'm not scared of her." I say it assuredly, pulling myself to my full height. But I feel like a little kid not even capable of convincing myself.

"No reason to be afraid if she can't find you. But that's not exactly true, is it?" Sarah shakes her head, her own tears finally falling. "They haunt us. The ones we run from. They hurt us every day without ever being here."

"Who are you running from, Sarah?"

"The person who destroyed my entire family." And I remember the article. The house fire that killed Sandra Wells's family the night she went missing.

"We're the same," I say. "Victims."

Sarah steps closer to me. "You shouldn't give up on Cassie. Not like this. Whatever happened to you, she wouldn't leave you, Lenora."

"You would tell me, wouldn't you?"

Sarah's head tilts. "Tell you what?"

"If she were here."

"There's no one here except me. I promise."

"I should go." I back toward the front door. "Cassie could come back at any moment. I need to wait for her."

"Wait, just a second—"

I walk out of Sarah's cabin and down the porch steps. My feet are sluggish. It feels like I'm wading through waist-deep mud. There are pieces of a puzzle bouncing around my skull that just don't fit together. I stumble toward Cabin Three, faintly aware of Sarah behind me, the sound of her door closing, and the light and warmth of her cabin fading.

Any hope of finding my sister fading.

Sarah looked at me like I was insane. Maybe I am. Maybe it finally happened, and Mom's DNA took over anything good inside me. Maybe I never saw someone in the woods wearing her clothes. Maybe nothing I see or perceive to be real is reality at all.

Something brushes my foot. I look toward the ground. My heart falls and drops, and everything in me stills.

My sister's walkie-talkie is lying in Sarah's driveway.

The police come in a flurry of red and blue, and it makes me want to vomit and cry at the same time. I file a missing person report. Tell them what I found in Sarah's driveway. "She might be in there," I tell them. "Where else would she be?"

We're in my destroyed kitchen, where I'm too nervous to sit. Which is probably a good thing since both chairs are still overturned. The officers stand near the door, their hulking figures taking up too much space. One cop is clearly older, with bushy gray eyebrows. His younger companion, a slender woman with observant eyes, stays right at his side. They're both holding tiny notebooks and taking vigorous notes.

They exchange a glance that tells me they think I'm as unhinged as I look. Covered in dirt and debris from being in the woods earlier, splashed in mud from my shoes to my calves. I think my arm is bleeding. Everything is so dirty and smeared, I can't figure out where the blood is coming from, only that it's just started to ebb.

"She wouldn't have dropped that walkie-talkie on purpose. She wouldn't have left it there."

"Ma'am." The older officer holds up his hands for me to slow down. "What are you suggesting happened?"

"Something happened to her. Someone took her."

"But her car is gone. Maybe she just took off to cool down? You mentioned the two of you got into a fight."

"She's never left without telling me before." I squeak out the words, and it almost sounds like a question.

"Did you see anyone? Any signs of forced entry at your home?" He scans the kitchen pointedly.

"No." I shake my head, realizing for the first time that I haven't really looked. Not when I was so consumed with anger over Cassie abandoning me. I never stopped to imagine the possibility that she didn't leave me on purpose. "I did this in the kitchen. I was, uh, upset."

"Right. We're going to file this report for you. But most of the time, these kinds of cases resolve on their own. She's probably out there blowing off steam. I'm sure she'll be home soon."

My nails click viciously together as I try my best to think. "She wouldn't have left that walkie-talkie just lying there like that. None of this is like her."

"You'd be surprised by how many relatives of missing people

say that. Just try and get some rest tonight. Let us do our job, and we'll do everything we can to find her."

"What about our neighbor?"

They stop, exchange a glance. "Your neighbor in the next-door cabin?"

"I think she's hiding something." I'm vaguely aware of how I must sound. My hands twitching, moving incessantly. The way I look. It all contributes to the expression on the officers' faces. Disbelief. Concern. Suspicion.

"You think she has something to do with your sister's disappearance?"

It doesn't make sense, even to me. Sarah has been nice and helpful. She's letting us stay in this cabin. She's given us clothing. Why would she have any reason to hurt Cassie?

Why would anyone hurt Tilly?

"Ma'am, are you all right?"

I'm zoned out, my nails clicking furiously. Can't think. Can't breathe. The tightening feeling at the base of my throat has only constricted since finding that walkie-talkie. Something is very, very wrong. "My sister is in trouble. You have to believe me."

"And you think your neighbor hurt someone?"

I stop. Force myself to take a breath. "No, I don't know. Maybe you could talk to her. Maybe you could have a look around her cabin."

"There's no reason—"

"A girl was murdered out here a few weeks ago. Tilly Meadows. And there's something else. Something she's lying about."

The older cop heaves a sigh of stale coffee breath. "Why do you think she's lying?"

"I don't think. I know. She isn't who she says she is. Her real name is Sandra. She must have changed her identity or something."

"So her name isn't Sarah?" the woman asks, her pen never slowing. Her partner lays a hand on her arm and flips his own notebook closed.

"Wait, what are you doing?" I plead as they step toward the door. "Please, just knock on her door. See if she'll let you look around her cabin."

"We'll talk to her, but you've got to hang back here."

I nod, knowing I'd agree to anything.

I watch them walk to the neighboring cabin.

Knock on Sarah's door.

Words are exchanged, and she invites them in. The nerves are too much. It feels like I'm going to burst from my skin. I do several grounding exercises. Breathe in with my tongue against the roof of my mouth. Hold it. Breathe out and release.

I focus on my breaths.

On my heartbeat.

Just when I'm beginning to calm myself, I hear them.

The door opens and the cops step out, immediately heading in my direction. I open the back door, but they stop a few paces away.

"She was extremely cooperative. Let us look through the whole cabin. No one else is there."

"Did you ask her about what I told you? Her name. She isn't who she says she is."

"She showed us her ID, Miss Lowe. Said she doesn't know what you're talking about. She mentioned you've been feeling unwell. You've had a rough few days."

The younger cop steps forward. "Perhaps we could call someone for you? Take you somewhere?"

I sway on my feet, barely keeping myself upright with a hand on the door. "No, that's OK."

"I don't think it's a good idea for you to be alone."

"I'm fine. I just need some sleep. I'm sorry." I straighten my shoulders, do my best to appear normal. "She's right. I'm not myself."

More words are exchanged, and it's hard to concentrate on anything except the growing hum in my ears. Eventually I get them to leave.

Watch their taillights disappear.

The campsite is silent once again. Even the lights in Sarah's cabin are off.

I'm alone.

The first raindrop takes me by surprise.

But the sudden downpour is welcome. It reminds me that as dead as I feel, I'm unfortunately still alive.

When Cassie and I were growing up, people used to say we had some kind of unexplainable twin connection. I knew when Cassie broke her arm before anyone. She knew when I started my period, bringing me a pad to the school bathroom where I was holed up crying.

It was true but not something I attributed to being twins. Anyone can have a connection like that if you know someone well enough. If your blood pumps for them and you breathe only because that person is breathing too.

That's why I expected to feel her more. Every moment. Every breath. Every phantom pain. I wonder if Cassie is feeling it. This anxiety forming in the pit of my stomach the size of a golf ball, does that come from Cassie too?

I don't sleep.

Every time I close my eyes, I hear the noises coming from our mother's room. Feel my sister's hand in mine.

Feel the moment she lets go.

We've never in our lives been separated for this long. I sit at the kitchen table, ignoring the aches and pains in my back, staring at the door. Waiting for it to open. For Cassie to burst through with some explanation for her disappearance.

The wind screams outside, trees beating against one another like the wind is trying to pluck them from the ground by their roots, and they're shoving against one another to avoid being next. The storm is even worse than last night. If Cassie is out there—

I can't finish the thought.

I grab my head and hold it. Will the images to go away. Images of my sister in pain or hurting. "Please," I whisper into the dark. "No more. I can't take any more."

I clench my eyes closed, and I'm back there. The dark hallway, Cassie's hand anchoring me to reality. That noise coming from our mother's room.

Thwack, thwack, thwack.

"Please, please, please." My eyes open, but I still hear it. Still feel the tremble in my skin. The sweat on Cassie's palms.

I lurch from my chair, a scream threatening to burst from my lips. The noise. It won't stop. It won't go away.

Thwack, thwack, thwack.

I freeze, my head tilted to the left. Listening. There.

Not a memory or a nightmare. The noise is coming from outside. It sounds like someone is hitting a board against a tree.

I walk to the door and open it, stare out into the dark abyss. The thought crosses my mind: *I can't go out there.*

But I have to.

For Cassie.

Because that night she ran, and I stayed, and both our lives changed forever. But she came back. That has to mean something.

My body shakes as I slip on my shoes, and my fingers linger on the doorknob, holding tightly. Unwilling to let go. But I make myself walk into the downpour, counting each step as I head in the direction of the noise.

I'm not as familiar with these woods as Cassie. I know the Blacktop, but I'm not there often. Not since we first moved in. Right off, I can tell that's not where the sound is coming from. The rain pours, soaking me to my skin, but I don't feel the wetness or the cold. There is a numbness that envelops me, stretching from the tips of my fingers all the way to my toes. There is no sense of danger. Or cold. Or pain. There is only Cassie.

The moon is hardly enough light to illuminate more than several feet in front of me. I count the fighting trees as I walk forward. As the noise gets louder.

And it's weird, but I know the exact moment I've found something important. The small clearing is around thirty feet long and ten feet wide. There's something about this space that's both foreign and familiar.

I close my eyes to listen, not knowing what I expect to hear. Cassie shouting for me. A clear sign of where my sister is and how to get to her. But there's nothing. Just the rain beating wildly against the trees. Thunder rumbling from the depths of the clouds, threatening a more severe storm.

Thwack, thwack, thwack.

The sound sends my eyes flying open. I want to retreat. To huddle in a ball and get lost in memories and the rain. The cold finally reaches me and gets tangled with my breath and highlighted by the moon.

Thwack, thwack, thwack.

I can't do this. I can't be here. But there. Right in my middle, right where a shared umbilical cord connected us for seven and a half months, there is a burning. A pull. Toward the noise. Toward the memory.

And like every nightmare I've ever had, I walk toward the sound. The storm shakes the trees angrily, but the sound gets louder, fiercer. I move with a carefully blank mind and an urging in my bones. I keep telling myself, *One more step and I'll be done. One more, and I can turn around.* But I keep going until I hit another clearing. A smaller one.

And it's there I place the noise.

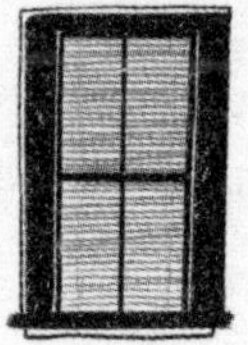

CHAPTER THIRTY-FIVE

THEN

When my eyes open, the first thing I notice is that you're not in bed. I stare at the empty spot where you usually sleep and wonder if it will be cold to the touch. I sit up, look around the room.

The window is closed. Locked.

You must be here. In the house.

That's when my pulse picks up, and I rip the covers back. I need to get to you. The worst thoughts pound into my mind. Dad. You.

I fling the door open and stop, nearly stumbling into the wall. Because there you are. A dark shadow. But it's you. I know it's you. You're at the top of the stairs standing perfectly still. Mid-step like I've caught you. Like you weren't expecting to see me.

"What are you doing?" I ask.

There's a long moment of silence before you answer, "I heard something."

A pit is opening in my stomach, and I listen, but there's nothing. "I don't hear anything."

"It's coming from Mom's room."

I glance down the hall. The floor might as well be water up to my waist, and I'm just trying to keep my head above it. My mouth is dry, and I lick my lips, but it doesn't help.

Suddenly, you're here. Grabbing my hand. You're sweaty. So sweaty. Like you've been exercising or running. "Hey," I say. "Are you sure you're OK?"

"I think we should check it out."

"Mom's room?"

You nod, and I wish I could see your face better, but it's too dark. "Is Dad here?"

"I don't know."

You pull me forward, and we're walking. Wading. Sloshing through mud. Something makes me want to stop, to pull back.

Mom's door is cracked. Just barely. Just enough to see a tiny sliver of light from her lamp.

"Wait," I breathe, but then the door opens.

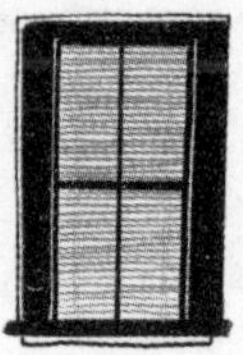

CHAPTER THIRTY-SIX
LENORA

Here's the thing about memories. You can't control or choose when they come to you. Like this one. Entirely meaningless—I forgot all about it. It's one of those memories tucked into the furthest corner of my mind. Not for any particular reason, only that it's odd enough to stand out but not spectacular enough to dwell on.

Wayne disappearing through the woods. The faintest sounds of hammering and drilling. Cassie noticed it first and yelled in for me.

I walked to the door and heard it too. "What's Wayne doing out there?"

"I don't know, burying a dead body?"

"Seriously."

She looked in the direction of the noise. "Sounds like he's hammering something."

Thwack, thwack, thwack.

"What though?"

"Who knows? It's Wayne."

Thwack, thwack, thwack.

The hammering bled into the night and the next day. For a week we heard the noises on and off. Suddenly, they stopped. The extraordinary bled into ordinary, and I forgot all about it.

But Wayne isn't hammering in the woods today.

I stare at the source of the noise. A board, not quite secured, flapping against the ground with the strength of the wind.

Thwack, thwack, thwack.

I prop the flashlight on the ground, and after sliding my fingers underneath, I pull up.

Not a board.

A door someone must have left open.

Unhidden.

Like a storm shelter. There is a ladder leading into darkness with only a tiny beam of light. A pinprick of pain pounds between my eyes, and dread begins its angry ascent up my esophagus. I think of Wayne out here in this exact spot. The sound of hammering and tools. But why would he build a shelter so far out?

Then, faintly, I hear something else.

Music coming from below.

Our mother told us a story once. She told us the night we were born, she'd screamed as they wheeled her to the OR. She felt everything. There hadn't been time for an epidural, and she knew, in that moment, the pain was only going to get worse. These babies, the ones she and her husband had tried desperately to conceive, were coming. And she wasn't ready.

She would later come to think of it as bright and fast. A rush down a fluorescent hallway. The smell of antiseptic. She remembered the looks on people's faces as she passed them. Nurses and visitors. The severe expression in their eyes must have matched her own, and she didn't know if they were afraid of her or afraid for her.

Suddenly she stopped, but everyone else kept moving in a frenzy, and the doctor, a woman with cool professionalism, looked—for the first time in the whole pregnancy—afraid. Mom told us nothing could have prepared her for this pain. The feeling of her whole body morphing, stretching, pulling, aching.

The first baby, Cassie, took twenty minutes of pushing and arrived in a bath of blood. Panicked nurses immediately whisked her to a waiting staff of neonatal doctors. Fuzzy was all our mother felt. Even the pain had started to numb.

She'd told us the story while standing in front of our kitchen stove, staring at a pot of slowly boiling water. Uncooked spaghetti noodles in her hands, an expression of pure stillness on her face. Our father was working late again. Spending a night at the office.

"One more," she said to us. "That's what my doctor told me. One more and you're done."

She'd begged to be cut open. Surely a knife in the stomach would be a better pain than this. "Anything," she told us, "would be better than that feeling of being split in half."

The doctor had only urged her to push. And she did. And there was more pain. And the doctor said something about a breach.

She bore down, grit her teeth, and closed her eyes. She pushed. She pulled every particle of strength and screamed through the agony of her doctor's hands pulling her second child from inside her by the baby's feet. In that moment, the world filtered in and out, and the white-hot pain melted into something more manageable.

Our mother said she'd heard her grandmother's voice. "Fitting isn't it, love? That we're born the same way we die. By blood."

She was sewn and stitched, treated and prodded. Eventually she was wheeled into a NICU room, where, with her husband at her side, she looked in on two little, tiny bundles. Two girls who'd arrived six weeks early, who'd shared a sac and placenta, who'd defeated all kinds of odds. Mom told us this part as she stared out the window behind the sink. The pot started boiling, but the pasta was still clenched tight in her hands. "I knew," she whispered, "that I should have felt the instant love deep in my soul. It's what all my friends felt. It's what I expected. But," she told us, "I could only feel the ache between my legs and the annoyance at the too-tight grip of your dad's hand on my shoulder." She touched her hand to her right shoulder at that moment.

"Mom," Cassie had interrupted her, "I don't like this story." Cassie looked bored. Her head on the kitchen table, her eyes on that pasta as if she could make our mother drop it in the water with only a look.

It was after 9:00 p.m., and we were both starving.

"Just wait," she said. "This is the best part."

She told us the rest of the story with a smile on her face. Later, when she'd gotten to hold her daughter for the first time—Cassie, I think—and that baby cried helplessly on her chest, our mother could only stare at her husband across the room and watch the way his eyes followed the pretty nurse down the hallway. When she was done with the story, she dropped the pasta in the water, and then she went to bed. Cassie and I finished dinner ourselves.

We girls would grow like gnarled tree roots, turning and twisting together. I always thought Mom would watch and wait for the shift in her heart. But, as we found each other and grew up, up, up, she could only watch helplessly as her husband grew in the opposite direction. His coping mechanisms. His own happiness. I always thought Mom didn't grow at all. In some ways she never left that OR room. Never forgot that ache and her grandmother's voice.

Maybe that explains everything she did. Her own beliefs.

We come into the world the same way we leave it.

By blood.

I think of my mother as I enter the shelter. As my feet step down into darkness and my hands brush cobwebs. As my body sinks into a pit in the ground. I think of the hardest thing my mother ever did and all the ways I never understood her.

I think of that night it all ended.

I wonder where she is now and if Cassie and I ever hurt her worse than we did the night we were born.

A tunnel stretches before me. One that is mostly dark except for a small sliver of light. And it's easy to follow it. Because I know deep in my gut that Cassie is down here. As I walk, the light gets brighter. The music gets louder.

Christian music, I think. Old-timey Christian worship music. In this dank cave it sounds eerie and out of place, but I keep pushing forward without thinking of the smell of mildew and the cobwebs and the entrenching blackness.

I only think of my sister, and I won't leave without her.

Even if that means I don't leave at all.

Mom used to say we'd leave the world the same way we entered it. When I entered the world, there was only Cassie, and I intend to leave it the same way. Even if that means leaving tonight.

The light comes from the crack of a door. I can hear movement behind it. Rustling. Two voices. I touch the door and press my ear to it. One voice keeps getting lost in the intensity of the music, but I recognize Sarah's. I lean my forehead against the door, grasp the handle, and get ready to open it.

"Lenora?" My sister's voice is crisp and clear and scared.

She must feel me too.

It's all I need to push through. The door swings open, and my heart stalls in my chest. There are three people standing in front of me. Cassie's eyes are wide with a fear I've only seen once from her. They seem to convey everything I'm feeling.

I was wrong.

So very wrong.

"Run, Lenora," she says.

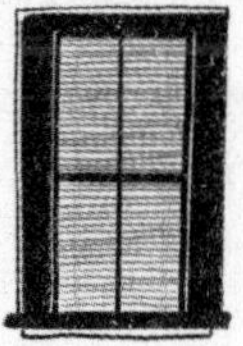

CHAPTER THIRTY-SEVEN
THEN

As my heart threatens to burst straight through my chest and the fear bleeds into panic, all I can see is the blood.

The wicked scene spreads out in front of me, and I cannot look away. It takes only a second to take in, to comprehend. Only a moment for my chest to deflate and my heart to stop, for me to see the truth for what it is.

"What happened?" That's everything that can come from my dry parted lips. Only words I can manage.

But it isn't a question. Not really. Mom is lying sideways across her bed. A knife sticks from her chest, but there's so much blood—over her, on her sheets. So much, I can't gauge the extent of her injuries.

And that's when I see you. I realize the wetness I felt on you isn't sweat. No, you're covered in blood too. I bring my hands to my face and stumble back. Red. So much red.

"You did it again," I say, numb. Because in every way that it's your fault, it's mine too. I knew what you are, what you're capable of. I've always known.

Still, you don't speak. We both must be remembering. Remembering everything. Even the hard parts. The night of the fire. Me seeing you slip from our window. Following you into the night, to Wellesley House. I stayed back, lingering near the woods. Perplexed about what you were doing. You went around the front of the house, and I waited so long that I almost left, almost went home. Sometimes I wish I had.

But then I smelled the smoke. "An accident," you claimed when I came running from the woods in a panic. But the words hadn't reached your eyes. And when I said we needed to get them out, you told me it was too late.

It felt so wrong not to try.

To listen to their screams from the second-story window.

I cried, and you hugged me. Rocked me. Said you lit the bushes on fire as a joke. To get Kate's attention. You didn't mean for the fire to spread, and you were crying too. I felt the wetness of your tears on my shoulder.

The house went up in flames, and I helped you hide the gas can you used. I told you I understood. I reassured you I knew it was an accident.

We came home filthy, smelling of smoke. When Mom's light turned on, I boosted you through our window, and I faced her. I told a lie. Something I can't even remember now, but ever since there was something in the way she looked at me that made me wonder if she connected me with what had happened at Wellesley House that night.

You wipe your face with your hand, smearing a streak of blood that you don't seem to notice.

"I'm sorry." But the look on your face is different now. More somber as you step to the side. I see what you were blocking. Monica slumped over. No blood on her or injuries. Almost like she's sleeping.

I gasp and fall back into the wall, pressing a hand against it, leaving a bloody print. "What did you do?" Then I move reflexively. I go to Monica. Touch a finger to her neck and find no pulse. Monica's face is angled away and down. Her features seem even prettier in death. And I was right before. The feathers do blend with blood.

"It was an accident."

The tears surprise me. The pain takes me off guard. Mourning a woman, a mother, who never really existed and a girl I didn't really like. I turn around in just enough time to throw up. When I'm finished, I rock back on my haunches and look at you. You're small in your blood-soaked pajamas. Your pants that are too short for your skinny legs. Fifteen and only a girl. Now my heart moves again. Now the sadness and agony and angst come roaring back because I can't lose you too. Not you.

"Mom wasn't supposed to be home," you say. "Monica was here. I snuck her in. We—Things happened. Got out of control. I didn't mean to hurt her. I asked her to come with us. To run with us. But she wouldn't. She won't leave her brother. It was never supposed to happen like this. Then Mom came in, and she made it so much worse."

"The knife," I whisper. "Where did it come from?"

You don't answer. But you don't have to. If this had played out like you said, if you never intended to hurt anyone, then how did the knife get up here?

"This is my fault. I should have protected you." None of this would have happened if I had watched you better. You wouldn't have been forced into this. But I see you now, the way your eyes roam over her body and Mom's. Even I can see the flash of pleasure, the flash of pride. The lack of remorse. I stand quickly and grab your face, streaking your chin with our mother's blood. "Why do you keep doing this? Why would you do this to us? We were about to leave. It was all about to be over!"

"I don't know." You're sobbing now, your shoulders shaking, your chest heaving. "You hate me, don't you?"

"No." My answer is automatic and requires no thought. I fold your trembling and bloody body into my arms. "Never." I have to remind you that there's something to fight for still. I can't lose you to the monster that lives in your head. I have to separate it from you. Split you apart piece by piece.

You're still my sister.

"I can't help it." The way you mumble it into my shoulder. Like you hate yourself for the words. For feeling the way you do. "I know it's wrong, but I liked it. Ever since Kate."

"No." My voice is high now as I pull back to look at you. "You don't get to do this. You don't get to be this. You don't get to leave me."

Your jaw is clenched, your eyes shrouded in darkness.

Has it always been that dark inside you?

I release you slowly. "This isn't who you are. Dad hurt you. Mom probably knew. She deserved this." My stomach turns violently again. "Wait, he hurt you. That's true, isn't it?"

You look down.

The room crumbles like a castle made of blocks. "But he was crying that night."

"He found a photo of Kate. I made a joke about her. About

the night of the fire. We got into a fight, and I said some awful things to him."

"What did you tell him?"

"That he shouldn't be so critical of me when every choice I make is his fault. He's the one who leaves us. He's the one who chooses the drugs over us. We all do things we regret. I thought if anyone would understand, it would be him."

A roaring in my ears. "So you told me he was abusing you?"

"I just wanted you to understand how much he hurt me. I wanted you to hate him like I did."

You're a liar, I think.

You're also so much worse than that.

"What about Monica? I thought she was your friend?" I stop and look down at her. Her body that suddenly seems so small.

"Can I be honest with you?" You wipe at the streaks of dried tears on your face. It leaves tracks through the blood splatter. "I didn't exactly want to kill her. I mostly needed to ask for her help."

An ice-cold tremor runs down my spine. "Help us do what?"

"Kill our parents. Run away. Our plan, remember?"

"No." I step back. "No. I just wanted to run away. I didn't want to kill them."

"Hey," you say. "Hey, it's OK. Just a misunderstanding."

"A misunderstanding," I mumble, blindingly aware of our mother's and Monica's bodies. The numbness spreads.

"No one will miss her. There's no reason our lives have to end because of one little mistake. We can still follow through with our plan. We can still run."

Our eyes meet.

But the only thing I can think is I have to get you out of here.

"You still love me, don't you, Sandra?" you ask.

There are pulsing memories like an artery severed. Hiding from our parents as they screamed at each other. Giggling under the covers. Riding bikes barefoot for entire summers until our feet were calloused and our hands ached. I don't know when it happened. When you changed.

I really don't know how you can morph into this awful thing and my love for you, Emily, not stumble an inch. It would be easier if I could hate you, and I try. I think of the cat. Of Kate. Of house fires. Life-stealing lies. Monica and the brother who will never see her again. Our mother. The good and the bad battle in my brain until I know what I have to do.

Until one side wins.

"It was a mistake." I say the words slowly, the truth of them settling into place like a rock. "This isn't you." You nod gently in agreement, and I take a step away. "Let's clean this up."

And we do. We pull the knife from Mom's chest. Drag Monica to your bed.

Then we do what we do best. We start a fire.

I tell myself the bad is being burned up until it's gone.

A baptism by fire.

You're new now. Different. Changed.

I'll never let you hurt anyone again.

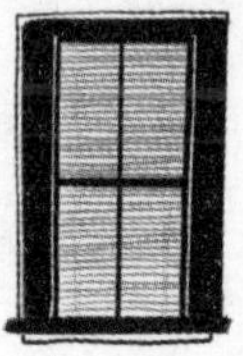

CHAPTER THIRTY-EIGHT
LENORA

The room is not very large. Eight by twelve, maybe. It looks like a bunker. Shelves full of dried and dehydrated foods. Jugs of water lining the walls. The music is coming from a stereo on a shelf. An old CD player that skips every few seconds.

My gaze then lands on Cassie. Lying on a mat with her feet tied together and her wrists behind her back. The image should be frightening. Horrifying. But the first thing I feel is relief. She's OK. My sister is OK.

The relief doesn't last long.

There are two others in the room. Sarah and a woman I don't recognize. This long, slender pale woman. But I know her. I know her alabaster flesh. I know her blond hair that hangs in two sleek curtains around her face. I know her smile.

They rush back to me in screaming color, the memories.

Waking in the woods, disoriented and trembling. The blurry world around me all looming shadows and dark shapes. But there. In the middle of the trees is a person. A girl or woman, I can't tell. She's dragging something. Hunched over. Grunting.

I squint.

What is she pulling?

With no contacts or glasses, it's all a blur that has me questioning what I'm really seeing at all.

Or if I'm even awake.

The woman stops moving.

So still, she could be an animal as easily as a shadow.

I can't see. Can't understand.

I don't know how long I stand there with neither of us moving before I turn around and run. Stumble. Trip. Scratches on my arms and legs. Can't see. Can't think. A dream or just me seeing things in the dark?

Until I'm back in between my sheets and unsure if I was ever even outside at all.

"It was you I saw that night," I say, not taking my eyes off this person. I wasn't dreaming. It had all been real.

She's taller than Sarah. Her hair is near waist length and hanging in oily clumps like she's in need of a wash. She's wearing clothes I recognize. Cassie's white UCLA T-shirt. A pair of my sweatpants I hadn't even realized were missing.

Things I thought were burned in the fire.

Sarah is looking at me as if she's seen a ghost.

"Run!" Cassie screams from her spot in the corner of the room. "Go, Lenora! Run!"

I look away from the woman to my sister. It must be clear on my face because the words die on her lips: I'm not leaving this room without her, even if that means I never leave at all.

I never was good at running.

Her eyes hold mine, tears leaking from the corners of them and down her cheeks.

Fear trickles in like slow-moving Antarctic water.

"I'm so sorry, Lenora." Sarah is unblinking and stoic. "None of this should have happened." It's the same Sarah who let the cops in. The one who served me tea and fudge in her kitchen. The Sarah who brought us dinner and gave us a place to stay.

It doesn't make sense.

"What's happening? Who is that?"

The woman is still watching me now, but her expression is indiscernible. And it clicks as I look between them. They're not perfectly identical, but they look strikingly similar.

"My younger sister. Emily," Sarah says, stepping in front of the woman. Then I remember the article. Sarah when she was Sandra. An escape from a house fire. A dead sister who clearly didn't die.

"You said you were running from someone," I say.

"Running from everyone," Sarah says. "We have been since we were teenagers. All I've ever wanted is to keep her safe."

"But the article said your sister died in a house fire."

"That wasn't my sister. My dad just identified her as my sister. It was someone else. A girl who died that night too. Emily didn't mean to do it. It was an accident that spun out of control."

Her words take a moment before sinking in. I look between Sarah and Emily. "You killed your mom and friend?"

Sarah shakes her head. "It wasn't like that. You make it sound so evil. It was a mistake. I promised her I would take care of her since then. That's why we're here. We needed something more private. I didn't know. I swear to you, I didn't know. I thought she was secure. The room she stays in doesn't even have windows. I swear, I didn't know anyone was in danger."

Sarah speaks, but it's Emily who has me fascinated. Her head slightly tilted, lips pulled up at the corners like she's amused. I recognize her now. A face in the window. The back of her head in Cabin Three. A growing shape in the dark. Walking down the hallway in my robe.

"It was you," I say to Emily.

Her lips inch up. "What was me?" I expect her voice to sound like something being dragged across gravel. A spine-tingling sound. But she just sounds normal. She looks curious.

"In the window that day when I thought it was Tilly or Karen. And that was you who left the camera on in the hallway. Put my robe on. You were in my room with me. That was all you."

Sarah swivels toward her sister, but Emily only has eyes for me. "I like you and your sister," she says. "You remind me of Sandra and me."

"I don't understand."

"None of this was supposed to happen," Sarah emphasizes through her teeth. "It was all an accident. A big misunderstanding."

"You weren't supposed to drag me down here and tie me up?" Cassie asks sarcastically. "I guess I accidently fell into these zip ties."

"I didn't know this was down here. I didn't know you were down here, Cassie. You have to believe me." Sarah is practically hyperventilating now.

Before I can comment, Cassie scoffs. "She keeps her sister locked up, Lenora. There's a room in Cabin One. A tiny room hidden behind a bookshelf. It was Wayne's panic room. Sarah didn't know it was also an escape room."

"I kept Emily in that room for her own good and yours. I didn't know she was able to get out. I never would have put her in there had I known," Sarah explains. Emily is looking at her sister, and I can't quite tell what she's thinking.

The dynamic between them is strange. In all the ways it counts, Sarah appears to be Emily's captor. The older one. The one in control. You'd think there would be resentment between them.

"It's a sickness," Sarah says with wet cheeks and shaking shoulders. "She's not a bad person. She's just sick. It's my job to protect her."

"You hide your sister in a cellar?" The shock wraps me up tightly. I look between the two women and try to make sense of this. "Your sister has lived here this whole time, and you've kept her locked up in a room? Why?"

She wipes her nose on her arm, smearing snot along her face. "She knows she needs to be here. She knows I keep her safe. But how was I supposed to know this existed? I didn't know any of this was down here. It's all my fault. Not hers."

Emily's eyes glint. Smart, I think. She's clearly smart, but when she looks at her sister, there's another emotion, and I can't decide if it's love or hate.

"I have to protect her, you know? She's my sister. I have to protect her from herself. But I never meant for any of this to happen. You have to understand. What happened to Tilly will never happen again."

My intake of breath is audible, and everything finally makes sense. "Your sister killed Tilly." The first thing I feel is anger. It's almost powerful enough to overwhelm the fear. But I'm shaking, and my knees are nearly buckling, and my sister is still tied up.

And I know it like I know I need air to breathe.

We're going to die down here.

The voice in my head says the words simply. Preparing me. My first reaction is to push them away. To fight them back and deny it, but my resistance transitions to acceptance.

I look at Cassie, who is staring at me, urging me with her eyes.

She still wants me to run.

Sarah's lips thin. "I didn't know this bunker existed. I didn't know there was a tunnel to the outside. None of this is Emily's fault."

"Sarah," Cassie says, her voice low and gentle. She's trying to maintain some semblance of self-control even as it all slips away. "I get it. I know what it's like to want to protect someone you love. We can help you do that. We can help you make sure Emily is kept safe."

A dark chuckle slips past Emily's lips, and our heads snap in her direction. She somehow inched closer to me. "Sandra," Emily says, looking at her sister, "they'll tell. You know they'll tell. We can't let them out of here. It'll destroy everything."

"Let me think. Just let me think." Sarah is looking at my sister and me, her expression crumbling.

"We won't say anything." Cassie's voice is soft and urgent. "We're friends, Sarah. I wouldn't hurt you on purpose. I trusted you. Now you have to trust me. I want to help you. Please."

"She's lying." Emily's brows pull low, and her eyes fill with tears. "I'm the one who's going to get in trouble when it's not my fault anyway. You know how I am. How could you expect me not to leave when you put me in a room with a door?"

Sarah flinches.

And the oppressor becomes the oppressed.

"You set me up to fail," Emily whispers. "I trusted you to keep me safe. I trusted you to help me. Now they're going to ruin everything, and you're going to let them."

"She's manipulating you," Cassie says. "Just listen to me. Let me go, and we can talk about this."

"We can't let them leave," Emily murmurs to her sister. Sarah looks torn, her gaze shifting between the three of us. "I don't want to hurt them either. I don't want to do this. I don't want to be this person. But if we let them go, then I'll never get a chance to make things right. You'll never get a chance to make it up to me for putting me in this position in the first place."

"No," Cassie practically growls. "No. Hurting us won't make anything right. That won't make anything better."

Sarah's eyes waver, and for one second, one long and short and spectacular second, I think she may just do it.

She may let us go.

Then her face shutters. "I can't."

Cassie's teeth grind together, and she looks at Emily. "You can at least untie me and make this fight a little more even."

My body jolts. This can't be happening. This can't be real.

"You want to fight me, Cassie?"

"I want to slam your face into the wall."

"Cassie." I keep my voice level, keep my eyes on Sandra and Emily. I have to keep my sister calm. Keep everyone calm for us to have any hope of escaping.

"What happened that night? I know I saw you out there," I ask Emily. Just keep her talking. I need to keep her talking. "If you're going to kill us, the least you can do is answer our questions first."

Emily says something to Sarah too low for me to hear.

Desperate now, I call out, "You owe us that much. Both of you. We deserve to know what happened to Tilly."

"I'd been out several times before that night. I'd been watching you both for days," Emily says, and I can see it. Emily lurking in the woods. Peering into windows. Me and my sister blissfully oblivious to what is waiting in the dark.

"How come you never hurt Cassie or me?"

"Because that was never my intention." The way she says it is almost believable. She tucks her hair behind her ears. "I just wanted to breathe some fresh air. To be entertained. And you two are really entertaining. So, every night when I snuck out, I'd come just to watch."

My skin prickles. "What changed?"

"The girl saw me. I didn't think. I had to act." She turns to Sarah. "You know I didn't plan it, don't you? You know I never would have risked us for something like that."

Sarah is silently crying, but she nods. Reaches for her sister's hand and squeezes.

It makes me sick.

"I think you're lying." Everyone turns sharply to Cassie. She's bracing herself on her wrists behind her back as she leans forward, still mostly lying down. "I think you did plan it. I think if you hadn't killed Tilly that night, then it would have been one of us."

"No, it was an accident."

"Are you trying to convince us or yourself?"

"How did you do it, Emily?" I ask quietly.

Her expression changes when I say her name. Almost softens. She holds her hands up so I can see them.

"You used your hands? You strangled her?"

"Yes." Like she's answering a question regarding the weather. "Right outside your cabin actually," Emily says. "Against the wall. Anyone could have walked out and seen it at any time. As much as you watch, Lenora, you sure miss a lot."

There is a part of me evaluating the situation. Going through scenarios. In each one I'll run a calculated risk. The door is to my back, and unless there's an inexplicable third sister I don't know about blocking that exit, then I'll have a clear shot. But if I try to run for help, it may not arrive before they hurt Cassie.

Strike that one.

I fight them.

But it's two to one, and Cassie would be vulnerable. They'd overpower me easily.

Strike that one.

"So, what now?" Cassie asks. "We're at your mercy." She shakes her bound ankles for emphasis. "What are you going to do with us?"

"It's not that I want to do anything. I'm sorry," Emily tells us. "I don't have a choice." She steps toward Cassie.

"Wait," I say, throwing my hands up, holding my palms out to her. "You said we reminded you of you and your sister. How?"

Emily lets out a breath of laughter. "You really want to know?"

"Yes."

"I see myself in you the most, Lenora. I think..." she whispers. "I think we have a lot more in common than you think."

"I'm nothing like you. I don't like hurting people."

Emily smiles. "Me neither."

At this, Sarah backs away slowly. "I'm so sorry. I can't be here for this. You have to understand. She's all I have. I'm sorry." She makes it to a ladder and starts her ascent.

"You're just going to leave us down here with her?" I yell. "You're going to let her kill us?"

"Emily doesn't care about you," Cassie says, and Sarah stops. One hand reaching toward the door over her head and one hand on a rung. "Don't you see that? She wouldn't hurt other people if she did. She would know that's the one thing that would make her lose you forever."

Sarah keeps her back to us but lowers her head. "I'm so sorry. I never meant for any of this to happen."

"What are you going to tell the police?" I ask as a last-ditch effort of survival kicks in, making the hair on my neck stand up. I'm close to death, and some innate part of my human psyche knows it and repels it.

"It doesn't matter what they think. Emily and I will be gone tomorrow. Same as you. Besides, none of that matters anymore." Sarah looks at Emily, not quite meeting her eyes. "Make it quick," she says. "Then we have to go." She doesn't look back at all as she goes up the ladder and disappears.

Cassie's face is twisted into torment. "Please, run, Lenora. Please go. There's no reason for you to die too."

And we're back in a long hallway. The last time Cassie told me to run. That time I didn't listen, not because I didn't want to, but because I couldn't. I was frozen in terror. Now it's different. I could run, and perhaps a part of me truly considers it. After all, if we both die down here, then no one will ever know the truth. About Emily. About Tilly. About the people Emily killed. Those things are important, and it's almost enough for me to leave.

But the sight of Cassie bound and lying there.

The thought of the terror I would leave her to experience alone is worse than any other type of torture.

"Yes, Lenora. You should run," Emily says. "You might make it." Gone is the docile, repentant Emily. This is the real Emily. The one who hopes I run just so she can catch me.

I only focus on my sister. Emily might take our lives, but she won't take this moment. Cassie's eyes fill with heavy tears. Each drop tells me something else.

I love you.

I'm sorry.

If I could do things differently, I would.

Please go.

I shake my head. Let my own tears say everything back. Everything I've wanted to say and couldn't.

I know.

Me too.

I wouldn't.

I'm not going anywhere.

Emily moves toward Cassie.

"Wait, please," I say, my voice rising hysterically. No, I'm not ready yet. "Please, you don't have to do this."

Emily steps toward me. "You're right. I should start with you."

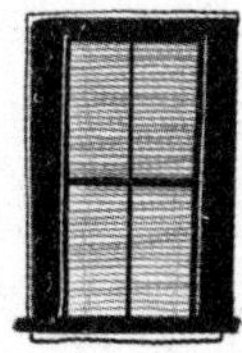

CHAPTER THIRTY-NINE

CASSIE

Sometimes I think of our mother. I think of her staring down at two tiny girls in the middle of the night. Both wailing for milk or warmth. And her, so lost and confused, she could provide neither. Her husband's side of the bed is cold. Her body is still bleeding. And if these two things make one more sound, she may just lose her mind.

That's what I picture at least.

That somehow Lenora and I were responsible for destroying our mother but saving each other.

Except now the thing that saved us might get us killed.

That's how I ended up here. A drive in the middle of the night. A figure in the dark that had me slamming my brakes before I even made it to the main road. I thought it was Lenora and left my car there, still running. Thought she was sleepwalking again. I followed her until she disappeared. Until there was pain, and the lights went out.

I woke zip-tied on a bed.

And if I had to guess, Lenora is here because of me too.

"Hey! Look at me, Emily. Only at me." I talk while working my wrists in the zip ties. Since they're raw and slick with blood, it makes what I'm doing just a little easier. "Start with me. I'm the one you want."

But she doesn't listen, and Emily lunges for my sister.

She slams Lenora back into the wall once, twice. My sister is like a rag doll. Her skinny body at Emily's mercy.

I bend my wrists, squeeze. A sharp pain zings up my arm, and a cry tears from my lips. Almost there. Almost.

Lenora's arms are up, her hands on Emily's face, her thumbs sinking into her eyes until Emily lets go. This is it. Lenora is finally going to have the upper hand—but Emily is there again. And somehow, they both tumble to the ground with Emily on top and her hands around Lenora's neck.

My left hand slides free first, and the pain intensifies. My whole hand is throbbing, pulsing with hot blood and agony. I start working the zip ties on my ankles. It only takes a couple of seconds to realize it won't be as simple to undo these. My hand is too messed up.

It's not going to work.

Lenora's legs are kicking; her body is bucking.

No.

Focus on the room. I scan it, look for something that could help. There's a glass jar filled with water. I swing my legs over the bed and hop sideways to grab it before smashing it against the side.

Lenora isn't moving now.

My heart picks up. Adrenaline spikes.

The glass cuts into my hand as I saw at the zip ties with my good hand.

Since I'm slippery with blood, it's impossible to get a good grip. I dig the glass into my palm deeper. Until it's steady. Warmth flows down my fingers. Blood.

"Come on, come on." Finally the zip tie starts to break. I keep going, sawing and pulling my ankles apart at the same time until it gives.

Then I'm free. Three paces, and I'm across the room, using all my body weight to heave myself onto Emily's back. She claws at my arm.

Lenora gasps for breath, her own hands flying to her neck.

I squeeze with my legs, with my arms, with all I have, shaking and hot. The pain is blinding. I look at my sister. "It's your turn to run now. I'm right behind you."

Eyes too wide and frozen, she shakes her head.

"I'm right behind you. Go, Lenora! You have to go."

She stands, stumbles back, looks at me one more time with turmoil in her eyes, and then turns, disappearing into the darkness.

All I feel is relief.

Lenora is going to live. Lenora is going to make it. Suddenly Emily surges up and uses all her body weight to slam us backward. I grunt, unable to maintain my grip, and she uses the momentum to straddle me, grabbing my wrist.

Her hands, covered in my blood, slide to my neck. Squeeze. "Just let go," Emily says breathlessly. "Just let go, and I'll kill your sister quickly. She won't even—"

Then suddenly the weight and pressure are gone. Emily is on her side, screaming, her hands gripping the back of her head. Lenora is standing over her, holding a brick.

We don't speak. There are no words exchanged because we're both on the same wavelength. "Hit her again," I say, wiping my mouth with the back of my arm. All I taste is blood.

Lenora swings the brick down. It connects with the side of Emily's face and slips from Lenora's fingers, crashing to the floor. Emily goes still and quiet.

I crawl forward and grab it.

Smash it over her face once more. Blood splatters and something cracks. My hands burn, and I let the brick fall to the ground. Emily isn't moving.

Her chest is completely still.

I rock back on my heels, shaking so hard, I wouldn't be able to pick the brick up again if I tried. "Is she dead?" I ask, barely getting the words out.

"I think so. Now come on. We have to go." Lenora helps me to my feet, pulling and tugging and leading me to a pitch-black hallway.

"It's this way. Just keep your hand on the wall. Go straight," Lenora says from right behind me.

It's so dark, I can't even see five feet in front of me.

The light and music edge away.

I hear my sister's heavy breathing.

Nearly silent sobs.

I sense it. The wall. The ladder. I step to the side. It's too dark to see my sister, but I nudge her. "Go," I say urgently. "Go up."

"You first."

I can hear the stubbornness in her voice and know there's no sense in arguing with her. I start to climb. With one hand bloody and burning, and the other most likely broken, I'm biting back screams with each rung.

I can feel Lenora at my heels. As close to me as possible, and I push up at the loose door. Heave with my head and hands to get it open. The moon looks brighter than I've ever seen it. I flop over onto the dirt before rolling to look down.

Lenora's head is just popping out when her eyes widen. She makes a mewling sound I've never heard before as she climbs the rest of the way out. I don't understand what's happened until I see it.

A knife sticking out of her back right above her hips.

She lies on her side, her legs still dangling in the hole, and Emily is here. Pulsing blood trickling down the creases of her face and into her mouth. Pulling herself out. Ripping the knife from my sister's back.

It doesn't make sense.

My brain can't fully understand what just happened. I call my sister's name. I press a hand to her cheek. But she doesn't move. Doesn't breathe.

Emily watches, swaying on her feet. "Are you going to run now?" she asks. Her words sound slow, sluggish.

"No," I say, moving to my feet. "But you should." I lunge for her.

There is pain in my arm, a pinch on my side.

But nothing is more painful than my sister without breath.

I don't care about dying. I'll go gladly if it means taking this bitch with me. I get Emily to the ground, pinning her wrist. The knife falls a foot away. I can't reach for it without letting her go, so I do the next best thing. I slam her head down.

Again and again and again.

There's a push and pull, and Emily is on top, and I can't move. There is only thrashing against her.

Her hands around my neck.

Still so strong even with a head wound pulsing blood.

Darkness creeps in.

If I tilt my head to the right, I can see Lenora. Lying there completely still. I always wondered what they thought. The victims. I wondered what crossed their mind when they knew they were going to die. When they knew they were breaths away from oblivion. What will be there? Who will be waiting on us? It must be different for everyone. For me, I think of Lenora. Just her. Her warmth. Her hand in mine. Her smile.

We will become a crime scene. Fodder for my very own community.

What happened?

Who did this to them?

They will wonder, but the answer will be far more complicated.

I close my eyes.

Then everything stops. Emily's hands release all at once. A strange expression is on her face as she falls forward, her body weight heaving on top of me. I gasp and choke for air, frantically trying to put out the fire in my lungs.

That's when I see her. Sarah. Standing in front of me. Behind where her sister just fell. A bloody knife in her hands.

She's looking at the knife and then her sister, a dazed expression on her face.

I lift my body. Crawl to Lenora. Place my hands on either side of her face. My throat hurts too much to try to speak, so I can only listen. Wait.

There.

The ragged draw of breath.

And there we are, Sarah and I.

Leaning over our sisters and crying for two very different reasons.

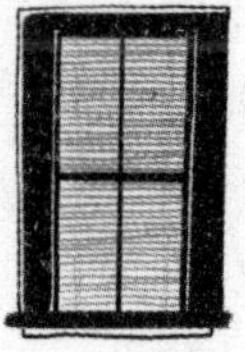

CHAPTER FORTY
SANDRA

There comes a time when we must make a choice. Every choice in my whole life has always been you. Will always be you. Even this one.

I tried, Emily. I tried to protect you.

The years we spent running together… I used to trust you. Used to watch you so closely and keep tabs on you. But you proved it wasn't enough. After Kate, Mom, and Monica, I still believed you. Still believed you were good. And things were great for a while. I started working at that restaurant in San Antonio. You got a job at that juice place downtown. I thought we were going to make it, you and I. We didn't speak of what happened in our home that night or what happened at Wellesley House. You were changed.

Then there was Beth.

I knew when she went missing that I had to do something.

Again, it was my fault. I should have watched you better. I shouldn't have put you in temptation's way. She was our neighbor.

Your bedroom window looked right into hers. So we came here. It was isolated. I told you about the secret room. Told you I would keep you in it. You cried and said you needed help. That you didn't want to be this way. You said you wanted to change too. You said you were sorry, and I thought things were finally changing.

I tried.

We came here and I met them. The twins. In them, Emily, I see me and you. Those women. Those sisters. I see what we could have been.

Their love and fear and panic, all intertwined. I understand them because we are them.

So you have to understand why I couldn't let you do it. Why I couldn't let you hurt them to save us. Because hurting them would destroy us.

Hurting them is hurting us.

Mom and Dad always loved you more, and I know why. We want what we can't have, and no one could have you. You are the sun and stars and moon. A meteor shower, brightly burning and then gone. The good parts of you are fleeting and persuasive.

I want to hold you.

Rock you.

Keep you safe forever.

You sink in front of me, and even more than the desperation and sadness so thick it coats my tongue, more than that is the relief. The tiny feeling in the back of my head that sings, *It's over. It's finally over.*

That's what I hate the most.

I whisper the Lord's Prayer under my breath, between gasping, hitching sobs. "Our Lord…hallowed be thy name…" But I can't remember the words, and I break. "Oh, God. Please take her. Please take her. Oh, God. She's sorry. I'm sorry."

But my cries are hollow.

I am empty.

And you're not here.

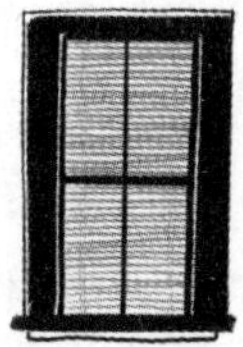

CHAPTER FORTY-ONE
CASSIE

There is no trash in the Blacktop. Hasn't been since Tilly died. Guess death keeps the teenagers away.

My hands curl around my knees as the breeze catches my hair. I close my eyes and feel it. I don't know how long I've been sitting on our rock. I only know I don't have anywhere else to be. Not for another hour at least.

"Hey."

I glance over my shoulder. Lenora is walking toward me. Hobbling, really. It's only been four weeks since she was stabbed. The wound has healed nicely, but she's still slightly off-balance. Still wincing every few steps. She walks out here anyway with her head high and a smile on her lips. It's still weird to see her outside the cabin. But she's done it more. A little bit farther each day. I was worried at first that almost getting killed would set her back, would be worse for her. But somehow it's had the opposite effect.

She is a beautiful sight.

"Thought I'd find you out here," she calls out to me.

"The cabin is suffocating."

She slides onto the rock next to me, her body instantly heating mine. Our connection buzzes with an energy that no amount of time or secrets can dim. "You all packed?" she asks.

"You know I am."

"Why aren't you acting more excited?"

"I would be if you were coming too."

"I told you." She rolls her eyes playfully. "This is your thing. Besides, you know I can't deal with the media." The press hasn't let up over the past month, and I can hardly take it—the phone calls, the request for interviews. So I know Lenora must be struggling.

She tells me I thrive in the attention. She says everyone loves a survivor, especially one as weird and quirky as me. It's true, I love the followers. The attention they bring to my channel and all the victims whose stories I tell. But I love Lenora more, and when the panic sets in about leaving her, even if it's just for a one-week trip to LA for an interview, it makes me itchy.

But I tell myself she's safe. Threats are neutralized. Even Karen and Robert are on decent terms with us. After everything that happened, we'll never be friends. But they returned shortly after Emily's death and Sarah's arrest. Karen apologized. So did we. They left together, clinging to each other as they walked back to their vehicle.

"Is Parker still meeting you?"

I cut my eyes toward her. "Not like that. But yes, he's going to be there."

"It's OK, you know? For you to be with him. I mean really be with him. Not just in the dark."

"I know." I stare forward at the Blacktop. "But neither of us wants to right now. We both think I should focus on me." Parker came by shortly after Sarah was arrested. He apologized to Lenora for insinuating she set that fire.

She accepted his apology and invited him to stay for dinner.

"Yes," my sister murmurs. "Be selfish for once. Besides, you'll be back in another week, and that's when the real fun starts." The thought eases my anxiety just a little. We're going to travel first before deciding where to settle down. A road trip up the East Coast. We don't know where we're going after; we only know we can't stay here. Lucky for us, we can afford it. Thanks to a six-figure book advance after an editor reached out to Lenora about telling our story. Her eyes lit with joy when she told me about it. No more ghostwriting for her. Lenora will tell her own story for the very first time in her own words.

"Where do you think we'll go when we get back?" she asks, staring forward at the forest. The wind shakes the trees. Peaceful noise.

"Somewhere with neighbors who don't have hidden tunnels under their house." Apparently, Wayne had a fake bookshelf in his spare room. Behind that was the panic room where Emily chose to stay. Sarah told the police that she never forced Emily and wasn't keeping her against her will. Emily had asked for the help and agreed to Sarah's terms. The way Sarah describes it, it's almost like she was helping Emily overcome a reluctant addiction. What Sarah hadn't known about was the offshoot to that room that led to an underground cellar and tunnel. Emily had a way out the whole time. She was in our cabin. In my room. In the bathhouse. She was everywhere.

Now she's nowhere, and Sarah isn't here either.

She took a plea deal, last I heard, and will spend a few years in prison.

It probably shouldn't, but the last part tugs at my heart. The agony on Sarah's face that night. It was the last time I saw Sarah.

I can't condone anything she's done. People died because of her choices. A young girl who went missing in San Antonio, and the girl who burned in the house fire that destroyed their childhood home. They even connected Sarah and her sister to another house fire in their hometown that killed another young woman. Kate Wellesley. The sister of that victim is very much alive and, last I heard, has never given up hope on finding justice for her own sister.

None of it is OK.

But maybe a small part of me understands that desperate longing to protect. To show love the best way you know how, as sick as it makes you.

I think Sarah was my friend.

Even at the end.

"Looks like a storm's coming," I say, glancing up at the hazy sky. But Lenora is turned back. Toward Sarah's cabin.

"It was wrong, what she did," Lenora murmurs more to herself than to me. "If Sarah had turned her in sooner, Tilly would still be here, and Emily would be locked up. None of this would have happened."

"Yes."

"I keep wondering." Her voice lowers. "How much better am I than her?"

A flock of blackbirds screams and lands in a flurry all across the field. Reminds me of a night not too long ago when I saw a person on the Blacktop. Emily.

"Maybe you should have turned me in, Cassie."

The birds' beady black eyes stare. Their heads and wings twitch. I brush my fingers against the rock. It's cold. So cold. But it's what's beneath the rock that's even colder. Our darkest secret. Our biggest tragedy.

Our mother.

"Why didn't you run, Lenora?"

She inhales sharply. Looks at me. "I saw her over Dad's body, and I froze."

I remember. I remember the creak of that door. The stillness in my chest as I took a breath that I physically couldn't release. I remember seeing our mother standing over our father. She had one bloody hand covering her lips while the other held a knife. Her mouth opened like she was calling out to us, but nothing came out.

It took several seconds that might as well have been hours for me to process the scene. For me to understand what our mother had done. In the months leading up to this moment, she'd stopped cooking. Stopped dancing. Stopped talking to Lenora and me. She'd spent nights in her room crying.

Dad would get home, and they'd scream at each other for hours, like a single closed door would protect our ears.

But how did she go from an unhappy housewife to a murderer? Our mother to a monster.

I tugged Lenora's hand and told her to run. But I didn't know Lenora was closing her eyes, too frozen to move a single step.

"I made it all the way outside before I realized you weren't with me," I say numbly. I still remember stumbling out the front door. Running toward the neighbor's house. Stopping when I felt the pressure of silence at my back. The front door was wide open, but you were nowhere to be seen.

The blackbirds shoot into the sky and move several yards away before landing on the green leafed trees. It feels like I could fly away with them if I really wanted.

"Why did you go back for me?" Lenora asks.

"I'll always go back for you."

I called her name in a broken whisper. Every bone in my body screaming at me not to turn around and go up those stairs. But my sister was there. I didn't have a choice.

When I made it to the top, everything was wrong. Our mother was slumped on the ground. Lenora's arms and hands were slick with blood.

"What happened?" I asked, bracing myself on my knees, choking back vomit. The blood.

There was so much blood.

Lenora couldn't speak through the hysteria.

I went to her. Laid both hands on her cheeks. "What happened? What did you do?"

Lenora only cried harder.

It had to have been self-defense. Our mother must have attacked her. Lenora had to fight back. That's when the fear sank in. What if they thought this was all Lenora's fault and they took her away too? What if I lost my entire family at once?

I couldn't let that happen.

"You have to calm down," I said to my sister, swallowing back the bile in my throat. "You have to breathe."

"The police." Lenora barely got the words out.

"Not yet." I looked at our mother's body, then back to Lenora. "We have to do something first."

"I'm sorry. I didn't mean—"

I shushed her. "It's OK. You didn't have a choice. It's all going to be OK. Now just listen to me."

It took all night. Rolling Mom's body in the hallway rug. Loading her in the trunk. We just drove. For hours. Off the interstate and down dirt roads until we found an abandoned field. And we dug and we buried.

We showered when we returned home well into the morning. Then we called the police. The story would always be that our mother killed our father and left. No one would ever know anything different.

When Lenora couldn't speak, they called it shock.

When she refused to leave the house, they called it PTSD.

We never spoke of that night again.

We visited Mom's grave every year. Never bringing flowers. Never staying long.

Until we came and her field was covered in tents, and two teenagers were sitting on her rock. Her grave was now a campground. It would be another three years before we came back again. After Lenora's breakdown. After we hit our lowest point. We decided to get away. To go camping.

We came here.

And we never left.

Lenora rubs her hands along the rock, a tear dribbling down her cheek. "She didn't try to kill me, Cassie."

My breath stalls. "What did you say?"

"That's what you assumed. You thought that was what happened."

"It was the only explanation, Lenora."

"No," she says. "Not the only one. I was freaking out. Begging her to call an ambulance. And I remember her lifting the knife. I remember thinking she was going to kill me, but I didn't fight back. I couldn't. I just closed my eyes. She grabbed my hand. Placed the knife in my palm. I didn't want to touch it. It was wet with Dad's blood. Warm." There's a faraway expression on Lenora's face. "And she just looked at me, and I knew, Cassie, I can't explain it. But I knew she wanted to die."

"No. No, Lenora."

"She kept her hands over mine when the knife went into her stomach." Lenora swipes under her eyes, making a sarcastic sound. "I still don't know whose hands were moving as the knife went in. Like when the girls on our bus played with that stupid Ouija board. No one could figure out whose hands were moving the planchette. It was like that. I didn't try and pull away. I just let her do it. She looked at me as she slid down the wall. I could barely breathe, but she was so calm. So peaceful. There was this look on her face. Like she was floating away."

I don't say anything. I can't.

Of every victim for every case I ever covered, the one I've never tried to understand is my mom. What she must have thought while taking her last breath. Did she have thoughts of her husband, whom she killed? A husband we learned after both their deaths was cheating on her and had been for the entirety of their marriage. A good father who never did learn to love his wife. Or were her thoughts on the daughters? The two girls who started draining the life from her the moment she conceived. Two girls she never loved in the way a mother should.

"I'm just like her," Lenora whispers. "I'm just like Emily. I killed our mother."

"No." My voice is hard. "The most selfish thing our mother ever did was put that knife in your hands."

The clouds suddenly look too heavy in the graying sky, like a grocery bag close to bursting. Lenora's face drops to her hands. She stares at them. Flips them over and looks at the backs of them. "Sometimes I expect to see blood," she says quietly. "It all feels like my fault. Everything wrong in our life. And I keep thinking of Emily. How she died. How Sarah lost it. Even after all that, she never stopped loving her sister."

"We're not them, Lenora."

"But are we any better?" Her tortured eyes meet mine.

There's a war waging inside her, and only one side can win. One side determines who we are.

"I know what it feels like to think I'm going to die." I stand on bare feet, my toes squishing into the soft ground. I grab my sister's clean hands as the first drop of rain falls. "And it wasn't lonely at all."

READING GROUP GUIDE

1. Compare Cassie and Lenora. In what ways are they similar or different? How would you describe their relationship?

2. Describe the campground setting. What role does it play in the story?

3. Cassie wonders if she's a cannibal for making true crime content. Do you think she's right? How can a person engage with true crime without exploiting victims?

4. Between the two sisters, Lenora seems to be more affected by the past. Why do you think that is?

5. Discuss the fraught mother/daughter relationships in this book. Can you draw any parallels between Tilly and Karen and the twins and their mother?

6. For a long time, it's unclear who is who in the past timeline. Did you try to predict which sister was Cassie and which was Lenora? Which did you think was the narrator?

7. Characterize Cassie's relationship with Parker. Do you think they could have a future together? Why or why not?

8. Explain Lenora's preoccupation with watching. Why does she do it? Is she the only voyeur in the story?

9. Sarah and Cassie seem to have an affinity for each other. Why do you think that is? Do you think Sarah truly cared about the sisters?

10. What do you think truly happened the night Cassie and Lenora's family was destroyed? Do you think each sister is still telling the truth?

A CONVERSATION WITH THE AUTHOR

First things first: What inspired you to write *When She Was Me*?

My sister had an intense pregnancy and birth experience with my identical twin nieces. I became so interested in twins and twin relationships, particularly as it compares to other types of sibling relationships, and the story just took off from there.

While true crime is still very popular, folks are starting to question whether or not the genre is respectful to victims. Why did you choose to dive into this issue in your book?

Like most people, I'm fascinated by true crime. I often wonder what that says about me or even us as a society. Some aspects of true crime can feel exploitive. For me, it's about finding the content that's wary of the line between the telling of another person's tragedy for personal gain and doing it give a voice to the voiceless for genuine education and awareness.

The wooded campground setting jumps off the page. What made you choose to place the twins' story there?

I chose it for the isolation factor, but as I wrote, the setting almost became a playground for the character's minds. A way to reflect their inner fear, guilt, and the unreliability of the narrative.

What does your writing process look like? How did you go about balancing the present and past timelines?

I start with an idea and then do a whole bunch of thinking. Then I'll make an outline and use that outline to write the first draft (which I usually spend a couple months writing on the couch while my kids are sleeping). With this novel, balancing the past and present timelines was a little trickier. My main thing was to make sure as the action ramped up in one timeline, it did in the other as well.

In this story you explore the blurred lines between characters' identities—can you talk a little bit about that?

I think there's something intrinsic in all of us, a need to identify who we are—good guys or bad guys. Like the characters, I think we struggle with this especially as we are often defined by our mistakes. Believing they can be placed nicely into neat, labelled boxes of "good" or "bad" causes a lot of inner turmoil for Cassie and Lenora because they aren't sure about the parameters in which to define themselves. Should it be by how they live their lives? What they contribute to the world? Or should you define them by the worst thing they ever did? I guess these are for the reader to answer.

There are so many unhealthy family dynamics in this story. Why did you choose to make that a facet of *When She Was Me*?

It's just so relatable and rich to explore. With Cassie and Lenora, I wanted to dive into a specifically codependent relationship and leave it to the reader to decide the morality of it. Whether it's a virtue or vice.

What are some of your favorite books?

Whatever I'm reading at the moment is my favorite. Sometimes it's a thriller, a book exploring world religion, a historical event, or psychology. I love to learn. Especially about people. I'm the one who meets someone and wants to immediately dive into their life with way too personal of questions.

For much of the book, the reader is left to guess which sister is which in the past timeline. Did you purposefully want to lead them to the wrong conclusion? How did you come up with that big, final twist?

The twist of any thriller is my favorite part, so I for sure wanted the reader to be at all the wrong conclusions. Funnily enough, in the first version of this novel, the past timeline wasn't as ambiguous. It was actually my wonderful agent's idea to make that change and to lean into the anonymity of the past perspective. Her incredible insight changed the whole book and really anchored the twist (which has always been the same).

What do you hope readers take from this story?

I'd be lying if I said I had some huge theme or purpose in mind when I wrote this book. My one hope is simply that a reader will enjoy the experience enough to pick up the next book with my name on it. But the best part about reading is how, through the lens of our own human experience, we can pull themes and ideas from books that others may not see. So that's what I hope. That maybe while reading a creepy, little thriller that a person may have a moment, a thought, a seedling of a feeling that makes them reflect a bit more on the human experience.

ACKNOWLEDGMENTS

I could write a whole book just naming people who've significantly impacted my life. First, I must thank my agent, Claire Friedman. This book wouldn't exist without your expert vision and your invaluable insight which completely changed the dynamic of the entire book in the best possible way. I couldn't be luckier to have you in my corner.

Thank you to my rockstar editor, Jenna, for taking a chance on this book. Your thoughtful questions and ideas not only made it better, but it made me a better writer in the process.

Thanks a million to Mandy and the marketing team for their enthusiasm in getting this one into the hands of readers. And thanks to the whole team at Sourcebooks who have had a hand in launching this book into the world. This debut experience was perfect because of your work and contribution. Thank you.

Thank you to Amy, who has become so much more than a beta reader (and the fastest reader I know). You are an integral part of my writing process. This book was better after you, and I hope you'll let me bother you for many more books to come.

Thanks to my favorite true crime podcast, *Crime Weekly*, and Stephanie and Derrick, whose respectful, consistent, well-researched, and timely true crime content shines so much light on the darkness in the world and inspires me to write more authentically.

I can't go any further without acknowledging the twins of my heart, Emery and Evie. You two are nothing like the twins from *The Shining*, but you do shine so bright to me. And my other favorite muses, Zillie—my oldest and wisest niece, who is way cooler than me, Waylon—who has the toughest feet but the softest heart, Maddux—your inquisitive mind makes me in awe of you.

Thanks to my family: Mom for the conversations and infinite understanding. I want to be more like you.

Donna and Daryl for always being willing to take my kids off my hands for an hour or two and for supporting me in more ways than I can possibly count.

Mike for the story ideas that are worth more than any inheritance.

Bev for reading with me for as long as I can remember.

For Cristie, Tony, and Ayden, the strongest people I know and the best house guests.

Grammie and Papaw for the endless love.

To Nanny Bush because your hugs could change the world, and I miss them.

Myrisa and the girls—you are a fearless woman, and you inspire me.

To Cole, who just keeps going no matter what life throws. I love you.

To Norma, Sam, Mateo, and Selena (but absolutely not to Matt) because you're my most loyal friend, and I'll love you and those kids forever.

Thanks to Debbie for your willingness to read and your honesty.

To Brooke for cropping my sweatpants out of my fancy author photos. Thanks, dude.

To my sisters (Maci, Ricki, Anya, and Anasophia) and brothers (Dimitri and Cyrus) and my in-laws who might as well be siblings (Kayla, Chris, Jay, Logan, Ashley, Larissa, Austin, and Chase). I'm so lucky to have you. I know I don't tell you that enough.

An extra thank-you to Maci for letting me borrow an experience or two for this novel. And to Austin for being one of my earliest readers.

Thanks to Ms. Drinkard whose enthusiastic reaction to a fourth grader's short story changed the trajectory of her life.

And a very special thank you to Jeanine, Davin, and Wil for teaching me about grief. The world noticed when you left.

To all my other loved ones, friends, and family—I'm lucky to have many—I wish I could write each of your names and share the ways you've changed my life for the better. Thank you for every interaction and every bit of support and encouragement.

And thanks to you. To the one who decided to pick this book up. Thank you for choosing my story and letting me be a part of yours. I wish I could have you over for dinner.

Finally, thank you to the ones who keep my world turning. Craton, who knows all my books before they're written. You are my most supportive friend, my confidant, and the best father to our kids (I guess you could say we danced, we cried, we laughed, and we had a really really really good time).

And thank you to Bow and Miles, who taught me how to love unconditionally. Every single word I ever write will be for you.

ABOUT THE AUTHOR

© Brooke Ledbetter

Marlee Bush loves to write the kind of stories that make you double check the lock on your door at night. She makes a home in Alabama with her husband and two children. *When She Was Me* is her debut novel.